More acclaim for the entertaining, moving novels of

Tara McCarthy

WOULDN'T MISS IT FOR THE WORLD

"Tara McCarthy takes us on a wild trip halfway around the world, where family, friends, and expectations collide in a funny, smart, and heartfelt story of making it to the altar without sacrificing yourself or your sanity in the process."

—Jennnifer O'Connell, author of *Insider Dating*

LOVE WILL TEAR US APART

"It's such a strange, weirdly appealing novel. . . . I think it's going to become some sort of cult classic."

—Alex McAulay, author of *Bad Girls* and *Lost Summer*

"Witty and funny and ironic and self-consciously politically incorrect . . . a really smart book."

—*The Stamford Advocate*

"Wonderfully creative and surprisingly dark."

—Popgurls

"A delightful satire."

—*Curve* magazine

who also writes as

Tara Altebrando

THE PURSUIT OF HAPPINESS

"Insightful, moving, and addictively readable."

—*The Philadelphia Inquirer*

"It's hard to imagine this book being more enjoyable."

—KLIATT

ALSO BY TARA McCARTHY

Love Will Tear Us Apart

Wouldn't miss It for the World

Tara McCarthy

doWn
tOwn
press

New York London Toronto Sydney

Downtown Press
A Division of Simon & Schuster, Inc.
1230 Avenue of the Americas
New York, NY 10020

First Downtown Press trade paperback edition August 2007

DOWNTOWN PRESS and colophon are trademarks of Simon & Schuster, Inc.

For information about special discounts for bulk purchases, please contact Simon & Schuster Special Sales at 1-800-456-6798 or business@simonandschuster.com.

Designed by Carla Jayne Little

Manufactured in the United States of America

10 9 8 7 6 5 4 3 2 1

ISBN-13: 978-1-4165-0325-5
ISBN-10:   1-4165-0325-0

Acknowledgments

I wouldn't have missed working with these folks for the world: my esteemed editor, Lauren McKenna; my fantastic agent, David Dunton; and my wonderful publisher, Louise Burke. Also, Megan McKeever: Thank you for always being so on the ball.

Thanks, as always, to Elizabeth Frankenberger, for her close read. And to Sara Zarr, for help with motivation and procrastination in equal measure.

Big, huge thanks to Trevor, for asking the exact right question at the exact right time.

And, of course, to Nick. For booking the honeymoon, for suffering E. coli falls with me, and for letting me borrow a song. Again.

Destination weddings can be a fun and relaxing experience for you and your guests. . . .

—*Destinationweddings.com*

If the world had any ends, [Belize] would surely be one of them.

—*Aldous Huxley*

Wouldn't miss It for the World

There is a band onstage, kicking ass, and almost everyone who means anything to them is in the crowd, bearing witness to the ass-kicking.

It doesn't even matter who, exactly, they are up there—what name they give themselves, what particular brand of music they play. It doesn't matter whether you've heard of them, or whether you like them if you have. What matters is that this is Big, as big as it's gotten for them. They've been at it for five years, and now this *is happening. They are opening for a band they revere—a band that you've most definitely heard of—by special invitation in one of the finest concert halls on the East Coast of the United States of America. It is a Friday night, and it is sold out. So sold out that the guy in Row G, Seat 41, has paid $250 for the privilege of being here, as he was on a business trip to London when tickets went on sale and then off.*

They are up there on that stage—where the lead singer (who also plays guitar and keyboards and upright bass and writes songs but whom we'll refer to simply as the Girl, for the time being) is doing that thing she does, gyrating and wowing, as lights fall on them like radioactive drizzle—because, almost six years ago, she graduated from college and took a thin-walled apartment with a girl whose boyfriend was "looking for his own place" while living with his parents; he spent

1

most nights in the roommate's twin bed with her. *The Girl tuned out their* mms *and* ohs *and* yeah babys *with her guitar. As the sex was apparently good, the songs she was writing accumulated rapidly. Before summer's end, the Girl—who has played guitar and piano since she was old enough to and who played out at some coffeehouses and such during college—knew, in a gonna-need-a-bigger-boat way, that the time had come. She needed a band. Joining a band that already existed seemed the easiest way to go about it. They wouldn't even know that they were "her" band until it was too late for them to do anything about it.*

She is up there now, putting down her guitar and moving over to the electric piano and saying into the microphone, "Thanks. This crowd is amazing," because she regularly read the back pages of the Village Voice *all those years ago and finally saw an ad that piqued her interest: "Alternative rock band seeks cool chick with mad guitar skills and a voice to back it up. No posers/no bs/no blondes." It was that last bit that intrigued her. So she called and arranged an audition for that evening, went out and had her brown hair bleached blond, and arrived at the appointed hour at a rehearsal room above a bodega in Williamsburg, Brooklyn. She was greeted at the door of the building by a huge chunk of a guy—the Bassist—whose hair, at least what little of it he had, was so dark it was surely also dyed. "We said no blondes," he said.*

"Well, I'm here," she said.

"Should we give it a go, then?" said the guy behind the drum kit, who was not in fact the Drummer. He put out his cigarette and got up and picked up a guitar, which would make him the Guitarist, but for our purposes we're going to think of him as the Boy to her Girl. More on that later.

Bassist said, "We were playing 'Hang On Sloopy.' Just for a laugh. You know it?"

Girl said, "I might be a little weak on the second verse, but I'll give it a whirl," then she stepped up to the mike and tried not to notice the boys looking at each other, no doubt silently communicat-

2

ing their shared hunch that her talent would be directly proportionate to the length of her skirt, which was the micro-est of minis. Girl thought it was a safe bet to imagine that countless chippies had responded to the ad and strolled in wearing similarly provocative attire only to belt out some mindless Top 40 pop/rock, thinking that that—plus the skirt—would blow the boys away. But our girl would have worn that skirt any other day of the week, and besides, she wasn't out to be "the girl in the band," wasn't there to prove to them the nature of her chromosomes. That much—even with A-cups—was apparent.

She is up there now, banging away on the Rhodes in a white dress that could double as a "Sexy Nurse" Halloween costume, because she sang "Hang On Sloopy" that night above the bodega the way she'd sing it if she were singing while cooking, or gardening (not that she has a garden, but maybe one day she will). She didn't try to "hit it out of the park" or "nail it" or "bring it home"; she just went with it, felt it, sang it sweetly, and it was good.

After that, Boy asked Girl if she wrote music, and she said that she did. And so she turned her volume down, then sat on a high stool and played one of her newest songs, "Recovering." What followed felt to her like awestruck silence. Even the air conditioner—secured in the window of the room with an assortment of tapes (duct, masking, and even, pathetically, Scotch)—seemed to cooperate, cycling off so that the only sound in the room was hers. She was half expecting a clichéd interview to follow: Who are your influences, that kind of thing. Instead, Bassist suggested she step out into the hallway for a minute. She didn't have to wait long before the door opened again.

"We practice Tuesday and Thursday and Saturday mornings," Boy said. He had already lit another cigarette, and she had already decided that she would marry him. Which would be tricky. Because she'd been spouting off for years about how she didn't believe in marriage.

She nodded once.

He said, "We're called the Co-op Board, by the way."
And she thought, Not for long.

Her mother is in a box seat, stage left, and she is a little bit drunk.
She flew in from Chicago not an hour ago and came straight from the
airport, but before that she had a glass of wine or three on the plane
to calm her nerves. She doesn't do this often. She's tipsy maybe once
a month, at book club, like most people in the U.S. of A. who belong
to book clubs. She still doesn't quite understand words like alternative *and* indie *as they relate to* rock, *and can't quite wrap her head*
around the fact that a lot of these people are here to see her daughter.
That their screams are for her. She finds New York in general too
big, too crowded, too loud, too intimidating—and this concert hall
is much the same in microcosm. She finds her children's generation
puzzling—with their piercings and gadgetry and irony and Swedish
furniture and jobs she's never heard of—and the band up onstage is a
fairly representative bunch.

"My mother's in the crowd tonight," Girl says from the stage, and
the crowd howls approval. The Mother thinks her ears might actually
burst from the combination of her heart and the screams; the drums in
there seem to be caught up in some strange wind. She thinks she might
cry. She is seated near Boy's family, and they smile over at her, know-
ingly. Her son, seated beside her, squeezes her shoulder. No one knows
that she thinks of him as the child she actually likes.

Girl says, "Mom had a little bit too much to drink on the plane,
which I'm pretty sure means she forgot to put in her earplugs" (and in
fact they are in her carry-on, which is stowed backstage). A swell in the
howls. "This next one's for you, Mom, 'cause you're probably gonna
be hungover tomorrow. It's called 'Recovering.'"

The crowd, if you'll forgive the expression, loses their shit.

The song is so beautiful—it has been described in numerous re-

views of the band's latest LP as "soaring"—and so powerfully performed this night that the mother's mortification gives way to a kind of pride she hasn't felt in years—maybe not since her late husband, a composer and music professor, played her a recording of his first industrial musical. It was an elaborate show written for a convention of employees of a major midwestern bathroom supply company and featured such rousing numbers as "We Put the Plumb in Plumber" and "Feeling Flush." She looks around the historic concert hall, and misses her husband anew, which she hasn't thought possible, missing him daily as she does. She thinks he would have known better how to process all this, what to say backstage, and why, exactly, their daughter's band is so good—if, in fact, it is. But even in her ignorance, Mom feels the electricity in the room and wonders if the actual guitars and the electricity that powers them are causing it, whether waves of it are coming off the stage. She feels literally charged, all the tiny hairs on her arms and everywhere else alert. Brush against her, and you'll get a spark for sure.

Fans of the band have left their seats at the back of the house to crowd the aisles near the stage, and it is all Mom can do not to leap from her perch and grab on to that big red velvet curtain and climb down and join them. But then the song ends and a new one starts, and it's so angry, so loud, that it leaves her wounded, confused, even mad. She watches her daughter convulse and shake—electrocution-style—and she wonders, How can that girl be capable of such beauty and such ugliness? More to the point, why does she insist on indulging the ugly? The mother feels as though she has spent the last twenty-eight years of her life, like tonight, grappling with one undeniable, unfathomable truth: this body produced that girl.

They are midway through a song that has topped the college charts for several weeks, and the crowd is singing along, because that first prac-

tice above the bodega was hair-raising in a good way, too. Then after practice, the Bassist suggested drinks. In a semicircular red leather booth in a dive bar across the street from the rehearsal space, Girl studied each of these guys and thought to herself, Now these I could take to the top with me. She could see the band photo already—a shot of them all at that very booth, light coming in at odd angles through a partitioned stained-glass window, Boy with his hand on a beer bottle, Bassist with a club soda in mid-swig, Drummer writing on a cocktail napkin, and our girl—only our girl—looking right at the camera. It was the kind of bar Girl loved—all dark wood, tin ceiling painted silver, mismatched pre-smoking-ban ashtrays spread out on the bar at a ratio of one per customer. It was the kind of conversation she loved, too—about music and life and nothing and everything and gear—*and she was happy that she'd probably be spending a fair number of hours here, with these guys, in the coming weeks and maybe years.*

They cut a fine figure up there. Even tonight, things are much as they were back then. Drummer is the scruffiest, and he seems to dress in no less than four layers at all times, even in summer. He has a perpetual five o'clock shadow and bushy, rarely washed hair. His face is wide and flat and curious, like he is looking at the world with his nose pressed against glass, window-shopping. He has lost both of his parents to cancer since Girl joined the band and has had three long-time girlfriends, the third of which he married. She is backstage, sipping water, pregnant, though nobody but she and the Drummer knows about the pregnant bit. It's too early to tell anyone, plus Drummer's a little bit scared of how the band will react, considering big things have started to happen.

Bassist is a bear, likely larger than any man you've ever known. He is not overweight, just huge. Tall and broad, he takes up the space of the rest of the band combined. He has shaved off the remains of his hair and wears thick black glasses and basically epitomizes a commanding presence. Though he puts up a good front and has a reputation for being somewhat of a "dog," he has not gotten laid in several months and hopes that the gods will look favorably down upon him tonight and send some hot little number his way. He hasn't taken a drink in six years and change because the band (pre-Girl) made it clear that it turns him into a really big asshole and that he's a big enough asshole to begin with.

Boy is the best-looking of the bunch—at least most people who've thought enough about it to form an opinion on the subject think so—but what matters most is that he is Girl's physical ideal. He is taller than her by a foot, wider than her by the same. From that first night, over the bodega, she felt like she'd fit perfectly in his arms and longed to prove she was right. His hair is brown and dynamic, and he often runs a hand through it or pushes a piece out of his eyes, which Girl took a particular liking to after a few drinks in that red leather booth. They looked to her that night like Mardi Gras beads, all shiny and blue and sexually charged. Boy only occasionally wonders what life would be like if another girl had walked into the room that night—one who wasn't quite so talented, quite so full of star power, quite so everything he was ever looking for in a girlfriend and not at all what he really wanted for a band in which he might have, otherwise, become the star. He writes songs, too, you see. And sings the songs he writes. But whenever he's singing one of his songs, he senses the crowd is looking at her anyway, wishing it were she at the mike instead.

Boy's Best Friend is in the crowd, on a fourth date that he has decided will not lead to a fifth, though he is on the fence about whether he'll have sex tonight anyway. It pains him to watch Girl and Boy sing this spirited duet together, and so he excuses himself to go to the bathroom. He goes, instead, to the bar. He orders Wild Turkey on the rocks.

It's not that he isn't happy the band has achieved this level of success. He's just annoyed that he had to buy tickets to the show tonight—that after all the years of supporting the band, he still doesn't make it onto their guest list, plus one. He has known Boy since high school, though they didn't really become friends until college, and he has been to pretty much every gig the band has ever played in the area, including one in an Irish bar in Woodside, Queens, of all places, and several in Hoboken. That's New Jersey. They are business partners, too, who run a Web design firm, just the two of them. Business isn't exactly booming, and he wonders if he could write off the price of the tickets come tax time.

At the bar, Best Friend is thinking back to the first time he saw the band with their new girl. She was nothing short of a marvel onstage even then, even though the stage wasn't so much a stage as a step up from the sticky-beer floor in the back room of a bar on the Lower East Side. She was thinner then—too thin, really, and Best Friend is the sort of guy who believes such a thing to be possible—with superlong legs poking out of a black leather miniskirt and a tight sleeveless silver top that didn't quite stretch over her navel. She had a spiky blunt cut and the coolest tattoo that Best Friend had ever seen on her right upper arm: a smear of black stars that seemed to twinkle, a Milky Way of ink right there on her milky skin. She sang a new song that night, something about ghosts and lovers and angels, and Best Friend felt like he was watching something big happening.

Boy introduced her after the show, and Best Friend could think of nothing more original to say than "You were great."

She glistened with sweat—"You think?"—and seemed completely genuine, like she really didn't know. His infatuation solidified.

As Best Friend is generally highly skilled at suppressing such memories—and the real reason why he's out here at the bar and not in there, where the band is really hitting their stride—we'll leave him be and check in with Boy's stepsister, in a box seat near Girl's mom. She has never been to a concert before—hell, she's never been to New York before—and is therefore having the time of her life. This band's music has provoked in her a sort of obsession—she has played only their CDs for weeks now, in anticipation of the show—and seeing them live like this tonight, she feels like nothing will ever be the same again. Like life is changing faster than she can keep track.

She lost her virginity eight days ago, with a geeky boy who's had a crush on her forever and whom she immediately swore to secrecy. To her knowledge, he is still the only other person on the planet who knows. She is watching the band and wondering when she'll have sex again, whether she wants to, whether it'll be better, somehow, the next time. Not that it was bad, but well, yeah, it was pretty bad. She's proud of herself nonetheless, for getting that out of the way—and with a guy who is moving away to another state, no less, so there will be no regret, no drama. She feels the bass parts deep in her heart and feels a sort of exhilarated melancholy about her life. She thinks Girl's brother is "hot." She and her mother have been fighting about clothes lately. A lot.

The song they're playing, the one that has sat atop the college charts, it's a cover of a song by one of America's greatest living songwriters that was later reinterpreted by that most famous of famous (and sadly deceased) country music couples. Girl and Boy are up there singing it because after that first practice, back in that red booth, Drummer and Bassist both had places to be, and Girl and Boy had another drink, just the two of them, before he admitted he had a girlfriend and that she was waiting for him. And Girl thought, Not for long.

She led the way out of the bar and onto the sidewalk and he offered her a cigarette, which she took, though she didn't really smoke. He lighted hers and then his.

"So I just have to ask," Girl said. "Are you named after the Man in Black?"

"I sure am." Boy held his cigarette in his mouth while he zipped up his jacket against the chill. Then he took it from his lips and said, "Dare I ask where your name came from?" with a raised bushy eyebrow that our girl knew she'd one day be in the habit of taming with her thumb. The affection she felt for that eyebrow was something en-

tirely new to her. So new that she wasn't sure whether to trust it but decided to anyway.

She went home that night with a happy buzz, and her roommate's headboard was banging but she didn't care. One day, maybe sooner than later, she'd be a rock star. One day, this would all just be part of her backstory, something to talk about with the press. "It ain't me, babe," she hum-hum-hummed, "It ain't me you're looking for."

They are up there now because for the last five years they have believed—in themselves, in each other, whether foolishly or not. They have gained and lost a keyboard player along the way, not to death or the dark side but to another band that has yet to have something this BIG happen, poor sap. They have collectively quit smoking nine times. They have been through three vans and somewhere between six and twenty-six lovers (Bassist is infuriatingly discreet for a "dog"). They have played in fifteen states, sometimes to a mere handful of people, sometimes to more, and they are up there now, taking their final bow, completely convinced, all four of them, that something this big can only mean the start of something bigger. Hell, the guy in Row G, Seat 41, had never even heard *the band before—only heard* of *them—but has every intention now of going to buy their record.*

They are up there, final note played, soaking it all in, every last clap and scream being sent their way, because they are equally convinced that they are completely wrong—that this moment, this night, is as good, as big, as it's ever going to get. That a few weeks or months from now, one of them will quit, and that will be that. That a few weeks from now, Row G, Seat 41, will be in a record store, thinking hard. He will know that there is a CD he really *wants to buy, and he will not be able to think of it for the life of him.*

The News

Alice Gilhooley Siren would never have heard of the Starter House had her daughter not been the band's lead singer. She might never have heard of Belize, either, had June not announced one Saturday morning, on a call from New York, that she and her longtime boyfriend and bandmate, Cash, had decided to get married there. Cash had called Alice earlier in the week to ask her permission to propose, and then had made her promise that she'd never tell June he'd done so. He'd never mentioned Belize.

"You're *eloping*?" Alice was midway through dusting her living room, which hadn't seen a visitor since the last time she'd dusted it. She'd been walking around the house for days practicing sounding surprised when she said things like "How wonderful!" or "Oh, June, that's so exciting!" She hadn't practiced "You're eloping?"

"No, Mom," June said, in her usual exasperated tone. "You can come. I mean, everybody's coming. Cash's parents and Abby, if she can get out of school. Billy. Hopefully Lydia. The band. A few others. Or, I mean, we're going to *ask* them to. We haven't actually told anyone yet."

"I'm the first?" Alice looked at a calendar on the wall, noted that the date was the first of June. Cash could be pretty cute.

"You're the first."

Alice wasn't sure she believed this. She had never felt first in June's life before.

"We're calling Cash's family next," June said. "And I'll call Grandma later, but you can tell her if you want. And I'll call Billy." Billy was June's brother.

"Well, that's wonderful." Alice went to get a tissue then. She wasn't crying, but thought she might. "Where did he pop the question?"

"Oh, just at home."

June wasn't forthcoming with any further details.

"Well, isn't that exciting!" Alice concluded. "Belize!"

When she rang off, Alice got the stepladder from beside the fridge and brought it into the living room. She opened it near the bookcase, climbed up to the top step, and reached for the atlas in the slot under the globe. She'd been planning on neglecting to dust that top shelf, but that seemed foolish now that she was already up there, Swiffer duster somehow still in hand.

Afterward, she settled onto one of her two identical couches (June had never had a kind word for their pink rose pattern) and looked for Belize in the atlas index. It wasn't there, and Alice all but harrumphed before remembering the computer. It still wasn't her first instinct—to Google. So she trashed the disposable part of the Swiffer duster in the kitchen and then went into the den. A moment later, staring at a map of Central America on the computer monitor, she sunk back in the office chair, and sighed. "Oh, June."

Alice, by her own admission, was not a world traveler.

She clicked her way to Belize.com, where pictures of blue waters and jungles appeared atop a page of links to other sites. She scanned the screen and clicked on "Getting Married in Belize," feeling a modicum of relief that the link existed, that people had done this before. She found the page that loaded sort of busy and hard to look at and read randomly. "In the jungle or on the beach. . . ." Then her eyes landed on, "Why go on vacation and get married?"

Alice desperately wanted to know. She read on.

"This concept is not new, it's been happening in Las Vegas for years, and the economics of getting married at a vacation destination make sense for those looking for the small to medium wedding."

This wasn't really helping. Alice clicked on the photo gallery, which looked nice enough—there were pictures of long stretches of beach, of monkeys, of toucans—but then she clicked on a photo captioned "Belize City Slum." Her throat tightened as the image appeared—two ramshackle houses, a haphazardly mended fence with posts of varying heights, and yes, there was a palm tree. She couldn't help but think that the people at Belize.com had a thing or two to learn about attracting tourists, an opinion she felt was confirmed when she found a Belizean news site that had an entire section for "Disasters." For the moment, anyway, Alice had seen enough.

She grabbed her jacket and keys and went out to the car. She drove twenty minutes through suburban Chicago over to the Renaissance Home for Active Living, where she worked part-time as a nurse and where her mother had very recently taken up residency. Alice had been planning on calling later in the day—one of her days off—but she felt the strong urge to get out of the house and to share the news. She had book club the next day, so it seemed foolish to call any of the girls. She so rarely had news; she would want to savor the moment.

Evelyn was sitting in a rocking chair in her room—distinctly not rocking—when Alice arrived. "Hi, Mom."

"You know what I've realized," Evelyn said.

"What have you realized?" Alice took a small square pillow from the bed and slid it behind her mother's lower back.

"No one ever calls me."

"I was going to call you today!" Alice said. "But then I thought I'd visit instead." She'd heard this particular lecture about no one using the phone anymore maybe once for every three times she'd heard the one about how people who throw their babies in the air don't realize they're doing damage to the baby's brain and the one about men being worse at taking care of their health than women. Alice always took the latter as a not-so-subtle criticism of Alice's late husband, Jack, ten years her elder, who'd died of a heart attack in his fifties and with whom Evelyn had never been much impressed. But then, having been abandoned by her own husband, Evelyn had never been much impressed with men in general. She'd never used the word *alcoholic*, but Alice, who was only two when he left, knew. She'd been raised by her mother and grandmother.

"People think you're in here, you don't have a phone, or you don't need the company." Evelyn gestured up at a calendar from a local florist on the wall; this month's photo featured tiger lilies. "I go days without talking to anyone."

"You do not, Mother. I know for a fact that you do not. Now, do you want to hear the news I came to tell you or not?"

"Well, you're going to tell me anyway, aren't you?" She started rocking.

"June's getting married!"

"Well, it's about time!" The rocking quickened. "Which one is this?"

"Cash, Mother. The only one there's ever really been. You've met him."

"Of course I've met him." Evelyn's silver hair seemed too soft for her. "You think I don't know who I meet and who I don't meet?"

Alice picked up her purse. "I can leave."

Evelyn twitched her nose and settled into her chair. "Well, that's nice news. Will you have it over at St. Mary's?"

"No, actually." Alice tried on bright for size. "They've decided to have a destination wedding."

"Come again." Evelyn leaned in closer.

"They're getting married on the beach, in Belize," Alice said more slowly. "It used to be called British Honduras." The Googling had cleared up the lack of Belize's presence in the old atlas. "It's in Central America."

"I know where it is." Evelyn tilted her head. "Does he have family there?"

"No."

Evelyn's face contorted. "She pregnant?"

Alice's brightness dimmed. "I don't understand it any more than you do."

"Well, I'm not going to Central America. You tell her that."

"You can tell her yourself," Alice said. "She said she'd call."

Evelyn snorted. "No one ever calls."

There weren't a lot of Gilhooleys—Alice was an only child, and her mother's one sister was long dead—and it suddenly dawned on Alice that it was just plain awful that June would choose to get married somewhere where there was no practical way her eighty-year-old grandmother could go. She made a secret wish then that her mother would promptly forget about the whole thing, like she did a lot of things these days. Alice's fifty-third birthday had just passed without mention.

"Now what's on the schedule for today?" Alice picked up the Renaissance's daily newsletter.

"Same ole shit," Evelyn said.

"That's nice, Mother. Real nice."

"Well, it's the truth."

Alice studied the event schedule, running her eyes over the local summer camp glee club visit, the movie in the lounge

17

(*Shrek 2*), the menu for dinner that night: turkey meatloaf and mashed potatoes. She laid the paper down and settled in for her visit. "So it is."

"Ohmigod! Ohmigod!" Abby McKay screamed. She had just come home to the Best News Ever. "I get to go, right?!"

"First of all," Maggie, her mother, said, "headphones out."

Abby let one of her iPod earbuds dangle.

"Both of them," Maggie said, and Abby complied with a huff.

She'd been listening to the Starter House on the way home from her weekend job at the Troc Center mall, so maybe she was psychic. Because she hadn't actually been listening to them that much lately, and then today she had, and now *look!*

"Second of all"—Maggie was unloading a bag of groceries—"we'll have to see, honey, once they set a date. They said December, so if it's during your winter break, of course. But I'm not sure how I feel about pulling you out of school."

"Please," Abby said. "*Please.* I'll do whatever it takes. Extra credit. I can chip in for my ticket." Her mother's face said, *Yeah, like that's gonna happen,* but Abby forged ahead. "Anything. I mean, Mom!" Abby paused dramatically. "He's my brother!"

Not three years before, under different circumstances, Abby had stood in this very kitchen and wailed, "But he's not even really my brother!" Abby was hoping her mother had forgotten about all that nonsense. Abby had only been fourteen, so how was she to know? She had since gotten to know Cash better, mostly via email, and had decided that he was her reward for having suffered through so much of her a-hole father's b-shit when she was little. Her boring, balding lawyer stepdad, Miller, was fine—sort of lame; a little bit rich, at least—but his son, Cash, was the coolest stepbrother anyone could ask for. She only wished she saw him more often; San Francisco was a long way from New York. She also wished that June hadn't scared the shit out of her the few times they'd met—the girl was just intimidatingly cool—but still. With this wedding news, Abby would be the envy of the senior class. Or at least of the handful of people who'd heard of the Starter House, which, fortunately, included Abby's current crush, Colin Murray.

"Well, it's not very thoughtful of them, if you ask me." Maggie put some bananas in a bowl on the island counter. "Though I guess at least it'll be warm. It *is* warm, isn't it?"

"Yes, Mom. It's near Guatemala. On the Yucatán Peninsula." Abby's mother's ignorance of simple facts sometimes astounded her. "Do you need me to draw you a map?"

Maggie put down a yellow Styrofoam package of chicken cutlets and clasped her hands dramatically. "That would be *lovely*."

Abby's mother had only recently discovered sarcasm, and Abby didn't have the heart to tell her that it should be used more like hot pepper flakes, less like black pepper. The lesson would probably be lost on her anyway, because Maggie didn't really know how to use either one of those things. Her salt-and-pepper hair, which Abby desperately didn't want to inherit, was the spiciest thing about her.

"I would just *love* for you to draw me a map," Maggie said. "Thank you *so* much."

Abby went to her mother and tugged on her arm, then pulled her into a hug. She'd learned that poor Maggie was so starved for this kind of affection from her daughter—so desperate to *connect*—that it worked to Abby's advantage to cough up a hug now and then.

"I'll be upstairs," she said, pulling out of the hug.

Maggie waved her off. "Dinner's in half an hour."

Upstairs in her room, Abby booted up her computer and looked eagerly around the room. She took a framed picture of Audrey Hepburn off the wall and stepped back and thought, Yes, that'll totally work. She took her digital camera out of its case and set it up on her desk, facing the wall where the picture used to hang. She looked at the display screen, noting the position of the nail, and said, "Cool." Next, she went to her vanity and brushed her hair and put on some lip gloss and a tiny bit of blush. She would have loved to do more—to put on some eyeliner, at least—but Maggie would freak, and that would defeat the purpose.

Back at the camera, Abby set the timer for ten seconds, then darted across the room and squatted to position her head in front of the nail. She smiled, but not overmuch, and the flash went off. She got up, nearly losing her balance, and checked the picture without moving the camera. She decided to take another one, and that one turned out better.

Abby plugged the camera into the computer, pulled up the photos, and within a minute she had sized, cropped, and printed two copies of the better one on Kodak paper. She then cut them into small squares, her face and shoulders against white. She went out into the hallway, then changed her mind and came back. She went to her computer, signed on to MySpace, and sent a bulletin to her 176 friends. She called it "Starter House Wedding!!!!!" And it read, "Cash (my stepbrother) and June from the Starter House are getting married. In Belize!!!! And I get to go! I'm so unbelievably psyched!" This wedding, this awesome new topic of discussion, was just the ammunition she needed, what with annoying junior-to-be Chelsea Lambert flirting with Colin Murray—a senior-to-be like Abby—whenever possible. She was always tossing her long blond hair this way and that and bragging about her father—who owned some hip nightclub that she got to go to—and the BMW convertible he said he'd buy her when she turned sixteen come winter and a million other things that made Abby wish that M and M (her shorthand for "Mom and Miller") were even richer than they were.

Abby rushed downstairs with the pictures, and burst into the kitchen. Maggie was frying the chicken cutlets, which she'd breaded, and they smelled good. Abby put the pictures on the counter, then put her elbows there, too, and looked up at her mother. She smiled and fluttered her eyelashes.

"What are these?" Maggie asked, turning from the stove.

"Don't be so clueless, Mom," Abby said, and she whirled around to leave the room again. "They're my passport photos."

"You're going to have to do them over," Maggie said. "New regulations say you're not supposed to smile."

Abby paused in the foyer. "Seriously?"

"Seriously."

Abby figured her mom, a convention planner who traveled a lot for work, would know. She heard a key in the front door, so she hurried over to open it and let Miller in.

"Hi, Dad," Abby said, and she kissed him on the cheek and took a newspaper out of his hands. The "Dad" bit had taken a while to get used to, but Abby liked the way it occasionally made her feel her family was normal. "Mom told me the news."

"Oh." Miller sounded disappointed. "Cash said he'd call later, so he could tell you himself."

"He did?" Abby would've liked that. It would have made for a better story. "Mom says she's not sure about me missing school, but you *have* to let me go. You *have* to!"

"Let's just wait until we find out more, okay?"

Abby sat on the stairs in the hallway and looked at the headlines—war and more war—as her stepfather went to say hello to her mom in the kitchen.

"You know this is all her doing," Maggie muttered, no doubt thinking Abby had already gone back upstairs.

"Oh, give him some credit," Miller replied. "He's not a puppy. Besides, it'll be fun. Something different."

"That's a word for it." Metal clanked against the sink, like a wind chime from hell. "My God, Miller."

"What?"

Abby's ears perked up, and Maggie said, "You don't think Tamara will be there, do you?"

"Well, she *is* Cash's mother." Miller sounded tired.

"Loosely defined."

"*Abby* seems excited!" Miller said, and Abby almost felt bad for all the times she'd been purposefully sullen or agitated in order to make Miller's job as stepfather as difficult as possible. He hadn't had an easy run of it. Tamara had abandoned him and Cash when Cash was really little. Just took off one day and never came back, then wrote to say she'd fallen in love with an inmate she'd met through a prison outreach program. No one had ever told Abby how much time he was serving or for what, but she'd heard Maggie on the phone once, right around the time she met Miller, talking to a friend about how Tamara had named Cash after her first love, Johnny Cash, and how Miller blamed the relationship's demise on "Folsom Prison Blues."

She joined them in the kitchen, all smiles, and put the newspaper down. "So who else is going to be there? Like, what's the deal with her family again?"

"Good questions, both," Miller said.

"Well," Maggie said, "her father died when she was in high school. Her mother never remarried. She has a brother. We met them at the concert."

"Oh yeah." Abby was at the fridge, filling a glass with ice and water. Her mind flashed back to New York last year, to the cute boy with the shaggy black hair and big blue eyes. How could she have forgotten him for even a *second*? "Her brother's hot."

Maggie just shot her a look and said, "Other than that, I'm really not sure who they'll invite."

Abby took a fork and pulled a string of spaghetti out of a pot she feared had been boiling too long. Maggie and Al Dente had never had the pleasure of making each other's acquaintance. Abby said, "Well, the rest of the band, obviously."

The bass player, Trevor, was cute, but he was really big. Like huge. Abby didn't have much experience in this department, but she couldn't help but wonder what it would be like to have sex with someone that large. The geeky boy she'd deigned to have sex with was a wisp of a boy, and Colin, too, was superskinny. Trevor, the bass player, could probably crush her to death, and the thought sort of excited and scared her at the same time. Joe, the drummer, was cute, too. But Abby knew enough about the Starter House to know that Joe was married and recently had had a baby girl. He maintained the band's MySpace page, and she felt like she sort of knew him.

"Dad, you have to promise me you'll let me go, no matter what this one says." She rolled her eyes in her mother's direction. "I mean, I'll make sure all my college applications are in way early, I'll talk to my teachers way ahead of time, I'll get notes from Hannah or Lisa, I'll do whatever it takes."

Maggie drained the pasta, and the kitchen window steamed up. "What's so exciting all of a sudden about what amounts to a weeklong family party the sort of which you usually hate?"

"The *Starter House* isn't usually at our family parties." Abby got the grated cheese out of the fridge. "And they're not usually *on the beach in Belize.*

"Ohmigod"—she took her seat at the table—"Can I have my own room?"

Dan Eshom arrived early for Sunday's arranged document swap with Cash—at an East Village bar they'd been frequenting for years—after which he was meeting his newish girlfriend, Becky, for a little while. He was already seated at the bar with a pint in front of him when Cash arrived at the appointed hour—noon. Dan had purposely arrived way early because he was woefully hungover and needed a drink to take the edge off. He had gone out with his former roommate the night before and had gotten drunk enough at one bar to agree to continue on to a karaoke bar, where he'd sung two songs: "867-5309" and another one he couldn't remember. That had been happening more and more lately, the drinking-induced memory loss, and he had promised himself, and Becky, several times, that it wouldn't happen again. It had been the martinis, of course. He'd have to lay off them. How many times had he used that line, about martinis being like breasts, and still he failed to heed the wisdom. He'd had three before switching to beer. Not good.

"So I did it." Cash had come in with way too much energy for Dan's liking, and had quickly flagged down the bartender. He was wearing long cutoff jean shorts and a T-shirt with some kind of iron-on depicting a 1950s housewife and a slab of meat. With sunglasses hooked over the neckline, he looked cooler than Dan ever did. "I popped the question yesterday."

"Yeah?" Dan felt for a second as if his rib cage were shrinking, pictured his heart being squished through prison bars of bone. "What'd she say?"

Cash looked at him sternly, shook his head. "She said yes, you idiot."

"Had to ask." Dan shrugged at the bartender, who presented Cash's beer, knocked twice on the bar, and said, "That's on me. Cheers! Congrats!"

"Thanks, man." Cash held the drink up, then took a sip. "Thanks a lot." He turned to Dan and said, "Now there's a man who knows how to respond to good news." He shook his head again, feigning offense.

"I didn't mean anything by it. It's just you want to be sure before you congratulate someone. So, congratulations." Dan raised his glass and they clinked, and then Dan drank hungrily.

He had been mentally preparing for this moment for years, but only in the way that people prepare for things that they don't really believe are going to happen. Like tax audits. And unwanted pregnancies. And the avian flu pandemic. Which was pretty much not at all. He'd just always thought that June would break up with Cash. That Cash would screw it up somehow, or that June would just plain realize that she could do better. Better with someone like, for example, Dan. Cash was nice and cool and normal, sure, but he was a bit of a bumbler through life in some ways. Back in high school in California he was always late for marching band practice. Then in college—they'd both landed at Fordham—he was always oversleeping, turning in papers late. Even now at work Dan was the partner with his head screwed on tight enough to handle billing, taxes, the details. He had long seen himself as a sort of grounding force for his pie-in-the-sky pal. And June—totally-got-her-shit-together June—was simply way out of Cash's league.

Dan had half a mind to leave the bar right then, to go pound down June's door and proclaim his love for her the way he'd dreamed about doing so many times before. If it hadn't been for the hangover, he might have. Instead, he soldiered on. "When's the big day?"

"We're thinking December." Cash was obviously all jazzed up with his news, and Dan was working hard to seem enthusiastic.

"That soon?" Dan said, thinking he'd have to work even harder, but Cash didn't seem to detect even an air of skepticism, and why would he? Dan was *his best friend*.

Fuck, Dan thought. I'm his best friend. There was *no way* he could be the best man at this wedding. It would be tantamount to torture.

"Yup." Cash raised one shoulder. "Why wait?"

"What's it going to be . . . Chicago or here?"

Dan was obviously rooting for New York, and June wasn't a traditional kind of girl, so he figured it was pretty much a done deal. Then again, he'd seen other women go bonkers once they had a diamond on their finger, so you never knew. His sister, Karina, had torn through a good portion of his parents' life savings because she suddenly had to have a 250-person wedding with lobster and orchids and Godiva favors and a twelve-piece swing band at a mansion on the waterfront in Monterey, a place she'd never be able to afford to live—at least not after blowing on the wedding what could have been a hefty down payment.

"No, man," Cash said. "That's the cool thing. We're doing it in Belize."

It took a moment for this unexpected sentence to assemble itself into sense.

"Seriously?" All too easily, all too vividly, Dan could see it: June, barefoot, with a flower in her hair, tattoo twinkling; Cash in jeans and a white jacket, in desperate need of a haircut and a shave. June would do something silly, like botch the vows, and it would make for a story that would stab at Dan's heart. How beautiful, how charming, how fully realized June was. Dan felt that most people were parbaked at best.

"No joke." Cash had said. "We're still nailing down some details, but we'll put together some travel info soon."

"Oh. Cool." This took a second to register, too. "I'm invited?"

"Yeah, man. We're not *eloping.*"

"Oh." Dan was already counting up the money this was going to set him back, already wondering whether he'd still be going out with Becky when it happened, wondering whether she'd want to go. He was wondering, too, where people got off making their friends and family travel to the ends of the earth just to see them do something they could just as easily do locally. Nobody would bristle at going to Chicago for the weekend. June grew up there. But to randomly spin the globe and decide to get married wherever your finger landed—Dan couldn't help but find the whole thing arrogant.

"Just please don't do it on New Year's," he said, thinking of a Fourth of July wedding he'd had to go to in Jamaica. "I hate when people do that shit."

"Really?" Cash asked. "Why?"

Cash's phone buzzed on the bar then, and he tilted it up. "Trevor," he said.

Dan looked at his watch: 12:15. "A bit early for Trevor, isn't it?"

Cash read from the screen. "'McCarren four p.m. Don't be a pussy.'"

Dan nodded. "A barbecue."

"Yep."

The phone buzzed again.

"What now?" Dan asked.

Cash read again. "He says, 'The missus is already on board.'"

"So he's heard?" Dan stroked condensation on his glass.

"Nah. He's been calling her that since practically before we even got together. You wanna come?"

"Yeah, maybe." Dan wasn't sure he had the energy for Trevor, his least-favorite member of the Starter House. "I'm meeting Becky. I gotta see."

Cash left then, and Dan finished his drink and ordered another, then waited for Becky to arrive.

Becky lived on the Lower East Side—which Dan, knowing Becky, took as a clear sign that the LES had jumped the shark—and now whenever Dan, who lived in Long Island City, which was not on Long Island but in Queens, was on the island of Manhattan, she insisted they meet up, even if it was just to say hi or steal a kiss. It had seemed cute at the beginning, but now, four months in, it was getting annoying. He knew that she, at least, would be thrilled about the engagement, so much so that he wasn't sure he was up to telling her. Like any single woman who was trying to find out if her newish boyfriend was the marrying kind, she'd see this as a glorious opportunity to talk about marriage without having to bring it up herself.

When she arrived, she kissed him and said, "How's Cash?" and so he felt he had to tell her. She was wearing a short khaki skirt and two tank tops—lime green over white—and looked irritatingly refreshed. Dan hadn't managed a shower.

"They're such a cool couple," was Becky's response, wrapped in a sigh, and Dan wondered whether he detected in her tone a tinge of dissatisfaction with their own implied lack of coolness. Was it possible that Becky would someday break up with *him*? Was it possible that Becky *thought she could do better*? She ordered a seltzer.

"They're doing it in Belize," Dan said. He wiped more condensation beads off his pint and made a mental note to drink it slowly. "I'm not even sure I'll go."

"We *have* to go," Becky said. "You've known those guys forever."

Dan noted the "we" but didn't flinch.

"Aren't you, like, his best friend?"

Hearing Becky pose the question actually made Dan wonder. *Were* he and Cash really that close? Best man material? They'd known each other longer than they'd known any of their other friends; that much Dan knew for sure. And they'd been roommates for years in college. And now they spent a ton of time together, since they were business partners. But were they actually *close*? The only thing worse than being asked to be best man would be not being asked. Because that would mean Dan had it all wrong.

"Yeah, but it's a lot of money," Dan said, returning to what he thought was the point. "And one of us needs to be here for work, and it obviously won't be him. And it's not like I even really *want* to go to Belize. If it were—I don't know, Tuscany or Australia or something—someplace I *want* to go, that'd be different."

"It's not about that."

Dan could only shrug.

"And anyway, how do you know you don't want to go to Belize? I bet you don't know anything about it."

Becky had once gone on a cruise to the Panama Canal with her grandmother and, best Dan could tell, thought this fact made her an expert on all things Central American. It was remarkable, really, how often Becky could bring up the cruise in conversation. They'd be out with friends, talking about Bush or TiVo or the new Richard Linklater, and *bam!* there it was. *Well, I took a cruise to Panama once, and . . .*

"I'll probably go," he said, as a way to cut short the inquisition. But he was already cooking up potential excuses—maybe a grandparent's ninetieth birthday or a family reunion?

Dan thought he saw Becky purposely divert her eyes from his when she said, "We must be getting old. Even our hipster friends are getting married and settling down."

Becky had recently grown keen on pointing out the milestones in other people's lives, as if to signal to Dan that it was time he thought about doing those things, too—owning a home, getting hitched, having kids. It was never a shit-or-get-off-the-pot kind of proclamation, but Dan could tell Becky had it in her to issue just such an ultimatum. And that he might get it sooner than he had with the previous two girlfriends. She was woman enough to roar. The state of his current apartment, in particular, provoked her lioness tendencies. Dan served as the super of the dilapidated mansion that housed his vast but run-down two-bedroom duplex; he liked to think it was out of the kindness of his heart but it was also because he got a cut rate on the rent, courtesy of the elderly, ailing landlord. He'd gotten used to the building's faults—he was willing to suffer for the extra space, the home office—but after a recent stairway collapse, Becky had declared that she would never again stay the night. To Dan's dismay—with regard to this, and to a certain sexual act that she said she'd never partake in—she proved to be a woman of her word.

It wasn't that Dan didn't love Becky. He did. She was sweet, and kind, and cute, and so generally good to him that she made him want to become a better person, a feeling he liked. In general, they were good companions, and the sex was frequent, varied (except for that one thing), and highly satisfying. On paper, it all looked fine. He just always thought he'd have some grand passion in his life, and Becky didn't inspire that. He wasn't sure he'd throw himself in front of a bus or a bullet for her, for example, and had a hard time believing that she—who had weird long hairs on the back of her thighs and did yoga three times a week and ordered *seltzer* in a bar on a lovely summer afternoon, one of the *first* genuinely nice summer afternoons of the year—was the great love of his life, the last woman he'd ever have sex with. June was another story. Just the sight of any of the band photos on the Starter House's website, which Dan visited way more often than he knew was normal, was enough to provoke a new swell of adoration for her. The one of June in a hoodie with the band on the beach was the worst, and whenever he looked at it, Dan found himself battling this undertow inside himself, knowing full well that the second he stopped fighting, disaster would ensue.

"You're not even thirty," Dan said, bringing himself back to the conversation at hand. "I, on the other hand, am going to be thirty-three soon. Jesus was thirty-three when he died." He shook his head and felt suddenly sad. "What the hell have I done with my life?"

"Oh, don't be so dramatic," Becky said. "That's just the hangover talking."

"I'm *not* hungover!" Dan protested.

Becky pulled a face and put on a New Yawk accent and said, "Whaddayathinkeyeyam? Dumbasometin?" which Dan had gleaned was a quote from some sassy old movie he'd never seen and didn't care to. It was actually the only accent Dan had ever heard Becky do, which sort of amazed him, as she worked as an accent-reduction coach with immigrants from Eastern Europe, Asia, South America, everywhere. Her sister was the one with whatever degree was required for that line of work, and she'd groomed Becky once her business got off the ground. Dan couldn't help but think it explained some of Becky's social awkwardness. Sometimes she herself seemed like an immigrant—not quite drawing on the right cultural references. She was especially useless when playing that game where you put famous people's names in a hat, then take turns trying to get your partner or team to say them. To Dan's complete astonishment, she'd never heard of Lou Diamond Phillips.

"Hey." Becky put a hand on his knee and squeezed. "Maybe we'll end up celebrating your birthday in Belize! That'd be fun, right? We'll turn the whole thing into a vacation."

"I guess." It would be the irony of all ironies if June and Cash got married on Dan's birthday, their anniversary forever unforgettable to him. With each passing year he'd think of them exchanging gifts of paper or glass or silver or gold over a romantic anniversary dinner and then going home and having passionate but totally connected anniversary sex while he ticked off another year in some crappy bar with a dwindling number of friends. He finished his beer and knew Becky would frown on his getting another one. "So they're going to be in a park out in Brooklyn later," he said. "Barbecuing. If you want to go."

31

"Can't," Becky said. "I've got that thing. For Sarah."

Becky's friend Sarah was engaged and, at thirty-five, was so concerned with her declining fertility that she was pregnant, having given up the pill the second she got the ring; her bachelorette party was going to be a Sunday-afternoon sparkling-cider affair at a jewelry-making shop in SoHo. The fact that Becky didn't find this *completely fucking insane* worried Dan immeasurably.

She said, "I should get going. But tell them I said congrats!"

"I will," Dan said, kissing her good-bye and watching her ponytail sway as she walked toward the door. He had a little bit of a headache, a little bit of a buzz, and was thinking of sticking around for one more drink. Becky turned at the door and said, "Don't drink too much!"

Their breakup was surely imminent.

The reaction to the news at the book club's Sunday brunch at Felicia's house, like the reaction to that month's pick—*Bee Season*—was mixed.

"Oh, it'll be an adventure!" said Mary-Anise, though Alice knew that if it were *Mary-Anise* who had to go to Belize for *her* only daughter's wedding, she'd have called an emergency meeting. If it were Mary-Anise, they'd soon be reading a book about Belize, and the wedding would be all they'd talk about until it was over, at which point they could talk about it some more. Alice sometimes wondered how Mary-Anise sustained such a high level of drama in life. Her neighbor's husband had recently left her, and you would have thought it had happened to Mary-Anise herself, her outrage was so palpable. Alice quite liked the drama, though—at least most of the time. Being friends with

Mary-Anise made life more interesting. No one else that Alice knew used the word *travesty* on a regular basis.

"My nephew went to Belize on his honeymoon," said Sue, and Alice was heartened. "He was sick for weeks when he got back. Some weird fever from a bug bite, so make sure you coat yourself in DEET!"

"Honestly, Alice, I don't know what you expected," said Felicia, in her breezy, passive-aggressive way. June and Felicia's daughter, Felicity, had gone to high school together but had never been friends, and Felicity now lived a few minutes away and had three children. Alice had shown June the family Christmas card last year, and June had laughed out loud at the image: Felicity, her puffy husband, and the three kids—all five wearing snowman sweaters. She'd handed it back to Alice and said, "You just reminded me I need to get my pill prescription refilled."

Felicia started clearing dishes from the dining room table, and Alice, who hadn't been much in the mood for eggs Benedict, made a last-ditch effort to make it look like she'd eaten more than she had. "Knowing our June," Felicia said, "she'll probably get married in a black leather string bikini!"

Alice inwardly bristled as she handed off her plate but kept her tone in check. "I've always encouraged her to carve out her own path," she said, "so I don't know what I'm complaining about, really." She was going to regret this next bit, but if it was true that Alice was most proud of her daughter in the moments when anyone else dare doubt June, then so be it. "So enough about my little rock star's exotic wedding! We're here to talk about spelling bees!"

After talk of *Bee Season* deteriorated into talk of the movie adaptation, which Alice hadn't seen, and Richard Gere's puzzling sex appeal, which Alice didn't find that puzzling, talk turned briefly back to Belize. "I think it was a British colony until pretty recently," Sue said. "So they speak English."

"Well, thank God for that," Felicia said with a sort of ignorant passion that made Alice want to run out and sign up for Russian language lessons or salsa dancing or a course in Pan-Asian cooking. They'd settled in the living room with generous glasses of wine.

"But what will you wear, Alice?" Felicia looked suddenly horrified. "The mother of the bride in a sundress and flip-flops? I think not."

"Oh, don't be so rigid, Felicia," Mary-Anise said, and then Felicia stood and corked the chardonnay.

When Alice got home, the phone was ringing and she assumed it was Mary-Anise, calling for their traditional book club postmortem. She picked up and said, "Wow."

"Wow what?" It was Billy.

"Oh, hi, honey."

"Wow what?"

Alice liked hearing her son's voice on the line, with the house all still and lonely. Billy was the one who had gotten her a computer, taught her how to surf the Web, called her more than once every few weeks. He came home to visit maybe three times for every one time June came and seemed to enjoy time with Alice, whereas June always acted like she had an invisible rash when she came home. She hated malls and restaurants that had more than one location and was only really happy when they were doing things in Chicago proper; Billy liked just being *home*. It genuinely amazed Alice how close to each other her children were when to her they seemed so different.

Billy said, "Wow, we're going to Belize?"

"Yes, I guess so!" Alice was standing in the kitchen, drinking water. It was bad to be tipsy at one in the afternoon.

"You should go get passport photos taken this week," Billy said. "Just to get that in the works, you know? She said something about December, so that's only, what, six months away?"

Alice said, "Good idea, I'll do it this week," but it didn't feel like a good idea. None of this felt like a good idea at all.

After they hung up—Billy was on his way to meet June and Cash at a barbecue—Alice took the Brita out of the fridge and poured another glass of water. She took it to her bedroom and put it down and felt drawn to a photo album on her bedroom bookcase. She knew exactly what pictures were in this particular album, but that didn't stop her from pulling it down and, still standing, beginning to flip. The first picture, of her pregnant with June, standing next to Jack's sea green Mustang, hit her harder in the gut than she'd expected, and then memories rushed to mind so quickly, so abundantly, that it was hard to separate one from the other: the hospital room she'd shared with Mary Ellen Pace, whose son would later meet June in high school; the way June had flown out of her and nearly slid across the room; the 101-degree day on which she and Jack had gotten married, in a hall without air conditioning. She so wished that he were still here with her. June had always been Jack's—he'd named her after one of his musical heroines, he'd taught her to play guitar. Jack would know what to say to Alice now, how to make her laugh about Belize, how to help her see it as some kind of grand adventure—because with him it would be. Without him, she couldn't help but think that she'd really, quite frankly, rather not go.

The phone rang again, and Alice picked up. This time it really was Mary-Anise. "Can you believe she cut me off? Like I'm a child. I wasn't the only one hitting the chardonnay."

Alice just let out a loud sigh, and Mary-Anise, now softened, said, "So how are you really feeling about it?"

"Well, I guess I'm going." Alice set the photo album aside.

"Well, of *course* you're *going*," Mary-Anise said. "You'll have fun. Remember Hawaii?"

Mary-Anise and her husband, Bob, had a time-share on

Kauai that her husband couldn't be bothered going to anymore, and so Alice had accompanied Mary-Anise last winter. It had been a wonderful trip, and Alice had been grateful to find a friend like Mary-Anise so late in life. They'd met maybe three years before, at a Barnes & Noble downtown, while standing in line waiting to have Karen Joy Fowler sign copies of *The Jane Austen Book Club*. Alice had taken a tin of Altoids out of her purse, and Mary-Anise had said, "I'll take one of those," and then they'd started laughing and talking and couldn't stop. Their own book club was born that week.

"Hawaii was different," Alice said. "I was with you. We were tipsy half the time."

"What, you don't think they have booze in Belize?"

Alice let out an inexplicable sound. She was suppressing sobs.

"Aw, honey," Mary-Anise said. "What is it? You want me to come over?"

Alice pushed her tears away, rubbed wetness from her cheeks, wiped her hand on her jeans. "I know it's silly, it's just this isn't how I thought it would be. At all. My daughter's getting married in a country I hadn't heard of before yesterday, and I'm alone and I'm miserable."

"Hey," Mary-Anise said sharply. "You're not alone. And you're going to be fine."

Alice sniffled and nodded, feeling pathetic.

"Remember W-W-O-D?" Mary-Anise asked.

Alice reluctantly said, "Yes."

"Well, come on. What would Oprah do?"

The question had become a sort of guiding principle in Alice's life of late. And even though she knew that a lot of people would find her foolish for thinking such a thing, she believed that the influence of Oprah on the world could not be overstated. Never mind the book club, Oprah changed lives and had inspired Alice to try to become more aware of herself as well as of the world around her. She'd participated in Oprah's bra and jeans revolution and now knew she wore the right size—and cut—all around. At Oprah's urging, she'd sent letters to her congressmen urging them to enforce laws against human trafficking. She'd educated herself about subjects like avian flu and global warming. So when Hurricane Katrina happened, and a group of nurses from the Renaissance decided to go down south to help, Alice had felt a sort of tug inside of her, a pang that she wished she could ignore. Then Trudy, her best friend at work, signed on and looked at Alice, wide-eyed, over a mug of coffee in the nurse's lounge, and said, "What about you, Alice?"

Alice focused on the mug—NURSES DO IT WITH INTENSIVE CARE—and wondered, for the first time, how Oprah would handle this specific situation. So she found herself saying, "I'll go, too." The words, once out of her mouth, took on a sort of power. She felt brave, for a moment, and proud of herself. This was the new Alice: bold, fearless, selfless. But the second Trudy got up and rinsed her mug before walking away, Alice felt a bit of her courage drain. Because it was one thing to act brave, it was another thing to be it.

Having given her word, Alice went down to some small, wiped-out Gulf Coast towns whose names blurred together and did some basic first aid, gave out supplies. The devastation she saw was simply that: devastating. But she'd been expecting that. The real surprise came weeks later, when the group from the Renaissance was invited to be in Oprah's audience for a show about the relief effort—only the show wasn't *about* the relief effort. It was one of Oprah's "Favorite Things" episodes—the one where she gives away thousands upon thousands of dollars in goodies. Like most people in the studio audience that day, Alice had cried, but Alice was certain she was crying for different reasons than everyone else. Alice wasn't a hero. Alice had guilted herself into helping. She was entirely unworthy of Oprah's loot.

She gave away the big-ticket items. The video iPod had gone to Billy; the UGGs to June; the BlackBerry, which had only made her depressed since she had so little to put into it, also to Billy, via June, who tried it and decided she didn't need it either. Alice had pretty much lived in the cashmere sweater until the weather got too warm, and she'd enjoyed imagining that the diamond necklace was a gift from Jack. Because of a variety of skin products—but especially Hope in a Jar—her epidermis had never looked better.

Hope in a Jar. It was right there on her dresser, and Alice wished the jar were big enough to climb into.

"Hellllllloooooo," Mary-Anise said. "Am I going to have to get you a T-shirt?" They'd joked about getting some "WWOD?" ones printed up.

What *would* Oprah do?

"Well, she'd stop feeling sorry for herself." Alice got up to get a tissue from the bathroom adjoining her room. "She'd also turn up in an *amazing* dress."

"Damn straight." Mary-Anise laughed.

"I'm serious." Alice took a deep breath. "I haven't got a thing to wear."

"So," Mary-Anise said in that way that made it sound like what she was going to say next was the most obvious thing in the world, and of course it was. "We'll go shopping." After a pause Mary-Anise said, "And I really wish you'd . . . ah. Forget it."

"What?" Alice asked.

"No, forget it."

"No, really. *What?*" Alice asked more forcefully. She knew Mary-Anise wasn't the type to let anything go easily. Ever. Apparently—this was one of Mary-Anise's favorite stories to tell about herself—when her daughter Bridget had gotten appendicitis on a trip down to Florida's Disney World, Mary-Anise had driven the rental car straight from the airport to a local hospital, where Bridget promptly had surgery. The next day the whole family had gone on to see Mickey as planned, even with Bridget in a wheelchair.

Mary-Anise said, "I just really wish you'd let me and Bob introduce you to Jack," and Alice had to concentrate on not hanging up.

Jack was Mary-Anise's husband's partner in his law firm and was recently divorced. The fact that he shared Alice's late husband's name was only one of the reasons Alice had avoided such a setup. The mention of it now left her stunned.

"I'm sorry," Mary-Anise said. "I know it's not a good time but I wish you'd . . ."

"You're right," Alice said. "It's really not a good time."

At work at the Troc Center on Sunday, Abby couldn't have been more bored if she tried. She was folding a stack of T-shirts with a handy folding board, and it was all she could do not to scream. Because seriously. A folding board? If there was a more retarded object in the world, Abby had yet to encounter it. Sometimes, on days like today, she wished she could just fast-forward and be grown up already, with her own apartment and wads of cash and fabulous clothes and a job that meant something—one that didn't just suck up endless hours, tick-freaking-tock. Surely subjecting people her age to working in a windowless mall—not counting the skylights above the food court——should be illegal.

As of this morning, Abby was officially living for the wedding in Belize. Before that she'd been living for college, but this was better because it was only six months away. There was so much to think about and so much to do. On her way to work she started making a list in the notebook she always carried with her—mostly for sketching purposes. She'd gotten a window seat on the BART, and she had her iPod playing the Starter House's second album, which had one of Abby's favorite songs, "Godspeed," on it. She wrote down

1. Buy a new swimsuit.
2. Buy—or make?—a new dress.
3. Finish college applications.

That last one was arguably the most important. Her mom was already up in her grill about them, and Abby would need evidence of real progress to show M and M when it came time for them to buy her plane ticket or not. So she'd dug out her UC application that morning and shoved it in her bag to look over. She didn't feel like doing it, though, and she lost interest in her list, too, and just listened.

God, the Starter House were good. It sort of amazed Abby that they weren't totally famous or huge, but she knew they would be soon. She was pretty sure they'd be her favorite band even if Cash were just some random stranger. Because a lot of the bands that were popular these days sounded a lot alike. They were all trying to be like some other band before them that had already sold a million records. But Abby couldn't think of anybody to really compare the Starter House to; they were just good. She mouthed some of the lyrics to "Godspeed," which had to be the best breakup song ever.

"Look up to the stars / Walk her to her car / because streetlights don't come on till late."

Cash's voice sounded so awesome on those lines, and it always made Abby wish she had a car that someone could walk her to.

"Watch her as she goes / taillights in the mirrors / wonder if she knows / she knows / Godspeed."

She'd asked him once what the inspiration for the song was,

and he'd said that he had no idea, that he started with music and then just waited to see what words came and that it was more about the sound of the words sometimes than their meaning. That had pretty much rocked Abby's world, because she felt somehow the same way about designing clothes. She was never inspired so much by an idea as she was by a feeling, so that was sort of the same, right? She bopped her head along to the coolest riff in the world and looked out the window on a miserably drizzly morning, hoping her days in San Francisco were numbered.

Everyone seemed to assume that Abby would go to college in the state of California—her friends, her teachers, M and M—though Abby had never stated or even implied such a thing. Some of the UC schools seemed okay, yeah—like Berkeley—and that was pretty much what M and M were pushing for. It was Miller's alma mater, and Abby suspected that her mother thought it would further cement their reputation as one big happy family if her daughter went to her new husband's alma mater. But the best fashion design schools—not to mention the coolest stepbrother in the world—were in New York. In Abby's mind, there was only one application that mattered. Maybe two. And she had a lot of work to do if she was going to get them in on time.

She was on line for Sbarro when she saw him, getting on line for Chinese food. Colin Murray worked at the Troc Center on weekends, too, and a group of them met for lunch pretty much every Sunday. His gaze fell on her, and he tilted his chin up to say "Hey," so she did the same, then Hannah and Lisa, both of whom worked at Forever 21, which Abby thought was pretty hilarious since they were only seventeen, cut in line with her and they ordered. She and Hannah had been friends since grade school, but Lisa was new to school this year, having just moved to San Francisco from L.A., which she never stopped talking about. Abby didn't really like her, but Hannah did—Hannah wanted to live in L.A. someday, in a house with an infinity pool and tiki torches—and Abby didn't dislike her enough to make a big deal out of it. She knew she and Hannah were tight as tight could be.

Once they had their food, Abby led the way to the seating area and slid into a chair next to Colin, who was one of her Top 8 friends on MySpace. "So did you see my bulletin? About my brother getting married in Belize?"

"Yeah, that's pretty cool," he said. His hair was dark and spiky, hipper than anyone else's hair that Abby knew. She was glad that when school ended in a few weeks, she'd probably be seeing even more of Colin here at the mall.

"Isn't he your *step*brother?" Lisa said.

Abby ignored her and kept talking to Colin. "It's in December. I might have to miss school for like a week."

Colin had a music magazine with him, and he was reading over the headlines on the front cover. He said, "You should go ziplining," and looked up with new interest.

"What's that?" Abby liked the way his hazel irises were darker around the edges.

"My brother told me about it." He sounded excited. "You go to these places and they've got these cables that connect to a bunch of platforms in the jungle and you hang from them in some kind of harness, I guess, and sort of fly through the air from one to the other."

Hannah cut in then and said, "Sounds awful."

Lisa, who pretty much never had an original thought, said, "Totally."

"No it doesn't." Abby turned to Colin. "It sounds awesome!"

"Well, excuse me," Hannah said, almost under her breath but not quite.

"Yeah," Lisa said. "You know what sounds awesome to me? Sitting on a beach."

Ignoring her—again! Abby was getting good at that—Abby asked Colin, "Where'd your brother do it?"

"Costa Rica. He said it was really cool. You totally have to do it."

"I will," Abby said. "I totally will. What's it called again?"

"Ziplining."

"Ziplining," Abby repeated, and even with Hannah and Lisa whispering to each other about something, and even under the cloudy skylights of the Trocadero, where the air smelled like some bizarro food hybrid like tacos lo mein or Cinnabon quesadillas, she thought that life—maybe, *finally*, a full seventeen years in—was starting to get interesting.

Dan had made plans to meet Cash and June at their place in Williamsburg, and then to walk over to McCarren from there. When he arrived and buzzed, June's voice came through the intercom. "I'm coming down."

Dan had been prepared to go up, but the door to the building didn't buzz unlocked, so he took a few steps down the street and looked in the window of the hat shop. What he saw confirmed what he already knew; Dan wasn't a hat kind of guy.

"He-ey," June said, finally. She was wearing slouchy black shorts that touched the tops of her knees and a cream-colored T-shirt with the Coney Island Cyclone rendered in purples and greens. Her hair was the same color blond it had been the last time Dan had seen her, and this surprised him. It looked, to him, like wheat.

"Hey yourself." Dan kissed her on the cheek.

As per usual, she smelled like lily of the valley. Because of *course* she'd have perfume that smelled like the one flower in

43

the world with which Dan had any positive association. His beloved aunt Jenny—his mother's twin sister—died from breast cancer in her forties, scaring the living bejesus out of Dan on account of his mom, who shared her genes but who was then and still remained cancer-free. Aunt Jenny was definitely the good twin in Dan's young mind, and though he'd finally, as an adult, grown fond of his own mother (he was still working on his dad), it was Aunt Jenny who had always turned up with cool toys and gifts. It was Aunt Jenny who always wanted to bake cupcakes and make mud pies and messes in general. It was Aunt Jenny who'd grown lily of the valley and then made and bottled her own perfumed water.

"So I hear congratulations are in order," Dan said.

"I guess! Thanks!" June nodded and her eyes got wide—"Scary!" she said—and Dan wondered whether she was having doubts about the whole thing already. He remembered those blissful months after June had joined the band but before she got together with Cash; she was working some temp job near Times Square, and he was nearby at a trade magazine publishing house, and they'd meet for breaks at a massive bar/arcade where June would play Dance Dance Revolution USA—a bizarre game where you have to move your feet in sync with symbols on the screen while loud electronica music blasts from the machine. Had he asked her out then, everything might have gone differently.

"Walk with me," she said. "Cash is gonna meet us at the store."

"Let's see the ring," Dan said before they moved.

"Really? I hate that shit." June started to walk off. "I almost left it home."

Dan stood his ground. "Be a girl for once, will you?"

June stopped and turned and presented her hand. Dan stepped forward and lifted it within an inch of his face and squinted.

"Very funny," June said, pulling the ring away. Dan's hand felt the cold void that her warm hand left behind.

Loath as he was to admit it, the ring was stunning. Not a traditional solitaire but a band of tiny glittering triangles and circles and squares. It looked like more of a wedding band than an engagement ring, and Dan wondered whether Cash's plan was to do the whole thing backward and give her a big rock in Belize. "He did good," Dan said.

"Yeah, right?" June studied the ring herself for a second, then ran a hand through her hair, patently embarrassed by her lapse into girlie girl. "I'm sort of shocked. Designed it himself. Or so he says."

"Well, he's a lucky guy." Lucky Dan didn't get there first, for starters.

"Well, shucks, Dan. Thanks."

Dan knew that June and Cash were both "cooler" than he was by popular standards, but even their supermarket was cooler than his, which seemed to add insult to injury: it had a refrigerated room. He and June pushed their way through thick slices of soft plastic that set off the cashiers and dry goods, keeping the frigid air where it belonged. Frigid air. Dan had never really put two and two together.

June instructed Dan to grab a twelve-pack of something cheap and maybe a six of something good. He did so, then joined her by the meat. He said, "So Belize, huh?"

"Yeah." June was eyeing steaks. "You excited?"

"Becky sure is!" He instantly regretted bringing her up.

"I like that Becky," June said, as if realizing this for the first time, and Dan realized, *not* for the first time, that June's body was perking up in the cool air. "She's got spirit."

"I'm glad you approve," Dan said wryly, sort of by rote, and they moved down to brats and wursts. "So, why Belize?"

"Because it's beautiful. And cheap." June picked up some chicken and apple sausages and said, "What do you think of these?" Dan shrugged, and they went into the basket. "And," she continued, "not completely overrun with horrible Americans, at least not where *we're* going. And I'd rather give some people there my money than give it to some wedding factory here that'll charge me two million dollars a head for crap I don't even want."

"Hey, man," Cash said, surprising Dan. "Let me help you with that."

Cash pushed his messenger bag around to his back, then went to relieve Dan of the twelve-pack, but Dan said, "I got it." He held out the six-pack instead. "Here."

"Ah." June put a flat palm on Cash's cheek. "Boys."

McCarren—thick with crabgrass and cut through with cracked paved paths—wasn't a nice park by any definition, but Dan had a soft spot for it, stemming entirely from these barbecues of Trevor's. He was, in fact, way fonder of Trevor's barbecues than he was of Trevor, who was sitting in a lime green lawn chair as if it were a throne when Dan, June, and Cash arrived. Trevor's friend Gary was there, too, and he introduced himself to Dan for what must have been the tenth or eleventh time, which pissed Dan off to no end. Why didn't this guy ever remember him?

Trevor said, "What the fuck is that?" and pointed at June's ring before anyone had a chance to say anything official, and Dan thought, This is just like Trevor; he can make anything about *him*. Though to be fair, the ring was catching all sorts of fire in the late-afternoon sun. "Am I gonna have to start calling you Yoko now?"

June tsked and said a singsong "No."

Trevor let out a short laugh and said, "I was talking to Cash."

"Ha-ha," Cash drawled.

"Holy shit, man." Trevor snapped open a Coke. "We going to Belize?"

Cash nodded. "That's the plan."

"Sa-weet," Trevor said. "Have Speedo. Will travel."

June said, "Well, if the trip doesn't kill my mother, that sure will," and Dan thought international travel with Trevor—Speedo or not—might be the death of him, too.

Trevor smiled. "How'd Alice take the news?"

Dan regretted that he hadn't thought to ask after June's mother on the walk over.

June said, "She was alive when we hung up. And anyway, it'll be good for her. You know. Leave the cul-de-sac."

June's brother, Billy, had arrived and was putting a six-pack of beer into a cooler. "It's not a cul-de-sac," he said.

June said, "It might as well be."

Billy handed some beers around by way of greeting, and Dan took one and said, "Hey, man. Good to see you. Thanks!" It occurred to Dan that he might be off the hook on the best man front, and since leaving Becky, he'd definitely decided that he wanted to be off the hook. Cash was pretty tight with Billy, so maybe he'd ask him?

Joe arrived then, with his wife, a hairdresser whose name Dan could never remember, and baby girl in tow. June, having learned her lesson, wasted no time in saying, "We have news."

"We heard," Joe said. "Some chick named Hearts and Stars or something is broadcasting it all over MySpace."

"Oh, shit." Cash scratched his head. "I mean, oh well! Whatever, I guess."

"That's his stepsister," June said. "You remember Abby?"

"Of course," Trevor said. "She legal yet?"

Cash rooted through his messenger bag. "Oh, crap. I forgot my gun."

The hairdresser, who had pretty lame hair in Dan's opinion, swooped in to hug June loosely—baby in a sling between them—and said, "Congratulations. It's so exciting."

47

Everyone settled in then, and some meats went down on the grill. This beer, Dan's fourth of the day, finally killed off the last of his hangover, and the park seemed to inspire a rather nice buzz, encompassing as it did everything that Dan liked about the outer boroughs of New York City. Nearby a small Hispanic girl with dark curly hair and pierced ears in a hot pink dress was tugging on a pink balloon tied to her wrist with white ribbon while her family grilled their dinner. Some festive music with a Latin beat blared from their boombox. Two dogs—one bulldog, one mutt—sniffed each other on the park's main walkway while their owners, one a hipster, the other an older Polish-looking woman, stood and chatted politely. Dan thought of Becky sipping sparkling cider at her jewelry-making party in SoHo and thought, for sure, life was way more fun as a guy, as Dan. Here at McCarren, he felt like he was a part of something.

"So who's all coming to this shindig anyway?" Trevor asked as he readied the coals for a second wave of cooking. Everyone had already helped themselves to the first wave, and June's steak and chicken/apple sausages had been a big hit. The air smelled of meat, heat, summer.

Cash said, "Well, Dan here's coming. Right, Dan?"

"I'm thinking about it, yeah. I mean, if I can."

"You're *thinking* about it? If you *can*?" Trevor's face contorted into a caricature of confusion and disgust. "What's there to think about? The man's getting married. You go."

"Well, I'll be there." Billy, sitting on a blue and white gingham picnic blanket, stretched long legs capped at the feet by bright orange sneakers. "Not like I have a choice in the matter, but yeah." June whacked him softly on the head. "I'm psyched."

Trevor said, "Joe?" and everyone looked at Joe, who looked like he hadn't had a decent night's sleep or a decent night out—or probably a decent lay—in months. He, in turn, looked at his wife, rubbed the baby's head with his thumb. "I don't know what we're going to do. It's not easy, you know. The baby."

June said, "Bring the baby! She'll be almost one!"

"To Belize?" Joe said.

"Sure, why not?" June cracked open a beer. "I mean, people in Belize have babies, you know?"

"Of course," Joe said. "We'll just have to see."

Looking at Joe—and also thinking of his own sister, Karina, and the dentist she married in her lavish wedding, and the baby that had come soon after—Dan couldn't help but think that having a baby was pretty much the end of the world. He'd been keeping a mental list, though, of things he'd swear he wouldn't do if he ever ended up having a kid. Like talk about the contents of a diaper, or ever refer to one as "poopy." Or change a diaper in a room where food was being served. Or beg off of every possible social event and blame it on the baby. Or talk about height and weight percentages. He was glad that Joe had deflected the heat away from him.

"Leah," June said, seriously, and Dan repeated, *Leah*. "I'm sure we can make arrangements. A crib. Whatever you need. And I'd be thrilled if you'd do my hair."

"Aw, thanks. Really." Leah shifted the baby's weight. "I'd love to. It's just we have no idea what we're in for, what things'll be like."

"Of course," June said.

Dan could tell she was crestfallen. This Belize idea was losing its zip, because when you actually started to think about the logistics, it was a pain in the ass.

"What's *your* excuse?" Trevor said, and Dan looked up and saw to his horror that Trevor was talking to him. June and Cash were talking to Leah and Joe, and Gary was putting some hot dogs on the grill. Billy and his orange sneakers, though, seemed to be awaiting Dan's response as eagerly as Trevor was, and

Dan found his gaze especially unsettling. June and her brother had the same sort of penetrating stare.

"It's not an excuse." Dan said. "I just don't know if I can really afford it. There's airfare and accommodations and a gift, and then there's the fact that I work for myself and don't get paid vacation days."

Trevor shook his head. "It's not about the money, man."

"That's what people with money always say."

"Yeah, I'm really rolling in it." Trevor turned and shouted, "Hey, June, what's airfare like?"

June turned and cocked her head. "Dunno. Three-fifty or so? Five hundred? I mean, it's not *that* far."

Dan nodded, feeling confident he was in the right. "Which means that the whole thing will cost me and Becky somewhere between a thousand and two thousand dollars."

"If that's how you want to look at it." Trevor cracked open another soda, and Dan sort of wished the guy would just have a freakin' beer already. People who didn't drink bugged him.

"Trevor," June said sharply. "Lay off it. Whoever can make it will make it. You don't have to start terrorizing people."

More like *trevorizing*, Dan thought. He'd been *trevorized* more times than he could count.

Trevor's eyes lit with a new idea, and Dan sensed his interrogation was over, that Trevor had lost interest anyway in the wake of such a scolding. "Hey"—Trevor moved toward June—"I thought we were recording in December."

"Yeah." June's gaze dropped to the ground. She suddenly seemed irrationally interested in the label on her beer bottle. "We might have to rethink that. Wedding-wise, it's really the only time that makes sense."

Cash stepped up next to June then, and then Trevor and Cash started getting into it about recording time—June said something like, "We don't even have enough songs"—and then Joe was involved, too, and it all sounded fairly heated, but Dan couldn't be bothered to pay attention. The band stuff bored the crap out of him most the time, and he was more surprised than anything that they were all still at it. Not that they weren't good, but it was such a long shot, and it had been, what, five years? He liked hanging out with the band, though, most of the time, and thought his association with them did wonders for his reputation. If you weren't naturally inclined to hipness, proximity to the hip could help. And it wasn't just that they were hip, they were a different kind of person than Dan. They were the cool kids, the ones who could skip class and not get caught. The ones who got tattoos and somehow pulled them off. He thought their energy was somehow different from his—though he couldn't exactly pinpoint why or how—and he liked it. Cash had been his pipeline to this kind of crowd for years.

But as for the nuts and bolts and amps and wah-wah pedals and studio time and "creative differences," it just wasn't all that interesting. He watched, instead, as Leah handed June her crying baby. June, taken off guard, said, "Oh!" and then started walking in circles near the group's splay of blankets and lawn chairs. She looked at Dan and raised her eyebrows and made her bottom lip tug to the left as if caught in a fishing hook—a sort of universal charade for "I have no idea what I'm doing"—and Dan just lay back on the blanket, perched on his elbows, and watched. The fact that June was holding a caterwauling baby gave him a nice excuse to just stare. She was shushing the baby and said, "Oh, Darla, you're killing me." So the baby's name was Darla. Leah and Darla. Dan made a mental note.

Suddenly Dan, whose bowel was as irritable as he generally was, realized that he was going to use the bathroom sooner than later, for more than a piss. So he decided it would be best to head home. The restrooms at McCarren Park left a lot to be desired.

"I gotta take off," he said, and everyone muttered good-byes. He started to walk off and said, "Have a good one," and heard Trevor say, "You have a better one."

God, that guy could be an asshole. Though to be fair, Dan sort of envied Trevor in this one regard: the man knew how to be somebody's friend in a sort of dramatic, knights-of-the-round-table way that Dan could never quite muster. Trevor was the guy who'd help you move when it was just you and him and five rooms of heavy equipment. In the snow. Without gloves. Or a van. He was the guy who'd loan you his car when your girlfriend's father, upstate, died and you needed to get her home in a hurry. He was the guy who went to see his friends' bands play out around the city probably once or twice a week, not because they all always came to Starter House shows, but because that's just what you did. He was a sort of friendship Knight in Shining Armor, and if there was one chink, it was that he expected everybody else to be the same way.

The whole bus ride home—it was a pretty quick trip from McCarren to LIC on the B61, which mercifully came right away—Dan stewed. But he wasn't just annoyed with Trevor. He was annoyed with himself, too. He couldn't help but think that his own lack of enthusiasm for this Belize venture was indicative of a major character flaw. Then again, if Cash hadn't been marrying *June*, Dan might've felt differently. The fact that he pined for his best friend's fiancée, though—he was sure again now; they *were* best friends—probably indicated an even worse character flaw.

At the dilapidated mansion he took a beer out of the fridge, snapped the can open, took a sip, then went to the stereo. His bowels had calmed. He cued up a Starter House song—one of June's slow piano songs—turned it up loud, and stood and listened. He did this more often than he cared to admit. There was something about her voice in his apartment—dilapidated or not—that made him feel close to her. She'd only ever been to the dilapidated mansion for parties, but when Dan played her records he could imagine her there with him, just the two of them. He turned it off just as quickly, though, having decided to go upstairs and not to come back down, since the stairs really were pretty treacherous. He went up them—taking them two at a time at the bottom in order to pass over a missing step—then went into his bedroom. He put his beer down and opened the closet door. An old Doc Martens shoe box on the top shelf looked down on him like a disappointed parent. He reached up to take the box down, then placed it on his bed and opened it.

It was there, all right. Right where he'd left it, and he was almost mad. If he'd lost it, misplaced it, thrown it out in a fit of jealousy or rage, then it would be gone and he wouldn't have to deal with it. It was a cocktail napkin with an autograph on it. He'd purchased it on eBay after tripling the price at the last minute in a panic because in that moment he'd felt that he just *had* to have it, that his destiny was at stake. The signature read "June Carter," and he'd bought it, of course, for June on account of her namesake, on account of the fact that they'd met up in Bar Code one day and she'd convinced *Dan* to try Dance Dance Revolution and he had, and then he'd fallen flat on his face and they'd laughed and laughed until Dan was sure the laugh turned into something else, a sort of charged—yes, sexually charged—silence.

He took the autograph out of the Ziploc bag it had arrived in and took it into the bathroom with him, put it on the back of the toilet, and picked up the matches he kept there for olfactory emergencies. He lit a match, then reached for the autograph and held it near the flame. He was playing out a scene he'd seen in how many movies and TV shows? He tried to think of specific scenes but couldn't, and wondered how often the paper gets burned versus how often it doesn't. Maybe there were universal rules about this sort of thing. Burn the item, and this will happen; spare the item, and that will happen. The flame singed his fingers, and he dropped the match in the toilet and said, "Ow." He sat down then—on the toilet—and made a decision with all the drunken conviction he could muster. He'd bought the autograph for June because he loved her. And goddamn it, he was going to give it to her.

*B*efore Radio City there was, oh, so much more. Like, for starters, this:

They are kissing for the first time, Cash and June, bar stool to bar stool, because earlier that night, they played a disappointing (lame turnout) gig in the downstairs room of a Hoboken bar where Cash's girlfriend, Cara, was being snarky with her gal pal Janine, saying things like "I don't think she's that great," and "She's not even that pretty." Janine was saying things like "Me neither," and "You're way prettier," but was really thinking, Cara's a complete idiot if she doesn't see the way June and Cash look at each other. They were loading out when Joe pulled his car around, radio blaring—all bass, like he was out cruising. Only it was their song, June's song, "Recovering," that was blasting, and Joe, who'd sent a CD to the DJ of this particular show and thus knew to tune in, said, "We're on the fucking radio!" They stood there in the street, annoying drivers who were passing by, determined to listen all the way through, even though they obviously knew the song's every note, lick, cymbal crash. They'd played it live maybe twenty minutes before. June, you may have noticed, is not the kind of girl who jumps up and down. She was jumping up and down. Nor is she the kind of girl who claps her hands excitedly, but, well, she was.

55

They are thinking of moving this little production from the bar stools to her place because things sound better on the radio than they do in a mostly empty club, and each of them had a moment out there on the street when they closed their eyes and imagined their song making its way into the world: into cars that reek of stale smoke on the FDR Drive and steamy kitchens on the Lower East Side and cluttered toll booths by the Brooklyn Battery Tunnel and maybe even swank beach houses out in the Hamptons. They imagined ears perking up, people thinking, What's that song? and then listening carefully to see who was by. When they opened their eyes, they were looking right at each other, and something had changed in that the something could no longer be denied.

They are walking silently now to her place, stopping occasionally to kiss with abandon in smelly doorways, because even after their radio debut, there was still the gear to contend with. After every stinking gig, the gear. Right when you should be able to bask in your glory, there is equipment to be packed up, loaded out, and driven back to the rehearsal space, where it needs to be loaded in again. Sure, you can load out and stick around, and risk your stuff being stolen from your car. Sometimes they do. But this time they didn't. Hoboken's just not that cool, and there's not much point *in sticking around. So they decided to unload back at the space and then toast their radio debut at their regular dive across the street.*

She is putting the key to her door in the lock because she rode back to the space with Trevor, and spent most of the ride hoping that Cash would drop Cara and Janine off before coming to the space and the bar. So when, a half hour later, he came into the rehearsal room alone, carrying an amp, she was hopeful. But then she went out for another load and Janine and Cara were coming up the stairs of the building—one carrying a guitar, the other a keyboard stand. Cash caught up to her out on the street, and she said—quite cryptically, when you consider that everything between them was still unspoken—"This is getting old."

They are at the bed now, grappling with buttons and snaps and zippers because he said, "What's getting old?" Then the girls barreled out of the door, and Cara came over and kissed Cash and said, "We'll see you at the bar," and he knew right then what: Cara.

Cara *was getting old. The fact that he was no longer in love with her was getting old.*

They are starting to relax now and slow things down because, after a few drinks and toasts at the bar, the band was mostly pretending not to notice that Cash and Cara were having a fight. A real doozy, by the looks of it. Janine, no fool, had already split, but Cara just wasn't letting go of whatever she was going on about, and she and Cash were having it out, big-time, by the jukebox. The band started joking, then, about good fight soundtracks, like "Beat It" or "Hit Me with Your Best Shot," but June's heart wasn't really in it (though she threw out "Saturday Night's Alright for Fighting" for sport; it was a Saturday). Joe and Trevor were beside themselves, all buzzed up from the night's events and mimicking the opening guitar riffs of "Eye of the Tiger." They had no idea what was about to happen between Girl *and* Boy.

Then Cara stormed out of the bar, and Cash returned to the table just as Joe said that he should probably call it a night. Everyone agreed it was time and started to head for the door, and then June said she was going to run to the loo and she'd see them at practice in a few days, not to wait. Clever girl, our June. Clever girl.

They are practically shaking from the thrill of discovering that their bodies just work *together because a few minutes later they were sitting silently at the bar, just the two of them, sipping whiskeys. Cash had only pretended to leave—went so far as to walk across the street to his car and get in it—and then came back in to find June sitting at the bar with two drinks in front of her. She'd only gone to the bathroom in the hope that Cash wasn't really as clueless as he sometimes seemed, and she'd prepared herself for the possibility that she'd wind up drinking two drinks if he was. 'Twould have been a terrible shame if the whole thing really were in her head.*

He is kissing her neck and it tastes of sweat and maybe whiskey and some delicate flower he can't quite place because June said, "Was that the breakup?"

She is squirming and heating up because he said, "Not quite."

He is holding back nothing now because he said, "I'm afraid to leave this bar with you."

She is pulling him into her because she shrugged and smiled and said, "That's going to make things kind of difficult."

They are moving in some foreign, familiar rhythm because he said, "I want to do this right."

And moving, still, because she laughed at the formality of it and then let her knee fall into his leg.

They are both saying things like "Oh God, Oh God," because he touched her bare knee and pushed it back to where it belonged and said, "No, I mean it. I don't want things to be messy."

They are hitting it and going straight through because she pictured Cara breaking things in the apartment she and Cash shared, screaming things like "That bitch! I bloody knew it!" (Cara was British), and she said, "Oh, Cash, honey. It'll be messy."

She's looking at the ceiling now, studying a fault line in the paint with his body collapsed on hers because he said, "Yeah, but it can be less messy."

She is stroking the back of his sweaty head—hot and cold in her warm fingers—because she said, "So what are you saying?"

He is rolling off her now and pulling her closer to his side because he said, "I'm saying not tonight."

The Pine Ridge

Saturday

Alice studied her first passport stamp—a barely legible smudged blur of ink—then stepped into the Belize City airport's main gallery. A flash of pink drew her eye as she scanned the small crowd that greeted her flight. A moment later, as her eyes were drawn back the same way, she registered that the pink was June's hair. Was it too late to turn around and go home?

"Mom!" June shouted, seeing her a split second later. "You made it!"

The pink seemed to fade away. Something about the way June's eyes crackled made Alice think that her daughter was at home here in a way she'd just never been in Chicago—maybe wasn't even in New York. Her skin glowed, and Alice had a flash of guilt over not having given birth to June in some tropical clime, over not passing on to her a gene for pink hair. Then again, maybe it wasn't Belize but another b-word that suited her daughter, who'd always liked being the center of attention anyway. *Bride.*

Still, as June rushed into Alice's arms, Alice couldn't resist. "Your hair," she said. It was longer than it had been in recent memory, falling in choppy layers down onto June's shoulders.

"*Mom,*" June groaned, still inside the hug. "Don't start."

She pulled away and nodded toward a luggage carousel. "We've got a two-and-a-half-hour drive ahead of us. We can talk about my hair all you want once we're on the road."

"Hi, Mrs. Siren," Cash said, stepping out from behind June.

"Cash," Alice said, opening her arms to him, too. "Don't be so formal. Please." It felt like a funny thing to say to a man who was wearing flip-flops, plaid shorts, and a T-shirt with a hole—like a scissor snip—in its sleeve.

"Okay then, Alice." He smiled. "Welcome to Belize."

"Thanks!" She peeled a layer off as they made their way over to the luggage conveyor. "It's hot." It had been 32 degrees in Chicago that day, the warmest it had been in a week, and Alice felt some of the same girlish giddiness she'd felt when she and Mary-Anise had arrived in Hawaii last December and walked into the open-air lobby to find a Christmas tree. There'd been a big snowstorm in Chicago while they were away, and they'd relished every opportunity to watch the weather reports, tropical cocktails in hand. They'd imagined Felicia out in her driveway with her snowblower, and they'd laughed and laughed and laughed.

As Customs had taken a while, eager bags were already spinning around the airport's one carousel. "That's mine," Alice said, pointing to her flowery rolling bag.

"Wow, Mom." June pointed out the bag for Cash, and he grabbed it, and Alice thought it was funny that June allowed him that much. "It matches your couch."

Alice looked at her watch and thought, That might be a record. Shortest time from hug to insult. But looking at her bag—which did now look more suitable for a trip to the English countryside—and knowing its contents, it was hard to defend. She imagined Cash's parents and all of June's friends having safari-tested luggage and luxurious tropical wardrobes, replete with wide-brimmed sun hats and rugged footwear. She pictured them talking in whispers behind her back about her clear one-dollar rain poncho, about her farty pleated shorts. She'd done her best, shopping for the trip whenever she could, but she still wasn't happy with what she'd brought or with any of the dresses—there were three—that she'd bought for the wedding itself. She'd packed them all, hoping against hope that one of them might magically reassemble itself in her bag into the perfect Mother of the Bride dress—something flattering, pitless (she was afraid of perspiration marks), and mature but not matronly. Something even vaguely, considering who her daughter was, hip. She was secretly hoping she'd spy something in a shop before the wedding.

On the road, Alice didn't feel like talking about her daughter's horrific dye job. She was too busy looking out the windows; too busy thinking, People live here. It wasn't a question—People *live* here?—not entirely. It was more of a silent reminder. She was not on a movie set. She was not dreaming. Those ramshackle houses, with burned-out or tireless cars out front, propped up on cinder blocks—those were people's *homes*. The proof was there: the laundry strung between the stilts on which the houses stood; the tire swings hanging under there, too. She wondered for a second whether swinging too hard could bring a house down right on top of you. It sure looked like it could.

In every direction, dark green hills and mountains and blue sky and in one direction a rainstorm—a dark, sagging belly of a cloud that seemed to be moving toward the SUV faster than possible. Alice remembered a day trip with Jack and the kids from another lifetime; they'd gone to a water park beside a mountain. She'd stopped once to regrip her loose flip-flop, and the others went ahead and they pointed to something behind her and she turned and she could see actual rain approaching—a wall of it—and then it hit her and she turned back and Jack and the kids were laughing because she was getting soaked but they weren't. Then the rain hit them, too, and she laughed, too, and they made a mad dash for the car, where the rain was louder than bombs and they got the seats wet and smelled like chlorine but didn't care. Alice watched this distant Belizean storm, wondering if it was some kind of sign, but it didn't appear to be moving anymore, if it ever was at all. She wondered whether June remembered that storm, that day, that mother who laughed freely. Alice so wished she were that person again.

She closed her eyes—she was tired from the trip and hadn't slept well the night before—and heard snippets of Cash's conversation with the driver up front. "What kind of fish?" he said at one point. "And what's the population there?" he said at another. Good, Alice thought. He's like June that way. Alice didn't know her future son-in-law very well but hoped this week might provide an opportunity to get better acquainted. She found the tone of his voice soothing and felt she could doze off if she wasn't careful. . . .

Her eyes shot open after the car hit a particularly nasty pothole. Signs of a village—bus stop posts, Pepsi signs—started to appear, and Alice sat up, stretched her eyelids to vanquish sleepiness, and prepared to see a proper Belizean town. But after they passed through a cluster of small buildings, the signs of civilization disappeared just as quickly. She hadn't been expecting thriving metropolises—she'd read about Belizean towns called Double Head Cabbage and Go-to-Hell Camp and Pulltrouser Swamp—but certainly more than a grocer and a bar. Every couple of miles someone would be walking down the road and Alice wondered how many miles they had to walk to get where they wanted to go . . . and back. There were young black men, older black women, young schoolgirls both black and white. Alice hadn't quite figured out the demographics of Belize but was confident June would make sure she knew all there was to know about the country's cultural history before the week was up.

"Are there any shops near where we're going?" Alice asked.

"It's in the forest, Mom." June sounded disappointed in her. "So no. Why, what do you need?"

"Mary-Anise drove me to the airport. I'd like to pick her up a little something."

"They have a gift shop, but when we go to Placencia there will be shops in town so you might want to wait."

Alice nodded and looked again into the distance. "Sounds like a plan."

She was lying about Mary-Anise. Though Mary-Anise had, in fact, offered her a lift to the airport, Alice had told her that someone from work owed her a favor for taking an extra shift. She'd taken a cab instead. There hadn't been a falling-out, exactly, but their friendship had definitely cooled. It was all very juvenile, really, but Alice had seen Mary-Anise and Felicia having breakfast together—or at least coming out of a neighborhood diner at the same time—on a morning when Mary-Anise had told Alice she had a doctor's appointment. Alice hadn't had the heart to ask Mary-Anise about it, but even their book club postmortems had lost their zest. Last month, the post-b.c. call hadn't come at all, and Alice figured Mary-Anise was upset that Alice hadn't been particularly impressed with Mary-Anise's pick for that month: *The Memory Keeper's Daughter.* In fact, if Alice had to read one more book about somebody's daughter or wife—be the somebody a pilot or time traveler or abortionist—she was going to quit book club for sure.

Alice spotted a kite way off in the distance. Book club had read *The Kite Runner* a year or two before, and Alice, who'd chosen the book and found the story just heartbreaking and wonderful, found her mouth turned up at the thought of getting out of the car and running off toward the kite so that she'd be there to catch it whenever and wherever it fell. She imagined herself crossing fields and scaling mountains. She imagined the kite plummeting into her hands. She imagined everyone she knew—June, Mary-Anise, Sue, even Felicia—getting there a second too late to catch the kite themselves and then celebrating her victory with her, toasting her success. Maybe in another lifetime, in another place, Alice would have been a great kite runner.

June said, "I'm excited you're here," and Alice took her daughter's hand and squeezed. She looked out the window again and felt, for a moment anyway, high as a kite herself.

Abby tried to watch the in-flight movie, but it was some dumb animated thing that she just couldn't get into. Not when she was still so pissed that she was here at all, that M and M hadn't allowed her to stay in San Francisco so she could go to Chelsea Lambert's Sweet Sixteen. Bad enough, she was missing the social event of the year. Worse, in the past few weeks, people had randomly decided that dates were the way to go—even though you had to be officially invited to go, so really you were just turning up with somebody who was already going to be there. This seemed stupid beyond belief to Abby until Will Sherwood, who was Colin Murray's best friend, asked Lisa, and Abby realized that Colin would never ask her. He already knew she couldn't go.

The party would take place at the nightclub Chelsea's father owned, the lucky bitch, and it was this big tropical-themed indoor/outdoor party where the outdoor part was heated so well that you could go swimming in the pool—the club had a pool!—even though it was December and San Francisco was hardly the tropics. All guests were expected to show up in swimsuits under formalwear or not at all. Hannah and Lisa had bought two new swimsuits each so they could decide which one looked best or felt right that night. Maggie didn't know it, but even Abby had bought a new bikini with the party in mind—not the sort of bikini Maggie would've approved of, either (black, barely there), but Abby packed it anyway. She looked kind of hot in it, if she had to say so herself.

Up until she got on the plane, even, Abby had been holding out hope she'd be allowed to stay behind and just spend the week at Hannah's—whose parents had said, Sure, no problem!

"I would never ask them to do that," Maggie had said.

"Ma," Abby had snapped. "They said sure, no problem. Those were their exact words. 'Sure.' And 'No problem.'"

Colin still hadn't asked anyone to be his date, but Abby imagined Chelsea Lambert herself might swoop in at the last minute. She'd probably task him with some ridiculous job like helping her jump out of a cake or leap through fire; maybe there'd be an elaborate ballroom dance. Then she'd invite him to go back to her house afterward with that whole little annoying blond clique of hers. So by the time Abby got back from this stupid trip her chances with Colin Murray would be shot because he'd be skanked up by Chelsea, and the rest of senior year would be ruined.

"You only have one brother," Maggie had taken to saying. "There will be plenty more boys."

"It's not just him," Abby had wailed on the day the plane tickets were purchased. "It's the social event of the year. It's bigger than the senior prom. I'm serious. The invitations came on MP3 players." Abby took the player out of her bag and shook it for emphasis. "You want to hear? It's Chelsea." She drew these next words out for emphasis. "*In-vi-ting me.*"

"You don't even like this girl." Maggie was flipping through a *Real Simple* magazine, and Abby snatched it out of her hands. "And you're seventeen. What do you care about a Sweet Sixteen?"

"Sooooo not the point, Mom."

"Give it," Maggie said, holding her hand out for the magazine, which Abby returned, though with the caveat that they should call it *Real Stupid*. Some of the articles, like "How to Brush Your Hair" and "How to Simplify the Holiday Season in 50 Easy Steps," really boggled the mind.

"Everyone's going. I mean, NOT everyone's going. That's the point. You have to be cool. Accepted. And I got invited. If I don't go, I'll be a social pariah! People are going to be talking about this party for years."

Maggie exhaled loudly. "Family comes first, Abby. And I hope to *God* you have better things to be talking about in *years*. You were so excited." She turned a page. "Hanging out with the band. All that."

"That was before I knew I'd be missing the most important party of my life! And before I knew Minky was going."

Minky, Miller's aunt, was the closest thing to a grandmother that Cash had. And even though she wasn't technically related to Abby, she behaved like a grandmother, giving her money for birthdays and for Christmas. She wasn't as annoying as movie grandmothers, the kind that pinch your cheeks or say embarrassing things about your breasts, but still. "I'm gonna get stuck with her," Abby said sadly. "I know I am." The thought of having to walk painfully slowly with Minky's crinkly arm clinging to her own was enough to make Abby cry.

"You're overreacting." Maggie unfolded a foldout perfume ad and rubbed her wrist against it.

Abby wiped her eyes and felt herself losing ground, and really, it was beyond pointless. The tickets had been bought. Her fate had been sealed. "There's even a rumor that Cordero's playing," she said weakly.

Maggie flipped a page and sniffed her wrist. "That means nothing to me."

"Cordero is only like the biggest R & B star in the world right now."

Abby was exaggerating, of course, and didn't even really like Cordero at all, but everyone else did, and that was part of what was making Chelsea Lambert's Sweet Sixteen such a big deal. Now that the party was only a week away, things had really started to heat up. People were selling their invitations on eBay for hundreds of dollars; others were rumored to be counterfeiting them; oh yeah, and one more little thing: MTV had started filming the whole thing for their reality series *My Super Sweet Sixteen*. So everyone at the party was going to be famous, and Abby would not be—unless they'd gotten footage of her listening to her invitation, fighting back tears as her friends jumped up and down and screeched and shouted and said, "Ohmigod, ohmigod," over and over. Abby had the invitation, the MP3 player, with her, in her carry-on. She was afraid to leave it at home, no joke, because someone might break into the house to get it. People were that insane about Chelsea Lambert's Sweet Sixteen. And besides, it was *her* invitation. She didn't want anyone else using it.

The movie had ended, and the plane's TVs were showing a program about tourist attractions in Belize; pictures of toucans and big stone temples and roaring rapids flashed across the screen. Luckily, Abby had done some research on the Web and found a place near where they were staying on the first leg of the trip where you could go ziplining. All she had to do was talk someone else into wanting to go. June seemed just the type; Cash, too.

Abby's mother poked her leg, and Abby looked over.

Maggie pointed at her ears.

Abby took out her earbuds.

"Have your little snit," Maggie said, "but it ends the second this plane touches the ground. Understood?"

Abby said, "Whatever, Mom," knowing that even she—the queen of the tantrum, the snit, the hissy fit—probably couldn't ignore M and M for a full week in a foreign country, not when

71

they were paying for everything. But for a little longer, anyway, she could try. She closed her eyes and imagined herself
flying through the rain forest, sliding across a wire through the
wet trees as the whole forest perked up to watch. She would
scream like Tarzan so loud that everyone back in San Francisco, at Chelsea Lambert's Super Sweet Sixteen Party, would
hear. Colin Murray would turn away just as Chelsea was about
to try to touch her nasty lips to his while slow dancing to some
lovelorn OC song, and he'd think, "What the heck was that?"
and their moment—the moment that should've been Abby's
anyway—would be ruined. *Check ya later, monkeys. Gotta fly.*

The pilot announced the beginning of their descent, and
Abby looked out the window. If she was excited by what she
saw—see-through turquoise waters revealing shadowy reefs,
deep green mountains that seemed to be watching her warily
from a distance—she didn't show it. She turned up the volume on her iPod and let the Starter House bring her in for a
landing.

Dan had been dreading riding two and a half hours to the resort in a van with Billy, who was on the same flight, many rows
back. He'd just never been comfortable around Billy—always
felt like June's brother had some kind of secret X-ray vision
into the minds of men who ever had a thought about doing un-
speakable things to his sister. Now, though, Dan was looking
forward to any diversion from the fight that Becky had picked
with him at JFK and which had managed to last through her
introduction to Billy, whom she'd somehow never met in the
city, and the whole way through a layover in Houston and onto
this plane—all without a word between them being spoken.

Apparently, Dan had taken too long after meeting up in

freezing rain to catch a cab to the airport with Becky to ask her how her day had been. Instead, he'd gone *on and on* about himself and the last-minute best man things he'd had to deal with, and so Becky had decided he was a selfish bastard who didn't really care about her at all. His side of the argument—that he *wasn't*—was a harder one to make, and so he hadn't. He'd simply said, "You're right, Becky! That's it. I'm a selfish bastard who doesn't care about you at all!" and then she'd said, "I think I liked you better when you were poor." After that they hadn't spoken, not even during their layover lunch; Dan simply followed Becky to a barbecue stand and ordered after she did, then ate in silence, opposite her at a tiny table. He'd snorted when she paid for her own pulled-pork sandwich.

Dan was pretty sure that the money hadn't and wouldn't change him, but then he probably wasn't the best judge. It was always other people who said things like "Dude, you've changed"; people never said that kind of thing to themselves in the mirror. But really, after taxes, it wasn't *that much money*. And he'd come into it through pure luck when his elderly, ailing landlord left him the dilapidated mansion when he died and a hot Long Island City developer wanted the land so badly that he was willing to pay three million for it. It's not like Dan robbed a bank or masterminded some ruthless business transaction to get it. That had to mean something.

The money had given his relationship with Becky a sort of jolt. Without it, Dan was pretty sure she wouldn't be here—ignoring him in first class with her *Ultimate Sudoku!* book on her lap. For a while after the windfall, anyway, she'd seemed to mellow, to just revel in her boyfriend's newfound wealth. Turns out Becky had a good head for wine, and a taste for finer foods. They'd been plowing through the city on a sort of culinary tour, and Dan had found her company incredibly pleasant. They were compatible eaters, and Becky felt about food the way she did about sex—she'd try (pretty much) anything once. He'd also discovered that his drinking didn't seem to bother Becky so long as he was drinking expensive wine in her company. Then, after the initial glow faded, the subject of what to do with the money had started to creep in, and all of Becky's annoying traits came back like seasonal allergies; Dan had pretty much forgotten both that he was susceptible to them and how god-awful they could be. The sudoku was almost the last straw, because it was all the rage, and if anything was all the rage it was a safe bet Dan wasn't interested. In this particular case, he just didn't see the point. Sudoku seemed like a supreme waste of time.

Tickets had already been bought, though, plans made. Besides, now that Dan had all this money, he was wary of breaking up with Becky. She'd liked him for who he was before the money, so in that sense she could be trusted above all other prospective women out there. He'd never in his life thought he'd have to worry about gold diggers, but now that he had a lot of money, he had no intention of giving it up. Or of doing anything with it, really, which was a problem all its own. He'd bought a spacious two-bedroom co-op with skyline views in a luxury tower called the McCarren—right on good ole McCarren Park—but that had been it. The rest of the money weighed on him.

The more immediate problem was, of course, Becky. She had her headphones on and her eyes closed, so he signaled a flight attendant and asked in a whisper for two glasses of champagne. He'd wake Becky up—if she was even really sleeping, which he doubted—when the bubbly arrived, and they'd toast the wonderful week ahead. Her eyes would light up the way they did when he actually did something unexpectedly sweet, and he'd think for at least a moment that he'd destroy the autograph on arrival. Yes, he still had that damn June Carter autograph, and yes, he was disgusted with himself. It was so pathetic that instead of burning it months ago, or even just reselling it on eBay so as not to be so overdramatic about the whole thing, he'd packed the damn thing. It was somewhere in the luggage hull on this very airplane because he was afraid Becky might find it in his carry-on. Could he be more of a fool if he tried?

The champagne arrived then, and Dan held both flutes in his hands and said, "Hey," but Becky didn't hear. He had no choice but to gently nudge her and she stirred, first wiggling her nose, then turning her head his way, then finally opening her eyes. She'd been sleeping after all, but he forged ahead. "Hey, sleepyhead," he said. "We're almost there. I thought we'd make a little toast." He lifted the flutes slightly for emphasis.

"You think alcohol's the answer for everything," she said. She softened it with a smile, then, and took a glass. "Is it *good* champagne?"

"For you, the best."

"Well, what are we toasting, exactly?"

"Us," he said, leaning in to kiss her. Fortunately his birthday was not this week but next. "And to Belize!"

They met up with Billy on the tarmac and then filed into the airport and got on line for Customs. The airport didn't feel air-conditioned, and Dan's jeans felt like heated blankets on his legs. Billy, camera in hand, took a picture of a WELCOME TO BELIZE sign.

"Uh," Dan said, studying the sign more closely. "You just took a picture of a sign that says NO PHOTOGRAPHY ALLOWED."

"Oh," Billy said. "Shit." He shrugged and Becky laughed and then he put his camera away and Dan was glad. He didn't like to call attention to himself in New York, let alone here, in a country he'd never been to. In general, he liked to blend in, and he already feared that the volume of Becky's typical conversation was going to be a problem.

"So here we are, eh?" Billy said.

He was unshaven and scraggly-looking and was wearing his sunglasses inside, though to be fair, the airport in Belize City felt very much outside.

"Yeah," Dan said. "Here we are."

Billy pushed his sunglasses to the top of his head; his hair was tightly cropped, a brunette cap. "So you're living the high life now, huh? How was first class?"

Dan felt suddenly embarrassed. "I'm not going to make a habit of it, but, well, it had to be done once, right?"

"Sure, man," Billy said. "Don't apologize. I'd make a habit of it if I could." He shook his head and smiled. "It's kinda funny, when you think about it."

"What is?" Dan said.

Billy was tapping his dark blue passport against his left hand with his right. "The way you were whining at McCarren about how much money it was going to cost to come to the wedding."

Dan's spine stiffened. "I wasn't whining."

Billy nodded slowly, smile intact. "You were whining."

"I hate to say it, babe"—Becky slid an arm around Dan's waist as they moved up in the line—"but I wasn't even there, and I practically remember you whining."

Once they passed through Customs and collected their bags, they found the driver holding the placard with Dan's name on it. He was black and friendly with spacious, even gaps between his teeth and a casual Jamaican sort of demeanor. He made Dan crave a tropical drink.

When they got out on the road, Dan was glad that there was a two-hour journey ahead of them. Because where they were? Well, it wasn't all that hot-looking. Billy had martyred himself to the front seat and was actively engaged in conversation with the driver about—at least this was Dan's best guess—the extra luggage in the van. The hatch behind them was jam-packed; their own bags had barely fit, and only after much unpacking and repacking and rearranging. Dan couldn't hear specifics, though, over the snaps and cracks the van was making with each bump. All the windows were down, wind whipping, to boot.

After a half hour or so, Becky fell asleep again—that girl could sleep through Jerry Bruckheimer—and Dan just looked out the window, wondering how it had all come to this. Heat spread through his body as he played out the looming drama in his head. Was he really here to try to stop the wedding? And if he was, why had he brought Becky? He'd fantasized about the moment, certainly—about telling June how he really felt about her. Each time, he imagined it going one of two ways, the only two ways such a conversation had probably ever gone, toward a kiss or a slap.

The driver said, "One minute," and pulled the van over to the side of the road. He got out, closed the door, and crossed the street, going into a shack that had a few signs on it. It was maybe a grocery store? Or a bar? He reemerged with another man a few minutes later, and the two of them went over to a garage that abutted the store. The road ahead stretched into more of nothing, and Dan wondered whether this was normal, stopping like this. The garage—open—housed an old car, beige and rusted.

Dan tried to imagine what the men might be talking about—maybe how much for the Americans, how they'd secure a ransom. Or maybe they were brothers or best friends and this was the only time they got to see each other, when the driver drove this road. He'd read some about Belize and knew that the people were mostly mestizos—descended from Mayans and Europeans with some Chinese and Spanish thrown in along the way—and he studied the two men for signs of their lineage, as if that would mean something, and even though at this point they were pretty much too far away.

Becky had woken up when the car stopped, and now she

looked at Dan, concerned. "Why are we stopped?" she said. Dan could only shrug.

Another uncomfortable minute passed, and the sun seemed to be baking them all through the roof of the van, which Dan was studying for clues, though clues to what he wasn't sure. It was a pretty crappy SUV—torn upholstery, floor mats splattered with dirt—and he noticed, just then, a hole in the windshield, with a spiderweb-like burst of glass around it. Had a rock popped up from the road and made the hit, or was it maybe—no, that was crazy—a bullet hole?

"Is that a bullet hole?" Dan said.

Billy said, "I was just wondering that myself, but no, probably a rock."

A CD dangled from the rearview mirror, and Billy reached out and spun it, sending refracted sunbeams across the interior of the car. Dan had to close his eyes, it was so bright, like a disco ball. Burn, baby, burn, he thought, as the heat sank deeper into his jeans. He couldn't wait to get out of them, should've risked looking like an idiot at sleet-encrusted JFK and worn shorts.

Dan didn't consider himself a racist, but at moments like this even he had to wonder. Even Becky, who'd gone on a cruise to Panama, looked slightly alarmed, the skin on her face tight. But racist or not, it was true that if they were to get murdered or kidnapped right now, they'd have no recourse. They had no idea where they were—the name of the road, or this town, if it even qualified as a town, how to make an emergency phone call (did Belize have 911?), none of that. They were being paranoid, for sure. And yes, probably racist—or at the very least classist—too. Though in what measure, it was hard to say. Dan knew how to gauge danger in New York—he only ever crossed the street in order to avoid packs of teenagers; white, black, or blue, they scared the shit out of him—but outside of New York he was clueless. Or was he? Fact was,

Dan just felt so *white* sometimes. And so *American*. He felt like an easy target—and he was not at all the kind of guy you wanted to have your back in a fight. He hadn't thrown a punch since, oh, eighth grade? And even that one missed its intended target entirely. But he had a ton of money now. Surely he'd be able to pay his way out of any trouble. The thought gave him some ease.

The driver and the other guy were walking toward the car now, heads down and tilted slightly toward each other, talking. Then the driver looked up, walked forward more intently, and climbed back up into the car, smiling and apologetic.

Billy said, "No problem," and they were on their way again.

Dan felt relief, sure, but also set about convincing himself he hadn't been flustered to begin with. He reached over and squeezed Becky's hand, and she smiled her own relief at him, then looked out the window.

After another hour or so of driving through small villages and past the occasional school or church, the road curved past a limestone quarry and there was no energy for conversation, as Dan and everyone else, apparently, concentrated on trying, literally, to save their asses. The road was so bumpy it was nearly impossible to keep your butt on the car's bench seat. So much so that it was almost funny, except it hurt. Becky looked over at him every once in a while, a broad smile on her face even as she winced. She loved an adventure, Becky. And this was definitely going to be one.

The terrain changed again before long, and Billy said, "What happened here? A fire?"

In every direction Dan saw nothing but tall, stripped tree trunks. It looked like something out of *The Lord of the Rings,* some forgotten forest in a plagued kingdom. He half expected a flock of giant black birds to fly overhead, or for a unicorn to appear from out of the gray mist, and he listened attentively as the driver explained about the pine beetles, about the replanting that had begun, about how there was nothing they could have done.

"It's so sad," Becky said, and Dan thought she was right.

Heads hit the roof at the next big hole in the road, and Dan said, "Fuck."

He honestly couldn't believe how awful the roads were. The place where they were staying was just past a resort owned by Francis Ford Coppola and Dan regretted he hadn't booked himself and Becky there instead. He hadn't wanted to seem richer-than-thou, but Coppola's guests arrived in style. Coppola's guests could come by plane.

You Better Belize It T-shirts pinned to the walls taunted Alice in the front office/gift shop of the Five Sisters Lodge. She almost laughed. She was really here. It was all really happening. Alice Gilhooley Siren was in Belize for her daughter's wedding. She couldn't help but think that Jack Siren, were he alive, really wouldn't believe it.

June, already best friends, apparently, with everyone who ran the resort, requested Alice's key—linked to a hunk of wood with the words "Roaring Creek" carved into it—and then they headed off down an impeccably landscaped pathway dotted with cabanas that looked like monster mushrooms made of straw. It was a beautiful spot, Alice had to admit. Pine forests covered the hillside in the distance while trees and flowers she'd only seen the likes of in botanical gardens filled out the resort grounds; she wished they were labeled so she could put names to them. The resort's main lodge—"That's where we're having dinner," June said as they passed—looked like a big log cabin the sort of which demanded festivity, and the sound of a waterfall dusted the air with white noise. They turned off the path and approached a mushroom cabana with a ROARING CREEK sign on the door; it was built into the side of the mountain, on stilts.

"Wow," Alice said.

"Yeah," June said, key in door.

The interior of Alice's private cabin was just as transporting—mosquito net, screened porch area set off by French doors, and not much else. It looked like something out of a movie.

"What do you think?" June swept her arm out across the round room as if to say "Ta-dah."

"It's lovely," Alice said as relief swept through her. She stepped out onto the porch and looked down, but it was hard to see through the trees.

"There are five waterfalls down there," June said from behind her mother. "The five sisters of Five Sisters."

"They're loud!" Alice laughed.

"I know. We're having dinner down there tomorrow night. There's this crazy cable car, sort of like a ski lift, that gets you down there."

Alice turned as June lifted Alice's suitcase onto a luggage rack by the door. "And what time tonight?"

"Seven. And then we're all booked to go on a tour of these Mayan ruins called Caracol in the morning. But it's not a full day, I don't think, except we might stop at this sort of swimming hole on the way back if it's hot enough. Then the day after that, there are a few options—canoeing and stuff. But we can figure that out as we go." She looked at her watch.

"Is Billy here yet?" Alice couldn't wait to see her son.

"Not yet, but he's with Dan and Becky, and they should be in a car soon."

"Who are Dan and Becky?"

"You know," June said, "Cash's business partner."

Alice nodded recognition of the name, though she'd never met the man.

"He's also the best man, though if you ask me Cash only asked him so he could avoid explaining why he didn't ask him. It's sort of a historical friendship more than anything."

"A historical friendship?"

June's voice held impatience. "You know. Went to high school together. Roomed together in college. Don't have that much in common anymore besides work."

"Sure." Alice didn't think she had any historical friendships of her own, but then again . . . Felicia?

"So Cash's crew is settling in over at Blancaneaux, which still pisses me off to no end." June craned her neck to look out a window. "I mean, who in their right mind goes to an exotic country and chooses to stay in a resort owned by a rich American filmmaker?" She turned and shook her head. "It boggles the mind, and I swear, if they say one thing about how great it is, I'm going to snap."

"Maybe they feel safer there," Alice said, crossing the room to her carry-on, which she'd left on the floor.

"Safe from what?" June's voice rang out against the falls. "Belizeans? Belizean food? What's the point in going to the rain forest if you're going to eat pasta freakin' carbonara every night?"

"I don't know what you're getting mad at me for. I'm not the one staying there." Alice had started unpacking her carry-on, placing items on the bedside table, on the bathroom vanity, on the ledge of the bathtub, which was right there in the main room.

"Well, anyway. Joe and his wife and the baby are coming for the Placencia part of the trip, and—"

Alice looked up, Hope in a Jar in her hand. "They're bringing a baby?!"

"Yes, they're bringing a baby." June put her palms out, face up. "What is it with everybody thinking you can't bring a baby to Belize?"

"I'm not everybody. I just think it's hard work, is all, traveling anywhere with a baby."

Just the word—*baby*—triggered memories of June as an infant, fierce, happy, prone to flirting with strangers; June as a determined toddler, unsteady on her feet, her soft hair hot from exertion; June as a peppy tween, learning the choreography to Michael Jackson's "Thriller" video, with Jack playing the part of a ghoul, in the living room; June as a gangly, vegetarian teen with better things to do and a guitar with which to do them; June coming home from college, newly feminist, and ripping down the June Carter quotes she'd long had stuck up on her bedroom walls. Alice sometimes felt like her children traveled with ghosts of themselves on their heels. The room seemed suddenly full of Junes.

"I'm sure it *is* a lot of work." June pushed the mosquito net open and sat on the edge of the bed. "But what's the other option—never leave the house again?"

"I left the house."

"I never said you didn't."

Alice shook off defensiveness. "Who else?"

"Trevor." June was trying to unpoke a hole that had been poked in the mosquito net. "You know, from the band."

"How could I forget?" Alice said. The band had once stayed at Alice's house when they played a club in Chicago, and Alice had gone downstairs early in the morning to start preparing breakfast, only to find a naked Trevor at the fridge, orange juice carton in one hand and private parts being scratched by the other.

June said, "And Lydia."

"With the kids?" Alice asked, then prepared to be scolded again. Lydia and her husband, Vince, had three, she knew. Lydia was one of the only friends June had from high school that was still in her life and Alice was looking forward to seeing her.

"No, actually." June got up. "Leaving them with Vince."

"Wow."

June went to the window and flicked a bug or something off the screen. "He *is* their father, you know."

"Don't get fresh. I'd just imagine it's a lot for him."

"Yeah, well, she does it every day, so he'll live." June turned again, and the sun through the window caught her pink hair, blistering it white. "The big scandal is that Tamara—Cash's *mother*—is threatening to turn up."

Alice felt suddenly irrationally intimidated. She'd so far avoided ever meeting Cash's actual mother, and from what she'd heard of the woman's life, she was pretty sure she was happier that way. "Really?"

"Really." June laughed, opening her mouth wide so that the pink of her mouth—dark, rich—made her hair look like another color entirely. "It's crazy, right? But we called the hotel in Placencia, and she hasn't made a reservation, so who knows. Poor Maggie is gonna flip her lid if that happens. It'd almost be worth the price of Tamara's plane ticket." She went to the window, craning her head to look out. "God, I just don't want anyone to die on their way here. The guilt would kill Cash." She walked to the bedside table and picked up Alice's book. "Jesus, Mom, *The Da Vinci Code*?"

"It's for book club." That was a lie, but Alice thought that since most of the free world had read the damn thing, it was probably a pretty good beach read. She'd resisted it long enough.

"Oh, well, in *that* case!" June tossed the book aside.

"So this may seem like a silly question. But you haven't actually mentioned the wedding." Alice unzipped her suitcase and made a split-second decision not to hang up her dresses; she wasn't feeling up to June's input and had a plan to hit up Billy as soon as possible.

"Oh, when we get down to Peggy's Place, I have a meeting with a wedding coordinator, but she's taking care of everything—cake, flowers, officiate. So there's really nothing to do, which is part of the joy of this whole kind of enterprise."

"What kind of cake is it?" Alice dared not ask whether that officiate would be an actual priest.

"No idea."

"And the flowers."

"Pretty ones."

Alice sat on the bed now. There was—except for a weird, not particularly comfortable-looking chair on the porch—nowhere else to sit. "You are the epitome of the low-maintenance bride."

"That was the idea." June sat on the edge of the bathtub.

"They bringing a dress for you, too?" Alice said.

"Very funny." June's legs were crossed, her front leg bobbing. "Actually, when we get down there, can I hang it in your room? I don't trust Cash not to spill something on it."

"Of course." Alice played with a stray string on the bedspread. "Am I hoping for too much when I ask you if it's white?"

"Yes, Mom, it's white."

"And your hair?"

"Haven't decided yet."

"June"—Alice looked up—"it's your wedding day."

June spoke slowly: "Which is just one of many happy days in my very fulfilling life."

Alice dropped her chin and gave June a look.

"What?" June got up and started to pace, hands on hips. "People are all crazy about how it's your wedding day, how it's *my* day, how it's the happiest day of my life, and I'm sorry, I just don't buy into it. I'm sure it'll be a happy day. Today's a happy day, and my hair happens to be pink. And if someday I look back and regret having pink hair on my wedding day, then

I'll probably look in the mirror and ask myself when I got to be so boring."

"Fine." Alice looked around for a hanger for her linen pants. "I can't talk about this with you."

"Why not?" June looked like she was about to laugh. "Talk!"

Alice couldn't think of any better way to say it. "But it's your *wedding day*."

June came forward to give Alice a kiss—making Alice wonder whether a kiss could be condescending—then left. Alice hated that she always enjoyed looking forward to time with her children more than she actually enjoyed the time with them. She almost wished she could be a fly on the wall instead—watching them interact with each other and the world without having to talk. Though knowing them—June, especially, and Billy was worse when he was in her company—they'd find a way to pick apart the fly.

Maybe if she'd met that Jack character that Mary-Anise was so keen on introducing her to she wouldn't feel that way. She wouldn't be alone all the time—wouldn't be alone here—and therefore wouldn't expect so much of June and Billy. Maybe by now her children would have embraced the idea of someone new—someone sharing their mother's bed—and this would be a happier occasion all around. She'd have someone to vent to about her children's obnoxious comments and hair dye.

But the thought of an actual date—a setup with Jack—had been too much for Alice to bear right out of the gate. A date required them to talk beforehand, to agree on someplace to go, and then to go there, just the two of them. Alice couldn't jump in like that. She'd hoped for something to happen somehow more, well, organically? So Mary-Anise had said, "I'll have a party." Her eyes had lit up. "You'll both come!"

"I don't know," Alice said.

"Oh, come on. It's Bob's birthday next month. It's perfect.

I'll ask a few of the girls, Bob can invite Jack. It'll be fun. And real casual."

"But—"

"But but but, Alice. Enough is enough."

And so Alice had agreed that a party sounded like a good way to go.

But this was the real reason Mary-Anise and Felicia were having breakfast, the real reason the book club postmortems had died. Alice hadn't actually *turned up* at the party. She'd showered and gotten dressed and gotten into the car. She's started it up, then looked at the tennis ball that hung from the ceiling of the garage—Jack had put it there so she'd always know how far to pull in—and then she couldn't go. She'd gone back inside the house instead, and put on her pajamas and turned off the ringer on the phone and watched an old VHS of that weeper of a film, *Message in a Bottle*. It was what she did when she needed a good cry, and the film was perfectly on topic this time. Kevin Costner plays a widower who can't move on . . . until Robin Wright Penn comes knocking. It was all too much, too tragic in the end, because when he's finally ready to move on, he dies a horrible death. See what happens when you move on! You die. Mary-Anise hadn't called Alice after then, and Alice knew that being friends with a widow wasn't that much fun. She wasn't even sure she'd want to be friends with herself.

It was time to shower, and so she did—mouth closed tight. June had left with a final warning about the water—fit for showering but not for drinking—and Alice didn't want to take any chances. Just being here was chance enough.

Abby wasn't sure if she'd ever seen any Francis Ford Coppola movies, but the guy sure knew how to build a kick-ass resort.

And her own bathroom? Her parents weren't as dumb as they looked.

There'd been an issue, she knew, about their staying here and not where everyone else was staying, but her parents had blamed it all on Minky, who would probably spend more time at the resort than anyone else—her plan was to take in the grounds, paint watercolors—and wanted to be as comfortable as possible. The words *eco resort*, which the other place was, hadn't impressed Minky as much as the words *Francis Ford Coppola* had. So M and M booked a three-bedroom/two-bathroom lodge for the three of them and Minky. They even gave Abby her own key.

"With freedom," Maggie had said, "comes responsibility," and Abby had said, "What am I gonna do, Mom? Sneak out and get drunk with monkeys? We're in the middle of freakin' nowhere."

"I'm just saying!" Maggie had said.

"Can I go unpack?" Abby asked when they got to the lodge.

"Yes." Maggie said. "We're getting a ride to the Five Sisters for dinner at seven, so that gives you—" Maggie looked at her watch.

"I can tell time, Mom," Abby said, and closed the door to her room.

She dug into her backpack then and took out her phone and turned it on. It buzzed and lit up, but then there was a whirling icon and it just whirled and whirled like a confused animal and Abby, finally taking pity on it, turned it off. A cell signal really would have been too good to be true.

Abby looked around the room, and there was no phone, so she went back out to the common room and looked there. Nothing. "There's no phone," she called out. She knocked on her parents' door, and Miller said, "Come in!" and Abby said, "Is the phone in here?" as she opened the door.

Maggie was hanging up the dress she'd bought for the wedding, and Abby congratulated herself on having helped her mom buy such an awesome, mom-appropriate dress. Abby didn't like her own dress nearly as much but hadn't had the time—or, in the end, the inspiration—to make one.

"Nope." Miller looked around. "No phone."

"This blows," Abby said, and her mother said, "Watch it."

Abby closed the door, went back to her own room, and thought, Maybe not so kick-ass, after all, Francis. It really was beautiful, though. Abby had never seen or been anywhere remotely like it, though there were aspects that reminded her of parts of Disney World. The Polynesian Resort bit. Lots of straw or hay or whatever it was. She kicked her shoes off, then tossed them across the room to see if they landed in a cool position. They didn't. She flopped down on the bed. How in the hell did you draw a pair of shoes and make it even remotely interesting?

Abby's application to Pratt was due a week after she got home, and she had yet to complete the required sketches—a pair of shoes, a still life, and a self-portrait, all drawn from observation. It had all sounded so easy when Abby first read the application, but for some reason it was turning out to be really, really hard. She had already wasted countless hours staring at bowls of fruit and looking in the mirror, growing increasingly displeased with what she saw: on the one hand, boring ole fruit, and on the other, a wide nose, boring brown eyes, weak chin. There were days when she thought she looked pretty good—striking, even—but those days only came a few times a year and, unfortunately, had yet to coincide with a day when she attempted a self-portrait.

Abby was pretty sure she'd never get into Pratt, which is why she hadn't told anyone she was applying. M and M would flip out about the East Coast thing, and if word got around school that Abby wanted to study fashion design, there'd be endless *Project Runway* jokes, with people telling her to "make it work" every time she walked down the hall. Hannah would want to apply, too, and would probably get in, and then their friendship would die a fiery death instead of burning out slowly like Abby was beginning to think it might once they graduated. Maybe it *was* a pipe dream, but Abby had been sewing since she was old enough to learn, and she was always getting compliments on her clothes in general and on the few things she'd designed. So it was worth a shot—even if her sketches sucked.

She got up and walked back out into the common room, barefoot. The furniture was all wicker, with cushions in deep tones of red and green. She guessed big fluffy couches were pretty much out of the question in such a humid place. And it really was humid. Any self-portrait she did this week would have to be called "Bad Hair Day." She flipped through a little rack of tourism brochures looking for one for the ziplining place, and found one. She'd bring it to dinner, show it to Cash. She couldn't wait to see him. In the meantime, there was an hour to kill. She looked around the room again. "Mom!" she shouted. "There's no TV!"

"You'll live," Miller said, and Abby got up, slipped her shoes back on, and said, "I'm gonna go check out the place."

"Don't be long," Maggie said. "And take your key!"

Abby found a pay phone in the lobby. A big group had just come in, and there were a bunch of loud men doing a lot of backslapping and laughing. On the phone, a sticker gave instructions for calling the U.S., so Abby followed them and used her emergency credit card to call Hannah.

"Hey, world traveler," Hannah said when she picked up. "How is it?"

"Eighty-five and sunny, but no phone or TV."

"Ouch."

"Yeah. So what's the latest? Did he ask anybody yet?"

"No." Hannah sounded almost disappointed that there wasn't news.

"So there's no news at all?"

"Well, there's some."

"Spill it." Abby pressed the receiver hard to her ear and formed a sort of cubby at the booth with her body.

Hannah's voice sounded surprisingly close. "Chelsea recruited some volunteers to go over to her house and form an assembly line to stuff these gift bags everyone's getting."

"Gift bags?" Abby snorted. "Like with yo-yos and bubbles? What are we, four?"

"Abs, they're supposedly worth a couple thousand dollars."

"Seriously?" Her heart stiffened.

"Seriously."

Abby wrapped her fingers tight around the phone's cold silver cord. "Please tell me you didn't volunteer."

"I sort of got roped into it." Hannah was trying to sound blasé. "Lisa's doing it. Some other people, too."

"Is *Colin* doing it?" Abby turned instinctively at a big burst of manly sounds.

"Yeah." Now Hannah sounded so very far away.

"I can't believe I'm stuck here." Abby wished the back-slapping guys would just shut the ef up—and they could all afford to lose some weight while they were at it. People in San Francisco just weren't really that big, and Abby had to wonder about the rest of the country if these guys were any indication. "You have to keep an eye on him. Promise?"

After hanging up, Abby stormed out the front door of Blancaneaux and hooked a right around the building. She'd seen the long path coming in and now bolted down it, reluctantly noticing the palm trees that lined the path—their tall green shoots smashed against a seriously blue sky—and plants she'd never seen, with leaves the size of surfboards, prickly flowers in Day-Glo colors. She walked and walked—faster, she figured, than anyone in Belize was walking at that exact moment—past a bunch of smaller cabanas with superhigh round roofs that made them look like dwarfs, then stumbled upon an ideal still life. Beside a river, amid lush ferns, sat two fat urns, one slightly bigger than the other. It was a unique, perfectly composed scene. But now just wasn't the time. Abby was in no mood. She looked around and noted the location of the urns, then went off toward a gazebo ahead. There appeared to be three blessedly unoccupied chairs there, looking out on that river. Abby started to run, hoping she'd make it there before she burst. *Gift bags worth a couple thousand dollars*. It looked like a good place for a cry.

"This is so frakin' cool," Becky said, and even though Dan agreed—the cabana, built into the side of the mountain, with stilts, *was* pretty cool—he had to roll his eyes anyway. He and Becky had been watching *Battlestar Galactica* on the Sci Fi Channel together pretty much ever since they started dating, and she'd co-opted the show's annoying faux cuss word. The show was brilliant, but Dan didn't see how actors could take themselves seriously when they had to substitute *frak* for *fuck*—and conjugate it correctly when appropriate. Recently, Becky had started using it in mixed company, eliciting confused looks.

"Easy with the fraking," he said, and Becky slid a warm hand into the waistband of his jeans.

"I don't think you mean that," she said.

Becky made a lot of noise during the quick, perfunctory sex that followed and didn't seem to care that the hut's windows weren't really windows. They were holes with screens, and Dan was sure people passing on the path could hear them. He tried to keep her quiet by kissing her, but she kept pulling her mouth away, digging her chin into his shoulder. Then he saw a really large insect—in the bed with them—and pulled out and jerked away from Becky and scrambled out of the bed, his foot catching in mosquito netting and nearly pulling the entire thing down.

"What the frak?" Becky said, her eyes wide with panic.

"Get out of the bed." Dan grabbed a local tourism guide from the night table. He climbed back under the netting and beat the crap out of the bug—nothing more extraordinary than a run-of-the-mill water bug, but he always hated those things and hated, especially, the fact that people called them water bugs instead of giant roaches, which is what they looked like to him. He thought that if a bug was large enough that you could actually feel its presence in a room, the way he had with this critter and several others back in the dilapidated mansion, then it wasn't really a mere "bug" after all. Fortunately his new apartment at the McCarren seemed impenetrable by the city's insect population. New construction—with walls that met floors properly—pretty much rocked, and Becky had taken quickly to Dan's new hood, now throbbing with hipsters and yuppies. She no longer had issues with spending the night.

"You scared the shit out of me," Becky said, because *Battlestar* offered no alternative for the s-word. She was across the room now, starting the shower, which was in the main room and not in the adjoining room that had the toilet. Dan had immediately thought of the erotic possibilities of the bathtub-shower combo, right there in the room with a ledge around it, but, well, with the bug situation—not to mention the warning they'd been given at check-in about the water being fit for washing but not for drinking—he wasn't feeling particularly horny anymore. The drooping condom drove the point home.

"Sorry," Dan said. He surveyed the damage. Bug bits were

smeared over a corner of the sheets. "We'll have to stop by the office and ask for a change of sheets."

"What's this 'we' thing?" Becky said, mimicking Dan, who was now solidly in the habit of correcting her use of "we" when he deemed it inappropriate. Things like "We went to a party at Nikki's" were fine, factual. Things like "We had a great time at Nikki's party"? Well, he preferred to speak for himself about whether he had had a great time or not. He would break Becky of this habit if it killed him.

Dan stripped the bed—no easy feat, what with the mosquito netting—and stuffed the sheets into a pillowcase. Then, wanting shorts, he unzipped his suitcase, which was perched on a luggage rack by the door. A Hawaiian shirt in bright blues and greens greeted him. A fish eye stared him down.

"No fucking way," he said.

Dan didn't own any Hawaiian shirts.

He flipped the top of the suitcase closed to look at it again—familiar enough, but maybe the leather piping was less worn?—and then dug under the Hawaiian shirt and pulled out a pair of tighty-whiteys and two packs of cigarettes. "Becky!" he screamed.

"I'm right here, Dan," Becky said from the shower. "You don't have to scream."

"I have the wrong fucking luggage!" he said. "So you'll forgive me if I'm not in complete control of my voice right now." He couldn't stop himself from just staring at the hideous assemblage of clothes in front of him, blinking as if they might change, presto, into his own carefully selected, meticulously packed tropical wear, most of it purchased specifically for this trip.

Oh no! It wasn't about the clothes, he realized. He pictured some old geezer opening Dan's bag, finding a Ziploc with a cocktail napkin signed "June Carter," and deciding to keep it, then going home and framing it in some Florida retirement home and talking about it over the Early Bird Special; the grand plan was no more. "I don't fucking believe this."

The shower stopped running then, and Becky pulled the curtain back, stood there naked and wet and calm.

"What the hell am I gonna do?" he said.

"First of all, calm down." She came forward, towel tucked atop her breasts, to try to give him a kiss, but he turned his mouth away.

"You calm down," he said.

"Was this the bag you took off the baggage claim carrier? Or do you think it got mixed up in the van?"

Dan hadn't considered this option, and he almost wept with relief. His bag was probably at the other resort, the Coppola place; even his luggage had intuited that that was where he truly belonged. The driver must've simply taken out the wrong bag. It would've been an easy mistake and was certainly more likely than Dan taking up the wrong luggage in broad daylight at the airport.

The cabana didn't have a phone, they realized then, and Dan zipped the suitcase back up. "You want to come with?" he said, heading for the front door.

"Well, if it's all the same to you, Mr. Potty Mouth, I'll be right here." Becky took a seat in one of the chairs on their terrace, with her book in hand. It was one of those horrible frothy pink concoctions that, according to the back jacket, tackled the age-old question of whether all the good ones really were taken or whether there really were more fish in the sea. Dan, whose taste in literature bent toward, well, literature, had half a mind to toss Becky's book into the churning pool at the bottom of the Five Sisters and try to get her to read something good for a change. He supposed he should be grateful she was the kind of girl who actually read books, but boy, did she know how to pick 'em.

Dan bumped into June on the main path, and she looked

lovely, even with the pink hair, which he'd seen once in the city but had forgotten about. He felt his stomach sort of drop the way he always did when he hadn't seen June in a while. She was and had long been his personal roller coaster. He should never have brought Becky along for the ride.

"Going home already?" June said, after they hugged, and Dan realized how ridiculous he must look; sheets under one arm, rolling suitcase trailing behind him. "No"—he indicated the sheets—"but I've officially declared war on the bug population. There was bloodshed."

"Oh, gross." June frowned. Beyond her, a flowering plant boasted a bloom in the same pale pink hue as her hair. "I confess I hadn't entirely thought through the bug thing," she said. "I mean, I'm terrified of them. So it's good to know I can count on you in a pinch."

This was the thing about June. Just when you felt like an asshole for freaking out over a bug, she made you feel good about yourself. You weren't a pussy. You were a fierce killer of bugs. You were climbing her highest peak with your hands in the air.

"And the bag?"

"Oh! Not mine!" Dan couldn't shake the creepy gaze of that fish eye. "I think mine's at the Coppola joint."

"Oh no." Her hand went to her mouth, then dropped again to her side. "I'm so sorry."

"Not your fault." He shook his head. "Not a big deal." The conversation was heading downhill fast, and Dan didn't like it.

"Do you need clothes?" She surveyed his jeans, his T-shirt. "I'm sure Cash can loan you something."

"I'll make do," he said, though how he would do that, he wasn't exactly sure.

"So we'll see you down at the lodge for dinner?" She was moving on now, rounding another bend.

"Yup. Seven o'clock."

"Great." She smiled and touched his arm and said, "I'm so glad you're here."

"Me too," Dan said, but inside all he felt was plummeting.

She suddenly said, "God, I'd kill for a cigarette."

Now, this was interesting. June had quit smoking, so far as Dan knew. Was she feeling angst-y? Were her feet maybe a teeny bit cold?

Dan said, "I think I may be able to hook you up later," as a plan formulated in his head.

"I'd be eternally in your debt," June said, and Dan wasn't sure he'd ever looked forward to a cigarette more in his life.

June walked off—the ride was over for now—and Dan didn't see anyone else around once she disappeared around a curve in the path. He unzipped the bag, bent down and pulled out a pack of cigarettes. Hawaiian Shirt Guy would be so grateful to get his shirts back that he probably wouldn't even notice the cigarettes were gone. But one missing pack was more conspicuous than two missing packs, so Dan reached for the other one and put them in his back pocket. Hawaiian Shirt Guy would think he'd forgotten them! And at least if Dan never got the autograph back, never got the courage up to give it to June, he could give her a smoke.

Alice was the first to arrive for dinner in the lodge, and was grateful for an extra moment or two before things kicked into high gear. Once everyone sat down to dinner, the week would be a sort of unstoppable train. There would be small talk and tours and meals and more small talk, punctuated by isolated moments of blissful solitude if she was lucky. It seemed odd, even to Alice, that someone so lonely would so love time alone, and yet that was the case. She hadn't spent seven days with anyone except Mary-Anise in years, and even in Hawaii, they'd somehow organically spent time apart. Like when, for example, Mary-Anise had been hell-bent on taking a helicopter tour, and Alice had been hell-bent on not.

The dining room—airy, bright—had screens for windows and slatted glass shutters that you could close against wind and rain. They were all open tonight, as the night was clear and lovely. There were maybe ten tables, set simply with bright woven place mats in blue and green and decorated with small bud vases. A table set for nine was obviously theirs. A small bar area in the lobby had only four bar stools and, with two of them occupied by a young couple, seemed crowded. Alice walked past the bar, through the building, and back out into the night.

A wooden deck extended out over pine tree tops and wrapped around the dining room. Tables hugged the building's exterior, and Alice thought that eating lunch out here one day would be neat. Farther out, built up on high stilts, was the section of the deck she'd seen described on the Web site as the Stargazing Deck. A chair similar to the one on her cabana's porch just begged to be sat in. Alice complied, then regretted it immediately. The chair was low to the ground—too low, maybe eight inches—and made of round pieces of wood, like logs. Its back was skinny and hard. In it, Alice felt like an emergency medical team might suddenly arrive, strap her into it, and take her away. Stiff as a board. Her butt would be dead on arrival.

She adjusted her position several times, but no improvements seemed possible, at least none that could be made without having to sit in or pass through an unladylike pose. Thank God she'd worn pants. The one thing—the only thing—the chair had going for it was that if you gave in to the chair back, your head naturally angled up at a sky littered with stars. Alice wasn't sure she'd ever seen so many, not even in Hawaii, and she sat for a moment, trying to pick out the Big and Little Dippers. She wasn't really sure she'd ever looked at the right clusters of stars, and she made a mental note to Google the Dippers when she got home. She wondered for a moment if she'd ever taught June how to find the Big Dipper, and how much of the stuff she told June when she was a kid was just plain wrong. Alice remembered thinking, when she was a young mother, that no one warns you about how much you have to *know* to be a good parent. Fractions, geography, congressmen; none of these things ever particularly stuck in Alice's brain, though she'd tried harder recently regarding congressmen, on account of Oprah. How her daughter had grown up to be such a fountain of facts, so generally knowledgeable, was a mystery.

Miller's booming voice, ordering a beer at the bar, snuffed the stars' twinkle, and Alice tried to make herself small. It wasn't that Alice didn't like Cash's father and stepmother; she just didn't like being around them, particularly. They were going to be June's in-laws, though, and for that reason Alice felt she owed them a certain sort of respect and affection. They were obviously extraordinarily fond of June—in fact, Alice was pretty sure that's how Miller himself had put it, over and over again—so who was she to begrudge them anything? Admittedly, the thought that June might start to call Miller "Dad" one day—less than a week from now!—pained Alice. She knew it was the way of the world, and she wished for June for that void to be somehow filled. And still, a part of her hoped June would just avoid the direct address altogether and skip right over to calling him "Grandpa" when she and Cash started a family. If they ever decided to do that, which was something—like money, and Jack's death—that Alice and June never talked about.

She felt a hand on her shoulder and turned at the neck to see Billy.

"Hey, Mom. Contemplating the vastness of the universe?"

"Something like that." Alice was thrilled to see him. "I'd get up and hug you, but I'm not sure I can."

Billy bent down to kiss her, and she said, "How was your flight?"

"Uneventful," he said.

"The best kind," Alice said.

He stood in front of her, leaning against the balcony railing, one arm extended out in each direction, the heels of his hands perched. "You're not going to get all weepy and stuff because your only daughter is all growns up, are you?"

"June came out of the womb grown*s* up," Alice said, and Billy smiled.

He stood with his feet planted wide, knees locked, and Alice couldn't help but notice what a fine man he'd grown to be, so very much like his father around the eyes, and the shoulders, too. So maybe she was feeling a little oversentimental. *A fine man?* But how could she not be?

Alice went to get up, and Billy stuck a hand out and she took it and let him help. She smoothed out her pants and noted Billy's shorts. "I hope you're wearing bug spray," she said.

"Swimming in it," he said.

"I was thinking you could come by my cabana at some point?" Alice gave him a proper hug now; he felt warm, sturdy; she was so grateful he was here. "I could maybe try on the dresses I bought, and you can tell me which one I should wear?"

"I'm sure they're all fine, Mom." Billy turned to look out at the view. "Wear whatever you want."

"But that's the problem." Alice heard her voice turn prickly. "I don't know what I want. Can you stop by in the morning?"

"Mom." He looked at her with a half-smile. "The wedding's not for days."

"Can you please do this one thing for me?" She was shaky with irritation.

"Okay, okay." Billy rubbed her back. "Jeez."

They stood side by side then, leaning against the railing, and Alice watched a waitress set a few large glass carafes of water on their table. Cash walked into the bar area then, with his stepmother and stepsister, and joined Miller. Billy and Alice watched them through pocked screens and slatted shutters as they took seats at the table. Cash's father helped himself to the head of the table, and Alice thought, What nerve. Then June walked in—pink hair up in an elaborate twist—wearing a short red dress and carrying a sweater, also red, and approached the table. When she draped her sweater over the back of the chair at the other head of the table, Billy turned to Alice and smiled again. "That's our girl," he said, then after a pause: "Something's up with her." He sounded puzzled.

"What do you mean?"

"I don't know exactly." Billy lowered his voice. "But there's a guy at work who asked me on Friday if I knew which way June was leaning on the job offer."

What on earth would June do for Nickelodeon? Alice wondered. Billy was an animator.

"When I tried to ask her about it on the phone yesterday, she shut me down big-time." Billy spoke in conspiratorial tones now. "I got the distinct impression Cash didn't know about it."

Alice said, "What job offer?"

"No idea, so I just played like I knew what the guy was talking about." Billy scratched his head. "I've heard rumblings about a show that's sort of based on that rock camp for girls, where June volunteered that one summer?"

Alice remembered June doing this, but hadn't heard many details.

"My best guess, it would be writing music for that."

Alice thought her heart might break open with joy. The jobs June had had over the years were awful, lifeless jobs, and Alice had long wished her daughter would find a better use of her talents than prancing around onstage in hot little numbers in a rock band. But maybe she and June weren't as far apart on the subject of her career as Alice had always thought. Because if June wanted a job like that—writing music for a children's program, composing like her father—surely there was hope.

Billy said, "Has she mentioned anything to you?"

Alice watched June talking to Abby. She was examining Abby's necklace, and through the screened windows they all looked like old film stars, all soft focus and slightly washed out. You could almost pretend June's hair wasn't pink. "She never mentions anything to me."

"I don't get it." Billy was shaking his head. "They're supposed to be recording, then touring next spring and fall. She can't just quit the band."

"Maybe she could do both," Alice said.

"Maybe," Billy said. "But I don't really see how. Everyone else in the band works for themselves. There's just not enough vacation days in the world. Never mind Cash, Trevor will never let it happen."

"Well, if anyone can make it work, June can," Alice said with an air of finality. She was thinking that in an ideal world, she could stay out here just talking to Billy all night. But it wasn't meant to be and, besides, Alice hated being late. "We should go in," she said, then led the way.

"There they are!" June came forward to greet them, pulling Alice into a hug and then Billy, too.

"We need to talk," he said, and June said, "Not now!"— two bright syllables—then turned back to the group to handle introductions and reintroductions.

Lovely to see you. So nice to meet you. Alice snapped into social mode. She'd agreed with her mother that it was probably best for her not to come, but now she wished that she and Billy weren't the only representatives of June's family. Not that Cash's family was huge, but Alice felt outnumbered. Then again, Alice pretty much always felt outnumbered. That happened when you were just one.

She wasn't entirely displeased, though, to find herself sitting next to Billy on the one side and Cash's great-aunt, Minky Dykstra, on the other. Maybe because of her work at the Renaissance, Alice found that talking to the elderly came easily to her, required less of her energy.

"Well, I think this is a marvelous idea," Minky said to Alice, apropos of nothing. "Was this your June's idea?"

Alice smiled and sensed, correctly, that Minky wasn't really expecting an answer.

"Imagine me, at my age, going to my great-nephew's wedding in Belize!" Her voice was high-pitched and artificial-sounding, as if she were a man trying to impersonate a woman.

Alice smiled. "How old are you now, Minky?" If Alice recalled correctly, it was short for Minerva.

"Eighty-nine in a month. But I don't feel it, I'll tell you. I look in the mirror and I think, Who's that old biddy? Of course I won't be here much longer." She touched Alice's arm and leaned closer, and Alice got a good look at her white-white hair. "People look at me funny when I say stuff like that. People don't like to talk about it. But I'm fine with dying. I've lived with death. Most people I know are dead! It's part of living."

Alice nodded and said, "That's the truth."

"But enough about me. And anyway, we're here for a wedding."

"Yes, very exciting," Alice said.

"Well, I've always said, being married is a good way to be." So apparently *not* enough about her. "If I had it all to do again, I'd get married. I would've worked harder at it. Nobody told me you had to work at it, and I was never all that interested."

Alice, having been raised in a house of women, had had the opposite experience. "And then there was the war, and I never trusted any of the men in the service. They were very flirty with me, some of them. But you never knew if they had a wife at home. There was one fella, though, who I liked. Paul was his name. Paul . . . now what was it? I forget things, words."

"It's okay," Alice said. "It'll come to you. Go on."

"Well, I would have liked to have married him, maybe. Being married is just a better way. Now I live alone, you see. I've lived alone most of my life. And you'd think that people would call me, but they really don't." Alice thought she should give Minky her own mother's number and vice versa; they could call each other all the time.

"I know," Alice said. "I live alone, too." And she had long given up on hoping people would call.

Minky went on and on about the realities of living alone—not particularly caring, apparently, that Alice knew them first-hand—then a camera flashed as Cash and June kissed at the end of the table, and Alice had a sudden vision of armed rebels bursting into the dining room and taking them all hostage. Alice had loved Ann Patchett's *Bel Canto*—Felicia's only decent book club pick ever—but thinking of it now, she wondered whether evil political forces lurked beyond the amber glow of the dining room. The book had been set in an unnamed South American country where a group of people at a party—including a world-renowned opera singer—was taken hostage for days upon days. Looking around the table, and out windows facing nothing but wild darkness, Alice wondered how this group would fare over the course of the next week if they really were confined to this very room and held at gunpoint with only an opera singer—or in this case, half of a rock band—to inspire the will to live.

"Now what's his name again?" Minky grabbed Alice's arm and nodded over at Billy.

"That's my son, Billy." Alice shook off images of machine guns and librettos.

"He married?"

"No."

"Well, what's he waiting for?"

Billy became aware that he was being talked about. "You're looking well, Minky."

"You wouldn't say that if you saw what I looked like when I was your age." Minky's laugh was a sort of squeak. "And anyway, you should use that charm on gals your own age and find a nice one to settle down with."

"Oh, believe you me." Billy smiled widely, obviously amused, though Alice wished he would take Minky's advice a bit more to heart. Alice didn't doubt there'd been dates and more, but Billy hadn't brought home a girlfriend in years. "It's not for lack of trying!"

Minky's face scrunched up as she studied him. She tapped a spoon on the table with her right hand. "I'm not sure I believe you," she said. "But to each his own, I suppose. Now, Alice, tell me. Are your parents still with you?"

"Oh, well, I never knew my father." Still such a strange fact to admit to, even after all these years. "My mother wasn't really up for the trip."

"Well, that's too bad." Minky reached for a bread basket that had just been put on the table. "You have to watch that, though. A lot of people stop living before they're even dead."

"Now, June," Miller said, loud enough that the whole table had to listen, too. "Don't be mad, but you really all *have* to come to see Blancaneaux."

"Yes," Minky said. "Why on earth did you pick this place instead?"

Alice watched her daughter's jaw stiffen.

"We thought it was important to support Belizean-owned business, and that we'd have a more authentic experience that way," Cash said, and June smiled at him with her mouth closed. His eyes lit up as he squeezed her hand. They seemed to be enjoying a private joke, and Alice thought "You and me against the world" was as good an approach to marriage as any. She ordered the Belizean beef stew.

If Dan wasn't already regretting bringing Becky on this trip, he certainly would have started now. Whereas June looked like she'd stepped off the runway of some spring fashion show in Paris, Becky's ensemble looked like last season's Kohl's. Dan had never actually been to a Kohl's, but he'd seen their commercials and also knew that there wasn't one in New York. That meant something. Her skirt was so flimsy that you could see the silhouette of her underwear through it. She had changed from orange and black leopard print to white only when Dan pointed out the gaffe. At first she didn't even want to bother—"It's dark out, who's gonna notice?"—but Dan had insisted.

"You care too much about what other people think," she'd said, sliding out of the jungle panties in the middle of the room, though to be fair, everyplace in the room was pretty much the middle of it. Dan thought June would never buy a skirt you could see through. Or if she did, it'd be on purpose, like because she was wearing leather hot pants under it.

Dan had seen that Becky was going to end up sitting next to Cash's father and immediately switched places with her, pushing her farther into the table. The thought of Becky trying to talk to Miller, whom Dan had met fewer times over the years than you would think, considering how many years he'd known Cash, was too much. Not that she couldn't be charming . . . not that there wasn't a certain appeal to her naïveté, her eagerness to talk at length about things she knew nothing about. Just not tonight. Dan didn't think he could bear it.

"Hello, Daniel," Miller said, extending a hand for Dan to shake. Not even his own parents called him Daniel, but Miller had insisted on it over the years. "You're doing well, I hope."

"I am, sir, thanks." Dan never called anybody sir, but around Cash's father it was a sort of tic.

"And who is this lovely lady?" Miller turned his attention to Becky.

"This"—Dan placed a hand on the small of Becky's back—"is Becky." He knew he should've said "my girlfriend Becky," but he was starting to lay the groundwork for a breakup, even if only in his own head.

"Nice to meet you," Miller said, and they all took their seats. "And welcome to Belize."

"Oh," Becky said. "Do you live here?"

Dan had to hand it to her on that one.

"Oh." Miller seemed taken aback. "No, no. Of course not."

"Hey." June was suddenly beside Dan, leaning down to talk. "Any news about your bag?"

"Well, they called down to Blancaneaux, but there's no sign of it yet." Dan was repressing how pissed off he was, how entirely uncomfortable he felt in his plane clothes. "I'm sure it'll turn up, though. And I saw they sell shirts and stuff in the gift shop. I'll be fine."

June winced. "There's nothing supervaluable in it, I hope?"

Dan's voice skipped at the back of his throat. "Nah"—he cleared it—"nothing like that. But," he added quietly, checking that Becky was involved in conversation and standing to talk to June properly. "I have, you know..." He touched his lips with his index and middle finger straight like planks, cigarette-width apart.

June leaned in and clutched her necklace, a long rectangular pendant made of Murano glass in shimmering reds and golds, dangling from skinny black leather. He'd complimented her on it before and thus knew that Cash had bought it for her when the band played Venice earlier this year. There was a photo album from the tour on the Starter House website and in one photo, June stands in Venice's famous Piazza San Marco with pigeons on her head and arms as the rest of the band—pigeon-free—looks on, nonplussed. Dan found it to be a symbolically precise image; people seemed to flock to June, too.

She said, "Ohmigod, can we go outside right now?" Then she put a hand on Becky's shoulder and said, "Hey, great skirt," and Dan thought she couldn't possibly be serious. Was she toying with him? Rubbing it in?

"Thanks!" Becky said, then returned without missing a beat to her conversation with Miller. "Well, it's my first time in Belize," she said. "But I once took a cruise to Panama."

On the balcony, Dan gave June a cigarette, then lit it for her, then lit one for himself. In New York Dan hardly smoked at all, but when he traveled, he liked to be his most free-spirited, flexible self. And that flexible self allowed him to have the odd cigarette.

June closed her eyes on her first exhale, and Dan felt like he'd caught a glimpse of her in ecstasy. "It's pretty crazy that we're here, right?" Her eyes were on edge, excited.

Dan looked out into the darkness of the pines and thought of New York—of sleet and rain, of the boxes he'd yet to unpack in his new place, of bulldozers taking down the dilapidated mansion, of the abandoned pool at McCarren coated in graffiti and ice. He said, "Sure is," and took another drag.

Even though the autograph was at Blancaneaux or wherever it was, it was practically burning a hole in his pocket. But the autograph was secondary, when you really thought about it. He should just tell her he loved her and that he didn't want her to get married before he'd had the chance to say as much. He'd tell her he didn't expect anything. He'd tell her he just wanted her to know. He'd tell her he was telling her now so that if, during the ceremony, he was asked to hold his peace, he would. He said, "Remember all those years ago"—the moment seemed long, loaded—"when we'd meet in Times Square at lunchtime?"

June laughed hard, and smoke came out of her in one big burst. "My God." She shook her head. "I haven't thought of that in ages. Dance Dance Revolution."

"Yup." The revolution was here and now. It was a coup against Cash. "You were pretty good at it."

June snorted. "And you were pathetic."

But he wasn't pathetic anymore. A pathetic man wouldn't have the balls to say, I've always regretted not asking you out on a proper date back then. A pathetic man wouldn't be here at all, readying himself to take down this house of cards, or at the very least to reveal his hand.

"Hey." Billy's hand on Dan's shoulder made the smoke in Dan's lungs turn foul. Billy pointed at the pack. "Can I get one of those?"

"You bet," Dan said, hoping Billy would take the cigarette and walk away. But he didn't. He said, "Actually, Dan, if you wouldn't mind, I'd like a word alone with my sister."

"Billy, don't be rude." June looked at Dan. "You'll have to forgive him." She put her cigarette out in an ashtray on a nearby table. "I should really get back inside."

"June!" Billy said.

"Not now, Billy," she said brightly.

"I heard about your luggage," Billy said, when June was gone. He blew a smoke ring. "Suuucks."

"Yup." Dan stubbed his cigarette out on the railing and watched tiny blood-orange embers float off into the night. "Like you wouldn't believe."

Gift bags worth a couple thousand dollars. Abby couldn't even imagine what you'd *put* in a gift bag that could amount to that much. Probably video iPods, which she didn't care so much about since she already had one. Maybe a digital camera? She already had one of those, too, but she wouldn't mind a newer one, and that wasn't even the point. The point was not so much to have the stuff as it was to be given it. The point was to be in with the in crowd, and how could she assert her "in"-ness without the right props? It didn't even matter what was in the bag—the bag itself was like a key to some exclusive club.

Now that Abby was away from Hannah and Lisa for a week, she was starting to worry about what things would be like between the three of them when she went home. This party—Chelsea's party—and the gift bag assembly line, they were things Abby was missing out on, and she knew Lisa well enough to know that Lisa would never let her hear the end of it. Lisa wanted Hannah all to herself, and this trip was giving her a huge opportunity to move in on Abby's turf. Abby had sort of talked with Hannah about this one day, when they were hanging out at Hannah's house, waiting for Lisa to come over, too.

"I think she wants to be your best friend," Abby had said bluntly, but not daring to look at Hannah directly.

"You think?" Hannah had said, all nonchalant.

"Yeah," Abby said. "I mean, do you even like her?"

"She's cool," Hannah said.

"Yeah." Abby's brain screamed, *Retreat! Retreat!* and she backed off. "She's all right."

Yesterday in school—it was weird to think she'd been in school only yesterday—Abby had come across Hannah and Lisa in the hallway, laughing hard, and when Abby had asked, "What's so funny?" Lisa said, "You had to be there."

You had to be there. That pretty much summed it up. And Abby was *here*.

At least June's brother, Billy, really was as hot as Abby remembered. He had long skinny fingers and a soccer butt and looked awesome in his army green shorts and black T-shirt. His haircut was way cool—though she sort of preferred the thick curls he'd had at Radio City. A silver-studded black leather belt gave him a sort of indie edge that Abby liked and was trying to cultivate not just in her designs but in her psyche. Sometimes she felt so painfully *normal.*

So yeah, hot brother. That, at least, was something. Abby had been sort of bummed to hear that Trevor and Joe wouldn't be arriving in Belize for a few more days, but Billy seemed cool—and she was pretty sure she'd caught him looking at her a few times during dinner, so he probably thought she was cute or whatever—and this Becky girl seemed like she might be normal, too, though maybe a primo candidate for a *What Not to Wear* makeover. Her boyfriend, Cash's friend Dan, seemed kind of like a dick, but Abby couldn't figure out exactly why. She hadn't really met any of Cash's friends before, since they'd never lived in the same city; she had kind of been expecting *more*.

"So, Abby," Becky said toward the end of the meal, "you're a senior?"

"Yup," Abby said. The Belizean lasagna she'd ordered wasn't really like lasagna at all—it was just layers of vegetables and corn tortillas, best she could tell—but it was pretty good anyway. Most people had ordered a shrimp curry, ladled into a bed of rice in a big neat scoop, and Abby sort of wished she'd gotten that instead.

Becky took a big gulp of water, which they'd all been told by their waitress was filtered and thus safe. "So where are you applying to college and all that?"

Abby looked to see if M and M were close enough to hear, but the coast seemed clear. Abby had overheard them whispering to each other about the color of June's hair, and was it permanent, and how Cash had better put his foot down about that one, so clearly they had bigger concerns. "Well, *they*"—she rolled her eyes toward M and M—"think I'm going to UC, but I'm applying to some schools in New York, too."

"Cool." Becky's eyes were brown and shiny, like tiny circles of silk. "Which ones?"

"FIT and Pratt." God, it felt good to say it.

"*Very* cool." Becky nodded a few times. "So you want to be a fashion designer?"

Abby nodded, but talking like this in such close proximity to her parents was making her nervous, even with all their whispering. Besides, time was a-wastin', and Abby needed to start a ziplining movement and fast. They were only going to be in the right part of Belize for three days. Becky looked sporty. She seemed as good a place as any to start.

Abby said, "Hey, so, have you ever heard of ziplining?"

Becky shook her head. "I don't think so, no."

Abby slid the brochure from her room out of her bag, folded it to the right panel, and handed it across the table. Becky took the booklet and studied it. "I think it sounds awesome," Abby said.

"Not to me!" Becky handed the booklet back. "I'm terrified of heights."

"It's not that high."

"Sorry," Becky said. "No can do."

Abby felt a sudden rush of gloom.

"What's that?" Billy said. She'd watched him outside, smoking with June and Dan, and she'd wished she could go

112

out and join them, like a grown-up. He was at the table now, looking over Abby's shoulder.

"Ziplining?" Abby held up the brochure, and Billy looked at it, bottom lip stuck out.

"Looks cool," he said. "You going?"

Abby seriously hoped she wasn't turning red. Her face seemed to be melting from the inside out. "I want to," she said. "Would you want to? I mean, if these guys want to?"

"Yeah, I'd try it," Billy said. "What the hell, right?" He took his seat across from her again. His eyes were this really neat color blue, more like gray even, and his black hair was so, so soft-looking. His T-shirt stretched across his chest in a way that made Abby wish she had X-ray vision. Was there chest hair under there? The thought of it made her uneasy, but not in a bad way. Billy was just obviously way more man than boy—Colin Murray was a boy—and Abby liked that she was talking to him.

"So, are you, like, a musician, too?" she said, then immediately felt ridiculous because she sounded like such a teenager. She took a sip of water for something to do.

"Not like these guys." He tilted his head toward Cash and June. "But I was in a band for a while, and I still play a little guitar."

"What was your band called?

"Ninety-nine Cents and Up."

"Cool," Abby said. She'd look them up when she got home. "So do you go see the Starter House all the time?"

"When I can." Billy shrugged.

"I'm completely obsessed with the new CD. Not that it's even that new anymore, but still." It wasn't quite real yet, the fact that the rest of the band was coming in a few days. The fact that Abby would be hanging out with them. "I play a little guitar, too," Abby said. Cash had taught her some basics back when they were melding their family together and bonding and all that. "But it's not, you know, my thing."

"No?" Billy smiled an amused sort of smile, and Abby felt dumb. "What's your thing?"

Abby shrugged. "Clothes, I guess. I mean, I make them."

"Did you make that?" He lifted his chin, indicated her top with eyes pointed at her chest, and she looked down. *Duh.* As if she didn't know what she was wearing. It was a black top she'd copied from something she saw in a store: two wide straps, empire waist, and a lot of cinching around the breasts.

"As a matter of fact," she said, "I did."

He nodded slowly, repeatedly, like he was trying to get his chair to rock beneath him, and Abby knew he thought she looked sexy. He said, "Cool. I like it," and Abby flashed hot with confidence.

"Thanks." She flipped her hair. "So what's *your* thing?"

"You know, I'm not sure I've even figured that out yet." He ran a hand over his hair, and Abby wanted to do the same. "But right now I'm an animator. For Nickelodeon."

"Wow. That's so cool." So he was creative, too.

"I guess!" He shrugged.

"I have these sketches to do." Abby adjusted her place mat for something to do. "While I'm here. For my application to design school. And they're really hard for some reason."

Billy picked up his beer and took a swig and then smacked his lips. "Well, let me know if there's anything I can do to help."

"I will." Abby sat back in her chair as Billy turned to talk to his mom, who needed a *What Not to Wear* makeover almost but not quite as badly as Becky did.

So maybe the week wouldn't be so bad after all. In a day or two she'd go ziplining with Billy, and after that he'd help her with her sketches, and then they'd sneak off and make out by a river or a waterfall and it would be scandalous and hot and way better than making out with Colin Murray at some bitchy rich girl's Sweet Sixteen party. And anyway, Colin still hadn't asked anyone. So maybe they'd pick up right where they left off when she got home. Maybe she should chill the ef out and enjoy herself. And she and Hannah had been friends for years. It wasn't like Hannah would just throw that all away, not in one week. *Gift bag, schmift bag.*

Becky leaned over and said softly, "He's cute, don'tcha think?"

Billy was still talking to his mom, and Abby watched his fingers caress his beer bottle. "Ohmigod," she said. "Totally."

"Does he have a girlfriend?" Becky asked.

"No idea," Abby said, but she was sure as hell going to find out.

Dinner was over, and everyone moved to the bar to mingle some more, and Abby miraculously ended up sitting on a bar stool between June, who was talking to Becky, and Billy. She hoped that no one heard her or cared when she ordered a beer. The girl bartender, who couldn't have been much older than Abby, didn't think twice about putting a bottle in front of her, and Abby thought, *Yes!* Things were definitely looking up. Dan had just announced that he was footing the bill.

Billy leaned in to Abby and said, "Dan's a millionaire. Did you know that?"

"No way." Abby shot her eyebrows up; maybe Cash's friends were more interesting than she thought. "Really?"

"Yup. Lucky bastard." He noticed the beer then. "Hey! How old are you?" He looked at Abby suspiciously, sizing her up with an amused look on his face.

"Eighteen," she lied, then took a swig and swallowed. "Which is the drinking age in Belize, just FYI. I looked it up. How old are *you*?"

"Twenty-five."

Eight years apart. Totally doable. If not now, then soon.

There was a wooden puzzle on the bar—three pegs on a board with a stack of seven circles in decreasing diameter stacked on one peg—and Billy asked the bartender, "What's the deal with this?"

"It's the Mayan temple puzzle," she said, and her accent sounded a little like a Spanish accent, with a tiny bit of sing-song. "You have to move this stack over to this peg, but you can only move one piece at a time, and you can't put any of the circles on top of a smaller circle."

"Heh," Billy said, and then June busted in. "Please, please, can I try?" she said. "I'm good at stuff like this."

Billy's arm touched Abby's as he moved the puzzle toward his sister. "You always were a game freak," he said.

Abby watched June work at the puzzle and was about to bring up the subject of ziplining when June looked at Billy and said, "Are you listening to this? Boggles the mind."

So Abby, who hadn't been listening to anything, only watching and waiting, started listening to the conversation behind them. Minky was saying that she thought everyone in the United States should learn to speak English. "Back when the Irish came over, people assimilated. That's what they did."

June turned from the puzzle, wooden doughnut in hand, and said, brightly, "The Irish already *spoke* English."

She turned back and said, "Where was this one again?" and Abby pointed to the left peg.

"Yes," Minky said. "But they were discriminated against, and they adapted. People today, they expect us all to change for them! They'd have us all singing 'The Star-Spangled Banner' in Spanish if they had their way."

"Actually," Becky said, "that's not true." Her voice was clear and strong, and Abby felt, momentarily, like she was in school, in a classroom, being taught. "I work with immigrants every day who want to get rid of their accents and learn to speak proper English. That's my job. Every day."

That shut Minky up. Or stopped her for a second anyway, and Abby, who was already sick of Minky, and who knew from

116

experience with her own grandmother that talking to elderly people was a lot like shouting underwater, thought, Nice one, Becky. Abby hadn't even known that a job like that existed in the world. Then Minky said, "Yes, but they're the minority."

"I honestly can't believe this," June said to Abby and Billy, shaking her head and shifting one of the wooden doughnuts on the peg back and forth with a hollow clicking sound as the conversation behind them went on and on, with Becky now saying something about the Spanish "Star-Spangled Banner" being a show of patriotism.

"I should've eloped." June looked up at Billy and Abby real fast—"I mean, no offense"—then back to the puzzle. "I mean that we should've eloped with just the young normal people."

Minky slapped a hand on the bar and said, "'The Star-Spangled Banner' should be sung in English."

Abby took a huge gulp of beer and watched as June stood, breathed out hard, and made a series of hurried moves on the puzzle. "Dammit," she said, and put one of the round dough-nuts down on the bar. She turned to face Abby and Billy and said, "The bride invokes her right to say it's bedtime!"

"I really do need to talk to you about something," Billy said, and Abby was disappointed to see that he was talking not to her but to his sister.

"I'm exhausted, Billy. Can't it wait?" She didn't give him a chance to answer.

On the way back to Blancaneaux, Minky fell asleep, and M and M were superquiet, probably because they didn't want to wake Minky up and get her all worked up about immigration again; Abby was surprised Minky wasn't standing on the bor-der with a gun with that attitude of hers. But when M and M woke her up for the walk back to the cabana, she kept her trap shut the whole way, thank God.

Getting ready for bed, Abby checked her room for any crazy-ass tropical bugs, and the coast seemed clear. But God, it was only the first night. Already it felt like they'd been here forever, and she felt sort of twitchy and restless and wished she could check her email or her voice mail or anything that would make her feel less far away than she was.

She climbed into bed and tried to read, but *Heart of Darkness*? Please. Her teacher was whacked if she thought the class was going to get through this one. So she put the book down and tried to sleep and could only kick herself for not asking June about ziplining when she had the chance. Though June was so worked up about things that Abby hadn't really had a chance at all. She'd have to try again first thing.

*T*hey are onstage at a dive Williamsburg bar called the Charleston, not far from their rehearsal space, on a Monday night, and the place is packed. It is the last night of a "residency," which means that they were given a crappy Monday-night slot, but that they were given it every Monday for a month. At first there was no one there but the girlfriends (Joe's and now Trevor's, too: more on that later), but they didn't particularly care. They needed to play out; they needed the practice. But at the end of the first month, people actually started turning up—the right kind of people, too: hip-looking ones, tastemakers—and then they asked for a second month of Mondays and got it.

They are tuning guitars and adjusting mike stands and getting ready to start a song to whoops of recognition on this last Monday night, the last Monday night they hope they ever have to play, because they've got an EP—four songs—out in stores now and it's generating buzz, big-time. They recorded it one weekend in a friend's home studio and pretty much played it once and left it alone, a little live gem. Three out of the four songs are June's, and she listens to them more than any sane person should because she's kind of shocked by how good they sound. She's quickly, almost unwittingly developed a distinctive guitar style—she's all over the whammy bar—and it's becoming a sort of defining sound for the band.

She is watching Cash now, with his cool new red guitar and funky *new black shirt—both of which she was instrumental in purchasing—and thinking that this is everything she's ever wanted. Cash. And the songs. And the Starter House.*

Oh yeah. They're called the Starter House now. (Co-op Board, RIP.) And it wasn't even June who suggested the new name. The hours and legal pads that she'd wasted had produced nothing with quite the same sense of, well, what exactly was *it that the Starter House so effortlessly embodied? Joe had suggested it when they were still riffing on the Co-op Board and trolling through the lingo of real estate, and they'd all agreed that it was potentially a keeper—mostly for its complete lack of pretension, its suggestion that they hadn't tried too hard—but then they'd set it aside and brainstormed a million other times only to come up with horribly contrived names like Common People and Wingding Nation, and, as they hailed from Brooklyn, Roebling. The Starter House had a nice rhythm to it. It looked good in print. They couldn't even explain why they liked it, they just did, and that seemed somehow right, perfect, destined.*

They are up there—one song down—feeling pretty good about themselves because a few music zines and websites have reviewed the EP, and the reviews have all been good. Pitchfork *called the Starter House the most promising new band to emerge from Brooklyn in years (or at least since last month).* The Big Takeover *called June's songwriting "inspired" and her lyrics "daring."* Aiding and Abetting *said, "Someday these guys are going to blow up something fierce," and* Space City Rock's *reviewer said, "You can't help but fall for these songs." Chiming in, too, were* Crashin' In *("top-notch songwriting") and* Geek America *("stuff this good just doesn't come along that often"), and* Delusions of Adequacy *called the EP "a treasure."* Swizzle Stick *had this classic, which speaks to both the rampant amateurishness and refreshing honesty of music criticism on the whole: "I listened to it dozens of times and I'm not really sick of it, which is more than I can say for most of what I review."*

There are a bunch of people from other bands in the crowd here at the Charleston tonight. They've got rehearsal spaces around the corner, too, and have heard the Starter House through the walls or through cracked doors, but they've started to hear (and envy) the buzz and want to see firsthand what the fuss is about. After tonight's set they will tell the Starter House how awesome they are and then they will go around the corner to another bar, where they will order drinks and talk about how the band's not really that tight, and how June's voice can be sort of grating, and how it's sort of annoying that they act like they're playing Madison Square Garden when it's just the freakin' Charleston. They'll convince themselves that they're just as worthy of Monday-night residencies and good press and that their song—whatever their favorite one of their own is—is way more radio-friendly and cool than anything the Starter House is playing. In most cases they'll be wrong, but it will take them anywhere from a year to four, depending on their levels of arrogance and disposable income, to figure that out, to give up the dream and move on.

They're up there onstage feeling sort of melancholy, all of them, about this being the last night of the residency because they've fallen into a sort of blissful Monday-night routine these last two months: loading in and sound-checking, then hanging out at the bar before they take the stage at nine, then mingling with fans for a while—collecting email addresses for their mailing list—then loading out and locking up the cars and walking a few blocks to a crazy Polish cafeteria-style restaurant where they order massive amounts of pierogi and kielbasa and slaw and run through the set again, verbally, picking apart each song. "That drum part sounds awesome," "Are those really the lyrics to that verse?" "Did you see that crazy guy dancing?" When the last pierogi is eaten, the last bowl of that weird pink soup that comes complimentary with any entrée slurped up, they drive back to the space, unload everything there, then call it a night. June and Cash often can't sleep on Monday nights. They're too jazzed up, and they talk through everything again, without Trevor and Joe there. They wonder sometimes if Joe's really committed, if Trevor's more trouble than he's worth, but then Cash shuts June down and reminds her that they were there first, and really, June loves them all—yes, even Trevor—and *wouldn't have it any other way. Except that she'd get rid of the very annoying, very loud girl Trevor is currently dating, who drinks too much and brings her too-loud friends down every Monday and then proceeds to talk through the set.*

"Can't you hear her?" June has asked Cash more than once. "I'm going to have to ask him to ask her not to talk. I mean, I can barely hear myself sing."

"You can't control the crowd, June. It's a bar. You can't make them listen."

"But she's Trevor's girlfriend or whatever. And I mean, it's just so rude."

So they are a couple now, June and Cash, and came out to the band a few months ago, which was a few months after the demise of Cara. They'd sneaked around for a while, faking going to separate apartments and doubling back and basically behaving like teenagers to Trevor and Joe's Mom and Dad, then one night, over drinks after practice, Cash made the announcement.

"So, uh," he said, because they'd talked about it and decided it should come from him. "June and I are sort of together now. Just so you know."

Trevor held out a hand to Joe and said, "Pay up."

Joe reached back for his wallet, pulled out a twenty, and said, "You guys would make horrible spies."

"So you're cool with it?" Cash took a swig of beer.

"No, actually," Trevor said. "We forbid it. Cease and desist immediately."

Silence really could be deafening, even in a bar where the jukebox is playing old Pixies songs.

"I'm kidding, man." Trevor smiled wide. "I mean, I'd tap that."

"Oh, fuck you," June said in a sort of weird outer-borough, Mafioso sort of intonation that made the f-word almost two syllables.

"God, you're easy to wind up." Trevor reached across the table and squeezed June's shoulder. "It really is like taking candy from a baby."

She pushed him off.

"But, uh, seriously," he said. "There's nothing we can do about it, right?"

June said, "Right."

"Then go for it, kids. Just don't let it affect the band."

Cash said, "We wouldn't."

June said, "We'd never."

"Yeah, well, you say that now." Trevor picked at the label on his nonalcoholic beer. "But seriously. I mean, if it all ends in tears, we're all pretty much fucked."

"It's not going to end in tears," Cash said.

Trevor pushed his bottle to the center of the table, where a few other empties had gathered, and repeated himself for effect. "Yeah, well, you say that now, but . . ."

"Okay, I think we're done talking about this." June got up and started to collect her things. "I mean, it's just started, and you've got it ending in tears. We're done here."

Joe and Trevor looked at each other and shrugged.

She is up there now in her miniskirt and dazzly red top, with two more songs to go, struggling to see features, faces, because there is an old man bartender who controls the stage light show, with a little too much verve, while also serving beers. But blinded by the light or not, she's getting used to being in the spotlight. She has recently discovered that she has some trademark moves that she does onstage, and while she doesn't ever want to seem studied, she's been practicing in front of the mirror, making sure she likes the way she looks when she does this and that, like shimmy this way or shake that way or pulse a hip like so. Cash makes fun of her, but she knows he likes it—and he does—when she plays rock star in her underwear in the morning, with her hair all mussed up and eyes still muted from sleep.

Last week, that reviewer from Swizzle Stick *suggested doing a Q&A with the band, and so they all met up yesterday at their favorite bar and geared up for their very first interview. The band were all situated in their favorite booth, Bloody or Virgin Marys in hand, when a guy with hipper-than-thou thick black glasses and a T-shirt that said* WILL WRITE FOR MONEY *came in, honed in on them, and walked over.*

"You must be the Starter House," he said, lifting his messenger bag strap over his head and revealing the faintest diagonal stripe of sweat across his T-shirt.

Trevor said, "Bingo," and then the guy went to get a beer and the band all looked around at each other and smiled. They were being interviewed. And even if it was just a scrawny, sweaty hipster who wrote for a magazine that was probably only sold in maybe a hundred independent record stores around the country, it was a start.

They hadn't talked about what they would and wouldn't talk about, and then June's body language must have given it away, be-cause after questions like "How'd you all meet?" and "So you dyed your hair blond just to spite them?" the interviewer guy said, "So wait, are you two like a couple?" and then June said yes and the interview went on and ended and the guy left, presumably to go and write for money, and then it came out that Trevor—and Joe, though to a lesser extent—was pissed. "Why'd you have to go and bring up the couple thing?" he said.

June said, "I didn't bring it up. And what did you want me to do, lie?"

"No." Trevor slapped a coaster around on the table. "But you don't see me and Joe slobbering all over each other, do you?"

"You're being ridiculous," June said, and then Cash said, "He does sort of have a point. We shouldn't, you know, sit so close, act like a couple."

June said, "We are *a couple."*

Trevor exhaled loudly. "You're two people in a band in which there are two other people."

"Fine. Whatever." June's beer was empty. "Like anyone's going to read the damn thing anyway."

She is up there, looking for Lydia through her squinting eyes because Lydia, pregnant with her first child, has come down to all but one of these Monday-night gigs, as she's convinced she'll never be able to go out again after the baby comes.

She is dedicating this last song to Lydia because last week Lydia said to June, "It's funny watching you up there." They were sitting at the bar after the set, and June said, "Funny how?"

"Funny because you're pretty much my best friend, and I've known you for years, but I don't really understand that." Lydia nodded at the stage.

"We're even," June said, and Lydia cocked her head. June pointed at Lydia's belly and said, "I don't understand that."

Lydia smiled and said, "Someday, you'll surprise yourself. Speaking of which, how's it going?" She nodded down the bar at Cash.

"Good," June said. "Really good. It just feels like how it's supposed to be."

"And not just because he's in the band and you like the idea of being this sort of rock star couple?"

"No, of course not." June was thinking back to that old roommate of hers and the headboard, and to the first day she laid eyes on Cash and his eyebrows. "Well, not just that," she said with a smile. "But here's the thing." It was the first time she'd said this to anyone other than Cash, to anyone whose natural inclination would be toward skepticism, since the odds are so, so stacked against them. She said, "I think we might actually make it."

"You and Cash?" Lydia asked. "Or the band?"

June nodded and felt, already, nostalgic for the Charleston, for this time in her life—the prime of it. She was talking about the band, but she considered the question again, then said, "Both."

Sunday

Alice opened the sliding wooden door to her porch and thanked the Five Sisters one by one for drowning out any of the nightmarish clicks and creaks that Belize's strange insects, unfamiliar birds, and unpredictable winds might have thrown her way. She would have to install a water-fall in her yard back home; she had slept that well. She stretched and turned back to the room and began to pre-pare for Billy's scheduled arrival—for the Mother of the Bride fashion show.

Alice had always had an idea of what kind of dress she'd wear to her daughter's wedding, but it had begun to dawn on her that maybe she'd formed that image before she'd realized that her daughter was June—and not some imaginary, perfect younger version of herself with whom she'd be the bestest friends. Oprah always said stuff about how our children were "of us" but not "ours" and that they were here to teach us about ourselves, and Alice thought Oprah had that one right. Though what Alice had learned she wasn't yet sure.

She'd tried on each of the three dresses—one gray, one sage, one red—so many times by now that she could easily imagine what June would have to say about each of them. The gray would elicit "It's the beach, Mom, not the Plaza." The sage would yield "Where'd you get that one, Seniors R Us?" And the red, "Wow, sexy momma!" Alice should've never bought, let alone brought, that third one, but Mary-Anise had insisted. "Oprah wouldn't let you walk out of here without buying that dress," she'd said in the fitting room. "You've still got a cute little body, Alice. Don't be afraid to show it." Alice had caved at the register only after Mary-Anise threatened to pay for it with her own money.

Alice was showered and wearing the gray dress when she heard Billy say, "Mom, it's me," and then knock.

"Coming!" she said, and she opened the door. "Morning, honey."

"Morning." He kissed her, and she could practically feel the transfer of sunscreen and bug spray. Her cheek felt sticky and warm. What was the point of showering at all?

She stepped back and held out her arms. "This is door number one."

"It's nice." Billy yawned and stepped into the cabana, then went to the wood chair on the terrace. "A little dressy for the beach, maybe?" he said. "And who on earth decided that this chair was worthy of being a chair?"

"So sit on the bed," Alice said.

"Nah," Billy said. "I'm good. It'll help wake me up." He lowered himself gingerly, and Alice saw that he traveled with ghosts, too. She could see Billy wailing in his crib and building model airplanes in the basement and playing drums in the garage and wearing that vintage pinstripe suit he'd managed to talk her into buying for his senior prom.

"Hold on, I'll put on another one." Alice ducked into the small bathroom with the red dress in hand. "How'd you sleep?"

"Like the dead. It's like sleeping with a noise machine set on 'Rain Forest.'"

"Me too." Alice realized they could talk easily, as there was no full wall between the rooms. "Did you talk to June?" She'd have asked June about this mystery job offer herself if they'd had a second alone. She wanted to know what the show was about—if the job was even *on* a show—how June had heard about it, and what exactly she'd be doing. She wanted to know which way June was leaning, too.

"I tried, but it's like she knows I know and she's avoiding me. Keeps shutting me down."

"I guess she's not ready to talk about it." The gray dress was off, and red was going on. "Or maybe there's nothing to talk about."

"Oh, now I'm even more sure there's something to talk about." Billy sounded excited, like a television detective who'd just found his guy but hadn't proven it yet. "I really think she's quitting. Because otherwise, what's the big deal?"

Alice stepped back out into the room.

"Nice. I like the color." Billy tilted his head and considered it again. "But it's a little, I dunno. Sexy? Maybe?"

Alice ran flat hands over her hips, smoothing out the fabric. "Well, I don't want to look like an old fart either."

Billy yawned again. "Let me see the other one."

Alice went back into the bathroom and slipped off the red. Last up was the sage. Mary-Anise had told her *not* to buy this one—"Not if you ever plan on having sex ever again," she'd said, which begged the question.

"Yeah. I think I like that one best," Billy said when Alice presented herself this time.

"You're just saying that because it's the last one, and you didn't say good things about the other two."

"They're all fine, Mom. Really." Billy got up.

"*Fine* isn't good enough." Alice ducked back into the bathroom with a pair of chinos and a white V-neck T—her clothes for the day. It was almost time to meet the others for the Mayan ruins tour.

"Sometimes it is," Billy said. "I mean, would you be this worked up if it were my wedding?"

"What kind of question is that?" Alice called from the bathroom.

"Uh," Billy said. "A good one?"

Alice came out and hung the sage dress on the shower rod. "Oh," she said, "before I forget. Will you *please* talk some sense into her about her hair?"

"Mom." Billy's voice was firm. "This is June. You're just gonna have to let it go."

Pickings for a guy like Dan were pretty slim in the clothing section of the Five Sisters souvenir shop. His luggage had yet to turn up, though, and he would burn the clothes he was wearing—the same ones he'd worn on the airplane, the only ones he had—before he'd wear them again. So he decided to be ironic and bought a pair of loud, tropical-print swim trunks that would double as shorts, and a YOU BETTER BELIZE IT shirt—cobalt blue with white print. He wasn't even really pissed about the luggage anymore. How could he be, when it was just so fraking typical? He'd been a fool to buy the autograph, a fool to bring it, and a fool to put it in his checked baggage. He'd only gotten what he deserved and was even starting to feel a little glad that it was gone, the pressure off for the time being. He could relax, breathe, enjoy the day.

Back at the cabana, he showered quickly and put on his new duds—"Wow," Becky said. "Those are really something," like she was one to talk—and then they went down to meet the group. Superfast, before they could all even say their good mornings, the driver closed up the sliding van doors and they were on their way, bouncing over potholes and sunken tire tracks this way and that. There was some small talk—*How'd you sleep?*—but not much. They were stopping at Blancaneaux to pick up the rest of their party, and Dan guessed no one wanted to have to repeat things again for the benefit of the newbies.

"Well, hello!" Miller said, as the van pulled up in front of Blancaneaux, which Dan now really regretted not choosing over the Five Sisters. It looked so luxurious, and Dan somehow doubted they'd have found a bug on their bed on their first day at Blancaneaux.

"I like your T-shirt," Becky said to Abby, who was wearing a pink girl-tight tee with black silhouettes of exercising women in a row across her chest, though Dan felt weird looking at it too long.

Abby looked at Dan's T-shirt and said, "I like yours," sort of laughing.

Dan didn't know if she knew his luggage had been lost, but he didn't have the energy to explain. He was just starting to admit that he was hungover. His brain, straining against his skull, was rightfully angry with him. He'd knocked back more of those Belizean stouts than he should have once Billy had interrupted his Dance Dance Revolution and he'd realized that there was no way he was going to get a second moment alone with June on their first night in Belize. Compounding the usual symptoms of a hangover was a foul taste in his mouth that Becky's toothpaste had done nothing to get rid of. There really was nothing worse than someone else's toothpaste.

They were in the van, three rows deep, for what must have been a solid hour. Dan had forgotten his watch and thought it rude to ask, considering it was a vacation, but when he started to see signs for Caracol closer together, he grew eager to get the hell out of the van. In general, the scenery was pretty cool but nothing spectacular. But then Dan was partial to oceans and ice caps, the really dramatic stuff. This was just hills and trees, and as for the Mayan ruins they were about to see, well,

Dan had never been big on ancient history. Though maybe he'd be more impressed if his head weren't throbbing. He'd have given his left arm to be on the beach with a beer in his hand instead.

It was kind of funny, too, to be cruising along unpaved rain forest roads with June and Cash. It seemed so very un-rock 'n' roll. Though Cash looked the part of a rock star today to a tee. He was wearing camouflage shorts down to his knees and a brown cowboy shirt with white stitching in an elaborate pattern over the neck and shoulders. The sleeves had been ripped off, so Cash's tattoo, some angel thing by William Blake, showed. Not for the first time Dan wondered whether Cash worked so hard to look the part of the rock-'n'-roll hipster because deep down he knew he wasn't all that interesting.

No, *that* was just mean. *That* was the hangover talking. Dan wouldn't have stuck around the guy for so many years if he wasn't interesting. Though they did seem to have less and less to talk about lately.

The driver spoke for the first time in ages. "Look." He slowed the van and pointed out his open window. "Those are jaguar tracks, you see?" Everyone strained their necks and murmured yes, and Becky said, "Where? Where? Oh yeah, I see them."

"Sometimes we get lucky on this road. Keep an eye out."

Miller asked how far away the ruins of Tikal in Guatemala were, and how they compared to the ruins the group was about to see at Caracol. By all counts, Tikal sounded more spectacular, but the guide expressed a preference for Caracol. "Only one percent of the buildings are uncovered at Caracol, so you feel lost there. I mean, you are in awe of how lost the city was, and how recently it was uncovered."

"There!" Becky screamed. "A jaguar!"

Marcos hit the brakes and everyone jolted and said, "Where? Where?"—Dan included.

"Right there." Becky pointed out the open window with a lean arm. "It just went up into the trees. I saw it, though. Its hind legs, anyway."

"Cool," June said, but Dan could tell from the way she said it that she didn't believe Becky had seen a jaguar at all.

"I saw it," Becky said to Dan quietly. "Did you see it?"

He shook his head. "Nope." He was imagining their break-up, and how he was going to play it. There'd be tears, for sure, and she'd probably be pissed, too, but Dan would just tell her that she deserved to be happier, that she deserved to be with someone who didn't have any doubts, someone who wanted the same things out of life. When he'd broken things off with the girl he brought to the Starter House's Radio City gig, she'd cried so hard she'd gotten a bloody nose. Dan hoped there wouldn't be any of that.

She was studying him suspiciously. "You don't believe me, do you?"

"What?" He laughed then. "Of course I do."

Becky felt pretty crappy this morning, too. Dan could tell. He heard her taking a painkiller and when he asked her how her head was she'd said, "Fine. Why?" He was sure she felt way worse than he did, since she didn't usually drink a lot and had had a bunch of Belizean stouts last night. Or maybe she'd gotten her period. He'd noticed a bushel of tampons in her suitcase, like a white bundle of TNT, and felt a little bit sorry for himself. Becky on the rag was his least favorite version.

Alice said, "Wow!" when Marcos, who was both driver and tour guide today and had striking blue eyes and skin the color of strong tea, led the group out of a jungle path into a clearing. All around them massive, gleaming pyramid-like stacks of stone rose up out of the ground like angry LEGOs. In Hawaii, Alice had felt like she'd somehow landed on Mars—the scale of Kauai was so hard to grasp—but this Mayan site, while just as foreign, was somehow creepier. Like Mars, but with evidence of actual Martians. Alice felt her skin go tingly, imagining the bones of Mayans beneath their feet.

Miller said, "Well, they don't call it the rain forest for nothing!" and Alice realized that a light rain had begun to fall. Miller chortled, but Alice felt sort of like he'd just said something inappropriate in church. No one else laughed, and Alice sensed she wasn't the only one of the group in awe. She took her rain poncho out of her bag and started to slip it over her body as the group moved on.

June came close—"Look at you, Mom"—and Alice felt the weight of her bag lifted. She let June take it.

"I'm nothing if not prepared." Alice took the bag back when she was slicked up.

The rain teased her nose, and she wasn't convinced any of the water was actually hitting the ground. It seemed to float. She felt so much like she was on another planet that it seemed possible that maybe water simply had different qualities here. She'd read that the Mayans had believed in the special, spiritual powers of things like time and stones and wondered how they'd felt about water.

"If you'll follow me . . . ," Marcos said, and led the group across the courtyard. "Amazingly," he said, "Caracol had a population nearly equal to Belize's today—roughly 200,000—and still contains the tallest human-made structure in the country, the massive sky palace, Caana." He gestured toward the largest pyramid, and Alice took in its many shades of gray, its countless steps and plateaus, carvings of gods and monsters.

"The Mayans possessed one of only five complete writing systems in the world," Marcos was saying, "so we know more about them than we do other ancient civilizations. . . ."

Alice tried to listen, to absorb, but she was too distracted by those most basic of traveler's thoughts: amazement that a place existed and that she was there to see it; awe over the scale of time, her life not even a blip.

"They had calendars, and they etched their history, names of rulers, and religious information on stelae—these stones that you see implanted in the ground . . ."

There was so much of the world Alice had never seen and probably never would, and she envied her children their backpacks and Eurail passes and strong stomachs and cheap ticket websites and Rough Guides and daring spirits.

"Look around and you'll see many uncovered structures, but this represents less than one percent of the city buried here. There were thirty-six thousand structures when Caracol was at its peak."

Alice tried to imagine what thirty-six thousand of anything looked like: three thousand at Radio City, forty thousand at a Cubs game Mary-Anise dragged her to. How many miles away, she wondered, was Mary-Anise? She had the actual book club pick with her, too, *The Thirteenth Tale*, in honor of their thirteenth book club read. Alice wasn't sure she should bother reading it, though, whether book club would be meeting again at all.

"So now," Marcos said, "we climb."

"Not me," Miller said, and Alice had almost forgotten that the others were there. "I've got a bum knee," he added. "I'll see you right here. " He snapped another picture.

"You know what?" Becky said. "I'm gonna hang out here, too. The last thing I need is for my vertigo to kick in. It looks pretty frakin' tall."

"Did you just say frakin'?" June asked, and Dan said, "She said freakin'," but Alice knew he was lying and was sort of confused.

Billy said, "I'm gonna climb *this* one." He pointed to another structure. "I'll try to get some cool shots of the rest of you over there." He turned to go, and Alice wanted to call out to him to stay with her, to climb with her. He could take pictures any ole day.

Maggie was standing beside Alice and looked over. "I'll go if you go," she said.

Alice studied the sky palace. Becky was right. Pretty frakin' tall. You wouldn't call something a sky palace if it wasn't. Alice wasn't sure she'd be able to do it, but she felt the need to try.

Abby thought the Mayans sounded pretty fucked up with their games that used heads for basketballs and the way they would bind their captives up into human balls and bowl them down the sides of their palaces. But the war in Iraq? All that Abu Ghraib stuff that went down? Things really hadn't changed much. People hadn't really learned anything at all, which was pretty depressing when you thought about it. Because, really, what was the point if we were all here just making the same mistakes over and over again? Abby sometimes thought she should have a more important, meaningful career goal—that she should aspire to some job that would "change the world." But the more she thought about it, changing the world was a lost cause. So she might as well design cool clothes.

She'd climbed to the top of the sky palace with the rest of the group—holy crap, was she out of shape—and found a spot to sit a bit off to the side. She was looking at her hiking boots, wondering whether she should try drawing them later. They were probably the one pair of shoes she owned that she hadn't taken a stab at. She thought the laces had potential, since they were long and thick, and there were those little triangular hooks the laces were woven through. The drawing might have more texture than some of the others she'd tried. But they were ugly, and she hated drawing ugly things. This, too, was the problem with the self-portrait.

Her butt hurt on the stone, and she wondered how many people in all these centuries had sat in that spot. She wondered whether someone had died and shed blood right where she was sitting. The landscape was distinctly lacking in flair—all gray and green—and some blood could really add a splash of color.

June looked really cool today, with long cargo shorts on and a sleeveless T-shirt with a cool Celtic design on it. Abby thought her stars tattoo was pretty, unlike most tattoos, and would have wanted to copy it if June had been a stranger, but because she knew June, copying now would seem lame.

"Isn't this amazing?" she heard June say to Cash. The two of them were looking out at the mountains, away from the courtyard. Cash squeezed her around the waist and said, "Yup," and Abby turned toward the other, smaller pyramid. She saw Billy's figure, small, like a Ken doll, with his camera pointed in her general direction. She smiled, just for the hell of it—eyes closed, mouth wide, teeth clenched, like little kids smile.

"Hey, look," Dan said. That shirt he was wearing really was ridiculous, and he'd still not said more than ten words directly to Abby, which she found weird if not just plain ole rude. "A toucan."

"No way," Cash said. "Where?"

"You're lucky today," the guide dude said. He was sitting on a rock atop the palace, not even remotely winded from the climb. "No jaguar for any of you, but a toucan, even better."

"Where is it?" June still hadn't found the bird, which Abby spotted easily on a treetop. There wasn't a lot of color from this distance, but the profile was unmistakable. It's a wonder the bird didn't topple forward, with that beak.

"There," Cash said. "You see it?"

"Yeah." June nodded. She smiled at Cash and said, "Rock 'n' roll!"

Cash walked over to where Abby was sitting, and she made room on her rock. "How's it going?" he said. He sat down and elbowed her.

"'S okay," she said.

"Did you see the toucan?" Cash pointed with his head.

"Yeah, I saw it."

"Not impressed?"

Abby shrugged. It was cool, she guessed, but it was still just a bird. If she'd had to draw a bird and not a pair of shoes and a still life and a self-portrait, maybe she'd have gotten more worked up about it. Why was it such a big deal to see one anyway? It was probably endangered—but Abby was pretty sure everything was endangered. People probably only liked it because it was—oh, yeah, and funny-looking, too. That beak! What kind of idiot bird has a beak like that? It probably made people feel good about themselves to laugh at toucans, but Abby was pretty much over it. And if their guide pointed out one more ceiba tree, she was going to have to smack somebody. It was just a tree!

"Minky driving you crazy yet?" Cash brushed some pebbles off his hands, and Abby wondered whether the sky palace wasn't falling apart bit by bit, tourist by tourist, whether they really shouldn't be here, poking around like idiots, at all.

"Not yet."

"Your mom said something about a dance or a party?"

Abby snorted and shook her head. "She's such a loser." She wiped at a scuff mark on her hiking boot. "It's not a big deal."

"Okay," Cash said. "Well, it means a lot to me that you're here, so I'm sorry if it is a big deal and you just don't want to say that it is."

Abby sighed. "Cordero's playing."

"No idea who that is."

"I figured you wouldn't. Huge R & B guy. I could've sold my invitation on eBay and paid for my plane ticket."

Cash winced. "Sorry, babe."

Abby thought she was going to cry, so she just nodded and was grateful that her stepbrother got up and walked away, squeezing her shoulder as he went. This was going to be the longest amount of time she'd ever been around him—a full week—and there was something surreal about it. She was always listening to the Starter House—and to Cash's songs, especially, since they were sort of related and all—and now here he was. Abby sometimes thought her life would have turned out better if she and Cash had actually grown up together and not just met when she was fourteen. Because his life was pretty freakin' fantastic and probably always had been—well, except for the Tamara drama—and she'd have turned out cooler if she'd been known as his little sister, if his reputation had preceded her. Cash had probably been totally cool in high school and never got made fun of or picked on. June, too; even though she had really no chest at all, she seemed like the kind of girl who just didn't give a shit what anybody thought. Abby really wished she could be like that. Bad.

"Hey," she called after Cash, realizing she was about to blow a golden opportunity. She unzipped her backpack and took out one of two ziplining brochures she'd taken from the cabana that morning. "I saw this thing that looks really cool." She handed it to him. "Ziplining? Have you heard of it? This guy at school recommended it."

"This guy at school, huh?" Cash studied the brochure. "You want to do this with *this* group?" He smiled wide.

"Well, not everybody." Abby hadn't ever imagined it would be hard to get people to go ziplining. Because what else was there to do? And there was no way she was the only one who'd die of boredom if any more of these little group expeditions involved Mayans and history; M and M were talking about taking a bus trip to Guatemala to other ruins, Tikal, tomorrow, and Abby was hoping against hope she'd be left out of their plan. "Billy said he'd be up for it." Abby tried to sound enthusiastic. "We talked about it at dinner last night."

Cash looked at the brochure again. "Could be fun, I guess. I'm just not sure if we have time. Everything's pretty scheduled out, but I'll ask June."

"Okay, cool." Abby zipped her backpack closed. "I mean, it's no big deal."

"Yeah, no, of course. No big deal. Got it." Cash held up the brochure. "All right if I hang on to this?"

Pain sluiced through Alice's lungs, then left her. She and Maggie had stalled midway up the side of the palace and were both catching their breath. Alice's breathing was shallow, quick, but she felt oddly determined now. "You ready?" she asked Maggie, but Maggie shook her head.

"Nah," she said. "I'm done for." She bent over, hands to knees, and said, "Whew!"

Alice looked up toward the pinnacle of the palace. June and the others were starting their descent, but it seemed embarrassing to get this far and not go all the way. "I'm gonna give it a shot," Alice said.

"Good luck." Maggie nodded toward the peak. "I'll wait for these guys and head down with them."

Alice put her head down and started climbing again. The steps were really steep, and Alice knew she'd ache the next day. She was nearly doubled over with each step, her knees coming as close to her chest as they could.

"You okay, Mom?" June was upon her.

Alice kept her head down. "Yup," she said. "I won't stay up there long."

"It's okay," Cash said. "Take your time."

Alice stopped, heaving again, and wiped actual sweat from her brow. She couldn't think of the last time she'd done that. When she and Mary-Anise went on their walks, they didn't really push too hard but instead mostly strolled around the neighborhood. Mary-Anise would remind Alice to walk heel-toe and to pump her arms to burn extra calories, but it was obvious now that Alice wasn't in the best of shape. She only had another ten steps or so to go, though, so despite the awful pull in her legs, she pressed on, counting the steps; *one, two, three, four, five, six, seven,* and she was there. She swayed from the strain of it and wondered for a second if this was how it was going to end, toppling backward off a Mayan palace and rolling down it like a ball. Luckily, she regained her balance.

Layers and layers of hills stretched into the distance in different shades of greenish gray, and Alice thought of King Kong and felt like letting out her best white woman scream. A flash of color in her periphery drew her eye to a toucan as it landed on top of the palace. She let out a little gasp and then looked around, foolishly, since she knew there was no one else up there. Apart from another small tour group—a family of Mennonites, as if straight out of a photo in Alice's *Fodor's Belize*—they pretty much had Caracol to themselves.

The bird's body was predominantly black, but it looked like it was wearing a bright yellow dicky. A circle around the eye—the one eye that Alice could see—was green, as was most of the bird's beak. The beak's tip, though, was red, on the top and the bottom of it, and there was an orange slash and a blue dash, too—toucan birthmarks. The bird made a noise then, a series of even high-pitched whistles, one of them a note higher than the others, that sounded like some cross between a tin whistle and a clarinet. Alice felt giddy inside, thinking of Froot Loops and wondering if two more ridiculous creatures on the planet had ever come face to face. She slowly went to get her camera out of her bag. The clean click of the clasp must've startled the bird, though, because it took flight. Alice said, "Dammit."

She heard June calling out, "Mom?" and went toward the steps so that June could see her.

"Coming now!" Alice waved, then she turned and took in the view once more, imagining monkeys swinging from vines and a city lit by torches, the echoes of ancient drums bouncing off stone.

"We saw a toucan," Dan announced to Becky and Miller. He was the first to reach the base of the palace—well, except for Marcos, who'd run down, taking the massive steps two at a time. Dan thought he could probably do that, too, but didn't want to risk cracking his head open in the middle of the Mayan jungle. Still, he was proud of himself for braving the climb with a hangover. It was a sort of twisted way of trying to prove to himself—or maybe just to everyone else—that he wasn't really that hungover at all.

"Yeah?" Becky said. He heard defiance in her voice and imagined it was the same tone he'd likely hear from her when he got up the nerve to say, "It's not you, it's me." He knew, on a certain level, that he was immature in relationships, that there was nothing wrong with Becky per se. He just couldn't help that there were just too many things about her that irked him. They didn't seem to irk anyone else who knew her, but what was Dan supposed to do? Pretend it didn't bother him that she always sneezed three times in a row, barely audibly (a sneeze was supposed to be one big *atchoo*) or reclined her chair back the second the seat belt sign went off on any flight, even if she wasn't planning on sleeping?

"I saw a jaguar," she said, "and you saw a toucan, so I guess we're even." She reached up and pinched his waist. It kinda hurt.

"Ow." Dan rubbed his skin through his shirt. "It's not a competition."

"I know." She pulled the elastic down the length of her ponytail and started twirling her hair up into a ponytail again. "I'm just saying." The elastic snapped, and the new ponytail swung into place. She did this ponytail routine a lot.

"I took a picture," he said. "You want to see?" He went to turn on his camera.

"No, that's okay. I'll see it when you put them on your computer or whatever."

Dan thought they were done then, but after a beat she added, "It's too bad I didn't get a picture of the jaguar." She got up and started to walk away.

"Yeah." Dan wondered how they would possibly last the trip. "It is."

Something about this whole situation was cracking Dan up, though he wasn't sure why. He wasn't intentionally goading Becky—or didn't want to be, really—but he felt this morning truly like he was on vacation, and something about being on vacation made Dan feel like a kid again. And maybe he'd been an obnoxious kid. It was just all too funny somehow—jaguars, toucans, who'd seen what. And now, on the way back to the Welcome Center, Marcos had them all taking turns stepping into a tomb—its passage barely one person wide. Dan felt like he was on some school trip, and it seemed somehow laughable that they were all here to see Cash and June get married. What kind of crazy person had ever decided that it would be fun to basically elope with your family and friends along and sightsee along the way? It pretty much defeated the whole purpose of leaving the country, and there was a part of Dan that thought that June and Cash were a pair of dopes for thinking this would be cool for anyone, let alone themselves.

After a quick lunch in the Caracol picnic area—fried chicken boxes had been packed by the Five Sisters—the car was full again and heading toward Rio on Pools. Whatever the hell that was. Dan gleaned from the conversation about the weather—it was sunny now, getting hotter by the second, the rain having cleared—that Rio on Pools wasn't somewhere you went in the rain. That they were lucky to be going. Everyone in the car, maybe awed by all they'd just learned of Mayan culture, seemed content to just look out the windows, and Dan was glad, because anyone who looked at him would probably ask him, "What's so goddamn funny?"

His family had taken a few RV trips when he was small—down to Florida, where they'd all go to Weeki Wachee Springs to see the "live mermaids." Becoming one of those underwater performers, long silky hair floating around their pale faces, had for years been Dan's sister's primary career goal. In fact, Dan was pretty sure the main reason for the second trip to the Sunshine State was Karina's desperate desire to go to Mermaid Camp, where she could learn how to swim and smile at the same time. Eventually, she met her dentist husband and decided to train as a hygienist instead, but the mermaids had made quite an impression on her—and also on Dan, who'd been thirteen and hormonal. For years, he had kept a bunch of Weeki Wachee postcards in his bedside table and, well, let's just say that even the thought of them now triggered a visceral memory down in his souvenir shop swimming trunks. Before that thought got too carried away, Dan concentrated on all the stupid ways they used to pass time in the RV: games with license plates, I Spy, that dumb word game Ghost, bad jokes.

"Knock, knock," he said, and was surprised he'd said it aloud.

June turned from her seat up front—Dan and Becky were in the middle row now, with June's mom—and she smiled. He pictured her underwater, pink hair like a halo of some exotic coral. "Who's there?"

"Toucan," Dan said.

"Toucan who?" June's smile broadened, and he saw her wrapped in sequins, swimming toward him with a flip of her tail.

He said, "Toucan not fit in the tomb at one time."

June shook her head. "That was pathetic," she said, and Dan could almost see bubbles coming out of her mouth, rising up to the surface of a shimmery pool.

"Hear hear," said Becky, whom Dan had almost forgotten about. He struggled to recapture the fantasy, the image of June's mermaid floating his way.

"Knock, knock," Miller said. The van hit a bump with a loud boom and hands went to the roof.

"Who's there?" Dan said this time, happy to have successfully engaged the group in his game, even if it was hard to keep up the mermaid fantasy with the likes of Miller in the car.

"Safari," Miller said, and then everyone in the car, it seemed like, said, "Safari who?" with the sort of amused disdain that Dan was used to hearing when people sang "Happy Birthday" in city restaurants.

Miller said, "Safari so goodie."

A collective groan filled the van; a moment's silence followed.

"What do you call twelve toucans?" Dan said. He started to laugh in anticipation of his own joke.

June began to laugh, too. "What?" she said.

"No, wait," Cash said. "I know this. A six-peck!"

"Is that it?" June asked Dan, who said yeah and felt the game, the mermaid, slipping away from him.

"You know!" Miller was trying to sound serious, but it

wasn't working. "Cash, June, now that you're getting married, there are some important things you should remember."

"Like . . . ?" Cash said.

Miller barely managed to spit out "Toucan live as cheap as swan" before losing a battle with laughter himself.

Dan could practically hear people's brains working—churning, clanking—as they struggled to find the next pun.

"Come on, people," June finally said. "That's enough." She turned to Dan and smiled. "Toucan give up now."

Dan shot back, "Toucan play at this game."

And just as fast June said, "The only question is feather they want to."

Dan thought for sure this qualified as flirting and, suddenly self-conscious, looked at Becky. Ponytail turned to him, she was looking out the window. Becky wasn't big on puns, and even if she was, she was clearly too busy looking for another jaguar. She held her camera with steady hands, poised at the ready, a sniper.

Alice had forgotten to pack a swimsuit for the day's outing. Actually, she hadn't forgotten—she'd decided not to—but that was what she was telling everyone now that they'd all arrived at Rio on Pools—a beautiful collection of swimming holes, replete with waterfalls and natural waterslides. Clever Maggie revealed that she'd actually been wearing her suit all morning, which Alice had never thought to do.

As the younger members of the party slipped off to change—some in the jungle, some in a nearby shack made of wood—Alice climbed down and across a few massive boulders and found a smooth-looking perch where she could sit and dip her feet in the water. She sat down and rolled up her pants, and the water felt like salvation on her toes. She hadn't even realized how hot her feet had gotten in her hiking shoes (she'd followed a Fodor's "what to bring" checklist down to the last check) but felt blissful now as the cool spread from her toes to the rest of her body. The sky had turned royal blue, and the sun seemed to be able to cover every inch of her at one time. She watched as June and Cash made their way over to a waterfall and then turned and dunked down with their backs to it. June howled as the cascades soaked them through. Alice took her camera out, zoomed in on them, and snapped just as June linked her arms around Cash's neck and kissed him. It was too bright for Alice to see how the photo had turned out on her camera's screen, but she thought about deleting it anyway. It seemed somehow too private a moment, one she hadn't intended to capture. Alice had never quite gotten used to watching her daughter with Cash.

Maggie was wading into a pool near Alice. "You coming in?" she asked.

"No," Alice said. "I'm happy here."

It was true on a certain level, yes. Alice was starting to warm to the idea of this destination wedding thing. Like any good skeptic, she was still clinging to her opposition, but in playing the part of the good sport, she was unwittingly starting to enjoy herself. Rio on Pools, just taken on its own, was amazing, like nature's water park. But it was also true that Alice was beginning to grow frustrated with her own limitations. It's not like she didn't know how to swim. It's not like she was in terrible shape. Maggie, for her part, had no problem showing off her legs, which may have been toned underneath but still had the crinkly skin of elephants and middle age. It was the simple fact that Alice wasn't in the routine of swimming, didn't like not knowing if and what kind of changing facilities were available. When had she become so content to live life this way, like she was just waiting out her days? In a mere half day in Belize she'd already had more new experiences than she'd had in the last, what, ten years? More? And how many of those others were June's doing as well?

Maggie had sunk slowly down in the water and had found a way to sit in it like it was a tub. "I admit I was wary of this whole Belize thing," she said, and Alice was happy to hear it. It was the first she'd heard of anything remotely resembling the skepticism she'd felt from day one. "But maybe there's something to it."

"Maybe there is," Alice said. "Though how I ended up with such an adventurous child I'll never know." Alice reached down and scooped water up onto her legs, white as snow; she should have invested in some self-tanner. "What are you wearing for the ceremony, by the way?"

"Oh, I brought a sort of sarong, wrap dress. Ivory with maroon flowers." Maggie closed her eyes and tilted her head up at the sun. "Abby made me try on a hundred dresses before she let me buy one."

"It sounds perfect." Alice imagined those colors looking wonderful on Maggie, with her hair—countless shades of white and gray, all muddled together like a blizzard. Alice spotted Abby across the way, sketchpad in hand. "You're lucky she'll even be seen with you in a mall."

"Oh, trust me." Maggie dragged some water through her hair, leaving dark finger trails in the gray. "It was only so she wouldn't be embarrassed by what I ended up with. She's an aspiring fashion designer."

"Oh, how wonderful."

"I suppose!" Maggie looked far away. "You know what it's like. You worry. Such big dreams. But anyway. What about you, what are you wearing?"

"Oh, I brought a few things." Alice deflated at the thought of them; Billy had been no help at all. "I'm still not sure."

"I like it." Maggie's arms were one shade above the water and another shade in it. "Decide that morning!"

Alice smiled up into the sun and tried to imagine doing just that. Deciding that morning. The wedding wasn't for five more days. She certainly couldn't obsess over the dresses the whole time. Besides, June said there were shops in Placencia. The perfect dress might be waiting for her there. All hope was not yet lost.

Abby saw Billy's Converse All Stars perched on a rock and took her sketch pad out of her backpack. She sat a few feet away from the shoes and tried to focus as Billy stripped off his T-shirt, revealing a lean muscular back, and then slid into one of the pools. "Ohmigod," he said. "This is awesome!"

Abby couldn't decide who she liked fantasizing about more—Colin or Billy—but right now Billy was definitely winning out. Because Colin was supershy. They'd known each other for four years now and had been lab partners for a few months, and he still hadn't made a move. But sometimes that happened when you really liked someone. So she had decided to be patient. But high school was almost over. There wasn't a lot of time left. So what in the world was Colin waiting for?

Abby quickly lost interest in the shoes—but took a picture just in case she ever wanted to revisit them—and flipped the page and started to draw Billy, who had found a rock on which to sit. His body was half submerged, his head resting back on another rock, eyes closed, arms spread wide to reveal dark bursts of underarm hair. Abby sketched furiously, and then he looked up and caught her looking at him so she quickly diverted her glance down to his shoes.

"So Abby," Billy said. "You have a boyfriend back in San Francisco?"

Abby studied the line of his hair on his forehead and thought out her response carefully. She didn't want to sound off-limits, but also didn't want to sound like she was naïve or never had a boyfriend. She opted for "Not exactly."

"What's 'not exactly' mean?" Billy's chest was city-white behind soft brown hairs.

"It means there was sort of someone, but I'm sort of over the whole high school thing." She kept her eyes on her sketch. "'Cause I mean, if I get into FIT or Pratt, I'll be moving to New York next year, so what's the point, you know?"

With his arms in that position, the cinch of his shoulders formed little peaks and valleys of flesh. "What are you drawing over there?" he said, and she looked up, no doubt guiltily.

"Your sneakers."

He got up and started to walk over, water sliding off him, glistening on his abs. "Let me see."

She closed her book. "No, it's okay."

"No, really. Let me see." He gripped the book before she was able to put it away.

"You're getting it wet."

His arms, wet and warm, touched hers.

"Let me see," he said.

"Please don't," she said—holding tight, eyes closed, praying *please please please*—and he let go.

"Are you coming swimming?" he said, falling back into the pool.

"Is it cold?"

"It's perfect."

"Okay, I guess." Abby stood and took her shorts off, not looking to see if Billy was watching. She just did it as fast as she could. Then she turned away and took her T-shirt off and adjusted her black bikini so that it was in the right place. She could hear Billy yelling something to June and Cash, and June and Cash were saying something back, and it sounded like there was some splashing, and then she turned and Billy looked up at her, and then down at her, and then up again, and then suddenly Maggie was there, covering Abby with a towel and saying, "What on earth . . . ?"

"*What?!*" Abby conjured all the attitude she could and shrugged a shoulder.

"You know exactly what," Maggie said.

"But I want to go swimming."

"Well, you'll do it with a T-shirt on, if you want to that bad."

Abby looked for Billy, who'd climbed into a different pool, where he was talking to June and Cash. He looked up at her for a second, and she thought he looked guilty. Her mother handed her her T-shirt, and Abby put her hands through the sleeves and only allowed herself a smile when a tent of cotton formed as she pulled the T-shirt over her head. The bikini, what little there was of it, had been worth every penny.

"I wish I'd had a body like that when I was seventeen." Becky was sitting on one of the porch chairs in the cabana while Dan took a leak. He contemplated the appropriate response to this while also trying to enjoy the image he had in his brain of Cash's little sister in that bikini. Holy smokes. Not so little! He called out to Becky, "I bet you were pretty hot." They'd all been deposited back at their respective hotels.

"Are you kidding me?" Becky was climbing into bed. "I was a total ugly duckling."

"Well, you turned out all right in the end," he said, then washed his hands and returned to the main room, feeling a strange warmth directed at Becky. It was this warmth that kept them together. Because Dan genuinely cared for her. He really did. He just thought there might be something better out there, and he thought it was June.

"That was one helluva bathing suit," Becky said.

Dan thought, Don't remind me!, but said, "You gonna come down to the falls?"

June, Cash, and Billy were all heading down to the valley where the Five Sisters met. There'd been talk of securing a few beers.

"I think I'll take a nap." Becky yawned and stretched. "If it's all the same to you."

He went to her and squeezed her bare shoulder. "You sure?"

"Yeah, you go. Have fun."

Dan stepped out into the late afternoon and felt liberated. He realized then that he hadn't been alone since meeting Becky to go to the airport, and that was a lot of togetherness for a guy like Dan. But he was looking forward to hanging out with the portion of the group that was his own age. Something about elderly and middle-aged people seemed to make for stilted conversation. Or, as last night's immigration battle had proven, pointless arguments that will never be resolved. He was looking forward to talking freely, unedited, though about what, exactly, he wasn't sure. He didn't particularly care.

Beyond the lodge he found the cable-car-type rig that took you down into the valley. He studied the setup for a second and then shifted a lever. The whole car shook and then started a slow descent down a steep track. He was glad he was alone, as he feared the car wouldn't even hold his weight. He had his first thought, then, of work—of the design business—and wondered whether his emails were piling up and whether he'd ever want to go back to being partners with Cash. He'd done his part to keep things up and running, of course, while the details of his inheritance and then lottery-size sale were finalized, but just being here in Belize made Dan think that maybe he should quit, travel a bit, figure out what he really wanted to do in life.

Dan arrived at the bottom of the hill, stepped out of the car, and walked down a winding path. It led him across a small footbridge over a river and into a clearing where the Five Sisters waterfalls all joined in a big pool. He found Cash and Billy splayed over hammocks, beers in hand. A wooden canopy shaded them from the sun.

"There he is!" Cash said. "The beers are over there."

Dan saw a bucket of beers submerged in water where Cash was pointing. It was hot out, maybe 85, and the water was maybe 68, so it did the job in a pinch. "Where's Becky?" Billy said.

"Napping," Dan said.

"So it's just us guys." Cash raised his beer. "And cheers to that."

"I thought June was coming," Dan said. The current plan was to hold off on the original plan of proclaiming his love until the autograph was back in his possession, but he was having a hard time letting go of the idea that he needed to be around June at all times so that he could find a moment alone.

Cash tried to balance his beer on his stomach, then gave up. "Yeah, no, she decided to hang out with Alice for a while, so she's off pretending to be a girl."

Billy said, "Fifty bucks says Alice straps her down and dyes her hair brown."

Cash said, "If she doesn't do it, I might." He sipped his beer, sighed loudly, and stretched out his legs. "This is the life, eh?"

But Dan's hammock was strung too high or too tight or something, and he couldn't get comfortable. He said, "These hammocks are crap."

Billy said, "You're ruining the moment."

Dan tried harder to find a good position, stealing glimpses of Billy and Cash to see how they were sitting. He said, "These hammocks are ruining the moment."

Finally Dan settled, and then he closed his eyes and took in the sound of the falls, the distant chirping of birds. He thought he heard a deep hum—the Five Sisters power generator.

They swung in silence then—well, silence except for the constant surge of the falls—and Dan felt the weight of cliché in the hammock with him. The Best Man Who's in Love with the Bride. It was practically a stock character, and yet it made the reality of his emotions no less difficult to bear. He was jealous of Cash, furious at himself, and increasingly pissed at June—for making the wrong choice, for never noticing.

Billy said, "So, don't take this the wrong way. But holy stepsister, Batman."

"*I know!*" Dan said, and then realized he and Cash had both said it at the same time.

"She seems to have taken a shine to you," Cash said to Billy, which was interesting because Dan hadn't noticed and had never really seen Billy with women or given a second thought to what his life/sex life might be like. "I hope that's not a drag."

"No," Billy said. "She's cute."

Dan cleared his throat in a classic "ahem."

"I mean"—Billy sat up, alert—"she's a cute kid."

"Kid?" Dan said. "Open your eyes. I'd say not a girl, not yet a woman."

"What am I hearing about the two of you going ziplining?" Cash asked.

"What? No!" Billy was on his feet, and Dan wondered whether he was protesting too much. "She wants to go and I said I thought it would be cool, but I wouldn't go unless other people were going. I mean, give me some credit. If you want to worry about somebody, worry about what Trevor'll do when he lays eyes on her."

"We may have to tie him up," Cash said.

"Wouldn't be the worst thing," Dan said, suddenly feeling oddly cozy in that hammock with an image of Trevor gagged and bound and begging for release.

"I'm going to go find Minky," Maggie said. "And you, missy"—Abby just stood there at the front entrance to Blancaneaux and took it—"are going straight to that gift shop."

So apparently Maggie wasn't going to let this one go.

"You'd better hope they'll sell you a nice, sturdy one-piece that'll cover your tush," she said, "or you won't be going swimming at all this week."

Abby tried her favorite argument. "You're being irrational."

"You try to pull something like that on me again, and you're in serious trouble." Maggie was actually shaking a finger at Abby; her skin had freckled in the sun. "I'd be tempted to ground you, but it would only embarrass us all more."

Abby rolled her eyes. "Hannah and Lisa bought practically the same bikini."

"Yeah, well, that's their mothers' fault. Inside." She pointed at Blancaneaux. "Now. Go!"

Abby watched her mother and Miller head off in search of Minky and her watercolors, then went inside the resort. She stopped in the lobby to call Hannah. Her suit was still damp from the swimming, and the lobby was just slightly chilly. A couple, probably newlyweds by the lovey-dovey looks of them, were sipping white wine on one of the couches in the center of the room, and a member of the staff was going around rearranging the flowers in vases spread around the lobby. It didn't feel like a hotel lobby. More like a rich someone's very busy living room.

"Hi, Abby," Hannah said when she picked up, and Abby thought it sounded weirdly formal.

"Hey." Abby gripped the phone's hard wire. It felt wrong to be stuck standing there. She hadn't ever had anything but cordless in her life. "So? Did he ask anyone yet?"

Hannah breathed loudly. "This is really hard, Abby."

"Ohmigod, he's going with Chelsea." Abby felt sick.

"No, Abby, he asked me," Hannah said. Then again, more softly: "He asked me."

Abby thought her head might explode. "What did you *say*?"

"I said yes."

Abby couldn't even compose a sentence.

"Abby?"

Still couldn't find a word. Hannah knew Abby liked Colin and that he liked her back. How many times had they agonized over every gesture, every thing he said and did, only to conclude he definitely liked Abby but was shy? What was he *thinking*, asking her best friend? And what was *she* thinking, saying yes?

"Abby, come on," Hannah pleaded.

"I don't know what you want me to say," Abby finally mustered.

"Say you're not mad. I swear, nothing's gonna happen."

The mere suggestion of something happening triggered visions of bikinis and bare skin and fake drinks with little pink umbrellas and some back room of the club, like maybe a coat closet, and then Abby would go back to San Francisco on Sunday and go back to school on Monday and it would be all anyone would be talking about and Colin and Hannah would have hooked up, because that's what people do, and she'd have lost her best friend and her potential boyfriend all in one go.

"I can't believe you," Abby said.

Hannah's tone turned. "Well, it's not like anything's ever happened between you two. I mean, I know you like him, but

I might like him, too, and he asked *me*. I thought you'd be happy for me."

"Wow." Abby felt possessed, like her head might start spinning, like the lobby around her might start to cave in on itself in a swirl of her evil energy. "I never knew you could be such a bitch."

She hung up without another word, then dialed another number. Lisa picked up right away and said, "Hey."

"Can you believe her?" Abby said.

"She told you?" Lisa sounded disturbingly excited, and Abby suddenly regretted calling her. But she couldn't help herself. She said, "What a total backstabber."

Lisa said, "Well, she does sort of have a point."

Abby couldn't believe this was happening. "What point?"

"Nothing's happened with you guys or even come close to happening." Lisa sounded thrilled to be in the middle of things, her voice bright, like she'd been practicing lines all day. "You can't just call someone off-limits if you like them. Not if they don't like you back. You should be happy for her."

The phone's metallic surface reflected a funhouse mirror version of Abby, and she wondered whether she should go grab her sketch pad and do the self-portrait right there and then. Her face would look contorted, stretched, and freakish like she felt inside. Then she heard Minky—"People look at me funny whenever I say that, but it's the truth." She turned and saw M and M—and M—entering the lobby.

"I gotta go," Abby said, and hung up, then ducked into the gift shop. She found a rack of plain Speedo suits and picked out a size 6 in navy blue. It didn't really matter how it looked, because she was never going to wear it in public anyway.

Back in her room, she peeled off her damp T-shirt and saw herself in the mirror, barely-there black bikini and all. She perched her sketch pad on top of the dresser and started to draw, thinking of Billy, and the jaw drop, and the fact that

Colin Murray had no idea what he was missing. She drew her breasts big and round and cartoonish and gave herself a huge puckered pair of lips, then started to hack black slashes across the whole thing as tears formed in her belly and made their way to her eyes. She threw herself on the bed then and gave over to the tantrum. Colin and Hannah. Together at Chelsea Lambert's party. Images flashed through her mind of Colin's hands on Hannah's waist, her arms around his neck—one wrist tossed lazily over the other. She saw them in the pool, and saw the way Colin's eyes were drawn to Hannah's own barely-there bikini, the way their cold limbs might brush up against each other under water. She saw them rooting through their gift bags, and IM'ing the next day, and then going out for the rest of the year and going to prom together and more. They'd grow up and get married and get rich somehow, and then Hannah would have her infinity pool in L.A. after all. Abby could see it all—Colin and Hannah and Lisa and Will Sherwood all sitting in the pool, cocktails in hand, as water ran off into the horizon, endless and free. They'd be laughing about that Abby girl they used to know in high school, wondering what ever happened to her.

Alice hadn't been able to stop thinking about that toucan. It was crazy, really, to come so close to a bird like that. A pigeon, sure, but a toucan? Even now, sitting at the Five Sisters Lodge with June, who was confounded by the Mayan temple puzzle, the thought of the whole scene made Alice giddy for reasons she couldn't quite pinpoint. Travel, she supposed, was full of moments like that, like when a rooster had startled her in Hawaii. Alice decided she'd buy postcards in the morning, send Mary-Anise a note. She'd apologize for being so . . . *pathetic,* and she'd hope that Mary-Anise would give her a second chance.

June pushed the puzzle away and sighed. "I want to tell you something, and I don't want you to get down on your knees and thank God for answering your prayers."

Alice sipped a tropical cocktail that the bartender had made special for her and June without the liquor once they'd both acknowledged headaches. She hoped she knew where this conversation was heading but didn't want to rush June along. She was feeling relaxed, as though the drink really did have rum in it, and she said, "Let me guess. You bought brown hair dye today."

"Very funny." June played with the ice in her drink. "And I'm not pregnant either." She took a sip. "I am, however, thinking of quitting the band." June looked over her shoulder, pink hair whipping around like a pom-pom. "It feels weird to say it out loud."

A warm breeze blew straight through the lodge. They were the only ones there.

"Why do you think that would make me happy?" Alice pushed ice around with her straw, then swatted a mosquito but missed it. "I've always just wanted you to be happy."

"We could debate that"—Alice could tell June was still eyeing the puzzle, hoping to unlock its mystery—"but that's really not the point."

"No, really." Alice picked up the puzzle and moved it to an adjacent table. June huffed, but her body seemed to relax. "I've *always* just wanted you to be happy."

"And not dress sexy onstage, and not have pink hair, and not vote Democratic, and a million other things."

Alice was guilty as charged—but was it any different that June wished Alice didn't watch Oprah, or read *The Da Vinci Code*, or buy floral upholstered couches? When had they gotten so locked in this battle over their identities? "It's only because

I worry," Alice said. "About the long term. I just don't want you to be left with nothing when the band—*if* the band—doesn't pan out."

"Well, I have a job offer." Again, June looked over her shoulder. "A nine-to-five thing. Writing all the music—the songs, the incidental stuff, the theme song—for a kids' program. The money's great."

So Billy had been right.

"And the show sounds totally cool." June almost sounded disappointed. "It's called *Lila Jay's Rock Camp for Girls*, and it's sort of based on that camp where I volunteered that one time." She poked the ice in her drink with her straw. "You know. Girls, guitars, empowerment. It's animated."

Alice said, "Oh, June, that sounds perfect for you." It really did. "So what's the problem?"

"Oh, you know." June shrugged with one shoulder. "A little thing called selling your soul, working for the man. And they want to know by the end of the week." She sipped her drink without picking it up, leaning in low to bring mouth to straw. "And I'm about to marry Cash, and he doesn't know that this is even happening."

"But can't you do both?" Alice didn't quite understand the conflict, but then she'd never really understood how the band worked, how June's life worked.

"It's really hands-on. Working directly with the writers and animators. So I couldn't tour. But I don't know. The band. You pour so much of yourself into something—it's been *five years*—and then it never really gets the sort of recognition you'd hoped for, and God, it's exhausting. But I honestly don't know anymore who I even *am* without the band."

"Well, I do, June. You're the same amazing girl you've always been. That won't change."

"I feel like I'm giving up." June sipped from her straw again, and another ghost appeared, this one making Kool-Aid and then selling it on the street in order to try to save up for her first guitar. "And I dreamed last night that my heart was being ripped out in a Mayan sacrifice, and here's the kicker." Now it was June's turn with the mosquito. It eluded her, too. "*Scott Haslett* was doing the ripping."

Scott Haslett. The name of June's elementary school nemesis could still get Alice's heart pumping faster.

"So now I keep thinking about that stupid class play."

Alice nodded. She remembered this fifth-grade drama of June's as if it had happened this morning. She remembered June coming home from school in a state—saying how unfair it was that Scott automatically got the part where he got to play piano and how she had said as much to her teacher, Mr. Sagapo, and demanded an audition. How June had gone in to school the next day to find that Mr. Sagapo had rewritten the play so that June got to play the piano, too. Alice remembered the production's every detail, remembered June in a plaid shirt with a frilly collar and a denim skirt and Scott Haslett, blond hair slicked almost brown. June played the piano—"Memory" from *Cats*—in the scene where she was supposedly rehearsing so that she could enter a talent contest and win money for desperately needed new uniforms for the town baseball team. But then when the actual talent contest came around, June's character—her name, randomly enough, was Begonia—fainted, and then Scott Haslett stepped up to the piano, played, and won. June had only realized many years later how "pathetic and sexist" (her words) the rewrite was. At the time, she'd gotten what she wanted. She wanted to play the piano. She wanted to prove that girls could do it, too.

"I feel like I've been fighting to get where I am since fifth grade," June said now, and Alice realized she'd been blind to never have seen how much the Scott Haslett experience had fueled June's pursuits in such a male-dominated field. Sometimes people's lives turn on a dime, and Scott Haslett's face had apparently been on June's particular coin.

"I don't know, honey," Alice said, as a new realization sank in. "If that story doesn't prove that you're perfect for a show about a rock camp for girls, I don't know what will."

"But what will Cash and the boys do?" June was playing with a long strand of hair from the back of her neck, twisting it and twisting it by her left ear with both hands. "The band won't be the band without me, and I'm not being egotistical saying that."

Alice believed her; she'd read enough about the band online to know that June was the band's heart. But her daughter also had a tendency to see the world with herself at the center of it, to take everything—things that had nothing to do with her—personally. Alice wasn't sure what she'd done to contribute to this aspect of June's personality, or whether it was inborn, but she couldn't remember a time when that hadn't been the case.

"You're only the center of your own world, honey," Alice said. "You only have to make yourself happy." Then she added, "But you really need to tell Cash."

"I *know*," June groaned. "Tonight. After dinner." She clapped the mosquito dead, then flicked the tiny carcass off her palm.

It always amazed Dan how different, how relaxed he felt once he left the city. He loved New York, of course. There was nowhere else he would want to be, but he loved leaving it, too. As soon as he did, the city felt like some bizarre fictional city from the movies, an oddity of human invention that made absolutely no sense. How did it sustain itself? How did it survive?

And why would so many people choose to live there when they could live, well, *here*? Even if the hammocks were woefully uncomfortable, they were still hammocks, and he was still in a valley where all he could hear was waterfalls and birds. The last hour had passed more slowly, more blissfully leisurely, than any he could remember. Ever.

Cash and Billy had gone back up the mountain to shower, but Dan had decided to just lounge for a little bit longer.

He could live here if he wanted to. The reality of that—the fact of his having enough money that he could probably buy an oceanfront condo in Belize (he guessed for maybe two hundred grand?)—was setting in, and he was half giddy, half scared out of his mind. Not that he actually would ever want to live in Belize—not the part of it they'd seen anyway—but there was such a thing as too many options, and money gave you options. Dan's mind had been rattling for months now—every quiet moment filled with thoughts of where to invest, what to invest in, whether to open a bar, join the Peace Corps, travel the world in a hot air balloon, donate it all to save the developmentally threatened Weeki Wachee, or just keep going to work every day and act like nothing at all had changed. Dan had never sympathized with lottery winners who complained that their massive jackpots had destroyed their lives—cost them family and friends. He'd always thought, *Boo-hoo*. But he could see now how money changed you simply by changing the way everyone around you perceived you. He hadn't changed, but everyone around him had. They all wanted something, and to pretend that they didn't. Whether it was a new car, or a couple of beers, or a plasma TV, or maybe a nice new dress to wear, everybody wanted something from Dan. Except for June—the only person he really wanted to give anything to. June had taken the news of his windfall like a star and had never once suggested or implied that it was anything other than fantastic news. *Fantastic*. That was the word she'd used.

162

Back at the cabana, Becky was up and dressed for dinner, wearing yet another tank top combo and floral skirt. "You look nice," Dan said, because it was, in fact, one of the better combos.

"I've got cabana fever," she said. "I'm going to go sit outside at the lodge and read until dinner."

"Oh," Dan said. "Okay."

Becky wagged her pink book in the air, then tucked it under her arm. She stopped in the middle of the room, cocked her head, and said, "So what are you getting them as a gift, anyway?"

Dan sat down on a chair on the terrace and kicked off his sandals. "I haven't gotten around to that yet, so I'll have to do it when I get home." Dan was always torn between registry gifts and trying to come up with something of a more personal nature. Though June and Cash's registry at a hip SoHo boutique oozed cool and seemed somehow more personal than your average Crate & Barrel one.

Becky wasn't letting go, though. "Are you doing anything special while we're here? As best man?"

"Besides my toast, I wasn't planning on it, no."

Her face seemed carved out of stone, and Dan went to get up, no small feat considering the chair. What kind of idiot had gone and made this the sort of national chair of Belize? It was actually—he could hardly believe it—worse than the hammocks. He decided to sit a moment longer and said, "You're not still pissed about the jaguar, are you? Because I believe you, okay?"

"I'm not," Becky said. "And I saw what I saw, I don't care if you believe me. Oh!"—she turned to go—"Someone just dropped off your bag."

"What?!" He saw the luggage then, upright near the door. "Oh, thank God." He dropped to his knees, closed his eyes, and clasped his hands in prayer, thinking that it would be funny, but also that it would be easier to get out of the damn chair that way. "Did they say where it—" he said when he opened his eyes, but Becky was already gone. The wooden door made a hollow smack as it closed.

Abby had managed to shower but had only thrown on shorts and a T-shirt and then climbed back into the bed. A knock on her door made her sit up and pull another tissue from the box beside her under the mosquito netting. "What," she said.

The door opened. *"What?"* Maggie echoed. "You're cruisin' for a bruisin', missy."

Abby sniffled and blew her nose.

"What's gotten into you?" Maggie's arms were crossed across her chest.

"The boy I like"—Abby could barely get it out—"asked Hannah to the party"—she started sobbing again—"as his date."

Maggie came forward, pushed the mosquito netting open, and climbed into the bed, where she sat beside Abby. Abby could practically feel her mother's reluctance to stop being pissed and to start being nice, and Abby only hoped that this stuff with Colin would get her off the hook on the bikini front.

"Oh, honey." Maggie took Abby in her arms, and as much as Abby wanted to squirm away, she wanted to stay. "I know you hate it when I say it," Maggie said, "but there really will be other boys. You're so young. There's no rush."

"But I thought he liked me"—Maggie somehow never got the point the first time out—"and he doesn't. No one likes me." Abby sniffled. She played with a wet tissue in her hand, trying to find a dry bit.

"I'm sure that's not true." Maggie pulled another tissue from the box and handed it to Abby. "*Jason* liked you. He *adored* you!" This only made Abby cry again; that was the geeky boy she'd lost her virginity to, the boy who, up until that point, she'd pretty much treated like shit because of said geekiness. Doing it with him had seemed like a good idea at the time, but now she wasn't so sure.

"Just don't be in such a hurry to grow up, sweetie. The bikini. The boys." Maggie ran a palm over Abby's head, pushed her hair back over her ear. "There are just so many better uses of your time and your heart."

Snotty and gross, Abby was sort of tiring of the pep talk. "I know."

"And this trip. The band. We're in such a beautiful place, for such a happy occasion." Maggie's shoulders curled in. "It'd be such a shame to let some boy ruin it."

But he wasn't just some boy. He was Colin Murray. The only person she knew who loved the Starter House as much as she did, the only guy in her class worth dating. "But now Hannah and Lisa are going out with guys who are best friends, and I'm all alone."

"I know it feels like the most important thing in the world. But Hannah will see through Lisa real soon, and if she doesn't, your friendship wasn't what you thought it was." Maggie found the remaining ziplining brochure among Abby's things on the bed. "Is this that thing you've been campaigning to do?"

"Yeah." Abby blew her nose again.

"Looks kind of neat, actually."

"Yeah, well, it's never going to happen anyway." Not that Abby even cared anymore. Because what was the point, now that Colin Murray was going to the party with Hannah?

"Why don't you try to sleep for a little bit?" Maggie made her eyes hopeful. "We've got about an hour before we need to get ready for dinner. Hmmm?"

"Okay," Abby said, but she knew she wouldn't sleep. She let Maggie help her get under the covers anyway, then when Maggie was gone, Abby got up and got her sketch pad and her camera and brought them back into the bed with her. She'd never finish these damn sketches if she didn't get down to business, and if she never finished the sketches, she'd never have any escape from Hannah and Colin and everything she hated about San Francisco. Hannah would be so jealous that Abby was going to design school that it was worth all the work her application was taking.

She flipped to the drawing she'd started of Billy's Converse All Stars and studied it. Not half bad. She turned on the camera and compared what she'd drawn to the picture she'd taken. The sketch was nearly done. She'd compare it to the picture again when she got home—and could view the pic larger on the computer—but the basics of light and shadow were all there. So she set about finessing some of the shading, highlighting some of the details around the laces. She had to admit it looked pretty good. So one down, two to go.

Abby turned to her drawing of Billy. She'd have been mortified if he'd seen it, and he might have, but she was pretty sure he hadn't. It was pretty good, more naturally drawn than the sneakers, probably because she was more used to drawing people—if only to draw clothes onto them—than she was sneakers. She'd taken a picture of him, too—shirt off in one of the pools—and she picked up the camera and looked at that. Butterflies went ape-shit in her stomach. God, he was cute. She wished there was some way—*any* way—she could get Billy to come to San Francisco. Colin Murray would see her with him, and he'd get so jealous he'd turn Hulk green and he'd ask Abby if he could talk to her in private and then he'd say that he was sorry, that he never really liked Hannah after all, and could he and Abby try it again. She'd say, "I don't know. I'm with Billy now," and then Colin would pin her against the wall and kiss her like he'd never kissed anybody, and then she'd say, "Colin. Stop. Please." And he'd say, "Please," and she'd say, "I need time," and then would go back to Billy, who'd say, "He bothering you?" and she'd say, "No, I can handle it."

God, life was torturous without television and internet. There was nothing to do except dream up all sorts of stupid scenarios. Abby put her pad and camera on the nightstand, then lay and watched as a breeze fluttered the mosquito net, moving pocked shadows across the bedspread. The sun through the window felt warm on her legs, and she thought that this spot was pretty great. Maybe she could get a mosquito net for home, just for effect. With a half hour to kill before dinner, she picked up her book. *Heart of Darkness* might suck, but her own stories sure weren't any better.

Alice hadn't yet been down the mountain to see the Five Sisters up close, so was happy that June and Cash had arranged a private dinner party by the falls. Again long-panted and coated in bug spray, she grabbed a light sweater and started up the path to the lodge, where hand-carved wooden signs for the falls pointed her down a path this way and that. The cable car wasn't in its dock, but Alice could see people getting out of it way down at the bottom—just flashes of color visible through the thick tree coverage—and then heard the cables clack and churn and saw the car start moving toward her. It was slow, for sure, but she didn't mind waiting, not when the night was so lovely. She thought of the likely weather in Chicago and gave herself a chill. When you were this thoroughly warm, it was hard to believe it was cold anywhere. Alice had started eyeing the clothes she'd worn on her flight—jeans, long-sleeve T-shirt, Oprah's favorite cashmere sweater, all at the bottom of her suitcase now—with a sort of disbelief. Had she really ever worn them?

The car clanked into place, and Alice opened a short gate and stepped in, then closed the gate behind her. "Mom!" June called, and Alice turned to see her daughter bounding down the path, carrying a big canvas box with a handle. "Wait for me!"

"What's that?" Alice asked, opening the gate again so that June could step into the car.

June plopped down and put the case between her legs. Her red dress—cut way too low and too high but with delicate stitching around the neckline and two cute front pockets—was typical of June. Alice marveled that this was the second red dress of the trip. How many red dresses did her daughter own?

"A battery-operated turntable." June moved the lever that set the car in motion. "Dan found all these old seventy-eights when the dilapidated mansion guy died. The basement was full of them. So he let us pick through them, and we shipped a bunch down and bought a turntable and sent that down, too." She smacked the case. "They're old Louis Prima records and Sinatra and stuff. All sorts of stuff that Dad used to love."

"What a nice idea," Alice said, and felt a surge—a sort of clog of the esophagus—at hearing June say "Dad." June had been a senior in high school when her father died and then had gone off to college before Alice had found her own feet again. She considered it one of her great failures as a mother that they hadn't talked—and still didn't talk—that much about Jack.

At the base of the hill, a stone path and a white footbridge cut across pools formed by the falls, and Alice stopped to snap a picture. June, who was walking ahead of her, turned and smiled at just the right second. The falls were twice as loud here, and Alice wondered whether they'd all have to shout all night. The sound made the whole setting somehow more festive—as did the torches lit around a large table, and small paper lanterns in primary colors that hung overhead. Small white votive candles in clear square vases intermingled with tropical flowers on the table—set in white linen—and Alice's heart choked on itself. It was just so very lovely, and yet so very June. She now couldn't imagine June's wedding festivities going any other way, being anywhere else in the world.

Billy was at a small bar at the far end of the canopied area and turned. He smiled and said, "Hey, Mom. What can I get you?"

Alice thought a glass of wine would be lovely. She said so.

"It might suck," June said. "Just so you know. This isn't really wine country." She opened up the turntable case on a table set off to the side a bit, then started poking through a box of records that had already been brought down.

"I don't mind," Alice said.

"The beer's local." June spun a record in her hands, then put it on the turntable. "The rum, too."

"And still I'd like a glass of wine," Alice said.

"June," Billy said. "Chill out."

"Fine. I will." Music intermingled with the whir of the falls then. It was a sort of swing beat with a trumpet blare, and Alice recognized Louis Prima's husky voice, if not the tune. Something about a banana. It officially felt like a party.

Alice watched as June walked over to where Cash was sitting, chatting with Dan and Becky, and kissed him on the lips. June said, "Isn't this amazing?"

"You've got to hand it to them." Billy's crisp white shirt highlighted the sun he'd gotten that afternoon. "This is pretty great. And they flew in their own records? Who *does* that?"

"I know," Alice said, then surprised herself when she added, "I wish your father were here." Only then did the stranglehold on her heart loosen.

"Oh, Mom." Billy rubbed her back. "Don't get all—"

"I'm not getting all anything. I'm just stating a fact. I wish your father were here." She was remembering dancing with Jack to records like this in the basement of their first house, the only room big enough to dance in. He'd been a great dancer, and Alice had been, too, though there wasn't any occasion to show it anymore. She imagined him here with them, poking through records with June, twirling them in his hands the way he used to—with such respect and ease. She imagined him making a wonderful toast to June and Cash, and charming Minky, and pulling Alice out onto a big flat rock to dance.

"Me too, Mom." Billy handed her a glass of wine, and Alice nodded, unable to get the words *Thank you* to her lips and meaning them in more ways than one. "She told me about the job," Alice said softly.

"Really? I gave up." Billy leaned in. "What's the deal?"

"It's like you said. Writing music for a show about a rock camp for girls. She has to let them know by the end of the week." Alice felt like a gossip and didn't like it. "She's telling Cash about it all tonight."

"God help us all," Billy said.

"What's that supposed to mean?" Alice's posture stiffened.

"I mean, they're supposed to be getting married." Billy shook his head. "And Trevor and Joe? It ain't gonna be pretty."

But Alice wasn't thinking about the other members of the band. She said, "It sounds like a great opportunity. And of course they'll still get married."

"I don't know, Mom." Billy shook his head. "If we were smart, we'd get the next plane out of here."

Alice was watching June and Cash, swaying together to the music. "You're exaggerating."

"And *you've* never been in a band," Billy said.

"Billy," Alice scolded.

"What? I'm just saying. They're like cults, bands. When you're in you're in, and when you're out you're out."

"Mom! Billy!" June was looking in their direction. "Let's take some pictures before we lose the light."

A fifteen-minute photo session ensued, with all sorts of different variations of the group taking shots near the table, in a gazebo at the bottom of the falls, and more. Alice took every picture she wasn't in and gave the camera to either Billy or Abby or Becky for every one she *was* in. When it seemed like every possible combination had been taken, June said, "Wait! How about just the girls?"

And so, after Minky said, "Oh, you don't want an old biddy like me ruining an otherwise perfectly nice picture," Alice, June, Becky, Abby, and Maggie stood together—arms around each other's waists—and smiled as the boys used every camera on hand to capture the image.

"Me first," Miller said.

"Now over here," Billy said, and Alice imagined each of these women as one of the Five Sisters, each with her own river or stream roaring along its own path in life—wending this way and that—and all coming together here. They were young and old and somewhere in between, and together, here in Belize, they were something entirely other than themselves, something they'd never be again. She wondered whether any of them felt, as she did, like this was her favorite moment of the trip so far.

Back at the dinner table, Alice realized she was ravenously hungry and set out to try everything on the buffet table. There was a big plate of a Belizean lasagna that some of the others had had the previous night, and a fish dish, which Alice dug right into; its papaya-mango salsa exploded with sweet-hot flavor. Alice thought of some of her staple dinners at home and promised herself never to trust the Gorton's fisherman again. She ate contentedly under the conversational radar as June and her friends talked about music and bands that Alice had never heard of, and she wondered if there was a place in the world where parents and children didn't reach a point at which they seemed to be speaking different languages. She wondered what that place might look like, then thought maybe it looked a lot like this very valley, untouched by time and trend. It was a place where extended families lived close, even in the same house, and not one where children left and never came home again. A place where you pretty much knew where your children were at any given hour—and where you never watched the news and heard about shootings and car accidents in New York only to be relieved when the victim stats (*forty-year-old mother of two, twenty-seven-year-old African American, Venezuelan tourist*) were all wrong.

Miller clinked a knife against a glass, and the sound rang out like a bell. "I'd like to make a toast," he said, "to Cash and June, for putting this lovely event together."

"Hear hear!" Billy raised his glass, and everyone else did, too.

"And—" Miller waited for the group to quiet down again. "And! I'd also like to invite you all to join us at Blancaneaux for dinner tomorrow night. Maggie and I would love to treat you all!"

It seemed to Alice that everyone at the table looked right at June, who was looking at Cash, frozen in horror or disgust or something. Surely everyone here knew how June felt about Blancaneaux.

"That's really generous of you," June began slowly. "But there's no need."

"I know you have some political misgivings, June," Miller said. "But really! The food's just fantastic—so far as we can tell from breakfast, at any rate! You'll indulge us, please, just this once! We insist."

172

Alice said a silent prayer that June would just go with the flow, and wondered whether there was a patron saint for this kind of occasion. If you could pray to Saint Anthony for the return of things you'd lost, maybe you could pray to somebody else when your grown daughter was acting like a petulant child? Not that she didn't see June's point about local businesses, but you couldn't go around imposing your political views on people. At least not without occasionally pissing people off or, in this case, seeming ungrateful.

June said, "Everyone's welcome to make up their own minds, of course, but—"

Cash cleared his throat loudly and said, "That sounds great, Dad. We'd love to."

"Cash?" June looked at him like he was a suspicious stranger, his own identical twin.

"June?" Cash looked at her the same way.

"A word, if you don't mind." She got up, and Cash made a face, threw his napkin on the table, then followed. They walked toward the bar, and everyone at the table seemed frozen in place. Alice tried hard to think of a topic of conversation to spark a thaw. "There was a child abuser who came down here to hide from the government back home," she said, then couldn't believe that's what she came up with. "Oprah did a show about it, and there were people here in Belize, in Belize City, calling in tips, and they caught him and had him extradited."

"I saw that one, too," Maggie said, and Alice was grateful.

"I didn't mean to upset anyone," Miller said, looking stunned, but Minky either didn't hear or didn't care.

"I like Oprah," she said, with wineglass in hand. She looked like she was about to toast the revered talk show host. "But I used to like her more. She's gotten very sexy lately. Very sensational. And the way she raked that poor alcoholic writer across the coals!"

June and Cash had returned to the table, and now Alice wished she'd just kept her mouth shut.

"My mom was in the audience once, you know," June said. Alice's trip to see Oprah was one of June's favorite topics.

Some "Really?"s and "Wow"s rose up from the table. Becky said, "It wasn't one where she gives away cars, was it?"

"Not cars," Alice said. "But yes, it was her 'Favorite Things' show last year."

"How wonderful for you!" Maggie said, but all Alice could remember was the fraudulent feeling, the tears, the fact that Oprah—in person—looked as odd, as alien, as today's toucan had. People that famous seemed like another species.

"The audience was made up of people who volunteered after Hurricane Katrina," June said. "My mother's the only person who came out of Katrina with a diamond necklace and a pair of UGGs."

Alice knew for a fact that this was not the first time June had used this line. She felt prickly all over. "Actually, there was a whole studio audience," she snapped. "Several hundred people. And I didn't ask for any of it. In fact, I think I gave those boots to you." Alice wanted to take a sip of her wine but knew her hand wouldn't be steady enough.

"I'm sorry, Mom." June drank from her beer bottle, and Alice thought it looked déclassé. "It's great that you went down to the Gulf Coast, really."

Alice knew she was making a scene—that she was probably doing the very opposite of what Oprah would do—but she didn't care. "I don't need you to tell me that."

"Mom. I said I was sorry."

For years of condescending to me? Alice wondered. Not likely. She turned to Miller. "Well, I, for one, have been dying to see Blancaneaux, Miller. So thank you—and you, Maggie—for your invitation." She didn't dare look at June. "And on that note"—she reached for her wineglass—"I think I'll have another glass of wine. I had the white"—she got up—"and it's really very good."

Dan had never been happier to see his underwear, and socks, and razor, and favorite new Banana Republic shirt—which he was wearing tonight, and which he thought made his shoulders look nice and broad and the rest of him look vaguely hip. He did, however, have slightly mixed feelings about seeing, once more, June Carter's signature: the big loopy *J* like a lasso, the *C* with that curly bit on the top end like a hangman's noose. His luggage had obviously been gone through, but all of his possessions were present and accounted for. He felt sort of bad now—getting up from the dinner table, and lighting a cigarette while Becky looked on in distaste—about stealing from Hawaiian Shirt Guy.

"Since when do you smoke?" Becky said.

"I don't smoke." Dan exhaled away from her. "I'm having a cigarette."

"Fine." She turned back to Abby. "Be that way."

She'd been talking to Abby all through the meal, and had started to sound like she was about sixteen herself. Some boy that Abby liked had apparently asked her best friend out or something, and Becky was throwing all sorts of girl power Abby's way with the "What a jerk"s and the "He's not worth it"s, and Dan just needed to get away from them lest he get up and scream, "He's just not that into you!" out into the valley.

June was alone by the turntable, so he went there. "You look like you could use one of these," he said, and held out the pack, flipping the lid open with his thumb, his own cigarette dangling from his lips.

"Yeah, I could." She bent down to flip through the box of records, and her dress rode up; she'd gotten some sun that day, too. "But Cash hated that I had that one the other night." She stood with a new record in hand. "And we've got bigger fish to fry at the moment."

Dan slipped the cigarettes into the thigh-high pocket of his cargo pants. "The Blancaneaux Debate."

"Well, there's that."

And for the record, Dan sided with Cash and Miller on that one. He would never admit to June that he was thrilled they'd be dining at Blancaneaux, but maybe the money had changed him. Because Dan was feeling a little bit like a second-class citizen at the Five Sisters, and it was a feeling—perhaps because he'd had it in his daily life for so long—that he didn't like at all.

June took the record off the turntable and slid it into its sleeve. "But that's not even the half of it, trust me." She took out another record.

"Well, I'm sure you guys'll work it out."

And if you don't, feel free to look me up! God, he was such a hypocrite. He inhaled again and felt the effect of the cigarette this time, like a cloud over his brain. He should've gotten another beer before starting this chat.

"Thanks again for the records," June said, placing the needle carefully on what turned out to be a Sinatra record. She pulled a few more records from the box and started sifting through them, like oversize playing cards. "They're really amazing. I can't believe they were in that basement all these years and you never knew."

Dan stubbed his cigarette out under his foot. Smoking alone wasn't as much fun as smoking with June. "Well, there's more if you want them. Some more boxes you never got to pick through."

"Really? I can have them?"

"Of course." This was good practice, right? Giving her these? "I'll never play them. I know myself well enough to know that."

"You do, do you?" She seemed to be mocking him. "Well, thanks, Dan. They're like my own little piece of the dilapidated mansion."

"Indeed they are."

Thunder grumbled far away, but June didn't seem to hear or care.

"So are you guys coming canoeing at Barton Creek Cave tomorrow?" She picked up her beer and turned to face him. "Don't feel like you have to."

She started to walk back over toward the party, and Dan followed. He said, "Becky said she wants to lay low, hike to the Big Falls or something?" The literature in the cabana included a sheet of things to do, and the hike to the Big Falls was on it.

"That sounds fun. You're probably sick of us all already."

"Never," Dan said, but he was actually looking forward to getting down to Placencia, where more people would arrive to tip the scales in favor of his generation. Much as it pained him to admit, he was sort of looking forward to seeing Trevor.

The wind snuffed a few of the votive candles, and the paper lanterns bent against the wind. "Whoa," Miller said, and Minky said, "Looks like Mother Nature has other plans for us all."

Staff started collecting plates and flower arrangements, and Dan went to the bar to get another beer while June got everyone's attention in order to get a handle on plans for the next day—namely, who was going canoeing and who wasn't.

Billy was suddenly beside him at the bar. "Are you going canoeing?" Billy said.

"Nah." Dan thanked the bartender for the beer; he was clearly preparing to shut operations down. "Becky wants to go on a hike, just the two of us."

"Sounds serious." Billy smiled.

"No, nothing like that," Dan said, awkwardly. It dawned on him that he was drunk. "I can't believe I'm going to say this," he said. Yeah, definitely drunk. "But I'm actually looking forward to seeing Trevor."

Billy smiled and turned to face the table. "Getting bored with this crowd, are you?"

"Well, considering my girlfriend has spent the entire night helping Abby recover from some apparently devastating boy news from home, it's been a rough night."

"Devastating, huh?"

"Oh, sure." He was on a roll now, having fun. "The guy she liked asked her best friend to this party, and, well, you can imagine the drama!" Thunder—closer this time—boomed, and Dan followed Billy's gaze to Abby, still talking animatedly with Becky. She seemed to notice them looking at her, and then she got up and walked right toward Billy. "Are you going canoeing?" she said, and Billy said, "Yeah, why?"

"Because my parents are going to Tikal and they're going to make me go with them if Cash and June are the only ones going canoeing."

"No, I'll go," Billy said.

Dan studied Billy and wondered now whether there wasn't something not quite right about the way he interacted with Abby. For his part, Dan had barely spoken a word to the girl the whole trip. He hadn't realized before that he had a strategy for dealing with jailbait, but this was apparently it. She and Billy, au contraire, seemed like bosom buddies.

Abby turned and shouted, "Billy's going, too." She walked back to the group. "Cash, please! Don't make me go with them!"

"Okay, okay!" Cash said. "You'll come with us."

Drops of rain started to fall—isolated thumps of water here and there—and Cash came over to the bar. "Why don't you guys make a run for it? It'll take us a while to get Minky over there. Just send the car back down, okay?"

"Sure thing," Billy said. But the rain was upon them before they could even leave, so they stood under the canopy—trapped—as sheets of rain began to slice at the air around them. The Five Sisters themselves seem to double in size—their surge, their sound intensifying as new water joined the family. Then Dan saw June, as if in slow motion, turn, and he watched her face drain.

"The records!" she screamed, and then she was running from her spot near the table to the box of records, where a sheet of water was pouring off the hut, right into it. The makeshift DJ booth was getting soaked, too. Cash ran over and snatched the turntable, then handed it to Dan, who quickly closed the damp box and put it on the edge of the dinner table, folding the tablecloth over it to keep any stray drips out. He turned to watch the rest of the rescue effort.

June was on the ground now, kneeling over the wet box of records and crying. "They're ruined!" she said over and over, and Cash held her and said, "Hey, what's gotten into you?" She clung to him hard, and Dan had to look away.

*T*hey are up there, onstage at a hipster club, the Galaxy Hut, outside D.C., playing their cover of "It Ain't Me, Babe" in public for the first time because one morning a few weeks ago June put on The Essential Johnny Cash at the apartment when her guitar just happened to be right there, out of its case. So she'd picked it up and started sort of playing along, and then she heard the song in her head differently, with her own sort of stamp on it. With the Starter House's stamp on it. She listened to it maybe ten times before Cash screamed from the other room, "For the love of God, June! Not again!" And then she'd switched off the stereo and started to piece together parts more earnestly.

"What are you doing?" Cash had come to the doorway of the room with a cup of coffee in hand. He sipped it.

"Just messin' around," she said. Then she started to sing along with the guitar, and Cash tapped a foot and nodded along and said, when she was done, "Sounds pretty cool." Then June said, "Maybe we should do it. With the band."

"A duet?" He turned to go back to whatever it was he was doing. "They'll never go for it."

Meaning, of course, Trevor and Joe. But they are up there playing it now, with June and Cash sharing a mike on the chorus—she thinks it's more fun that way—because they'd brought in a big crowd who were demanding an encore. The band had already played every song *they had, so June didn't bother to ask the boys whether they'd go for it. She just said, "We're gonna try a little something different here," into the mike and then, "Boys, follow my lead."*

They are up there now, watching as the crowd shouts their own "No! No! No!" after each "It ain't me, babe" because Trevor and Joe knew the song, of course—from the first line June sang, which, technically, if you were going to be strict about such things, should've been Cash's. June's whammy subbed for harmonica, and Joe found the beat right away and started building drums one on top of the other—first bass, then tom-tom, then snare. Almost instantly Trevor's bass was thumping along, and the crowd was digging it, you could just tell, and when they hit that last big "It ain't me, babe"—that last "No! No! No!"—the crowd's fists punched the air and made the band smile. The roar at song's end was louder than it had been all night.

"What the hell was that?" Trevor said, at gig's end, when they were loading out the gear. Always the gear. He was sweaty with excitement.

June hefted her guitar amp into the back of the van they'd rented for the drive up from the city and said, "Just something I've been playing around with."

Trevor readjusted the position of the amp in the truck bed. "A heads-up would've been nice." He's single again, and a little snippy as a result.

"Sorry. But we needed another song." She shrugged. "I thought of another song."

He smiled then. "We should work on it this week. Maybe slow it down a little bit more?"

"Maybe," June said, but she knew the tempo was already just right.

Joe came out with another amp and said, "That was awesome."

They are playing it again, a month later, at a recording studio in Greenpoint, where they're midway through recording their first album, because they've been in the studio for ten hours and are getting punchy, and since they've been having so much fun playing the cover out, they're recording it—live, one take. Just to see how it sounds. Out of curiosity. And it turns out it sounds amazing.

So Joe, unbeknownst to the band, because he figures nothing'll ever come of it anyway, decides to send it to John in the Morning, the Seattle DJ he worships and whose show he listens to on the internet every morning because there's no decent rock radio in New York. John flips for it, however, and starts playing it every day, and then Trevor decides to find out how to get the song on iTunes, and when it is, it gets bought a couple hundred times every time John in the Morning plays it on the air. They pay all the appropriate royalties to Mr. Dylan.

"I'm not sure this is a good thing," Trevor said one morning a few months later. They were at Cash and June's apartment, where they were sequencing the songs on the record before having it pressed. They've been working with a sound engineer, putting finishing touches on the final mixes.

"People are hearing about us." June came from the kitchen with two coffee mugs in each hand. "How can that not be good?"

"They're not hearing our songs, though," Trevor took a mug, and it looked like an espresso cup in his hand.

"But they will! When the record comes out." June sat down with her own mug. "When the record comes out, people will review it because we've already had this sort of novelty hit."

"Did you just say novelty hit?" Trevor had already drained his mug. "We're doomed."

"Not a *novelty* hit," June corrected, slightly annoyed. "It's a Dylan cover. It's not like it's Al Yankovic."

"Still"—it was becoming clear that Trevor and June rarely saw eye to eye—"it makes me nervous that this is the first thing people are hearing of us."

"But that's the whole point." It's not that the cover—with its obvious nod to her name and Cash's, too—had been part of her grand *plan. How could it have been? But it had started to feel like it was. "People are* hearing *us."*

"Cash?" Trevor said, because Cash had developed a tendency, during band meetings, to speak only when spoken to.

"I don't know, man." He put his feet up on the coffee table; they were bare, and June swatted them away. "I think she's got a point. And the song just sounds awesome. I mean, it's not like it's an embarrassing cover."

"Yeah." Trevor's tone softened. "It's pretty kick-ass, I have to admit." John in the Morning was still playing it all the time.

"Okay, then," June said. "Now to the matter at hand. Here's the list of everything we recorded." There were eleven songs, including the cover, and she'd printed out all the song titles four times. "Everyone put them in the order you think they should be in for the record, and then we'll compare."

Nobody took very long or had to think very hard, as they'd all already spent countless hours with the near-final mixes, playing the beginnings and ends of songs to see what worked well before and after what else. June had one of her songs in the top slot, and Cash had one of his. Joe had June's song there, too, and Trevor had Cash's there, too. This was going to be a problem. So they talked and talked about which song was grabbier and catchier and more accessible, then about the extent to which they, as a whole, wanted to be grabby or catchy or accessible. They talked about which song was more representative of the overall sound of the record, and about anything and everything they could think of to say about songs except for which one was "better," because everybody knew that wouldn't work, would only cause trouble.

Finally, June said, "Fine. Let's open with 'Arsenic,'" which was Cash's song, but then Cash said, "No, I think you're right. Let's go with 'Fire in the Hole.'"

"Well, aren't you both just too sweet?" Trevor said. Then he took a quarter from his pocket. "Heads, Cash. Tails, June."

It flipped in the air, and they all watched as it went round and round, then Trevor snatched it and smacked it onto the top of his left hand. Tails. June wasn't one to argue with a quarter.

"What about 'It Ain't Me, Babe'?" Joe said, when they'd finally agreed on the order of songs.

Cash said, "What about it?" and Joe said, "Should we put it on the record?"

Trevor said, "Hell, no," and June, for once, felt she couldn't have said it better herself.

Monday

At breakfast with Minky—M and M had already gotten up super early and left for Tikal—Abby's patience was shrinking. Minky was going on and on about some World War II veterans thing she belonged to, and Abby kept saying "Uh-huh" and "Right" and "Sure," but she wasn't really listening because she really didn't care about any story that anyone could tell that involved *Robert's Rules of Order*. She was counting the seconds until she got picked up to go canoeing at Barton Creek Cave.

Abby had started to detect a pattern in Minky's stories: they usually climaxed when Minky said something to a person that no one in their right mind would ever say, like "You have a problem with listening" or "Your hair looks better the way you used to wear it." When telling these stories, Minky would leave a dramatic pause after such statements, then chuckle and say, "And she looked at me!"

Minky was lucky all they did was look at her. There were times when it seemed like a slap across the face would be more justified. Because, really. Who says stuff like that?

Abby finished her pancakes and imagined a world in which she could be Minky for a Day. She'd go around school telling people what she thought of them, and when people reacted badly, she'd say, "I'm a good observer of people, you see. I notice things about you that you might not notice yourself," which was how Minky justified telling people that their pants were too tight or their wardrobe too drab. Abby imagined walking up to Chelsea Lambert and saying, "You have a problem with not realizing that the world doesn't revolve around you." She'd tell Hannah that she should go see a dermatologist or at least buy some dandruff shampoo. She'd tell Lisa that she should grow a personality. She'd tell her teachers that listening to them talk about Conrad was actually way more boring than reading Conrad himself. She'd tell Colin Murray that he's scrawny and should work out and that just because he has good taste in music doesn't mean he has good taste in girls. And she wouldn't care what anyone else thought of anything she said. Minky never did.

But today would not be that day, and next Monday wouldn't be either. That first day back at school—that whole first week—was going to be the worst ever. People would be talking about the party in endless detail, and Abby would have nothing to say at all.

"I'll be right back," Abby finally said, then spat out her prepared lie. "I forgot my sunscreen for my face." Cash was going to be there any minute.

"Fine, go. Don't mind me," Minky said, so Abby left the dining room.

That morning, Maggie had apparently made Minky promise to make sure Abby was wearing the Speedo, and so Abby had worn it. But now, knowing that Minky didn't know enough to mistrust her, she slipped back into the cabana and changed into the bikini. She wasn't sure whether they'd get wet or not but figured it was best to be prepared. When she passed the front desk on her way back to the restaurant, Cash was waiting.

"Hey!" she said, and he said, "I told Minky I was going to grab you. Let's go."

She followed him out to the car.

Billy and June said hi but then nothing else, and Abby sensed that the mood of the car wasn't great. She looked at Billy—seated between her and June in the backseat—and raised her eyebrows, and he shrugged. He laid his head back against a headrest and closed his eyes. Abby thought, Yeah, good luck with that, as they hit their first hole in the road, the road that was getting beyond boring. Because seriously, how many times could one sane person drive this same road without going insane? First the forest that got eaten by beetles, then the limestone quarry, but thankfully they turned off, drove through—yes, through—what must've been a river, with water spraying away from the car like it was the center of a fountain, and then wound around a bunch of even tinier roads that were barely roads. There was no pavement to speak of at this point, and at certain times the car was definitely at risk of turning on its side. Mr. Levine, Abby's math teacher, would have loved these angles. Abby put the car at 45 degrees on one super-flooded and pocked part of the road.

A bunch of people wearing black clothes and hats sat in a horse-drawn carriage by the side of the road. They were white. Abby had seen some white girls walking on the main road on the way up to the Pine Ridge, and she'd wondered what the heck they were doing there, but Belize was once a British colony, so there were probably some Brits—white Brits—who'd settled there. But these people looked like Amish, like people out of another era.

Billy said, "Did we take a wrong turn and end up in Pennsylvania?"

Abby had never been to Pennsylvania, but she wasn't in any rush if this was what it looked like. There were farms and hills and trees and it was pretty and all, but God, Abby would just die of boredom. Not that folding T-shirts with a folding board was riveting, but she was a city girl, she knew that much. And just like Hannah had her L.A. infinity pool fantasy, Abby had her own New York penthouse fantasy. She saw herself moving to the city to go to design school, finding some awesome roommates with which to share a cool apartment in some hip neighborhood, and then opening her own boutique. She'd probably have to work for some bigger company for a while, for the experience, but her designs would be so cool and original that she'd be sponsored by some wealthy patron, and then she'd get rich, too. If she ever went to Pennsylvania at all, it would be to open up another store in Philly, but only after she'd opened ones in cities like London, Paris, maybe Miami.

"They're Mennonites," June said. "Not Amish."

"Close enough," Billy said.

"That's the spirit."

Billy took his camera out, and then the driver said, "No cameras." Billy let it sink to his lap, and the driver explained: "The Mennonites don't believe a person should leave any memory behind when they die."

Abby thought for a second and said, "That sounds hard. I mean, how would you even . . ."

She trailed off and no one answered and Billy looked over at her and shrugged again. They rode on—on the tilt-a-whirl road—and Abby wondered, What was the point of living if once you were gone you were gone, like erased? Her whole goal in life was to do something that would make people remember her when she was gone. Not leaving any memory sounded like something out of a science fiction movie, but then Abby had always thought that most religions sounded pretty insane.

They were about to round a bend, and so she turned to

look out the back of the car and lifted a hand to wave. A Mennonite waved back, and she thought, Ha. Gotcha. I'll remember you when you're dead.

At the butterfly farm, Alice paid the admission fee at a small wooden booth by the gate and joined a group of other Americans—she spotted a Mets cap, a Martha's Vineyard T-shirt, and other giveaway details—as they walked across the grounds. A tour was just beginning.

The farm, just a few miles down the road from the Five Sisters, looked like any other kind of farm: random buildings here and there—some small, some tall—strange pieces of machinery scattered in distant fields. Here, however, the focal point was a big screened-in structure—maybe the size of your average fast-food joint—straight ahead down a dirt path through the grass.

The guide, a soft-spoken Belizean woman with a six-month baby-belly and a loose ponytail, instructed the group—there were maybe ten of them—to step into a sort of screened-in antechamber, where some butterflies were loitering. Once the group was inside the chamber, with the door to the outside world closed behind them, the guide opened the door to the larger butterfly sanctuary. There must have been thousands of butterflies in there—some midflight, others clinging to all sorts of tropical plants, and still others dangling from the screened walls and roof. The air flashed with color—gold, blue, green, red—as if full of confetti with wings.

Alice, who hadn't expected such proximity to the butterflies but had hoped to enjoy them from a comfortable distance, tended to flail wildly whenever anything foreign grazed her skin—flies, mosquitoes, the works—so she gripped the front straps of her backpack tightly near her armpits. She had had nightmares when book club read *The Secret Life of Bees*—imagining yellow jackets sneaking through her windows and building hives in her walls—and in real life the presence of a bee could practically result in pulled muscles as Alice jerked to get away. Butterflies she generally liked, thankfully. Though, yes, from a distance. She didn't want to kill any today; she wouldn't be able to stand the guilt.

A small wooden case—the size of a minifridge—where butterflies in various stages were hanging upside down drew the group's attention as the tour guide, standing by its side, spoke in lilting tones about Belize supplying various parts of the world with the butterflies that they raised here, about the life cycle of caterpillars, about cocoons and wings that needed to dry before the butterfly could take flight. Alice was only half listening, because right now, before her very eyes, a butterfly was being born.

First a toucan in the wild. Now this.

The guide noticed, too, and pointed the newborn out to the group, and they all craned their necks and made it harder for Alice to see. Still, through a space between a big bald head and a poofy burst of gray, she could see it: a butterfly, slick and new, emerging from the inside of a fractured black cocoon. The cocoon fell away, and the butterfly, looking now like one wet wing with legs, clung to a tiny perch upside down. Alice tried to imagine what the insect was thinking in that moment, how much patience must be required. But she knew it operated entirely on instinct, something she was never quite able to wrap her head around. She'd seen a documentary on PBS about red crabs on Christmas Island, and though she couldn't remember exactly where on earth Christmas Island was, she'd never forget the images she'd seen, of hundreds of thousands of crabs emerging from the forest and walking across the island to mate and then lay eggs in the sea. A lot of them would get run over by cars and trains as the people who lived on the island went about their lives. Alice, mostly, was grateful she didn't live there. Alice felt like she had no good instincts at all.

She spotted a butterfly wing on the floor, then, and a live butterfly—both wings intact—right near it, right in the path of the tour. She held her breath as the group moved its way. The butterfly didn't budge, but miraculously, no one stepped on it. Relieved, Alice moved into the next room with the others and suddenly wished she could fill one of the empty rooms of her house with butterflies. She'd take down June's old posters or move Billy's old baseball collectibles into storage, and then she'd be able to tap into this kind of feeling of joy and beauty on a daily basis. In the place where ghosts of her children lived, there'd be, instead, an explosion of butterflies. Every morning, over coffee, she could go and sit there, feel their flutters on her cheek, and watch the light play on their wings. She'd be calm and happy and wouldn't flail at all.

Alice hadn't realized before *how much* she liked butterflies. Sure, she'd point them out in the yard, when anyone was there to see them. Alone, she'd just marvel over the fact that the daylilies she'd planted actually fulfilled the promise of their plastic tags: Attracts Butterflies. She'd planted her first batch of them years ago, when Jack was alive and they all, the garden, too, were young. She'd scoffed at the tag in the store, but she planted the flowers and lo!—not five minutes later—a butterfly had flown over. "Oh, for the love of God!" she'd said, and Jack had laughed.

Most people probably liked butterflies. June had been the one to point out that a lot of the small things that Alice took pleasure in, a lot of her favorites, were commonplace. "Everyone loves weeping willows," June had said when Alice had said something about the tree in the neighbor's yard, the tree she'd always wished were hers. "Everyone likes seeing the moon during the day," June had said, when Alice had pointed out an airy white crescent against a blue sky and marveled. Alice didn't think June was wrong, necessarily, she just didn't think that fact should ruin things. Maybe there was a good reason so many people liked such beautiful things, and what was wrong with that?

The tour moved on to a feeding station, and as the guide explained what the butterflies were feasting on—fresh papaya—and how often they were fed, a butterfly landed on her head. If she felt its tiny legs clinging to her hair, she didn't indicate as much. For her part, Alice tightened her hands on her backpack. The butterflies feeding in the birdbathlike structure seemed to be staring at her suspiciously. They all featured a big black dot surrounded in white that looked like one big eye. Frankly, they were freaking Alice out, and then one took flight and fluttered about and landed on Alice's hand, still hooked around her backpack strap just inches from her face. Some members of the tour noticed it there and snapped a few pictures, and Alice didn't know whether to look down to the left at the butterfly or smile for the cameras. She hoped they were zooming in so that they only got her hand and the butterfly in the frame. The thought of her face appearing in strangers' photo albums unnerved her.

The group's attention moved on, but Alice just stared at her new passenger as she moved through the rest of the sanctuary. She wasn't listening to the guide anymore at all. She was figuring out what to do about the butterfly and remembering, too, last night's storm, and June's complete breakdown over the records. Wet and ruined—and during one of her father's old favorites, too. She would have run over to hug June herself had Cash not gotten there first. Poor, puzzled Cash. What must he have thought!

Alice imagined June had told Cash about the job offer by now. That was the only reason Alice wished she were canoeing with them and not here. So she'd know how it had gone. And also so she could apologize for her own contribution to

June's meltdown. She'd thrown a fit when she shouldn't have. Because yes, they were here in Belize, and the wedding was all but organized, but you couldn't discount the stress of just being a bride. And June, with the weight of this decision on her, too. Alice should've known better.

Alice shook her hand a tiny bit, hoping to dislodge her hitchhiker, but it didn't take off—only opened then closed its wings again, almost in greeting: take me to your leader. And so Alice joined the group again, as they clustered around what the guide was describing as an especially rare butterfly; blue morphos, she said, would probably be extinct if it weren't for sanctuaries like this one. The next time Alice looked down at her hand, the butterfly she'd been carrying was gone, and she felt sad that she hadn't seen it leave. She should've paid better attention.

Once more, the group stepped into the antechamber. A couple of butterflies had to be picked by the guide off people's hats and shirts, and she slipped them through the door back into the main chamber. Alice saw a butterfly right above the door and wondered whether it was plotting an escape, whether it had prepared long and hard—prison break style—to get to this point just inches from freedom. The guide opened the door back out to the world, and Alice, secretly hoping that the butterfly would make a break for it, hung back as the group exited single file. But when she could delay no longer, she exited the chamber and wondered whether the butterfly hadn't tried to escape because she'd been watching too closely, and she might've snitched. She thought then that she must be getting old and crazy. Imagining the thoughts of butterflies, as if they had any at all. It made her happy, somehow, though, to think that they did. *The Secret Life of Butterflies*. Now there's a book she'd like to read. Book club could meet in her butterfly sanctuary, and even Felicia would have to admit it was spectacular.

"Are you traveling alone?" a woman asked Alice as the group walked up a small incline to an open-air hut. The tour was to continue, apparently, though Alice could have happily slipped away and called it a day.

"Oh no," Alice said. "We're here for my daughter's wedding. They went canoeing today, and I'm not the canoeing type."

"How exciting!" the woman said, and Alice repeated the words inside her head, wanting them to stick, wanting so much to think so and wishing this business about the band, the job weren't a factor at all. "Well, it's very brave of you to come here on your own. I haven't left my husband's side for a second since we got here." She indicated the man in the Martha's Vineyard T-shirt.

Alice felt a ventriloquist's hand up her back when she said, "Well, I've never been canoeing with my husband before, so why start now?"

She flashed hot, but she just couldn't bear the look of pity the truth would elicit, and what was the harm? It felt nice, actually. To pretend.

"Are you at Blancaneaux?" the woman asked.

"No," Alice said. "But we're having dinner there tonight." She realized her error immediately and kept talking so as to bury what she'd just said. Though she'd only implied her husband was still alive, hadn't she? "My daughter wanted to support a Belizean-owned place, so we're at the Five Sisters."

"Oh," the woman said, and Alice regretted if her simple statement of fact sounded judgmental. "I hear that's nice, too. We're here for a few more days, then we're off to Coppola's other place down on the beach."

"I didn't realize he had two." Alice was happy that dinner had gotten lost somewhere.

"Well, three, really. He's got another one in Guatemala."

194

They were in the hut now, surrounded by Tupperware containers that held caterpillars, leaves, and twigs. "Is the wedding up here?" the woman whispered, apparently about as interested in caterpillars as Alice was.

"No, it's in Placencia."

"That's where Turtle Inn is!" she said, and Alice thought she'd really stepped in it now, with her living dead husband, too. "I'm sure it'll be beautiful!"

"I'm sure it will." Alice tried to picture the scene, then tried to picture herself in it. "But I can't for the life of me decide what to wear. I brought three dresses."

The woman's eyes grew tall. "Three!"

Alice nodded, ashamed.

"Well, if it were me, I'd start by narrowing it down to two." The woman held up her index and middle fingers and nodded.

Dan wasn't much of a hiker—and in fact didn't much like people who were—but it seemed stupid to not hike to the waterfall when there was so little else to do. He was looking forward to getting down to Placencia because of the ocean, too, not just because there would be more people there. Rain forests were okay, but he thought he'd feel more relaxed once they were all at the beach. Besides, now that the autograph was back in his possession, he was back to Plan A—Declare love. Present autograph—and everything here in the Pine Ridge was too scheduled, too dependent on tour guides and drivers. There was no room for spontaneity. Things down at the beach would surely be more low-key—and the beach, too, was closer to civilization and escape routes should one become necessary. If Cash—or even June herself—decided to run Dan out of town for his proclamation, there'd actually be someplace to run. The local airstrip was barely a mile from the resort.

The hike wasn't that bad. The sun pounded the crap out of them as they walked down the road out of the Five Sisters, but they soon turned off and climbed down the side of a hill. Before long they were walking across huge rocks, the falls roaring maybe half a football field away. They passed some wet tourists on the way down into the valley, and it was definitely hot enough to swim.

There was only one guy down at the falls; well, two. A photographer, and a guy who was sitting a little bit away from him, reading a book. Dan assumed it was the photographer's guide, but maybe it was just an employee of one of the resorts on his break. The falls were running a sort of golden brown, no doubt on account of all that rain. The image of June, wet record in hands, still pained Dan. It was such a ridiculous thing, really, to get so upset about some old records. But an amazing thing, too. And things between Cash and June clearly weren't great. She'd said as much.

Becky, being Becky, asked the photographer guy if he would mind taking their picture, and so they posed with the falls behind them. Dan, frankly, had been expecting something a bit more spectacular, seeing as they were called the Big Falls. They really just weren't all that big.

"So I'm just curious," Becky said, after thanking the photographer and retrieving her camera; the two men soon left the valley. "You know how people give each other gifts on their wedding day?"

"I guess."

"Is Cash giving June anything special?"

Dan took his shirt off and sat on a sunny rock. "Not that I'm aware of."

"Fascinating." Becky took her river shoes from her backpack, put them on a rock, then squirted a tiny bit of sunscreen on her finger and put it on her nose. She'd already coated herself head to toe back at the cabana, but must've realized she'd missed her nose.

"If you say so." Dan lay back on the rock, but it wasn't that comfortable, so he sat up.

"So you know what's weird?" Becky said, putting her river shoes on.

"What's weird?" Dan took his baseball cap off and ran a hand through his hair.

"I could kill you here, and no one would ever know."

Dan looked at her, feeling like he'd been slapped. "What the *frak* kind of thing is that to say?"

"Just making conversation. I mean, it cuts both ways." Becky stood and walked over to a pool of water. "You could kill me."

"Here's 'just making conversation,' Becky." Dan put on a friendly voice. "'Sure is nice weather we're having.' 'Read any good books lately?' That's making conversation."

"Oh, calm down. I'm just making a point about how remote we are right now. How if one of us cracked our head open on a rock, we'd be fraked." Becky slid into the water. "Frak, it's cold!" she said. "You coming in?"

"Yeah," Dan said. "I guess."

"Well, if you're going to be that way, don't bother." She turned to face the falls.

Dan put his own river shoes on—they were the first pair he'd ever owned—and started to climb down, but damn the rocks were slippery, even with the shoes' rubber soles. He slipped and found himself in the water much faster than he'd intended.

Becky sank down into the water, dunked her head under while holding her nose, and then floated. "So do you think you'd ever have a wedding like this?"

Dan thought, Oh, here we go. "Hard to say." What grown woman still holds her nose when swimming?

"Why?"

"I just don't go around picturing my wedding, is all." He took a deep breath, closed his eyes, and went under water, then wished he could stay there a really long time. He could find some pipe to breathe out of and swim all the way to Florida, to Weeki Wachee, where the mermaids would welcome him with open arms.

He ran out of air and resurfaced, wiping water from his face. It smelled like dirt.

"Do you even *want* to get married?" Becky said.

This was not a conversation Dan wanted to have thousands of miles from home, effectively trapped. He'd already had it twice too many times in his life for his liking. He looked at Becky, then away at the falls, then back at Becky, then down at his finger, feigning some kind of splinter or cut.

"God, Dan. You look like a deer in headlights." She made a wide-eyed scared face. "Forget I asked."

"It's hard to explain, is all." Or at least it was hard to explain to women.

"You want to try?"

And so Dan began his spiel. "I guess I don't really feel any strong urge to do it. I mean, I sort of wish I did, because it's what people do, and I don't want to be old and alone and all. I just don't see it for me right now."

"You mean for us?" There was an edge to Becky's voice that Dan thought meant tears were on the way.

He stepped gingerly up on a rock and out of the water and grabbed a towel. "Why are we talking about this now?"

"Have to talk about it sometime!" Becky half yelled. She started to walk off toward the falls, dragging her legs through thigh-high water.

"What the hell has gotten into you?"

"I'm late, Dan." She turned and faced him again and, seeing that the valley was still theirs alone, she yelled at full volume, "I'm fucking late!"

A flock of black birds took off from trees above them, and Becky just kept walking off toward the falls, no doubt thinking about that broken condom a few weeks back and how maybe she should've given the pill more of a shot and not bailed after it made her feel "weird." Dan sat on a rock and waited for the sun to dry his skin and for the reality of how completely screwed he was in every way to set in deep, like a burn.

Back at the Five Sisters, Alice decided to check out the screened-in sunroom near her cabana. It didn't have any butterflies, but it did have a few hammocks, so Alice decided to settle in there. The canoeing trip wouldn't be back for another few hours, and dinner wasn't until seven.

The hammocks were made of a weave of skinny plastic ropes that didn't easily make room for a person. Alice couldn't quite make an opening for her butt. She put her book down on the ground—below where she imagined her head would end up—and then spread the mesh wide so she could sit. When she tried to lie back, she had to reach behind her to spread out the ropes there, too, and she nearly fell over the first time she tried to lift a foot off the ground. Finding her balance, and looking around to see whether anyone had seen her first awkward attempts—no one, whew!—she tried again, and ended up settling her butt and straddling the hammock in her shorts. Spreading the net around her ass wide, she was finally able to lean back, but she had to struggle to get her feet into a resting place, and when she did, she wasn't comfortable at all. The hammock behind her back was stiff against her spine; she felt like she was lying on a balance beam made of wood. She shimmied around a bit, wiggling her hips, and tried to find a more comfortable spot, which she finally did, though even then, it was less than ideal. This was possibly the worst hammock ever made. She couldn't help but wonder if the other hammock was any better.

So she repeated the whole ordeal with the other hammock, ultimately finding a slightly more comfortable position. She sighed with relief, and thought how it sort of defeated the whole purpose of the hammocks, this having to work so hard. Only then did she look down to the ground, where her copy of *The Da Vinci Code* lay beneath the other hammock, firmly out of reach.

"Oh for chrissakes," she said, then she closed her eyes, deciding to give napping a try. Her brain was too alert, though, too hopped up. Sue from book club, who did yoga and meditated, called it "monkey mind," and Alice thought it fitting she'd have monkey mind here in monkey country. She wondered if monkeys ever had human mind, and if they liked it when they did.

Alice's butterfly farm lie had revealed to her only that she was basically living a lie all the time—not just on butterfly farms in Belize—and had been for some time. And while it seemed like most of America was living one sort of lie or the other—and all too ready to talk about it on Oprah—Alice's lie was this: she was lonely. She pretended she wasn't. She pretended she liked it, but she didn't. After Jack died, she was too busy recovering, and being strong for June and Billy, to think about other men, and then, somehow, so many years had passed that she just couldn't even imagine it. But now, in her low moments, she could work herself up into such a state—imagining her friends at home in the evening cooking with their husbands while she cooked for one—that she could go from zero to crying in under sixty seconds. She liked to try to convince herself that the memories of happiness were enough, enough to keep her happy now, and that she wasn't really alone because she had her children. But she didn't really. Have them, that is. They were off in their own worlds, and Alice didn't belong there.

Oprah and her favorite guest shrink, Dr. Robin, would say that Alice was *here*, however—in Belize, specifically—for a reason. And that it was important that she didn't leave before figuring out what the reason, the lesson, was. Maybe it was that it was time to show her children who she really was? Maybe that it was time to show herself? When had it become so hard to just be Alice? Had she ever really been herself?

Well, if it were me, I'd start by narrowing it down to two.

Such a simple piece of advice from a complete stranger, and now Alice felt compelled to act on it, grateful to have an excuse to behave like someone else entirely. She went back to the cabana and started to get organized for tomorrow morning's move down to the beach. Packing, on the one hand, was easy. There was no deciding. Everything had to go. But when Alice got down to the dresses, she looked at that matronly one—the one that Billy had told her to wear, the one that Mary-Anise had advised her against buying—and knew for sure she'd never wear it to the wedding. It made her feel too old, too far gone.

So she left the cabana—door unlocked—and speed-walked up the path to the front desk before she changed her mind. A few groundskeepers watched her long march—sage dress on a hanger, sleeved in clear plastic, trailing behind her—and she had to resist the urge to wave.

In the gift shop, Alice exchanged greetings with the girl working reception, then selected a postcard with a picture of a toucan on it, and brought it to the desk. She hooked the dress over her elbow, picked up a pen, and asked, "Is there any way you mail this to the U.S.? If I leave the address. You can charge the cost and the postcard to my room? Roaring Creek?"

"Yes, I can," the girl said, and Alice finished writing out Mary-Anise's address. In the place for the note, she wrote, You WERE RIGHT: OPRAH WOULD NEVER DO THIS!

Bats were the sort of thing that Abby knew existed but liked to remain in denial about—like dust mites and rapists and sleeper cells. And yet here she was, in a canoe inside Barton Creek Cave, being told about the bats overhead. She held a plastic yellow light, weighed down with a couple of C batteries by the feel of it, and pointed it up at the bats, while behind her, Billy rowed. Their boat was tied to Cash and June's, where their guide was seated, too.

Abby had once gone to an outdoor movie at sunset at a neighborhood park at home, and in the flicker of the projector a shitload of bugs had appeared, and then, not five minutes later, a couple of bats started whipping around in front of the screen, in the funnel of light, feasting. It was totally gross and sort of cool at the same time, and Abby forgot about the movie and just started watching this other drama. Then a bat had darted by way too freakin' close and she yelled, "Oh shit," and a bunch of people around her laughed and she had, too.

She didn't like the feeling she had now, though, of being in such an enclosed space with so many bats. Sure they were way up there and she was way down here, but she had a vision of one of them getting caught in her hair and pretty much gave herself a chill. She felt a tiny fleck of something on top of her head and smacked at it in a panic. It was Billy's hand, and he laughed. "Gotcha!"

"Quit it," she said, but she smiled into the dripping darkness of the cave ahead and then ducked as the boat slid under an especially low stalactite.

The tour guide was pointing out piles of broken pottery and high perches on which the bones of Mayans—sacrificed to the gods or just plain old left here because it was once used as a tomb—were supposedly found. Both boats turned the lights they were carrying off, then, and the darkness hurt Abby's eyes. They desperately wanted to focus on something, and then finally they adjusted—there was the slightest amount of light still coming from the mouth of the cave—and it was all so quiet and weird, and Abby thought maybe Belize was pretty cool after all.

It was Monday, which meant that tomorrow they would go back into Belize City by car—that same damn road again, but for the last time at least—and then fly down to Placencia, where the beach and the rest of the band would be waiting. More important, according to M and M's guidebook, there was an internet café in Placencia. So Abby could check her email and find out what was going on at home. For all she knew, Hannah and Colin had already had a fight and called off their date. For all she knew, the club where Chelsea Lambert's party was going to be had burned down. The gift bag loot could have been stolen. Hell, for all she knew, Chelsea Lambert had dropped dead of *E. coli* or died in a car crash. For all she knew, Colin Murray was dead, too.

They had turned around and were heading back out toward the mouth of the cave now, and they passed a bunch of boats loaded with tourists and tied together. It was a big group, maybe twenty people, and they were all wearing matching T-shirts, yellow like caution signs. Some of them waved as they passed, and Abby waved back—she sure was doing a lot of waving today—and then they were gone, though you could still hear their tour guide, who sounded American. "You'll need to duck up here, folks! I haven't lost anybody yet . . . this week!" Laughter echoed.

"Somebody please shoot me if I ever end up like that,"

June said, and then Cash said, "Why do you have to be like that?"

"Like what?"

"Criticizing every little thing and every other person on the planet who does things differently than you?"

"*That's* the fight you want to have with me right now?" June said. "Really? That's what you want to fight about. Tour groups with matching T-shirts?"

Cash didn't answer, and the boats cruised out into the daylight. They unloaded at a sort of natural dock area—Billy got out first and then held out a hand to help Abby across some water—and June was already on her way off to the restrooms, across a field where construction workers were framing out some kind of barn, maybe?

"I'm sorry we're not that much fun today," Cash said, as Abby walked beside him back toward the car.

"It's okay," she said. Her T-shirt was cold from the cave, wet drips here and there, so she took it off and let the sun hit her skin; at least that was her excuse. Really, she just wanted to show some skin for Billy, who was trailing behind them. "I'm sure you've got a lot on your mind. Getting married and all."

"It's not just that." Cash looked sad, and like he hadn't slept. "June's got a job offer. A good job. A *dream job*, really. She's thinking of quitting the band."

"What? Why?" That just wasn't possible. It would be such a total waste! "But she can't!"

"She just dropped this bomb on me this morning, and I haven't had a second to talk to anybody about it. I don't know what to do."

"Tell her she can't!" Abby said.

"That's not how it works, Abs." He rubbed his eyes behind his sunglasses. "I wish it were."

June came out of the bathroom then, and Cash didn't say anything else and Abby didn't either because she wasn't sure if it was bad that Cash had told her, whether June was going to be pissed.

"Give us a minute, will you?" Cash said, then went over to June. The two of them spoke softly, but urgently.

Billy came to Abby's side. "I thought your mom put the ixnay on the ikinibay."

"Yeah, well, she's not the boss of me." Abby felt like she could cry. She pretended to look for something in her backpack as a distraction.

"You mean she's not here."

Abby was in no mood. "It's just a bikini. I really don't see what the big deal is."

Billy smiled and said, "Me neither," but Abby knew he didn't mean it and he was annoying her, talking about the bikini—and in pig latin!—when *this* was going on. Something about it all felt like it was his fault, too. He and June were related. She crossed her arms across her chest.

"He told you, didn't he?" Billy took his baseball cap off and ran a hand through his hair.

"Yeah," Abby said. "He did." She was thinking of the show at Radio City and how she'd felt more alive then than she maybe ever had in her life, how the band could give her chills in a way that maybe only a handful of bands could. She felt like she was going to cry. She said, "She can't quit."

Billy put his cap back on, twisting it down onto his head and squinting up at the sun. "Oh, Abby," he said, all condescending, like he was a wise old man. "I'm afraid she can."

There was actually something kinda cute about the idea of Becky pregnant. Sitting at one of the outdoor tables on the terrace of the Five Sisters Lodge, halfway through his second beer while Becky napped, Dan imagined she'd make a pretty good mom. Not the hippest mom in the playground, of course, but a good, loving mother. And since he was prone to thinking about things in grand terms ever since his windfall, Dan had to wonder whether this wasn't its own kind of windfall. They could get married, have the baby, and that could be Dan's life. They'd never worry about money, and they'd learn to love each other more fully, more passionately, along the way. Not everyone had fireworks in their marriage. Most people didn't, best Dan could tell. And what was the other option? Walk away and be a total shit? Pay fuckloads of child support and never see the kid? Dan wouldn't stand for it. He would not be that kind of dad. He'd marry Becky and have an affair with someone else before he'd go down in history as a deadbeat.

But maybe he wouldn't want to have an affair. Maybe this was the universe telling Dan that it was time to grow the fuck up. He had no real idea what else he wanted to do with his life anyway, so maybe this was it. The path for him. If Becky was pregnant, they'd get married and have the baby. They'd consult his list and refrain from precious baby names and talk of poopy diapers. They'd hire sitters so they could still go out to the kinds of restaurants that served foie gras and didn't have children's menus. Becky would go to Mommy and Me yoga and take the kid to all sorts of Gymborees and make a bunch of mom friends, and then, after a while, they'd buy a house in Westchester and send the kids—they'd have another, of course—to the best schools around. They might not live happily ever after—did anyone, really?—but Dan would try his best. He could see himself in the role of the doting husband, of the fun-loving dad. He could almost smell the leather of a baseball mitt, the sugar cookies, the Johnson & Johnson shampoo.

June came out of the lodge and put two beers and a pack of cigarettes on the table.

"Having a bad day?" Dan asked, wondering where she'd procured the smokes.

June said, "You have no idea."

"Becky's late," Dan said, to prove that yes, he had some idea, though of course once he said it, he realized it was the last thing he should be telling June, all things considered.

"Shit." June sat down across from him, pushed one of the beers his way. "Really?"

"Really."

"Wow." June took a sip of beer, swallowed, put the bottle down. "How do you feel about that?"

"Like I'm glad there are hills around"—Dan looked out at the Pine Ridge—"so I can run for them." Impressed with his own joke, he smiled.

"Well, I've been offered a job that would mean quitting the band, and I have to decide by Friday. Not that that's in any way on the same level as Becky, but, well, Cash is pissed. I'm not even sure he understands the levels on which he's pissed. And there's this little thing called a wedding that's supposed to be happening on Saturday."

"Supposed to be?"

June shrugged.

"He'd never . . ."

"Wouldn't he?"

"He adores you."

And I do, too. The fantasy life with Becky and baby dissipated like mist.

"Not right now he doesn't." June picked at her Belikin label and shook her head. "And he's got a right to be annoyed. I mean, the job offer sort of fell from the sky, but I should've let him know it was even a possibility."

"What kind of job is it?" Dan couldn't think of many jobs she'd be qualified for.

"Musical director for a new animated show at Nickelodeon." June drank from her beer, then lit a cigarette. "It's inspired by that camp I volunteered at over the summer?"

Dan nodded that he remembered the quasi School of Rock for girls. "Cool."

"Yeah." June took a drag, exhaled. "I've been offered the senior music position, which means I'd pretty much be working hand in hand with the animators and writers, supplying whatever music they needed: incidental stuff, songs, the works. I don't know. I probably shouldn't have let it get this far."

And Dan should never have let things get this far with him either: he should never have agreed to be best man. He should never have kept Becky around this long. "Will you promise to stay here and not move an inch—well, except to smoke or drink—until I get back? There's something I need to go get. I'll be back in two seconds."

"Okay." June laughed.

Dan picked up his cabana key and went up the path. He would get the autograph, give it to June, tell her how he felt, and then he could move on one way or the other. He would know whether to extract himself from Becky or whether it was worth giving it a real go, without this fantasy of being with June hanging over him all the time.

He opened the cabana door softly, stepped barefoot onto the room's cool tiles, and went to his suitcase. The autograph was zipped into a side compartment now, and he slowly, very slowly, unzipped it. It was torturous, really, like pulling a Band-Aid off over the span of a minute, but he did it. He had the autograph in hand when he heard a moan from the bed, and Becky said, "Dan?"

"Shhhh." He started for the door and whispered, "Go back to sleep."

"Dan?" She sat up in bed.

"Yeah?" His hand was on the door handle.

She sounded fully awake when she said, "Who's June Carter?"

Alice couldn't get over how lovely Blancaneaux was. It was just like the Five Sisters, really, only grander in scale and somehow fancier. Like it was dressed up in its Sunday best. And she hadn't realized how desperately she'd been craving pasta until she'd looked at the menu. The restaurant was easily four times the size of the dining room at Five Sisters, and the outdoor area—where Miller had insisted the group be seated—featured plush seating and huge potted plants and outdoor ceiling fans, which seemed to Alice the epitome of tropical luxury. Even the lighting—golden brown—seemed rich. Best of all, the tables around them were all full, and the woman from the butterfly farm was nowhere to be seen. On the one hand, Alice wanted to thank her for her advice—it felt great to have unburdened herself of one of the dresses—but on the other, the husband thing could prove awkward.

Miller ordered a few bottles of wine from Coppola's own vineyard, and Alice and June shared a look. June whispered, "Best behavior," and dragged a finger across her heart, twice, to make a cross.

"You better be," Cash said, not realizing the whisper had been for Alice, and then June kissed him on the cheek. So they were talking, they were okay. Not that they could really ignore each other under these circumstances, not even if they wanted to. But Alice hoped June and Cash were able to compartmentalize things. They were marrying each other, after all. They weren't marrying the band.

Alice had actually gotten used to the pink hair over the last several days, and it wasn't as bad as she initially thought. Or maybe it had gotten lighter in the sun? June's hair had been a wheat blond, last Alice knew, and the pink on top of it was almost the color of cotton candy or strawberry frosting and triggered a memory of what Alice thought of as her grandmother's bathroom, though it was really just the bathroom of the house Alice herself grew up in. When you stepped onto the cool tiles, it was as if you were literally looking at the world through rose-colored glasses; the sun shone through a window of muted pink stained glass so that even things that weren't pink seemed to become so by association. There was a fuzzy pink throw rug by the powder pink sink, a big pink bathtub, and flowery pale pink wallpaper. There were three different pinks in the mosaic of square-inch tiles on the floor, towels with pale pink designs threaded through a hot pink background, and little glass dishes filled with fancy pink soaps. Cut to look like roses, they smelled like poor replicas of the real thing, the aroma of which shrouded the backyard. This room had felt like heaven to Alice when she was a girl. Until bathtime, at which point either Alice's mother or her grandmother would invade this pink paradise and supervise.

Clearly, these women had never let Calgon take them away. The bath would barely be running—that soothing swish accompanied by the thundering thump of the flow hitting the tub—before it would be turned off. With barely two inches of lukewarm water in which to bathe, goose bumps were pretty much inevitable. If they didn't come from the cold, they came from the stories Alice's mother and grandmother told as they scrubbed. They had a disaster story for every occasion and acted as if staying in the tub too long would ruin Alice in ways she was too young to understand. When she'd become a mother herself, Alice had reminded June of Isadora Duncan's untimely death every time she ventured too close to a car without her winter scarf properly secured, and Alice had no doubt it was a result of her own childhood bath ritual. It was a wonder June hadn't grown up sharing all of Alice's anxieties.

When the food arrived, talk turned to television, and specifically to *The Amazing Race*. Alice really enjoyed the show—seeing the far-flung cities and towns the contestants were sent to, watching the human drama play out faithfully. She occasionally tried to imagine who she'd want as her teammate if she were to sign up to be a contestant and was pretty sure she'd fare better with Billy than she would with June, who, for all her knowledge, also had a way of acting like she knew things she didn't. And if Jack were alive? Well, it was hard to say how they'd do. He was generally good with maps, but he also refused to stop for directions. Truthfully, her best companion would likely be Mary-Anise. She was in great shape, and she was a go-getter. She was also mostly without shame.

"It's just ridiculous to me," June was saying, "that people watch this show where a bunch of Americans storm into a town and run around like idiots, trying to win this huge sum of money that the people in these towns could eat off for a lifetime."

Here we go, Alice thought, wondering what it must be like to be so concerned with right and wrong all the time. Not that Alice wasn't principled or moral, but couldn't she enjoy a goddamn reality TV show without reproach? "I think it probably sparks a lot of interest in travel," Alice said. "Boosts tourism."

"Tourism isn't always a good thing. I mean, look at Venice."

The irony of June's saying this was not lost on Alice, but neither was it, apparently, lost on June. "I mean, I know, I contribute to it, too. But I just mean there's a way to travel that's respectful, and *The Amazing Race* ain't it."

"Cash, you didn't tell me your bride was such a cynic," Miller said.

Cash's eyes lit up. "You have met June before, haven't you?"

And then Minky, apropos of nothing, said, "She looks like a desperate housewife!"

June's mouth went agape in amusement, and the table fell silent. The dress really was cut pretty low.

"You let her out of the house like that at home?" Minky asked Cash, but he didn't answer. Then Minky turned to June. "You won't be able to dress like that if you take a real job," she said.

"Yes, June," Miller said, and Alice hoped he was going to divert things so as to avoid this train wreck. "Cash tells us you're thinking of quitting the band. Taking a job writing music for TV, though I guess on a show that isn't the root of all evil?"

"Thinking about it, yes." June looked at Cash, who said, "What?! They're family."

"June's father was a composer," Alice said in an effort to spare everyone currently on the spot. "Of industrials."

Across the table, June mouthed, *Thank you*.

Alice said, "Most people don't even know what those were, but they were really quite interesting." And then Alice launched into her industrial musical routine and felt as if the woman from the butterfly farm, were she to walk by, would sense Jack Siren was very much alive.

Abby felt like she was in a movie, but not a movie she'd actually want to see. It would be some very adult, intellectual thing—probably with a pretentiously lame name like *June's Friends* or *A Wedding in Belize*—and everyone in it would be witty. June would quit the band, and all hell would break loose. Maybe someone would outdo her and announce that they were dying. Cash would admit to having had an affair with Becky, and maybe Abby and Billy would get caught in bed together. Maggie would somehow get a gun. Or maybe the Abby character would pull a Natalee Holloway and wind up missing. There'd be people searching the surrounding forests for days, and then they'd find her body atop a Mayan palace. She'd be headline news in San Fran and no one—not Chelsea Lambert, or Hannah, or Lisa, or Colin—would ever be able to forget her when she was gone. Screw those Mennonites.

The food was normal, at least. Abby and her mother had ordered in cahoots and so were splitting lobster and also spaghetti carbonara. Abby's interest in lobster came around maybe once a year, and she had to admit that the middle of the rain forest was a pretty stupid place to get it. But whatever. This Coppola guy probably had fresh ones flown in every hour.

June came over to her just as dessert menus were being circulated. "I know you're not that happy with me right now, but I have good news!" She bent down beside Abby. "I was able to get you, me, Cash, and Billy on a slightly later flight. And we're all booked for ziplining at nine a.m., then we'll meet everybody else in Placencia."

Abby watched her mother's face ignite with the news. "June, that's really unnecessary. But thank you. Abby's really had her heart set on it."

"It's okay, really." Abby said. "We don't have to go."

"No, I want to." June stood up now. "I'm glad you thought of it! It'll be fun. You only live once, right?"

Maggie pinched Abby's leg and made her eyes wide.

"Thanks," Abby said to June. "Thanks a lot."

Abby knew she was on thin ice, so she didn't bother asking M and M if she could hang out with June and Cash and Dan and Becky and, most important, Billy at the bar at Blancaneaux while everyone else went to bed. She dutifully said good night to everyone, then went back to the cabana with M and M and M and pretended to be going to bed. M and M went off into their room, and Minky was pretty much asleep on her feet even at

213

the best of times, so Abby just waited and waited. It was torture, really, the waiting, but she had to be sure. Then she got up—she'd gone so far as to climb under the covers fully clothed—and snuck out of the cabana and into the night, which was dry and sticky at the same time, like ChapStick.

The path was quiet, and Abby took off running once she was sure her footfalls wouldn't alert M and M to her escape. The main lodge and bar were only a short way down the path, but Abby didn't want to get attacked by spiders or lizards or crazies, because there were probably crazies in Belize, right? There were crazies everywhere.

"Well, look who it is," June said, exhaling smoke as Abby, breathless, came upon them at the bar. It was a small enough space—they were pretty much the only people there, though a guy and a girl were playing a game at a small table in the corner. It looked like Parcheesi, a game that Abby had totally forgotten how to play. Seeing it, seeing them playing it while she joined this cool group of people at the bar, made Abby sort of sad and at the same time empowered. She felt brave and grown-up and had a sudden flash of other things in her life that she'd long stopped doing or thinking about. She suddenly couldn't think of the last time she'd done a cartwheel or jumped rope.

"M and M know you're here?" Cash asked.

Abby pulled up a stool. "What do you think?"

"Can we get another beer, please?" Cash said to the bartender. "For my sister."

Abby tried hard not to beam. She loved it when he called her that, without the "step."

"Why don't we get Abby's opinion on the subject currently on the table," June said, and Abby thought she sounded kind of drunk. "Abby, what do you think of the fact that I'm planning on getting married with pink hair?"

"June, you've already made your point loud and clear," Cash said. "I'm not allowed to tell you what to do."

"No, I really want to know what Abby thinks." June aimed her eyes at Abby's. "Abby?"

Abby was trying to figure out something to say that wouldn't piss anyone off and was hoping they'd keep arguing among themselves, in order to give her more time. She thought the pink hair was pretty harsh, but kind of cool in its own way. But pink hair and a white dress? It just didn't work. Though the fact that June was tanning more richly and deeply by the day was helping to pull the look together.

"Fine, then," Cash said. "Tell her what you think, Abby."

"I think—" Abby took a swig of her beer. "I think that you'd look prettier without it. But that the point of fashion isn't always to look pretty."

"Very diplomatic!" June said. "The point of *life* isn't to look pretty."

"Well, you're certainly not looking very pretty right now," Cash said.

"I'm not trying to," June said, and Abby still couldn't tell if this was a real argument or a fun sort of argument.

"I'm stepping out for a smoke," Billy said, and June said, "You're allowed to smoke in here."

Billy said, "I know," and Abby stood up and said, "I'll come, too."

Billy looked at Cash, who looked at Abby, and she said, "Oh, please. It's not like I've never smoked before." Which wasn't entirely truthful. She'd had a puff, once. But, well, she was curious. She liked the idea of it. The idea of her and Billy stepping outside for a smoke.

"You really shouldn't smoke," Billy said.

"You'll give me one, though." She'd decided she couldn't blame him for his sister's actions and was no longer mad about the pig latin.

"One. But this is it."

"Fine, whatever."

She took the cigarette and put it between her lips, and then Billy presented a lit match and she leaned in and inhaled. The cigarette glowed and she almost coughed when the smoke hit the back of her throat, but she didn't. She exhaled and swallowed to make the itch go away. "So what's going on in there, exactly?"

"Oh, it's all stupid. Cash just assumed that June was going to dye her hair brown before the wedding, which she probably was until he assumed as much. And of course now it's not just about the hair, it's about the job and the band and God only knows what else."

"Do you think they'll break up?"

"I have no idea."

"Wait." Abby realized her question had two meanings. "June and Cash, you mean? Or the Starter House?"

"Well, both. But I don't think they'll call off the wedding. The band, though, I think it's a goner. But don't be so glum. Hey, I mean, you got your wish about ziplining, right?"

"Yeah, right."

"It'll be fun."

"Yeah, whatever." Big freakin' whoop at this point.

"Hey, what happened?" Billy elbowed her. "You were all excited about it."

"Yeah, well, not anymore."

"Don't let my sister ruin it for you."

"It's not that."

"Then what?"

Abby just shook her head, and Billy said, "Come on. Tell me."

She breathed out hard. "I only wanted to go because of this guy at home. And I found out he asked my best friend out, so there's really not much point anymore."

"Except that it'll be awesome." Billy smiled. "And he sounds like a jerk, for the record."

216

"Thanks," Abby said, and the sight of the cigarette between her fingers made her feel strange and bold. She felt like she must be some other person, because the Abby she knew a few days ago would never be having a cigarette and drinking a beer with a cute twenty-five-year-old in Belize. She said, "So, do you have a girlfriend?"

Billy studied her curiously over his cigarette, and Abby put hers to her mouth and inhaled, and it felt like her first true breath as an adult. His eyes had followed her cigarette to her lips, and she looked at his lips and decided then and there that she would kiss him. Not now. Not with everybody else around. But before the trip was over, for sure.

T̄hey are hanging out in the Maintenance Shop, on the Iowa State University campus, in Ames, Iowa, because bands can only generate so much buzz and so many record sales without leaving the comfort of their home city, and because their cover of "It Ain't Me, Babe" landed them an appearance, playing themselves, on a popular WB—check that, CW11—show that shall remain nameless. They are officially "on the road" with a van they purchased for $1,000 on eBay.

They are looking at the framed, signed black-and-white concert pix on the wall of this sort of brick basement club—with stained windows behind the stage—because they argued and argued about the TV appearance but then decided to do it because they weren't just playing the cover, but an original song as well. It was the sort of exposure you couldn't turn down.

*June alone had a speaking part, a fact that was more than mildly irritating to Trevor and Joe and Cash, all of whom were reluctant to admit that they cared—*Come on! It's the CW11!—*until they realized that they all cared. The lines went like this:*

> *JUNE: Actually, I've seen bigger.* (In response to a kid who claims to be her biggest fan.)

And then,

> *JUNE: Cool. We were happy to do it.* (When the prom
> committee cochairs thank her for the great set.)

*It was really nothing to get in a huff about, but the boys, who'd
already finished their sound check and run-through and were hanging
out in their green room while June was on set rehearsing the lines,
huffed and puffed big-time.*
  "This is ridiculous," Trevor said.
  *"Didn't this happen to No Doubt?" Joe slumped on a couch in the
corner. "And now the only one people even* know *anymore is Gwen
Stefani."*
  *Cash scanned the snack table but wasn't really hungry. "If you ever
compare us to No Doubt again, you're out of the band."*

*They are seeing the likes of the Hoodu Gurus, and the Replacements,
and Meat Puppets, and Robyn Hitchcock, and Wilco among those
signed pics on the walls of the Maintenance Shop, and they're feeling
good about the show now that they're here because June said, "It's
not my fault I had lines," over dinner in the Standard Hotel in L.A.
after the CW11 shoot. "If you'll recall, I didn't even want to go on the
damn show."*
  *It was true that the band had actually been more in favor of
it than she had been, and she suspected that Trevor was secretly a
fan of the show's barely legal female lead. "What's done is done,"
Trevor said.*
  *"What was I supposed to do?" June drank from a tall, red, grainy
plastic cup of fountain Coke. "Refuse the lines on grounds of gender
discrimination? I mean, I am, unless I'm mistaken, the lead singer.
And lead singers historically get more attention. Not my fault."*

"You don't have to ham it up so much, though." This from Joe.

"Yeah, okay. I'll be a little mouse, curl up in a little ball." She shook her head. "That'll work."

"I don't mean . . ." Joe trailed off. He didn't really know what he meant.

"You know why we get press?" June didn't like being criticized. "Because I say things that are interesting. I'm handing them their copy, and they eat it up." (e.g. "I'm the Mae West of rock," "I play guitar better than any guy in any band in this week's Billboard Top 40," "George Bush should be shot.")

Joe took a bite of his burger, spoke while chewing. "Maybe you don't have to be so, you know, controversial?"

"Are you kidding?" June pushed ice around in her Coke. "You're kidding, right?" She looked to Cash and Trevor for support, but they were attending to their own burgers.

"I'm just saying. You know"—Joe shrugged—"I'm a Republican."

All three of his bandmates said, "You are?"

"Yeah, so I mean, when you go off on Bush or whatever, well, I don't like you speaking for me, for us as a band I mean."

June dug into her own burger at last. "Last I checked, I wasn't gagging you all during interviews."

No one said anything for a while then, and then Trevor looked up at Joe. "Seriously, man? A Republican?"

They're looking at the guitars up there on the stage—waiting patiently to be brought to life—and feeling good about the tour, on which they've mostly had full, if not sold-out, houses because the appearance on the show that shall remain nameless helped push "It Ain't Me, Babe" onto the college charts, and the time to tour seemed nigh, and then the song got picked up by a car commercial and they actually had the money with which to buy that van on eBay.

WOULDN'T MISS IT FOR THE WORLD

They mostly aren't speaking to each other now—or rather, they're refraining from talking—because when you spend hours upon hours in a van crossing some of the most boring parts of the American land-scape with someone, you don't want to talk to him or her when you don't have to. They've been on the road for two weeks, and they're craving comforts of home, and that most treasured thing: solitude. Trevor has an annoying whistling habit. Joe's feet smell like scrambled eggs. June drives too fast (they've gotten three tickets), and Cash can't read a map (they've been lost, like way lost, just as many times). There are just some things about people that you'd never know unless you drove across the country with them.

They are up there, playing their last song—an up-tempo, danceable song called "Wonder Woman"—having left "It Ain't Me, Babe" off the set list tonight because they're sick to death of it, but also because the show was rebroadcast on the CW11 the night before. They watched in a motel on the side of a highway and relived their initial horror over the fact that their original song was cut, gone, left on the editing room floor.

They've used up all their time onstage, intentionally, figuring the booker will just have to call it a night, but he doesn't. Because when they go offstage and grab bottles of beer and/or water, the cries for "It Ain't Me, Babe" from the Maintenance Shop crowd—and God, all these college kids look so young and wholesome and white—won't stop. So the booker comes over and says, "I think you'd better give them what they want." And so they take the stage, and June, who's overtired and really pissed about the CW11, answers a call from the back of the crowd for "It Ain't Me, Babe" with her own "No! No! No!"

She steps up to the mike and says, "It ain't our song." And then she turns to Cash and says, "How about we do 'Thirst'?" and Cash says, "If you want to cause a riot," and June says, "Maybe I do."

Then Trevor steps over and says, "We made our bed," and starts playing the "It Ain't Me, Babe" bass line. The crowd whoops recognition, and Cash starts singing.

    June pulls a couple of college girls up from the front rows and hands one a tambourine and positions them in front of the mike, and then she doesn't sing at all. Her guitar parts sound as pissed as she is. There is such a thing as regretting what you started, and this is definitely it.

Tuesday

So Becky was killing him after all. And he deserved it. What kind of slimeball shares his bed with one woman while he's in love with another? And what kind of asshole actually admits it—*to the girl he's sleeping with*—when she's thousands of miles from home and possibly knocked up with aforementioned asshole's baby?

But no, Becky was asleep. So she wasn't killing him. Still, Dan couldn't imagine knife wounds could hurt any more than the stabbing pains in his gut. He curled up, fetal, but no, that wasn't the answer. He sat up and scooched down to the end of the bed, escaped the mosquito net, and rushed toward the bathroom. He almost didn't make it to the toilet before the explosion came. This wasn't going to be pretty. Not for Becky either, what with the lack of proper walls. He wanted desperately to be quiet, of course, but this was beyond his control. He could only hope she'd sleep through it.

"You okay?" she asked, after the next burst, and Dan guessed he was louder than Bruckheimer.

"Go back to sleep," he said, strained.

"Are you all right?"

Another burst of pain and expulsion. "I've been better."

Becky was quiet then, the way she'd been when Dan fessed

223

up about the autograph. He had tried to play it like his crush on June was just that—a crush—and that it was in the past, but that he wanted to give her the autograph anyway, since he'd bought it for her. Becky had said, "Oh, Dan," sadly, and he'd said, "What?"

"You still think you're in love with her, don't you?"

"Sometimes," he admitted, because maybe Becky would break up with him and he'd be off the hook in the decision-making.

"June would eat you alive." She'd sighed. "And you're not in love with her any more than you're in love with me."

Dan almost quoted from *Battlestar Galactica* then, because, as Admiral Adama once said, if you think you're in love with someone, then you are. That's what love is. And who was Becky to decide that he wasn't really in love with June? She had nerve, really. But he didn't feel like picking a fight. Not *that* fight, anyway.

"What does this mean," Dan had said. "For us?"

"I don't know, Dan." Becky had reached out and pulled his arm, his watch, closer so she could see. "But right now we have to go to dinner. And when we get to Placencia tomorrow, I need to go to a drugstore and buy a pregnancy test."

They'd gone to Blancaneaux then, and Dan had apologized to June for leaving her hanging outside the lodge—"No worries," she had said, "though I'm still intrigued"—and Becky hadn't acted like anything at all was wrong. Dan had actually been sort of impressed.

On the toilet, the pain was gone. Dan cleaned himself up, went to wash his hands—the water was running slightly brown and had been since the rain—and returned to the bed, sweating.

"What time is it?" Becky asked, holding the mosquito netting back for him.

"Late. Or early. Let's go back to sleep."

The pains started to build incrementally just a few minutes later. "I think I have to go back in there," Dan whispered, and Becky just squeezed his hand.

Round two was just as bad, more voluminous if anything. Some kind of horrible acid had obviously liquefied Dan's intestines. Surely it was they themselves coming out of him, his disintegrated pipes. It hurt that badly.

That quickly, again, it passed, and he prepared for his move back to the bed.

It was probably nothing. Probably just a combination of rich food and too much of Coppola's wine. Becky hadn't wanted any but hadn't wanted to call attention to herself, and so Dan had been drinking out of both of their glasses, which Miller—determined to be the perfect host—had kept refilling. Dan had no idea how many bottles the table had put away, but he'd certainly done more than his fair share. And then they'd gone to the bar. God, the bar. Where they'd drunk even more. And smoked. And watched the tension between June and Cash mount. And through it all Becky was calm and sober as a judge on account of the possibility that their baby was growing inside her. Maybe she was made of more high-quality stock than Dan had ever given her credit for.

The pain stabbed again, and Dan had to wonder if this was anything at all like what giving birth felt like. It was hard for him to imagine more pain than this, and then he knew it would only be another minute before he had to get up and go in there again. "You okay?" Becky said.

"No," Dan said. He seriously thought he might cry. "I feel like I'm dying." Was this his punishment for being such a shit? If so, God really did have a sick sense of humor.

Becky put a hand to his forehead and said, "You're not dying. It was probably just the rich food. And all that wine."

"It's bad, Becky," he said. "Really bad."

"Can I get you anything?"

"A proper bathroom."

"Don't be stupid," Becky said. "It's just me." Then after a moment she said, "You *did* remember to brush your teeth with bottled water last night, didn't you?"

He thought of the brown water at the sink and at the Big Falls, and tried to remember brushing his teeth last night. "No," he said. "I don't think I did."

"June told everyone at dinner to be extra safe, after that rain. Didn't you hear?"

"No! When?"

"You must've been in the bathroom."

Oh, the irony! "You should've told me!"

"Sorry!"

Dan got up and made another run for it. When he was done, he waited there for the next wave, but it didn't come, so he climbed into bed, where Becky snored lightly. Dan had never heard her snore before and wondered whether maybe it was a sign—like out of some old wives' tale—that she really was pregnant after all. God, he hoped she wasn't. He'd never wished for a woman to get her period more. Because she seemed pretty calm right now about the fact that he was in love with someone else, and they were pretty obviously going to break up after the trip, but surely that would change if she were pregnant.

The stomach pains were far off again, but Dan knew they'd soon be upon him, and he'd blown through the cabana's entire toilet paper supply. There were maybe ten squares left total. So he slipped out of bed and went down to the lodge to see if it was open, and if it was, to see if he could steal some toilet paper from the bathroom.

It was almost daybreak. The sky was white, and birds were chirping to life. Dan only hoped he'd make it to the lodge and back before another attack came upon him.

June was sitting at the bar with a steaming mug, elbows on

the bar, hands dug into her hair, staring at the Mayan temple puzzle.

"Step away from the puzzle," Dan said as he approached. "Repeat. Step away from the puzzle."

June pulled her hands out of her hair and turned. "Ugggh. I officially hate this thing." She pushed it away. "I seriously want to hurl it off the side of this mountain."

"Maybe it's not about the puzzle, grasshopper."

"If there's one thing that you and I both know, Dan, it's that it's not about the puzzle." She seemed to become more alert then, her eyes more sharply focused on him. "You look like hell."

"I think maybe they should call the Big Falls *E. Coli* Falls."

"No!"

"Either that or food poisoning from Blancaneaux. And, ironically, I was in the bathroom when you made your announcement about not brushing your teeth with the water."

"Oh God, Dan. You poor thing."

"I came to swipe, no pun intended, some toilet paper." He pointed toward the bathroom.

"I'm so sorry, Dan. Feel better, okay?"

When he came out of the bathroom with a roll in hand, June was gone. He went back to the cabana, hoping to get a few hours of sleep before having to leave. How he would last the two-and-a-half-hour ride back down to Belize City and then the flight, he had no idea. Back in bed, he lay and watched Becky sleeping. "I'm really sorry," he whispered. "For everything."

But he knew she was asleep, knew she wouldn't hear.

Abby took her backpack and made her way down the path—so quickly her calves hurt and her arches ached—to the urns. She took out her sketch pad and began to draw the scene, making sure to get all of the basics in place: the position and size of the urns, their relationship to the ground and to the plants surrounding them. Nearby there was a tree of some kind—Abby could only guess papaya—and she went over and took a loose papaya from the ground and placed it in front of the urns, where the picture had been revealing itself to be dull. "Much better," she said aloud, then she sketched the papaya and its shadow, and then put her sketch pad away. There wasn't time. So she took out her camera, and took pictures. She'd have to finish this one later.

Gathering her things and putting them away, Abby turned back up the path. She had just enough time to walk back at a leisurely pace. She stopped midway and turned to take in the setting one final time. She wondered whether she'd ever come back here. Whether, when she was older, she'd come here with her husband, maybe even on her honeymoon, though definitely not to get married, or maybe not until she retired. She had a feeling now that she was going to end up marrying Billy. It'd be a few years before he'd admit to his feelings fully, for sure. But she'd be living in New York and hanging out with Cash and June, and finally he'd cave in. Then they'd come back to Belize someday as lovers, and they'd reminisce about how it all began: with that look, that bikini, that double take and sharp inhale of his at Rio on Pools when she took off her T-shirt. She closed her eyes and tried to imagine him being right there, kissing her, his arms around her, his hands in her hair. It was so real she could almost step outside herself and draw it. She'd insert herself into that sketch she'd already done of Billy. Was there a rule that said you had to be alone in a self-portrait?

So only Billy knew that she really couldn't give a flying fuck anymore about flying through the jungle on some weird series of cables. She felt dumb, now, that she'd made such a big deal out of it, considering it was Colin Murray who put the idea in her head.

228

She couldn't believe how mad she still was. She'd forget about it all for hours at a time, sure, but then it would all come back, Mack truck. The only thing she wanted more than to never have to go back to school was to go back immediately, so she could tell Colin and Hannah off, Minky style, or give Colin the cold shoulder and tell Hannah stories about Billy that would make her jealous beyond belief. In her head she was playing scenes over and over in which Colin was with Hannah at the party, but Abby somehow showed up and he came over to her and said, "She asked me, Abby. I felt bad saying no." He'd say, "It was really you I wanted to go with," and then Abby would say, "I met someone. He lives in New York. I'm going to college there, so it all worked out in the end." Either that, or Colin would take her hand and lead her to some quiet empty room and they'd make out and then Hannah would walk in on them and Abby would say, "Now you know how it feels."

She felt pathetic, now, that she'd gotten everyone interested in going ziplining all because of some asshole guy who didn't even like her. She felt more pathetic, too, when she thought of everything he said or did that she'd misread. Because she must have gotten it all wrong while Hannah and Lisa got it all right. Nothing had ever happened between Colin and Abby, and that was evidence that nothing ever would; he didn't really like her at all. It was supremely unfair that life put you through crap like this. She knew that in the grand scheme of things this wasn't a big deal. She'd live. Worse things than unrequited crushes happened to people every day, every minute of every day. But that didn't make her any less sad. Or maybe a little less sad. But still sad.

But she'd have to go through with the ziplining anyway— even if it cost her her life. The whole production, once they got there, looked kind of ramshackle, and the guy explaining the harnesses seemed sort of sleepy. But there had to be all sorts of safety regulations and laws about this kind of thing, right? She and Billy and Cash and June were all standing on the first platform, surrounded by nothing but trees.

After some quick instructions about how the harness should fit you and how to get into it—and also, most important, how to work the brake, which was this sort of locking clamp that latched onto the line and which you worked with one hand— the instructor said, "Okay, who first?" He held a helmet out in his hands.

There was no way Abby was going first—it looked pretty scary—so it was a good thing Cash and June both said, "I'll go."

"Ladies first," Cash said, with a wave of the arm, and June said, "In that case, forget it. You go."

So Cash stepped up, put on a helmet, got strapped in, and then stood on the edge of the platform.

"Ready?" the instructor said, and he made a hand signal to a guy on the next platform.

"Sure," Cash said, and then he pushed off and yelled "Woohoo!" as he flew down the line like runaway laundry. He slowed down perfectly when he neared the next platform and then he stood on it, turned, and yelled, "That was awesome!"

The instructor on that platform did stuff with Cash's line clamps, moving them over to another line, and then Cash was off again and out of sight through the thick forest of green. His next "Woohoo!" faded away into the distance.

"You're up," Billy said to June, though now Abby was eager to try it, wished she'd been brave and volunteered to go first.

"Catch you on the flip side," June said, as she stepped into her harness. Again, the hand signal was made and then June was gone with a "Yahooooo!" and Billy laughed. "I wonder if it's possible to zipline without making any noise," he said, and Abby shrugged and smiled. "You can try!"

"You want to go next?" he asked, but Abby was too embarrassed to go with just Billy watching.

"No," she said. "You go."

So it was Billy's turn, and he got ready quickly and then took off with a sort of reluctant "Aaaaaah." Abby watched his muscular arm, stretched out overhead to touch the brake, and thought he looked pretty hot.

"Couldn't do it!" he shouted from the other platform, and Abby only shrugged as she herself got into a harness and put on a helmet. She hadn't had much time to fuss with her hair that morning, so it couldn't look much worse.

"Ready?" the instructor guy asked, and Abby nodded.

When he gave her the okay, she jumped off the platform and let out an "Aaaaaaggggggggh," unable, like Billy, to stop the noise. It was hardly the Tarzan cry she'd imagined, but it felt good, and so the next time, she yelled some more, and then some more as she zipped through the jungle, wind whipping past her ears, birds flying up and out of the way. And so what if nobody at the party could hear her (because, uh, the party wasn't happening yet)? So what if wimpy Colin Murray and his music magazines liked Hannah better than he liked her? In a few months, she'd be moving to New York, and only an idiot wants to go away to college and have a boyfriend back home. It completely defeats the purpose of being away in the first place.

She caught up with Billy on one of the platforms—maybe the fourth or fifth. He had his camera out.

"This was a great idea," he said. He snapped a picture of Abby, who smiled dutifully, then put his camera back in its case and in the lower pocket of his cargo shorts. "But the guy's still a jerk."

"Thanks," Abby said, unsure whether that was the right response.

Billy looked ahead toward the next platform. There were maybe four left, by Abby's count. "You want me to bring up the rear in the home stretch?" he asked.

"Sure," Abby said, stepping up so that the guy manning the

platform could hook her on. "See you soon," she said, then she took off into the air, and this time she was quiet without trying to be. She still felt the release, the elation of the screams, but somehow it felt like they'd turned inward, like she was shouting inside at herself, cheering herself on. She closed her eyes and let her head hang back for a minute and felt, for the first time in ages, truly alive and free.

"So what did you think?" Cash asked Abby, when she climbed down from the final platform, and even though she wanted to gush about how amazing it was, June was standing there, drinking from a bottle of water and looking nonchalant. Abby felt the need to act nonchalant, too.

"It was cool," she said with a shrug, but what she was really thinking was how grateful she was that it had all worked out okay in the end. It had been really fun—*so* fun that she wasn't sure she'd even tell Hannah or Colin about it. She didn't want to give them the satisfaction of knowing she'd done it.

"Well, I loved it," Cash said.

"Me too." Billy had arrived. "But my ass hurts."

"Mine, too," June said, and Abby suddenly feared that June had hated every second of it, regretted the whole stupid idea.

They started heading back toward the car then, and Billy and Cash ran ahead and started playing catch with a papaya.

"That was really fun," Abby said to June. "So thanks." She kicked a rock. "I didn't mean to seem ungrateful or like I'm mad."

"Ah, but you *are* mad!" June raised an index finger in the air.

Abby shrugged. "I guess I just don't get why you would want to quit."

"I know, Abby." June sighed. "But the band's not all bright lights, big city. It's a shitload of hard work for no money."

Abby hadn't ever really thought about the money part, had just assumed they were somehow raking it in.

"And I've got this crap job as a bartender," June said. "And I do boring office temp work because it's flexible, but I'm sick of it. This show, this job, would be a way to make some good money doing something I love. And the show sounds really cool. I mean, it's about a *rock camp for girls.*"

The thought of June working as a temp was too depressing, but not as depressing as the thought of the band breaking up; it didn't matter whether the show was cool or not. "But you don't even realize how amazing you are. I mean, the last album? It's incredible. And I'm sure it'll be the next one that will break through in a big way. You can't give up. You just can't."

June just smiled.

Abby said, "And I mean, what about my brother?"

June looked off toward Cash. "Between you and me, I give him maybe another half a day before he admits he actually wants me to quit the band."

"Why would he want that?" Abby looked in his direction, too.

"It's complicated, Abby."

Cash was running hard and fast as the papaya sailed overhead, and June called out, "Cash! Look out!" just as he was about to run out of flattened dirt and into brush but then he went down and there was a snap—either a twig or a bone, Abby couldn't tell—and then his ankle was all wrong. "I'm okay," he said, then Billy helped him up, but when Cash went to walk, he yowled.

"God, Cash, how could you be such an idiot?" June said, and Cash threw an arm around Billy and started hobbling toward the car.

"If I'm such an idiot, June"—Cash pulled his leg into the car and put it down carefully—"maybe you shouldn't marry me."

Placencia

Tuesday (More)

"Panty rippers for everyone!" Trevor barked. "And Dan here's paying!" He was standing at the tiki bar on the beach at Peggy's Place Beach Resort, wearing a black T-shirt with "girl-friends are for pussies" in lowercase white typewriter font, and his sunglasses were clutching his bald head, upside down. The next four days would surely be the longest of Dan's life.

He and Becky hadn't even made it to their cabana before Trevor spotted them coming out of the reception building and waved them over to the bar, where he was hanging out with a guy and a girl that he introduced. They weren't related to the wedding, and Dan promptly forgot their names. The Caribbean Sea—flat and blue, nary a wave to speak of—was just a few paces away and stretched beyond to the horizon. The TV playing an American football game actually irked Dan. He wasn't much into sports and, well, it sort of ruined the tropical vibe. The pool, right there on the beach, helped.

"What's the matter, Dan?" Trevor was passing pink drinks around.

Becky took one and pulled on the straw, but Dan knew she was fake-drinking. She still hadn't gotten her period. It was only maybe four days late, she'd said, so Dan had hopes that she was getting herself worked up over nothing. But she swore she was like clockwork otherwise. They hadn't had sex since

Becky made her announcement at the Big Falls, and Dan sort of wished he'd paid better attention that last time, now that it seemed like he might not have sex with anyone for a while. Not that he was in any shape to have sex now.

"Dan's having some stomach problems," Becky said. "Best we can tell, it's because he brushed his teeth with tap water in the Pine Ridge after it had started running sort of brown."

"You idiot." Trevor shook his head, and his new goatee—which was longer and more goatlike than any goatee should actually be—swayed.

"Speaking of which," Dan said to Becky. "Do you think they sell bottled water?"

"The water here's fine, man." Trevor sipped his own "virgin" drink through a straw, and Dan thought, Men should never drink with straws. "We got down here yesterday, and we've been drinking it no problem."

Dan didn't care. "I'd just really feel more comfortable if . . ."

"Holy shit, man." Trevor's smile over Dan's shoulder was wide, and Dan turned to see what was causing it.

Cash was making his way across the beach on crutches, and it didn't look easy. June was a few paces behind, trailed by Billy.

"What the hell?" Dan said when they finally made it to the bar. "What happened?"

"Yeah, Junie," Trevor said. "What did you do, try to cobble him?"

Cash lowered himself into a chair at a table by the bar, and June helped with his crutches. "Just a game of Kill the Man with the Papaya gone horribly wrong,". he said. "It's just a sprain, though."

"Give me some sugar." Trevor spread his arms, and June let herself be embraced.

"Great to see you." She sounded subdued, tired. Dan hadn't

238

seen her since the wee hours and wondered whether she'd slipped the Mayan temple puzzle into her luggage and brought it down to Placencia. She came over to him and said, "Hey," then said, "We just missed you at the airports. We ended up on a flight that was like fifteen minutes after yours."

"Funny," Dan said.

She asked Trevor, "How was your trip?"

"Fine. This place rocks." Trevor raised his drink. "Where else in the world can you order a virgin panty ripper without people looking at you funny?" He introduced his new friends—landscapers from Boston, he said this time—and June seemed about as interested in them as Dan did.

"So who else are we waiting on?" Trevor said. His landscapers went back to watching football. On a field somewhere in America, it had started to snow.

"Bunch of weekenders." June took a drink from Trevor, who'd ordered her a panty ripper, too. "Lydia, my maid of honor. She's coming Friday on the same flight as Leah and the baby. A few aunts and uncles, a couple of random friends. Possibly Cash's *mother*." She looked around. "Where's Joe?"

"Napping." Trevor stroked the goatee. "He enjoyed his first night out without the baby a little overmuch last night."

Dan looked at Becky at the mention of the word *baby*, but she was talking to Billy: "Was it scary?" she asked him. Dan didn't much care about ziplining.

"This Lydia." Trevor's smile seemed to catch the sun, and he looked like a dental commercial—with effects to show sparkling teeth. "Is she single? Or am I going to have to find myself a local hottie?"

June rolled her eyes and said, "You know Lydia. She used to come to gigs. She has *three kids*," but, really, she should know better by now.

"Is she bringing her kids?" Dan asked, horrified at the thought.

"No." June sighed. "Little Darla will be the only little one, provided Leah doesn't change her mind at the last minute."

Trevor had a one-track mind. "Okay, so local hottie is the way to go," he said. "And I think we have our first contestant." His gaze had landed down the beach, so June turned around and Dan did, too. Abby was coming their way, walking past the pool in a low-cut tank and short shorts.

"Uh, that's Abby." Dan said, happy for the opportunity to put Trevor in his place. "Cash's *seventeen-year-old* step-sister?"

"Fuckin' hell, really?" Trevor's whistle seemed to say, "Damn!"

"Really." June said.

Billy piped up with "I thought she was eighteen"—which only fueled Dan's impression of Billy's inappropriate relationship with the girl—and June shook her head. Billy looked at Becky and shrugged, then continued talking: "So, no. It wasn't that high. You probably would have been fine."

Trevor was still staring.

"Hey!" June snapped her fingers in front of him.

"Oh, come on." Trevor finally looked away. "You were strutting your stuff when you were seventeen, too."

Dan didn't doubt it, though even now June had less stuff to strut. It really was a shame about her breast size, and Dan thought, again, that he should've paid better attention with Becky, because what if June and Cash really did fall apart, and he and June actually got together? No more C-cups for Dan.

Abby reached the bar, and June said, "Abby, c'mere." She put an arm around her future sister-in-law's shoulder. "You should study Trevor, here, from a comfortable distance. He's the kind of guy you'll spend the rest of your life avoiding. The kind that thinks 'That's what she said' is a witty comeback."

"Ouch!" Trevor said, but he laughed. "Nice to meet you, Abby."

"Actually, we met at Radio City last year." Abby and June's arms were entwined behind their backs, and Dan imagined it would have turned him on if he'd been feeling better. "I'm a big fan."

"Oh, right! Of course. Cool." Trevor sat back in his chair, somehow managing to look like a peacock. "You're in San Francisco, right? We'll have to play out there the next time we tour."

"Yeah," Abby said. "That'd be awesome." Dan followed Abby's gaze to June, but June didn't appear to be listening anymore. Her hand was at the back of Cash's neck, playing with the hair there, and she was looking out at the ocean. So this was going to be interesting. Because everyone knew that June was thinking of quitting the band except for, well, the band.

"Does anyone want to go into town with me?" Abby said. "Please!"

"I'll go." Becky stood and gave Dan a meaningful look.

So this was it. They'd know for sure in a matter of hours whether Becky was pregnant or not. Dan's legs felt soft in the thighs, and he leaned back against a bar stool. His stomach woes had obviously weakened him, and he suddenly wanted nothing more than a nap despite his not being a napper. But he could feel a distant rumble in his bowels.

"Really?!?!? You'll go? Like now?" Abby looked like she might start jumping up and down, an image that Dan, once he thought of it, had a hard time shaking, even in his woeful state.

"Sure." Becky put her drink—still full—on the bar, and Dan considered sticking around after she was gone, to drink it, but the rumble let him know how it felt about that idea. Becky said, "I need to find a pharmacy. Want to meet me at the front desk in ten minutes?"

Abby said, "Awesome."

Becky picked up her carry-on and turned to Dan. "Can I have the key?"

"I should settle in, so I'll come, too." He put down his own half-emptied drink—he couldn't remember the last time he'd left a drink unfinished—then picked up his own carry-on. He was pretty sure he'd seen their luggage being carted down the beach in a wheelbarrow.

They'd been told when they checked in that their cabana was second from the end, so they headed down the beach toward one of a row of turquoise-and-peach-painted beach bungalows. They were right there on the beach, and Dan decided that when he was feeling better, he'd find a good rock, and check to see if the bungalow was a literal stone's throw from the sea. He had a sudden flash of anger that he wasn't able to enjoy it all as much as he would were he feeling better, were he not sure that he'd walk into the cabana, put down his bag, and head straight for the toilet. Again, the pain, the pressure were like distant thunder, but he could feel the storm approaching. The lightning strike was closing in.

The trip down from the Pine Ridge had been a blur of sky; he'd spent most of the ride with his head in Becky's lap watching clouds outside the window, feeling like complete crap. In fact, there had never been a time in Dan's life—even with all the hangovers—during which the words *complete crap* were more fitting. He was surprised there was anything left of his body at all, that it hadn't all been expunged from him by now. It had been all he could do not to soil himself in the car, and then when they'd stopped for lunch he just sipped water and picked at his lunch—he'd developed nausea, to boot—and read the signs over the bar: CAUTION: HOT AIR USUALLY PRESENT; TRESPASSERS WILL BE SHOT—SURVIVORS WILL BE SHOT AGAIN; THE CUSTOMER IS SOMETIMES RIGHT. These Belizeans sure liked their funny signs, and Dan inwardly groaned at all the tourists taking pictures. There was some kind of caged animal, too, drawing crowds and their cameras, though Dan never bothered to ask anyone what it was. He'd excused himself, instead, and sat in a stall in an outhouse kind of men's room with flies buzzing around his head, wondering how he was going to survive the second leg of the trip, until he heard Becky's voice calling out to him. "Dan?" There was no ceiling. "We're hitting the road."

"Coming now," he'd said.

He'd had another attack in the airport in Belize City, and this was not the kind of airport in which you wanted to have an attack of diarrhea. The international airport would have been one thing, but this was just an airstrip with an office, for a puddle-jumper airline. The check-in area was about the size of your average hotel room, and the bathroom—there was one, with one toilet—opened right up into the waiting area. A line had formed by the time Dan was able to shut down his pipes again, and it was all he could do to stop himself from apologizing for the smell, which thankfully had weakened incrementally with each episode. Still, there was no blaming it on the guy before him. He'd been the only one in there for maybe twenty minutes. The whole thing was now beyond tedious. His ass hurt enough that he didn't want to sit down anywhere else but the bowl, so the plane ride—fairly bumpy—had been a real treat. Because if you've ever been on a plane that held only nine passengers, and if you've ever watched your girlfriend chitchat with the classically handsome British pilot from the copilot's chair, *distracting him from flying the fraking plane*, and thought that death was surely imminent, well, at least you weren't also dealing with the fact that you might crap your shorts.

The bathroom in this cabana, at least, had proper walls. And a nice big window. Dan didn't have much of a chance to take in the rest of the room—he'd noticed a kitchen and a big air-conditioning unit over the bed—before he was on the bowl.

This attack was short and powerful, and he washed his hands while reading a sign about the water being fit for drinking.

"I could go with you," he said to Becky when he returned to the main room. She was putting sunscreen on her face.

"You'd be a burden more than an asset," she said, and he said, "Thanks," and lay down on his side on the bed.

He honestly couldn't believe this had happened to him. *Only* him. If a bunch of them had come down with the same thing, well, there'd be some humor in it, running (ha!) jokes about *E. coli*. This solo plague, however, just really wasn't funny. And God, Trevor would probably never let him hear the end of it. Years from now, they'd be barbecuing at McCarren with their wives and kids, and the trip to Belize would come up, and Trevor would say, "Yeah, and remember how Dan had the shits the whole time?"

Dan hoped he'd someday forget.

Abby waited for Becky on a bench outside of the main building, watching a hummingbird hover near a huge red flower. At first she hadn't realized what it was, had thought maybe some sort of monster killer bee. Weren't there always news stories about swarms of them flying up from South America? She wasn't sure she'd ever actually seen a hummingbird, but she must have, in a zoo at some point, right? Or maybe just on TV? You could barely see its wings, they were flapping so hard, and the rapid blur made Abby tired.

After leaving the bar, she'd gone back to the bungalow and told M and M that Becky wanted to go into town, too. She'd had to beg them to let her go meet Becky alone, without their coming down to make sure it was okay, and that Becky was really going. They'd pulled that crap all the time when Abby was even just a little bit younger—calling Hannah's mom to see if it was really okay for Abby to stay for dinner, and most of the time they didn't even let her stay at all. They had a thing about dinner: thought you should eat it with your family. They seemed to feel that way about going into Placencia, too.

They hadn't taken news of Cash's ankle sprain that well either, and seemed pretty unhappy with Abby and her ziplining until she'd explained that it hadn't actually *happened* ziplining.

"It's not like he fell off a cable," she'd said. "It was in the parking lot."

She felt guilty anyway, though. If she hadn't made such a big production about going ziplining, then they never would have been there at all, and Billy never would have picked up that papaya and thrown it, and Cash would've never fallen while going long. The ride to the hospital in Belize City had been entirely silent—what was there to say after what Cash said, about how maybe they shouldn't get married?—then June had gone with Cash through the double doors to an examining room, and Abby and Billy had been left in the waiting room. Hospitals were pretty much the same everywhere, or at least the waiting room looked like any old hospital waiting room. Maybe more in need of a paint job than some, but that's all. There were TVs bolted into the walls, and Abby had tried to make out what she could of a show that had just started called *Noh Matta Wat!* It looked like a low-budget soap opera about a bunch of Belizeans. Someone was pregnant. Some other chick wasn't too happy about it.

Billy said, "You want a soda?" and got up and dug for change in his front pocket. "Nah," Abby said, "I'm okay, thanks." He crossed the room, and Abby went back to the show, trying to pick out dialogue. A man said, *"It wa be sweet fu me, and fi you,"* and it sounded sinister.

June had burst through the doors again maybe a half hour

later, and Cash was on crutches behind her, his ankle in an Ace bandage. "It's just a sprain," Cash said, and June reached out and stroked the hair at the back of his neck. Something about them seemed to have changed in that emergency room. They looked like something had been decided, and Abby made a secret wish that June had decided to stay with Cash, idiot and all, and with the band.

The hummingbird whirred away out of sight, and Abby looked up the path. Becky was passing under an arch made by two coconut palms.

So far Placencia pretty much blew the Pine Ridge away. The grounds at Peggy's Place were gorgeous, and the cabanas on the beach were just too freakin' cute. Bright and happy, they reminded Abby of those paint-by-number kits she used to do when she was little. They even had little foot baths, which pretty much blew folding boards out of the water in the invention department. You could step off the beach into the foot bath, and then right onto the steps leading to the porch. Pure genius in the field of sand management.

Becky said, "Hey, let me take your picture with that sign." She took her camera out, and Abby turned to see what sign she was talking about: NO SHOES. NO PROBLEM. NO SHIRT. NO PROBLEM. NO PANTS. PROBLEM. Becky held her camera out in front of her and said, "Smile," and Abby complied and then the camera whirred. Becky cupped a hand by the screen and said, "Cute," then put the camera away. "What do you need in town, anyway?" She clicked her backpack shut.

"Well, you know. That guy. The party." Abby was suddenly embarrassed to admit: "I want to check my email."

"Are you sure?" Becky had her hands on her hips, and with her ponytail and her baseball cap, she suddenly looked like a camp counselor. "Once you let your life at home back in, it's not a proper vacation anymore. Personally, I wouldn't check my email right now if you paid me. I mean, if anything really bad happened, someone would find me. Really bad news doesn't come by email."

"That's one way of looking at it." One really weird and morbid way of looking at it.

"I just wouldn't do it if I were you." Becky shook her head and looked superserious. "Not with everything that's going on. It's not like any of it is going to change."

"I think I'll feel better." Abby picked up her backpack—just her wallet and water and some sunscreen—and put it on her back.

Becky shrugged. "If you say so."

They went into the office and paid for bikes, then picked two off a rack around the side of the building.

"This way, right?" Becky said, aiming her bike away from the way they'd come from the airstrip, and Abby nodded. There was one road, and the guy at the front desk said it would lead them right into town.

Abby hadn't ridden a bicycle in a while but discovered it was, well, like riding a bicycle. They cruised down the road—there were no cars so far—and past a huge resort, like some massive fenced-in circus tent made of thatch.

"Ohmigod," Becky said. "That's the other Coppola place."

They slowed and studied it.

"It's gorgeous!" Becky said.

"Yeah," Abby said. "It's pretty cool." Though she wondered about this Coppola guy now, and why he was so big in Belize.

"Why couldn't they have gotten married there?" Becky whined, but you could tell she was pretty much joking.

"Probably a lot more expensive," Abby said.

"Oh, yeah, definitely. We looked into the rates. It's like triple."

Not like she and her millionaire boyfriend couldn't afford it! It was too bad Billy wasn't a millionaire, really. That would be the best ammunition ever against the likes of Chelsea Lambert.

Abby said, "So what's it like to have a millionaire for a boyfriend?"

They continued on, past a pink stucco building that looked like it had been hit by a hurricane and abandoned, or like the builder ran out of money, and something way deep inside Abby made her wonder if maybe she should be scared.

"I don't know." Becky rode hands-free for a minute—it was weird that someone from New York was that confident on a bike—and adjusted her ponytail. "Same as having a regular boyfriend, but with better food, I guess." She looked over at Abby and smiled, so Abby relaxed, because Becky didn't seem scared. "It's not like Dan grew up with money, so he doesn't really know how to spend it, which I guess is good for him, in the long run."

Cash had made Placencia sound so cute—"a tiny fishing town"—but it didn't look cute here on its outskirts. They biked past a field of long grass dotted with some rusting agricultural equipment—a burned-out tractor, some rusty barrels—and then sped up, without even looking at each other, when they saw a man on the road whose clothes seemed to be about to fall away from his skinny body. Abby's heart rate picked up as she passed, trying to look and not look, and then she relaxed; he was obviously high on something.

"That was a little scary," Becky said.

Abby just said, "Yeah."

After a few more pumps of the pedals—everything was so flat!—they were in town. Shops with handmade signs advertising handmade jewelry, cold sodas, coffee, and souvenirs sprang up on both sides of the road. A group of tourists eating out of small cups stood outside an ice cream shop, which, like most of the shops, looked more like a house. Even the grocery store looked more like a barn than a supermarket. Only the bank looked like what it was. Oh, and the gas station, too. Abby saw a sign above the grocery store sign—PHARMACY—and pointed at the side of the barn. "There," she said.

They pulled off the street into a parking lot alongside the building.

"You want to wait here with the bikes?" Becky asked, climbing off hers. "Then we'll hit the internet café together?"

"Sure," Abby said, though she didn't really like the idea of hanging around alone in this town. She didn't want to seem like a baby, though.

A dog tied up on a long leash attached to a fence around the gas station auto-body shop ambled over, looking thirsty. It was small, no bigger than a shoebox, and Abby put the kickstand down, or tried to, but it was broken, so she laid the bike down on the ground and bent to pet the dog. She took a bottle of water out of her backpack and poured a bit in her hand and the dog drank from it. "That a boy," she said.

At the sound of a whistle, the dog turned and trotted away. Becky was still there, probably looking for the source of the whistle the same way Abby was. "Actually," Becky said, "let's stick together, okay?"

"Okay, sure. If you want."

They walked their bikes around to the front of the building. A "GONE FISHIN'" sign hung crookedly on the door to the pharmacy, and Abby wondered how literally to take it.

"Let's go in here real quick," Becky said. She leaned her bike against the front of the building. Abby did the same, then followed her inside.

"Excuse me, hi, good afternoon." Becky stepped up to the cashier.

"Hello," the woman said. "What can I do for you?" She had deep brown eyes and deep brown skin and her features were sharp and angular, like carved out of stone. Abby wondered whether she was Mayan.

"Do you know when the pharmacy might open again?" Becky said, and Abby was suddenly really glad Becky was here. Maybe she'd do the talking over at the internet café, too.

The woman shook her head and said, "Never know with Libba." It was pretty clear from her eye roll and *tsk* that she didn't approve of Libba.

Becky looked around, then breathed audibly. "Is there another pharmacy in town?"

"That's the one." The woman shrugged.

"Okay," Becky said brightly, like it was no big deal. "Thanks." But back outside Becky looked like she was going to cry.

"I have a bunch of extra stuff," Abby said. "Shampoo and, well, tampons and stuff. And my mom's got a ton of stuff, too."

"I *wish* I needed a tampon," Becky said.

But why would someone *want* to get their period? The answer came to Abby the second she'd formed the question. *Duh.* After that one time, she'd been so terrified, because sure, they'd used a condom, but Abby didn't know if they'd done it correctly, and you always hear stories anyway. Abby just said, "Oh."

"I'm sorry." Becky took her cap off and then put it back on again, this time without the ponytail strung through the space at the back. "I really shouldn't drag you into this, but I'm late, and, well, I'm freaking out."

Abby didn't know what to say.

"But I mean, it's probably nothing." Becky shook her head and her hair swished behind her. "Sometimes air travel screws me up."

"Yeah, it's probably that." Abby nodded her head and tried hard to control her mouth, but she really, really wanted to know. "You think you'd get married?" Marrying a millionaire sounded pretty awesome, even if Dan would never have been her own millionaire of choice.

250

Becky's hand went to her stomach, which Abby noted was superflat—not like she'd be showing yet at all. "I think I'm going to be sick."

"I'm sorry." Abby couldn't have felt more dumb. "I didn't mean—"

"No, this is good." Becky took a few deep breaths. "It's good to know how you really feel about things, right? But I really shouldn't even be talking about this with you, of all people. What are you, sixteen?"

"Seventeen. But, you know. It's not like I don't know about"—the phrase "the birds and the bees" came to mind, but Abby couldn't bring herself to say it—"stuff."

"Well, if you're having sex, you'd better be using protection."

"I am." Abby looked down at her shoes, thought about maybe trying to draw them again. She'd never tried this top angle. "I mean, I did." She was pushing away thoughts of that afternoon with Jason. "It was just one time."

"Well, don't rush into anything." Becky pulled her bike away from the wall. "I mean, I'm twenty-seven, and I might not meet someone to marry for another *ten years*. Even one guy a year means I'd sleep with ten more guys before I met my husband. For you it's more like twenty."

That was a pretty weird way to look at it, but then there was actually some logic to it, too. Abby had never imagined she'd sleep with twenty people.

Becky put a leg over her bike, and Abby did the same.

"Did you not use protection?" Abby asked. "I mean, you don't have to answer that."

"No, it's okay." Becky started riding, and Abby followed. "We did. But it broke one time. And it really would be just my luck considering things with Dan, but, well, there's no point in going there." She seemed to shake it off. "So where's this internet café?"

"It should be right on this road." Abby couldn't get there fast enough. "It's called the Blue Iguana Galaxy Café."

Abby was pretty sure there'd be a long email of apology from Hannah waiting for her. She wasn't really feeling like forgiving her, though. What was really the point so close to the end of high school? It would really depend on what Hannah said, though, how sorry she seemed. Either way it would be fun to see her grovel. Maybe there'd be an email from Colin, too. He'd ask her not to be mad. He'd say Will had pressured him since he was already going with Lisa. He'd say he really liked Abby and that he hoped they could start over.

Rounding a curve in the road, Abby saw the sign then for the Blue Iguana Galaxy Café, but it was all wrong. Singed curtains blew in the breeze through burned-out windows, and the air smelled of ash. Abby came to a stop and put a foot down and stared at the café, now a burned and blackened shell of a building. She said, "You have *got* to be kidding me."

Alice had unpacked the two remaining dresses and hung them on hooks on the wall of her bungalow. She studied them for new inspiration now that she'd seen the actual wedding location: the flat white beach dotted with coconut palms. The dresses looked more unappealing than ever. The gray was, well, gray. And that was suddenly the last color Alice wanted to wear. It would seem like a scar on the otherwise bright setting. Everything here was pink and green and blue, and—never mind that it was too dressy—gray was all wrong. Which left red, which Alice wasn't sure she'd ever worn in her lifetime. It really was too sexy. She'd have to brave a trip into town.

Laughing announced June's presence on the stoop, and

there was a knock at the door. "Mom?" June shushed some laughing—Billy's—and Alice could see them playing in a fort they'd built with sheets in the living room when they were maybe six and eight, and working together on that thousand-piece puzzle of some Dalí painting at the old wooden table in the basement. "Your children are here!"

"Come in, come in," Alice said, and gave them hugs when they did. "How was ziplining?"

If they asked her about her trip down, she'd spare them the details of her having spent the entire time envisioning tragic headlines about the wedding party that died in the crash, leaving the bride and groom to practically celebrate their wedding alone. It was a wonder planes like that could fly.

June was holding a garment bag and started looking around for a hook. Alice moved her own dresses out of the way quickly, sticking them in a wardrobe.

"Disastrous," Billy said. He sat in the corner nook, where there were some bench couches. "Cash and I were messing around, throwing a papaya around, and he sprained his ankle."

"He's on crutches." June was sliding the plastic off her dress, now free of the garment bag.

"Oh, no! Billy!"

"What? It's not my fault. And then these two had a fight."

"We didn't have a fight."

"If it looks like a fight and sounds like—"

"It wasn't a fight. And even if it was, it's over now."

Alice had stopped paying attention because June's dress was uncovered now, and it was beautiful. Strapless with a shimmery gold sash around the midriff. "Oh, June." Alice felt tears coming. "It's beautiful."

"Put it on for the poor woman," Billy said.

"What? No!" June said.

"I'm serious. You don't want the first time she sees you in it to be that day." Billy was flipping through Alice's *Fodor's*

Belize. "Back me up on this, Mom. We need to get some tears out of the way."

Alice got up to get a tissue from the bathroom and said, "He might have a point," on her way. Once there, Alice pulled a tissue out, dabbed her eyes, and looked in the mirror. She looked nothing like she'd imagined she'd look when she'd imagined this day when June was just a baby girl. She looked old. She looked sad. And nothing about their surroundings was right. She'd envisioned them dress-shopping together, standing in big plushy rooms with white couches and walls of mirror. She'd imagined them having lunch someplace fancy and girly—like at the Plaza—and then repeating the whole mother-daughter ritual when the time came for fittings. She'd never imagined the dress would simply be presented—a done deal. And in Belize.

"Okay, then." June said from the other room, and then, "Billy, close your eyes."

June's voice was muted as Alice stared herself down. She was having a sort of out-of-body experience. She must be.

"I might need a hand with the zipper," June said.

Billy said, "Say when."

Alice's eyes in the mirror and her hands on the tissue—everything looked foreign. She couldn't think of the last time she'd looked herself in the eye, really looked, and now she knew why. It was a weird feeling, unsettling. The eyes really were the windows on the soul, and Alice felt like hers were sort of grimed over, hard to see through.

"When." June was no longer in Alice's periphery.

"Pretty smokin', sis," Billy said.

"All right, Mom," June said. "We're ready for you."

Alice blew her nose for sport, then stepped back into the main room, where June was standing by the front windows, silhouetted by blinding sun reflecting off the sea. Alice felt dizzy, then stepped farther into the room so the sun's glare wasn't in her eyes. June's dress came into the natural light of the room then, and the sun made the gold sash sizzle. Alice's chest felt like it might cave in upon itself, and she put a hand over her heart.

"I told you," Billy said. And then Alice started to cry. "It's beautiful, honey."

"Thanks, Mom. I thought you'd approve."

Alice kept on crying.

Billy stood and stretched. "Now that I've seen it, I just have to say." He put his hands up as if protecting his face from a punch. "You really should ditch the pink hair."

Alice wiped her eyes and waited for June's response.

"I don't tell *you* what to do with your hair," June said.

Billy said, "*My* hair's not pink. And while I'm on a roll with brotherly advice, I highly recommend you tell the rest of the band about your job offer. Everyone else here knows, and, well, you know . . ."

Alice said, "Loose lips sink ships," an expression that didn't make her feel any younger. Maybe she should've hung on to the Seniors R Us dress after all.

"Exactly!" Billy pointed at Alice. "Or wait." Billy picked up the *Fodor's* again, flipped to an early page, and read: "Don't call the alligator Big Mouth until you have crossed the river."

"What the heck does that have to do with anything?" June asked.

"It's a Belizean proverb," Billy said. "It sounded fitting!"

Alice laughed.

June presented her zipper to her mother for unzipping, her arm raised over her head. She said, "You two are quite the pair."

Dan was on the toilet reading a Colson Whitehead novel and thinking that Colson Whitehead was probably not the type of writer that people typically read on the crapper when Becky came back from town. He wasn't doing much in the way of, well, you know; he was just sitting there. At this point, it seemed easier to just stay there than to get up and go out to a hammock only to have to come back twenty minutes later. He'd obviously perfected some mind-over-matter skills—he'd been able to shut himself down to a relative degree for the trip here—but his body was rebelling now. Unleashing all its fury. His ass burned raw. On the bright side, he was starting to begin to conceive of actually leaving the cabana again. It was sort of like the opposite of labor, really. Instead of contractions getting closer and closer together, Dan's were getting farther apart. He was feeling farther, too, from ever clinching his dream life with June. It was hard to feel romantic on the toilet.

He flushed when he heard Becky come into the cabin so he could clear the way for her and her pregnancy test. He said a quick prayer at the sink, just "Please God," figuring God, if He existed, knew the rest.

"No luck," Becky said. She was sitting at the kitchenette table drinking water.

"What do you mean?"

"Pharmacy was closed." She got up and walked over to the bed and lay down and Dan lay down next to her, not touching her. Already, thoughts of being physically intimate with her were defunct. "Then we went to the internet café, which was burned to the ground."

"Really?"

"Really." Becky sipped her water again. "Then we went back to the pharmacy, and it still wasn't open. And it's the only one in town." She squeezed her breasts then, and said, "They're sort of sore. So that's something." Dan knew he'd never touch them again; a door had been closed.

He got up. "I have to shower."

"I'm gonna go do some yoga on the beach." Becky got up. "Maybe if I relax, I can trigger my period or something."

"Sounds like a plan."

Becky looked at him, blinking her eyes in disgust. "You're such an asshole."

"What?" Dan hadn't even really meant anything by it, but now he did. "I just don't think yoga is going to trigger your period. But you should do it anyway. Definitely. It always calms you down."

Becky started pulling yoga clothes from her suitcase, and Dan went into the bathroom before she could ask him for privacy in which to change. They hadn't had a moment like that yet, but Dan was pretty sure this was going to be it.

Dan showered, grateful for decent water pressure but with his eyes and mouth mostly closed. It was, after all, possible the water was fine for some and not for others. Certain people have immunities to things that others don't, and that doesn't make them any less anything. The soap was latherless, though, which bugged the shit out of him whenever he traveled. Would it really break the bank to spring for some decent, brand-name soap? He hadn't yet absorbed the fact that he could probably stay in much nicer hotels now than he used to. He could probably request his own brand of soap.

He dried off and went to the front door of the bungalow with a towel around his waist. Becky was sitting on a beach towel, hands open and propped facing up on her knees, her legs crossed. She liked to meditate in this pose, eyes closed, on the terrace of his new place at the McCarren, so she probably didn't see the creepy-looking dude walking up the beach. He was stumbling in the surf, and his shirt was ripped. He stopped and swayed on his feet, and then looked to be making a beeline toward Becky. His hair looked dirty, wild.

Dan's body went prickly; he had to do something, and fast. And he did not want to go out onto that beach. But he had to get Becky out of harm's way. He looked around the room, and items registered in his mind—bug spray, sunscreen, water, Belize guidebook, Becky's dress.

"Becky!" he yelled through the screen door. "I got sunscreen on your dress!"

Her head started to shake, and she got up, picked up her beach towel, and shook it out, then stormed up toward the cabana. "How could you possibly? I hung it up!"

He held the door open for her, and she stepped into the bungalow. Her dress was hanging right there on the wardrobe door, completely fine. She turned and huffed. "What the frak, Dan?"

"That guy. On the beach." He went to the front door and pointed, and Becky followed the line of his finger. "I thought he was about to start bugging you."

"Well, I appreciate the effort, I guess." Becky moved away from the door.

"I can't believe this," Dan said as Becky bent into a stretch. Why couldn't the damn rumble have started before he'd showered? He said, "I have to go in there again."

How a town could have only one internet café—and how they could let it burn down—was beyond comprehension. How did a town like this survive? And the drugstore situation was even more pathetic. You'd be out of business pretty fast if you ran a business like that back home.

Poor Becky. Abby really hoped she wasn't pregnant because if she had the baby she'd be stuck with Dan as the father for the rest of her life, and her chances of finding somebody else to marry would drop dramatically. And even if she didn't keep the baby, she'd have to live with that for the rest of her life. *Noh matta wat!* Abby shoved a pillow from her bed under her

258

T-shirt and imagined herself pregnant with Billy's child. That would sure cause a little soap opera action in her life. Like if they hooked up on this trip and then Abby went home to San Francisco and realized she was knocked up. People would sure stop talking about Chelsea Lambert's Sweet Sixteen then.

But scratch that. No way. Abby threw the pillow back onto the bed. She didn't want a baby. She wanted to move to New York and go to design school and go out all the time to cool bars and clubs and restaurants with Billy as her boyfriend. She wanted to bring him home for Thanksgiving and then take him to the homecoming game and make out in the bleachers while wearing all sorts of hip clothes she'd made. More than anything, or most immediately, she wanted that kiss. Now that they were in Placencia, halfway through the trip, it felt like the clock was ticking.

She'd seen Billy walking into one of the other bungalows, farther down the beach, so she grabbed her sketch pad—ripped out the sketch of him, and the one of her with big cartoon breasts—and headed for the door. "I'm gonna go sketch," she said to M and M, who were reading books on the front porch. "Don't go far," Maggie said.

The same creepy guy from the road into town was walking along the shoreline, and Abby almost didn't want to step off the porch, but then she realized, yes, that'll work. She walked down to the shoreline, then down the beach a bit, away from the guy, then back up toward the bungalows. She rapped urgently on Billy's door.

"Coming," he said, then stepped up to the screen door, shirtless and rubbing his eyes.

Abby looked nervously back toward the guy on the beach. "Can I come in? There's a guy following me."

Billy pushed the door out to let her in and seemed to wake up instantly.

"Thanks." Abby stepped into the room. The bed was unmade, Billy's stuff tossed everywhere: flip-flops here, T-shirt there, swimsuit hanging over the back of a chair, Converse All Stars by the door. "Ohmigod." She decided she should ramp it up a little. "I was just looking for a place to sit and sketch, and he was completely freaking me out."

"You shouldn't be out alone." Billy kept watching out the front door, and Abby liked how easily he snapped into the role of her personal protector and hero. "Looks like he's moving on," he said, and turned to the room.

She held up her sketchbook and made a scrunchy face. "Maybe you could give me some pointers?"

"Sure." Billy looked around the room, then crossed it. He reached for a T-shirt on the bed and pulled it over his head. Abby wished he hadn't. Some of the charge of the room seemed to fade.

He gestured toward the table near the window and took a seat. Abby did the same. He said, "You lied to me," as she flipped open to her sketch of his Converse All Stars; thankfully, it actually looked like the sneakers that were sitting right there.

"He really was following me, I swear." She should've acted more scared, breathless.

"Not that. I believe that." He studied the sketch, and Abby studied his hands—so manly and hairy—on the book. "At least I thought I did." He tapped her arm, and she looked up. He said, "You said you were eighteen."

"Oh," Abby said. "That." She looked away.

"Yeah, that."

"The bartender was right there," she protested, and could hear in her voice that she sounded like a child. "I had just ordered a beer, and I didn't want to get in trouble."

Billy wasn't buying it, but that was okay. Abby wanted him to know she had a secret agenda. She wanted him to know she wished she were older for him. It was good that he knew she lied for him.

He adjusted the sketchbook so he could see better. "I don't like being lied to."

She intentionally brushed her arm against his when she said, "I won't do it again," and he seemed to shift farther away in his chair. When it came to this kiss, she might have her work cut out for her.

Alice had expected she'd be sick of everyone by this point in the trip, but as she watched the group trickle in and take seats at the dinner table on the restaurant veranda, she found the opposite to be true. She'd somehow grown fonder of these people—even Minky—as the days wore on. And she'd begun to realize what a disservice she'd done herself these past however many years, eating dinner with nothing but *CSI*s and *Survivor*s for company.

She felt unusually still in her seat, watching the action around her as if it were all being fast-forwarded while she herself moved in slow motion. Her mind seemed to jump from one conversation, about the ankle sprain, and how swimming, thankfully, is recommended as part of the healing process, to another, about the location of bars in New York called The Room, The Other Room, and Another Room—it was like something out of Abbot and Costello. Who's on first?—to still another, about the difference between watercolors and oil paints. It was as if she suddenly had one of those fancy gunlike, sound-seeking contraptions in her head: she could look at anyone at the table and somehow block out everything else but what they were saying.

They'd hit the halfway point of the trip, and it was bittersweet to think it'd soon be over. People always said that you really need two weeks to make a proper vacation, and that felt true. Alice very much didn't want to go home. There'd be mail to deal with, and her mother, and work. And she'd have to mend fences with Mary-Anise. She wondered, then, where the sage old-lady dress was. On a plane? In the back of a postal truck? Or in a sorting facility in some town she'd never heard of? She hoped it beat her home—that Mary-Anise would have a few days to soften after reading Alice's note. That she'd leave a message for Alice so that Alice would know, as soon as she put down her bags and hit the button on the machine, that everything was going to be okay.

It was strange to think that June would have made her decision by then. That she'd be married to Cash but potentially no longer in the band. It seemed fitting, really, to start two grand adventures around the same time, and the prospect of June's actually, seemingly, growing up tickled Alice pink. Now if only she'd get rid of the pink hair! Billy was right. It just didn't work with the dress. But if that's what June needed to do to cling to at least a little bit of her rebelliousness for the time being, so be it. Alice couldn't wait to hear all about the new job, of course, and imagined that June would thrive in ways that the indie rock world had never allowed her to. She saw her married, settled, fulfilled, and no longer needing those aspects of herself that were more in your face, up front. She imagined liking this new version of June a lot more than previous ones.

"You okay, Mom?" June said. "You seem kind of out of it."

"Do I?" Alice said. "Because I feel very much in it."

"I'm not sure I know what that means," June said. She was wearing yet another dress, this one a bold floral pattern.

Alice smiled. "I'm not sure I do either."

The only thing worse than hanging out with Trevor when you weren't feeling 100 percent was hanging out with Trevor when he *knew* you weren't feeling 100 percent. Dan was going to have to try really, *really* hard to act like he'd made a miraculous recovery from his *E. coli* or whatever it was. And also to hide the tension between him and Becky. He couldn't count on Becky to play her part particularly well, so it was going to be a sort of one-man show.

"How's the patient?" Trevor said, coming over to stand behind Dan's chair just as entrees were being served.

"Great." Dan looked at his plate and saw only one thing: food that would have to come out of him eventually. "I took a killer nap, and I'm feeling a ton better."

"Cool." Trevor looked down at Dan—well, he always looked down on Dan literally, but he seemed to be doing it meaningfully, too. "So you're coming snorkeling tomorrow?"

There was no way in hell Dan was going on the all-day snorkeling trip. He said, "Unless I have a relapse, yeah, absolutely."

Trevor smiled and said, "You're such a bullshit artist."

"I am not." Dan's hand went for his beer.

"Look at you. You're pale, and your eyes are bloodshot." Trevor leaned in but didn't lower his voice. "You've been on the crapper all afternoon, haven't you?"

Dan didn't have the strength. He said, "Would you keep your voice down?"

"Everybody here knows you've got the runs, man. Don't sweat it."

"Still," Dan said. "It's a restaurant. People are eating." It was no better than talking about a poopy diaper.

Trevor slapped Dan's back, once, and left his hand there for a few seconds. "Oh, Dan. I'd call you anal-retentive, but obviously that's no longer the correct term."

"Trevor. Please."

"All right, all right." Trevor took the seat that Becky had abandoned—she was going to the bathroom for the tenth time, presumably to see if she'd gotten her period—and leaned forward in excitement. "Hey, man, so I've got the best idea."

"Yeah?" It was hard for Dan to get excited about anything.

"There's this private island that Peggy's Place owns, and you can rent it. Like for a night."

"I'm not following." Dan sipped his beer.

"We should do it! It's not massively expensive." Trevor diverted his eyes and shrugged a shoulder. "You could totally handle it."

Dan's neck jerked his head forward. "*I* could totally handle it?"

"Yeah, like as a wedding gift type thing." Trevor drank from a bottle of Coke, and Dan thought, How quaint. Trevor set the bottle down. "You're not going to be one of those stingy rich guys, are you? Always whipping out the calculator in the restaurant."

"No, of course not." And of course Dan had never made any such scenes in a restaurant, when a check was being split, but had only, over the years, perhaps complained *afterward*, to people who weren't actually present at the dinner, about people who order appetizers and dessert and don't kick in anything extra.

"I just think it'd be awesome." Trevor saw Becky coming back their way and got up. He was his own kind of gentleman. "And maybe it'd make you feel better after all this literal crap you've been through. But whatever, man. If you're not up for it, no biggie."

It was true that Dan needed something to snap him out of his funk. And he was feeling pretty good now, away from the bungalow, beer in hand, rumble-free for close to an hour. Dan got up, too. "You think they'd want that? I mean, they might have other plans."

"They'd flip for it," Trevor said. "June was the one who told me about it."

"How much we talking?" Dan said.

"Couple grand. Not even."

Dan whistled. "That's a hell of a wedding present."

"Come on, man. When else can you get a private island for that little money? And it's available. I asked about it. They'd take us out Thursday noon and bring us back Friday morning before the weekenders arrive. What do you say?"

Dan wanted to say, "I'll think about it." But he knew exactly what would happen next. Trevor would say, "You do that, Dan. Think about it the next time you're on the bowl," or something equally irksome, and then Dan would want to kick himself for not just being, for once in his life, a little spontaneous. So he said, instead, "Let's do it."

Trevor had to come back, since he'd already started to walk away, figuring Dan would be lame. He said, "You're serious."

"I'm serious."

Trevor reached for a knife and clinked it on his Coke bottle. "Dan the Best Man has an announcement to make."

Becky's eyes went wide when Dan looked at her, and Dan sort of shrugged. Maybe she imagined he was going to declare his love for June right there in front of everybody, and for a moment Dan thought that would be one way of doing it. Other faces looked over at him, expectant.

"Well, um, thanks, Trevor." Dan quickly composed his thoughts. He picked up his beer to buy a few extra seconds. "This has been such an amazing week so far, and I just wanted to do my part to make it really memorable. Some of you may know that Peggy's Place here has a private island. So I'd like to invite you all to join me there Thursday afternoon and overnight!"

June got up and stormed over, and Dan wasn't sure if it was a good storm or a bad one. She grabbed his arm and said, "Are you serious?" His eyes grew big.

"Yeah." Dan was thrilled to see her so excited about anything having anything at all to do with him. "I mean. If you want."

"Oh, Dan, that's amazing. Really?" Her hand still clung to his arm as she turned. "Cash, isn't that amazing?"

She grabbed Dan's arm with her other hand now, so both hands were clutching him. "But it's too much." She looked over at Trevor then. "Did Trevor bully you into it? He has that look on his face." She squinted suspiciously at Trevor, then at Dan.

"Trevor? What? No!" Dan was a pretty good actor when he tried.

"Oh, Dan, thanks so much." She kissed him on the cheek. "You're awesome."

Trevor raised his glass and said, "To the private island!" and the table echoed, "The private island!" and then Dan returned to his seat. Everyone settled back into conversations, most of them about the private island, from what Dan could tell, and started to eat their dinner.

"How's yours?" Dan asked Becky after he'd had a few bites of his own meal and decided he must've crapped out his taste buds. She just ate silently, and he said, "What now?"

Becky wiped her mouth with her napkin, then put it back on her lap. "Money can't buy you love, Dan."

"I thought it could be fun for all of us," he said, but he'd been a fool to think so, and now he knew.

M and M and M all came down to the tiki bar after dinner, which put a serious cramp in Abby's style, but she was on her best behavior tonight anyway, so they'd let her go to the private island. They hadn't said they wouldn't, when Dan made his announcement, but she could tell from the looks on their faces that they would rather pluck their eyelashes than spend a night on a private island in Belize.

"So Trevor says you guys are in a band?" The landscapers were at the bar, and had joined the party. Abby was sitting between Billy and Cash.

"Sure are," Cash said. His foot was propped up on an extra chair. "Or I mean, I am. And June. And Joe over there." Joe raised his beer.

"Have we heard of you?" the girl landscaper asked. She was wearing some kind of landscaping company T-shirt and a pair of khaki shorts and looked crazy underdressed compared to all the other girls there. And it was such an obnoxious question. *Have we heard of you?* How were the Starter House supposed to know who had and hadn't heard of them? And if you hadn't heard of them, it only meant you weren't cool enough to have heard, not that they weren't worth hearing about.

"Somehow I doubt it," June said, and·Abby knew what she meant. There was nothing alternative at all about the landscapers from Boston. They probably listened to really boring sensitive-guy rock if they even listened to music at all.

"We're called the Starter House," Cash said.

"Nope. Haven't heard of you," Guy Landscaper said, then turned to Girl Landscaper. "You?"

"Nope."

Abby tried to picture them digging holes and planting shrubs, but it wasn't easy. All they seemed to do was drink and watch football. She'd heard they were here for three months, since business in Boston shut down for the winter, and for a moment landscaper had seemed like a pretty cool job.

"Who do you sound like?" Guy Landscaper asked, which had to be the most annoying question ever. They sounded like they sounded.

"It's kind of hard to say." June said.

"They're awesome," Abby said, and she was determined

that the Starter House be reminded of how famous they really were. "Maybe you've heard their version of that song 'It Ain't Me, Babe.' It was in a commercial?"

"Oh yeah!" Girl Landscaper said. "Cool!"

"Yes, we've finally achieved superstardom in a car commercial," Trevor said. "We might as well break up now."

"But you can't!" Abby protested. She couldn't believe Trevor was just going to roll over and let June ruin everything. Her face turned red.

"Easy, kiddo." Trevor clasped his hands behind his head, leaning back in his chair. "I was only kidding."

"Oh." Abby looked guiltily at June and then back at Trevor, who looked suddenly suspicious. Abby had never actually heard a record scratch and drag off of an LP, but she imagined this was what it was like. The air around them seemed still.

"Uh"—Trevor didn't take his eyes off Abby—"something you want to talk about, Junie?"

"It's nothing definite," June said.

Trevor just looked at her for a second, then he looked at Cash, who didn't look any less guilty than Abby imagined she looked. Trevor said, "Oh, this is priceless," then got up and walked off toward the pool, which glowed aquamarine.

"Trevor! Come on!" June followed him. "Wait!"

Joe followed, too. Abby couldn't believe what she'd done.

"I'm so sorry," she said to Cash. She grabbed his arm. "I didn't mean to."

"It's okay." Cash was watching June and Trevor. "We were going to get the band together tonight. It's really okay." He reached for his crutches, and Abby helped him, then watched him make his way over to the pool. June and Trevor and Joe were talking animatedly, but Abby couldn't make out the words. Until Trevor said, "*About that rock camp for girls?* Gimme a fucking break, June."

Maggie came over and put an arm around Abby, oblivious

as usual, and said, "Time to say your good nights," like Abby was a child being sent up to her room while the parents busted out the obscure liquor bottles and turned up the music. Abby let herself be led away from the bar and back to the cabana.

God, she was such a loser. In her room, she took her sketch pad out and started to draw a new version of her self-portrait. The drawing was comprised entirely of one big mouth. With a foot inside of it.

Alice jerked awake at the tail end of a bang or boom. The air conditioner was running, groaning to clear the thick humidity of the air, but still the thump, the bang, rang out like gunfire. Alice's breath caught and her head pounded, heart attack style. The noise stopped then, and she lay back and waited. The room was darker than dark, and there was only a faint orange glow from her travel alarm clock. It was 3:00 a.m.

Thump! Thump! Like someone trying to hack through a wall, and Alice didn't know whether to run out onto the beach and scream bloody murder or to stay so very still. She thought of her mother and of the burglary at the old house with the pink bathroom. This was long after Alice's grandmother had died, long after Jack had died, too, and Evelyn had been home alone during the break-in. She had slipped into the pink bathroom and hidden in the tub behind a pink shower curtain. Alice could imagine her curled up in the bathtub, trying hard to keep her breath quiet and praying for them to take what they wanted and just leave. The next day, Alice had asked her mother to move in with her, but Evelyn would have none of it. She'd asked for a tour of Renaissance instead.

But there was nothing to steal in Alice's cabana, really, and if you were looking to steal, why not break down the front door?

Just come in, and wag around something vaguely gun-shaped, and Alice would roll over for you easy.

All sorts of rational thoughts fought their way into Alice's brain—it's just the wind, or a maintenance man, or a harmless drunk, and it doesn't even matter what it is because it's so loud that surely other people are hearing it, too, and help is on the way—but the adrenaline was all the more powerful, and when the sound came again, Alice thought her cardiac might arrest.

A weapon. She needed a weapon. The kitchen. A knife.

But was it better to alert whoever/whatever it was that there was someone inside? Would they give up their quest, whatever it was, if she got up and turned on a light? She thought about shouting, "I'm calling the police," but they would know there were no phones. They would have picked their target well. Alice remembered that man she'd seen walking on the beach, stumbling in the surf, hair wild and dirty, and wondered if he'd watched them all that evening, chosen her specifically as his mark. A predator would see someone who was alone, unguarded, unloved.

A long stretch of silence brought no relief, so Alice lay alert in bed, covers to chin, and waited for help, or morning, to come.

*T*hey are a few notes into their set in the back room of a dive bar in the middle of nowhere—or so it seems to them—somewhere on the outskirts of Milan, Italy, because the same famous band that invited the Starter House to play Radio City asked them to play a gig in Venice, too. They have booked their own club tour in advance of that show because the money from the car commercial (the bulk of it, of course, went to Mr. Dylan, but still) gave them an excuse to tour Europe, which they'd all always wanted to do.

They are staying, lest you get any grand notions, at a hotel that leaves much to be desired. This is a strictly low-budget operation, with a strict policy that rooms cost under a hundred euro per night. The beds here in Milan are saggy, the walls dingy, the courtyard onto which their windows face more of an eyesore (and nose sore) than anything. Because of mental and physical exhaustion, they ate a light dinner before the show—which was late—at the closest restaurant to the hotel, a low-rent place called Le Chalet. The food, at least, was Italian, and an Italian patron in the restaurant was pretty sure he knew who the band was, and racked his brain, to his date's supreme annoyance, before concluding that they were the

271

Canadian band Metric. He thought June was sort of staring at him off and on there for a while, and he was right. She does that sometimes, for sport.

They are up there playing instruments borrowed from an Italian band called Spezia—and sounding kind of off—because their own gear was stolen out of their rented van the night before. It doesn't help the overall sound that they're all pissed off—at each other, at no one. Actually, that's not true. June sounds kind of awesome when she's pissed off. Looks it, too. And they're all pissed off at Joe, including Joe, who's pissed off at himself. He may or may not have locked the back door to the rented van.

June is saying "Grazie" after their first song and keeping her eye on a loud group of guys by the bar that might bode trouble because a few nights ago, in Paris, she engaged in a battle of wits with a rowdy group of drunken frogs who kept shouting out things she couldn't understand between songs; she just sensed that the content was sexual, insulting. Then somebody screamed "Fuck Bush," and June said, "If you think we support him, you're a bigger asshole than he is," at which point somebody threw a plastic cup at the stage, and June, to her own mortification, said, "Oh, fuckez vous," before leaving the stage three songs shy of done, apologizing to Joe the Republican on her way past the drum kit. She was warned by the boys over dinner at Le Chalet that she had best keep her mouth shut up on that stage, and she knows they're right: she should not engage. She's not sure she can tell the difference between harmless Italian drunks and harmful ones because when you leave the U.S. of A. all the cultural markers are different, all the T-shirts and caps and haircuts mean different things. She does not know how to curse in Italian any better than she does in French.

She's really tearing it up on that borrowed guitar because if she thinks about the fact that she's never going to see her beloved Rickenbacker again and how stupid she was to have brought it overseas, she'll be really pissed, but she's mostly pissed that the band knows her business. It came to light on this tour's stop in England that Cash's ex-girlfriend got pregnant way back when, right around the time Cash was leaving her for June. June doesn't want to know exact details regarding bedroom overlap—of which she'd been assured there'd been none, a fact she liked to believe, never having seen herself as the home-wrecker type, though really, June, get real. There's no baby to deal with—June feels horrible guilt over the relief she feels about that—since Cara lost the pregnancy before she'd even told Cash it existed, but Cara saw that the band was playing in London, where she now lives, and decided to serve up her grief to Cash on a sort of silver platter and then invite him to brunch because her therapist (she'd seen one back in America, and they were still in touch by phone) said it was a good idea to seek closure. So Cash's past is woo-woo haunting him, and June is feeling spooked, too. She is up there singing with her eyes closed, trying to escape into the music, where there are no ghosts.

Trevor is watching her closely, and while it looks like he's shaking his head to the groove, he's really shaking it because he should've known better than to let Joe take responsibility for the van keys and also to let June into the band that day over the bodega. The ad should've said "no broads," not just "no blondes," though June would've probably strapped on a dildo and turned up anyway. The ad had been written in a moment of weakness, when the boys were all single, horny—dumb, dumber, and dumbest. He's pissed that this bullshit with her and Cash and the Ex and the Baby That Wasn't is a dark cloud over this European tour—which marks his first time ever abroad—and he can't help but feel that there'd be no drama if there weren't a Girl. Then again, his band wouldn't likely be touring Europe—and how amazing is that—if it weren't for June. He hates to admit it, but she now defines the band with her guitar style—he's never met a guitarist who could use a whammy bar like that—and everything else about her. She's at *the forefront of every picture of the band; or the best ones, anyway. The only ones anyone wants to use.*

Joe's up there, trying to make eye contact with Cash or anyone, but it's hard to make eye contact when you're the drummer, and besides, they're all still too pissed at him, or at least that's how it seems. He's thrilled about the fact that he's about to become a father and terrified of how it's going to affect his life in the band. He's especially grateful that Leah isn't the kind of woman who put her foot down and said that he couldn't go on tour and leave her home, six months pregnant. He hopes to God she doesn't have any complications or go into premature labor, because as much as this tour is everything he's ever dreamed of, he also knows he'd never forgive himself if he weren't there to see his daughter born. He's sort of sad on this trip, Joe, having been to Italy the first time when he was in the eighth grade, with his parents, now both dead. He remembers having fettuccine Alfredo in Rome, and touring the Vatican, and taking horrible pictures (horrible because he was fifteen and hadn't quite grown into his face) in the Colosseum, and visiting some lush gardens somewhere outside of Rome, where there were fountains and all sorts of trees he swore he'd never seen in the States. He likes to imagine that his parents are looking down on him now and that, even if they might not like the music he's playing, they'd be proud of him for doing his own thing, going after his dream. He wishes Leah were here in Italy and that the baby would just hurry up and get here, too, so that he'd have a family again.

Cash is up there, singing one of his own songs now—one of two in the set they're playing these days—and wishing June would get over herself just this once. It's not about her. It's about him, and Cara, and the Baby That Wasn't. He knows he should be relieved, and in a way he is. He's really happy to not have a child with Cara. But he's feeling nostalgic for that backpacking trip he and Cara took through Europe when they first started going out, right after she'd moved to the States—how they drank ridiculously cheap beer in the Czech Republic and sunned on a beach in Spain and were so young. Besides, he al-

ways felt bad about how the whole thing went down, and now he feels worse, and if June can't understand that, then she's not the woman he thinks she is.

The crowd is eating it up now—except that rowdy group, which has retreated to a bar elsewhere in the club, and it's just as well—and so the band is starting to relax into itself, into the songs. They are playing "Wonder Woman," a new highlight of the set, and the crowd is throbbing and sweating, and up there onstage, they start to feel themselves becoming a band again. Cash botches a guitar part, and June turns at him, mid-chorus, and he's already looking at her, having botched it on purpose to get her attention, and she knows this instantly and smiles and the look they exchange says it all. It says, We'll get through this. It says, Have brunch with her for all I care, it's the least you can do. It says, We're the Starter House, and we're playing in Italy.

They are in bed that night, all of them—not together, of course—and June curls up behind Cash and says, "I'm sorry," because she knows she was being irrational about things and also because the night ended on such a high note. Even with borrowed gear, they rocked the house. You just don't get crowds like that back in the States. Crowds that actually dance.

Cash says, "I know."

"We'll have babies someday," she says, though the very thought of it all—diapers, spit-up, drool, sippy cups, talking toys, lunch boxes, Sears portraits, homework, bullies, acne—fills her with horror.

Cash says, "I know."

She thinks they're done talking then, because silence follows, and they're so very tired, but then Cash says, "How long do you think we can do this?"

June whispers, "Do what?"

"This." Cash turns and props up on his elbows. In the dark she can only see darker shadows for his eyes. "The band."

June has been asking herself that question lately, or a variation of it at least. And she's afraid of some of the answers she's coming up with. Because yeah, she likes the rush of being onstage—she has ever since the first time she played piano in public, in her fifth-grade class play—but what she really loves is the music, writing the music. *The industry b.s., the touring, the PR, the CW11 she could do without.*

For years the Starter House had felt like what she was meant to do—like breathing, like being with Cash—but lately she's not so sure. But she can't say any of that. Not yet. So she says, "I don't know," and pulls Cash close. "As long as they'll let us?"

Wednesday

If Abby could have turned up for breakfast in some kind of disguise she would have, so as to avoid the band entirely, but since there was no sign of them yet, she was free to be herself and nearly die when Billy—rumpled from sleep, eyes all dreamy—walked into the restaurant alone. He looked around and saw they were the only ones there from their group and came over to where Abby and her family were engaged in their new morning ritual, eating yummy breakfast burritos and fresh fruit and homemade yogurt.

He said, "Morning."

Everyone said, "Morning," back.

Then he said, "Would it be okay if I joined you?" and Abby's stomach somersaulted. "I'm just having a cup of coffee," he added.

The whole thing was so boyfriendly that she almost couldn't stand it.

"Of course," Miller said. "Please. We were just talking about this whole private island scenario."

Billy pulled a fifth chair over to the table. "Well, it should be interesting, to say the least." A waitress came over, and Billy asked for coffee. Minky said, "And I'd like more juice."

"They won't let me go," Abby said. She felt childish then, and wished she weren't here with her parents. She wished, too, that she didn't need anyone's—not her parents' or the government's—permission anymore to do anything at all in life.

Miller explained. "We've decided to take a pass and go on the—what's it called?" He looked at Maggie, and she said, "Monkey River tour."

"The boat leaves from a canal right through the woods across the road," he went on, "so Minky can come with us very easily."

"I've about had it up to here with my own watercolors," Minky said. Her blouse was a shrill floral pattern. "And I'm more interested in monkeys than in Mayans."

Miller said, "Then we're going over to check out Coppola's other place—what's it called?"

Maggie said, "Turtle Inn," and Abby had to wonder whether Miller even knew the name of the place where they were staying.

Miller finished: "For dinner."

Maggie said, "We just don't want anyone feeling like they have to be responsible for Abby."

"I'm sure no one would mind," Billy said, and Abby wanted to stand up and cheer. She wasn't sure June or Cash would vouch for her right now, but if she didn't get to go to the private island, she'd never get to make it up to them, or get that kiss from Billy. She felt suddenly like she was a character in some Jane Austen novel and her suitor had come to ask for her hand. It was all very old-fashioned and Abby felt as dumb about the whole situation as she did sort of excited. Billy added, "And Abby and Becky have really hit it off."

"Yeah," Abby said. "Good point. Talk to Becky if you want to. Because I mean, come on. This is a once-in-a-lifetime opportunity."

"You're seventeen, Abby." Maggie dunked her tea bag around in her tea. "Nothing is a once-in-a-lifetime opportunity yet."

"Well, I understand this is a family issue, and I wouldn't want to interfere." Billy drained his cup. "But if you decide to let Abby go, we'll all keep an eye on her. I give you my word. Now if you'll excuse me, I've got to get ready for the snorkeling tour."

"I'll see you there," Abby said, and Billy said, "Cool."

Billy walked off, and Minky said, "Well, he certainly seems like a nice young man," and Abby wanted to give her a hug. "Now if he could only talk some sense into his sister. Seems to me a *job* would do the girl wonders."

That quickly Abby wanted to smack her upside her white head instead. "I'll bet you've never even listened to the band," she said. "Because if you did, you wouldn't be in such a hurry to have them break up. They're amazing. You just don't get it. None of you do."

"Everyone knows how you feel about the band," Maggie said.

"It's not about how I feel about the band"—shouting underwater for sure—"it's about the fact that they're amazing. Everyone acts like 'Oh, Cash and June and their little band.' You have no idea how many people there are out there who worship them. It's like you're too close to it, or something. And too old."

"Watch it," Maggie said.

"You'll never get it." Abby's self-portrait now would have steam coming out of her ears. "And you're the same with me. 'Your little fashion designs.' And 'Oh, Abby likes to sew, isn't that cute?' I'm applying to fashion design schools in New York. What do you think of that?"

Maggie's tea bag was wrapped around her spoon a few inches above her mug and froze there. She said, "I think you might want to watch your tone if you want to cling to what little hope remains that we'll let you go to that island."

Minky said, "They never brought my juice."

Dan woke up to Becky coming through the door. It slammed behind her, and she took a box out of a brown bag and then opened it. An instructions booklet fell out, and she went into the bathroom.

"Are you sure you want to do this?" Dan asked from the bed.

"What kind of dumb question is that, Dan?"

He got up and sat at the table and read the instructions and tried to distract himself from the sound of Becky's pee. He said, "It says here to wait a week after your period's late for best results."

"I know, Dan." Contempt wafted his way. "But it might know that it's positive and if it does, I want to know." Only Becky would talk about a pregnancy test like it was some kind of oracle. "If I still don't get it by the time I get home, so help me God, I'll take another one."

Dan looked at the box then, which was dusty, so he blew on it, then regretted that and coughed. He read the back of the box, for the shortened version of the directions. Three minutes and they'd know. He called out, "Tell me when to start timing."

"I'm already timing," Becky said. "One more minute."

So Dan read the bit about how to read the results again, though you'd have to be an idiot not to know how to read them. Then he looked to see what other handy info made the cut and got put right there on the box. That's when Dan saw the expiration date, stamped onto the box's white end flap:

FEB06. "Uh, Becky?" He got up and walked toward the bathroom. "We might have a problem."

She opened the door and said, "Negative," and he held up the box and said, "Expired."

She whipped it out of his hands. "You're fraking kidding me."

"No, look. Didn't you check?" He sat on the bed. It had long been Dan's impression that only women did stupid stuff like buy expired items, or track paint through their apartments, or bounce checks.

"It was the only one they had! And I didn't even know they could expire." She went for the instruction booklet on the table. "What does that even mean?"

"How am I supposed to know?"

There was no point in arguing. They both knew it. Dan said, "I'm sorry that you're dealing with this."

"Not as sorry as you are that you're dealing with it."

"Can we please, please try to be at least a little nice to each other?" Dan rubbed his eyes, elbows on his knees. "'Cause honestly, I can't handle it."

"Okay." Becky turned the instruction leaflet over. "I'll try." She started to read with interest, then she put her face in her hands and started to cry. Dan went over and read from the leaflet: "Expired tests can give unreliable false readings."

"Mom! You have to get out here!" Alice stirred in bed at the sound of June's voice. "There's a huge iguana on your roof."

"Oh, for the love of God!" Alice said. She got up and pulled on her robe, then went out onto the porch. The day was hot, and June was standing on the beach, looking up at the roof. Her black sunglasses covered half her face. "It's huge!"

Alice went right to June and gave her a deep hug.

"What's gotten into you?" June said, and Alice pulled out of the hug and turned to look up at the iguana, the source of all of last night's woes. It was army green and four feet long and its head perked up, on alert.

Alice stood with an arm linked through her daughter's. June's skin was soft and warm. "I've never been so happy to see an iguana in my life."

June put the back of her hand to her mother's forehead. "Are you feeling all right?"

"I didn't know what it was." Alice was still studying last night's menace. "It must've been stomping around on the roof, or getting comfortable, in the middle of the night. I thought someone was coming to kill me."

"Oh God, Mom, no. I'm so sorry."

"It's not your fault. But, well, you know. Strange place. Middle of the night. I didn't know."

"Well, we both got a proper Belizean welcome from the local wildlife then."

Alice just looked at June, confused.

June adjusted her sunglasses. "Promise you won't freak."

"I'm not sure I can, no."

June reached up again and took her sunglasses off. Her left eye was swollen shut, purple and pink and blue.

"Oh God. June!" Alice's hands went to her daughter's face, tilted it so she could see the bite—was it a bite?—better.

"Cash found the damn thing this morning." She held two fingers out about three inches apart. "Spider this big. He trapped it and took it down to the front desk. They said it's not poisonous or anything. But boy does it hurt."

"I can imagine."

"And before you ask, I put stuff on it. And they recommended another remedy I can buy in town. But I don't really have time to go to town. The snorkeling boat leaves in half an hour."

"I'll go." An image of that NURSES DO IT WITH INTENSIVE CARE mug flashed through Alice's mind. "I mean, June, the wedding's only . . ."

"I know." June turned the bite away from her mother. "We'll have to face this way in all the pictures. Or I'll wear my sunglasses." She put the shades back on. "You'll be okay? In town?"

"I'll be fine."

"It's probably just a local kind of cortisone, but it's worth a shot." June handed Alice a piece of paper with the name scrawled on it. "Thanks."

"Are you all right?" Alice asked. "I mean, otherwise."

June looked up and down the beach. "Let's go inside for a minute."

Alice stepped in the foot bath, then onto the stoop, and June did the same. Inside, they sat at the kitchen table. Alice's wet feet felt cold, alive.

"Well, you were right about the loose lips and the ships." June reached out and felt a flower in a vase, checking, Alice could only assume, to see if it was real. It was. "Abby sort of let the cat out of the bag—this was after you called it a night. So I told Trevor and Joe everything last night. About the job. We were up late talking. I'm just tired."

"Any closer to a decision?" Alice's mind had already been made up.

"I don't know." June slid down in the chair, hands folded in her lap and neck tilted back over the chair's edge. "It feels like I'm cutting off my arm or something. I mean, all of my friends, everyone I know, except for, well, Lydia, is in the band or related to the band somehow. I'll be a leper." June got up and looked out the window. "But at the same time, I'm already hearing music in my head. I'm more fired up about writing cool music for this show than I've been about the band in ages. And I don't know, I keep thinking that if there had been a show like that on when I was younger, I would've really loved it, and benefited from it."

"Well, you did all right. You went up against Mr. Sagapo and Scott Haslett on your own."

June smiled, and Alice got up to straighten the bedsheets out at least a little bit. Her tumultuous sleep had made a real mess of them. "And you make friends wherever you go, June. You get that from your father, so you shouldn't worry about *that*."

"I know, I know."

Alice untwisted a sheet. "He would be so thrilled that you were composing."

"Well, it's not exactly *composing*, and God, Mom. Don't lay *that* on me, too." June flicked a bug off the window screen. "Trust me, it's bad enough already."

Abby wasn't particularly interested in bumping noses with eels or sharks, but the coral reefs were supposed to be really cool. Mostly she was hoping for an opportunity to apologize again to Trevor and to June for last night's foot in mouth. Everyone was pretty quiet when they met up, though, and Abby wasn't sure if people were avoiding her or not; it was hard to make eye contact with everyone wearing sunglasses.

The whole trying-on of fins and snorkels was pretty gross, but her snorkel smelled only like rubber and salt, so that was really the best you could hope for. Nobody seemed to be trying their masks on, so Abby didn't either. She just followed along as a guide—tall, lean, and dark-skinned—led them down a wooded path across the street, where a red, white, and blue boat, half of it covered with a frayed awning, awaited them. Billy was the first one down the path behind the guide, and he turned and raised an eyebrow. Sure, the paint was chipping, but it had to be seaworthy, right?

The guide started helping them all aboard. First Billy, then Abby, who sat across from him, so as not to be too obvious, then Joe, then June. When he got a load of Cash and his crutches, he said something like "You went bliggity blam boom boff!" and June said, "What's that mean?" and he said, "What you think it means!" Then Trevor stepped up.

"You follow baseball, man?" he asked the guide, who had just put on a blue and orange cap with an overlapping N and Y; Abby wasn't sure if it was the Yankees or the Mets. The boat rocked hard as Trevor's first foot came aboard, and Abby wondered for the first time about the boat's weight capacity.

"You sit in the middle, mon," the guide said, then he tipped his hat and said, "World Series this year. Put money on it."

Trevor said, "All this sun must be going to your head." And the guide just smiled. He was wearing sunglasses, and Abby wanted very much to see his eyes, was hoping they were the sea green she imagined they were.

The guide revved the boat's engine, and soon they were pulling out and traveling down a long canal dotted with resorts, all of them like something out of a movie. Then before long, they were out on open water, moving too fast—it was too loud—to talk. The water's odd color reminded Abby of a jade necklace she had at home, one of the few relics of life with her father that she had.

She should've kept her mouth shut about fashion school at breakfast, but M and M had taken it in stride. Her job now, or so they had said, was to prove she was serious about her fashion designs and also—and today's snorkeling trip was going to be the first big test—that she was mature enough that she could go away to college and live on her own. That last bit really cracked Abby up. Because it didn't seem like most people who went away to college and went down to spring break booze-and-boob fests in Florida and Mexico and wherever else were very mature. She was being held to a ridiculously high standard. But she thought she had it in her to pass their test. There would be no more black bikini, for starters. At least not until she got to the private island, if she even did. And she wouldn't throw any more hissy fits about the Starter House, at least not in front of M and M. She'd be the picture of politeness with regard to the other, elderly M. Just let Minky try to say something that would get a rise out of her. Couldn't be done. This was the new and improved Abby—Abby 2.0—with new maturity standards and grown-up plug-ins.

June took off her sunglasses to wipe something from them, and Abby screamed, "Your eye!"

June shouted, "Spider!" and put her sunglasses back on and smiled a smile that made Abby admire her big-time. Because if Abby had a huge swollen eye two days before her wedding, she'd be crying for sure. It'd be a miracle if June could get a snorkel mask over that thing.

The boat slowed after another ten minutes or so, near a small island, and the guide dropped anchor. "We'll start here," he said. "You can swim around this end of the island"—he pointed— "and come ashore on the other side. I'll meet you there."

Abby had never been snorkeling before, but she was a strong swimmer and hadn't been too worried about it—until now. She could do jackknives and cannonballs and forward flips. She'd taken surfing classes once in California, and she'd always been comfortable in the water. But swimming around an island? Was this guy out of his tree? The water was really, really choppy.

"And whatever you do, don't touch the coral," the guide said. "Coral is an animal, and if you touch it, you kill it."

Yeah, so no pressure. Abby jumped off the side of the boat after Joe and Cash did—nobody else seemed fazed by the idea of swimming around the island—and struggled to tread water while she put her mask on. Note to self: should've done that first. Her feet, with fins on them, felt like they weren't moving fast enough to keep her head afloat, and yet they did. Her thighs ached already. She breathed through the mask, and it seemed to work, so she dunked her face in the water and took a breath and got water in her mouth and coughed.

"You okay?" Billy said. He was just about to jump in.

"Yeah." She was working harder now to tread. "I just can't get it to seal."

The boat was rocking on chunky waves, and Abby tried to move away, afraid of getting hit. This wasn't like being in a pool, or swimming off the ocean's shore, at all.

"You got it?" June said from the boat. She was wearing a cool art-deco-patterned bikini with a bandeau top and boy trunks, and Abby felt especially dull by comparison in the Speedo. "You have to really close your lips around it."

Trevor, still on the boat, said something Abby couldn't hear, and June snapped, "Trevor! Don't even."

Billy said, "Yeah, come on, man. Grow up," then jumped.

Abby tried the mouthpiece again, and this time she caught air but she knew she was breathing too fast, had to slow down. At least the water appeared calmer with your face underneath, but she could still feel herself being pushed around, water swishing near her ears. Below, everything looked gray; she'd been expecting tons of color and felt maybe this whole snorkeling thing was overrated. She flapped her feet slowly and then looked up quickly and realized she was drifting faster than she was heading in the right direction. In fact, she was about to run aground into a high coral reef. She tried to back up but couldn't and turned instead, brushing a fin against coral, she was sure of it. Surfacing again, she found that the water was so choppy that she could only see people's heads every few seconds. Her breathing was hard. "I can't do it," she called out, but no one reacted. "Help!" she finally yelled.

"Swim this way," the guide yelled from the boat, and she headed for him, her breathing fast and shallow. For ages it didn't seem like the boat was getting any closer—she could see the guide giving a thumbs-up to the others, waving them on—and then she was right there, about to get hit and go under. There was no ladder.

"Put your foot there, on the engine," he said. "Now give me your hand."

He pulled her up, and the shock of it—and the banging of her leg against the boat, which gave her a blue splinter on her thigh—triggered her tears. "Oh my God," she said. "Oh my God."

"Is she okay?" she heard Cash yell, and the guide said, "Yeah, mon."

"It's"—well, hard to breathe, but also—"too choppy."

The tears were leaking, and Abby stopped whipping them away since she was covered in salt water anyway, so what was the point? God, she was glad to be on the boat again. She kicked off her fins and bent her leg so she could pick out the splinter in her thigh. She tasted salt water, or tears, she wasn't sure which, and as she watched the others make their way around the reef and off toward the end of the island, she felt sad, too, because she was missing out on all this cool stuff. Everyone else was doing it, so what was her problem? Why was she so scared? Why had she totally wigged out? Was she just destined to miss out on *everything?*

The guide started up the boat then and cruised around to the other side of the island, where there was an actual beach. There were people snorkeling right there off the shore—where the water was calm as a puddle—and Abby felt like yelling at the guide, "Why couldn't we have started here?" She grabbed her bag and put her swim shoes on and struggled to shore over rocks that hurt like mo-fos. Onshore, she pulled a towel from her bag, spread it out, lay down, and thought, Thank freakin'

God. The sun felt amazing, and Abby figured she'd just have to accept that she wasn't cut out for snorkeling. She would refuse to admit to anyone that she cared.

"What happened?" June said when she came ashore with the others. Billy helped Cash across the rocks, which was no easy task, then they all scattered around the beach, laying out towels.

"I don't know. I guess I freaked out."

"Well, yeah. It's ridiculously choppy over there. Unlike here, which looks like the perfect spot to learn. Come on, I'll show you." June started heading out toward the water again.

"No, it's okay." Abby just sat still. "I don't want to bother you."

"No bother. Come on."

Abby didn't think she could win an argument with June, so they made their way back out to the boat, and leaned in to get their fins and snorkel gear.

"I feel really bad about Cash's ankle." Abby put her first fin on and figured she might as well apologize chronologically for everything she felt bad for. "I mean, if I hadn't made such a big deal of going ziplining, then it—"

"Hey!" June already had both her fins on. "Quit it."

"And I'm really sorry about last night, too. Me and my big mouth."

"Abby." June fake-strangled her. "If we'd never made everyone come to Belize, you would have never had a chance to go ziplining or to tell Trevor anything. And you didn't exactly put the papaya in Cash's hands."

That sounded funny, and Abby laughed.

"And swimming is supposed to be good for preventing stiffness, so it's really no big deal." June looked more serious then, her eyes sharper. She dipped her mask in the water, then spit in it and rubbed the saliva around. "It was good for us, anyway. Helped us to put things in perspective."

289

"Yeah?" Abby liked the sound of that a lot. She did the spitting thing, even though it grossed her out. "So, like, you're not quitting?"

June breathed out hard and shook her head. "It means the world to me that the band means so much to you. Or that the music does. And we're always going to be making music, Abby." They were walking out a bit—beyond the edge of the tourist boats—where the water was maybe waist high. "It just might not have the name the Starter House, and if we're smart we won't let anybody use it in a car commercial."

Abby didn't know what to say. She'd always thought it was cool that the song was in a car commercial, but she could see how maybe the Starter House would regret it. It wasn't even their song.

"Now, come on," June said. "Let's try this again."

And so June walked her through it. And it turned out Abby's mouthpiece kind of sucked, because when she used the one June had been using, she was able to breathe easily, and it was so peaceful, the sound of the air, even though it reminded her of life support machines, with a sort of whir and then a suck. She swam straight out away from the shore, where the water got deeper, and there were some fish here and there, and then all of a sudden, a whole school exploded in front of her, turning just the right way so that their colors—yellow and black—popped, and then just as fast she was right there in the middle of them, and they were tickling her legs and her arms, and Abby had to stifle a laugh, and then she stopped kicking and just floated there and watched as they fluttered and twisted and then, like an army called to attention, swam away. In the clearing they left behind was a starfish—all shimmering orange and gold with the sun playing off its skin, if it was even called skin. Abby's own shadow, stretched long and thin by the angle of the sun, danced around, while tiny waves on the surface created a meshlike pattern of white lines—they looked electrified—on the sand below. She stretched to touch the starfish, but it was just out of reach.

Alice asked about the walk into town at the front desk and was told it was maybe fifteen minutes, did she want to rent a bike? She most definitely didn't, so she set out on foot—sticking to the edge of the road as there were no sidewalks—and found herself soon passing the manicured lawns and imposing walls of what must've been Coppola's second Belizean resort. Sure enough, the sign read TURTLE INN, so she hurried past, though really, she would just have to lie again. She'd never been snorkeling with her husband before, so why start now!

It already seemed like a long time ago, the butterfly farm, and now, from what felt like a distance, she wondered what had gotten into her in the Pine Ridge. Lying about her husband still being alive. That was crazy! Were the mountains of the Pine Ridge high enough that she could blame altitude sickness for her break with reason? Had she been oxygen-deprived?

Alice waved to passengers in cars that passed, but only if they waved first, which they did maybe half the time. She walked by a few large pink-faced buildings advertising to potential retirees or snowbirds, and a row of lots with FOR SALE signs. The road took a turn then, and when it wound around, Alice could see a man sort of staggering down the road toward her. He was still a good twenty yards away, but Alice slowed and thought about turning around. That might call more attention to her, though, and she certainly didn't want to do that. So she walked on and studied his figure, which was definitely not walking a straight line. He had dark skin and wore shorts with ragged edges. Alice couldn't tell from this distance, but he looked like he might be barefoot. She felt her pulse quicken, could actually feel and hear her heartbeat in her ear. She turned to look over her shoulder, hoping for a taxi, a car, someone on a bike, anything, but the road behind her was empty.

He was almost upon her now, and she had to decide whether to get a firmer grip on her bag and how to do so without being conspicuous, whether to make eye contact. This was an empty stretch of road, with only a field on the left where some kids were kicking a soccer ball around. They came closer to the gate and she imagined they were trying to get a better view of some local ax murderer attacking a tourist. She'd never felt more foolish in her clothes in her life (except maybe at a Starter House concert). She'd worn a hat, since the sun was so strong down here, and now it seemed like a flashing neon sign that read TERRIFIED AMERICAN.

She looked at his face—he was too close to ignore—and their eyes locked. His were unfocused, and Alice thought she noticed a sort of fog over one of his eyes, like something had burst, or was infected. She held her breath, felt her abdominal muscles tense, and then the moment was gone and he was past her. She didn't turn around to confirm that he was still going about his business and not doubling back to jump her, but she did pick up her pace. She was walking now past houses that looked like the slums she'd seen in photos, and she couldn't believe her folly. A bike would have been well worth it, a cab even more so—or hell, screw it and let June's bite heal on its own. Two men passed her this time and didn't seem to pay her any mind, and then she saw a sign for a restaurant she'd read about in her guidebook and followed it. It pointed off the road, down a sort of sandy path, and then there was another sign that pointed down a more established path, this one blessedly full of shops. She ducked into the open-air restaurant, which was technically right on the beach but set back from the sea a bit. There were loads of college types eating from big plates of food. Alice went straight for the bathroom, where a fly buzzed around. She locked the door and put the bowl cover down and sat. She swatted at the fly a few times and took a series of deep breaths, shaking off the fear.

When she came out, she didn't quite know what to do with herself. A waitress was taking one table's order in the patio area and there was no one behind the bar—not that she would've ordered a drink anyway. Should she ask for a table and sit? Order something even though she wasn't hungry?

"Everything okay?"

Alice turned and saw a man seated at a table give a little wave. He was middle-aged and fit and tan and seemed somehow American, though Alice wondered if she only thought that because he was white. A black-and-white chessboard sat pieceless next to his beer. He held an open book.

"Oh." Alice straightened her top. "Fine."

"You seem a bit"—he put his book down, spread-eagled—"lost."

"No, not lost. Flustered, maybe?" Alice had taken her hat off in the bathroom and now ran a finger through her hair; she couldn't imagine how awful she must look. "The walk was, well . . . I should've taken a taxi."

"Ah!" He nodded his head. "Turtle Inn?"

"No, Peggy's Place."

"Really?" He looked her up and down blatantly, then started to get up. "Well, I was about to have a beer. And you look like you could use one. Care to join me?"

Alice thought for a second she should be offended, but he was probably right. "Sure."

He came to her and said, "I'm Kurt," and she said, "Alice," then he went behind the bar, reached down, and pulled up two bottles of Belikin. When he went back to the table and took his seat, Alice took the seat opposite, hung her bag on its back, and took up her beer. That first sip was pure relief.

"You're sure you're okay?" he asked with a furrowed brow. He had short silver hair and brown eyes and wore a brown leather band around his wrist. Alice had never before known a man who wore a bracelet. She put him at about fifty-five or sixty.

"It's silly, really." Alice shook her head. "I passed someone on the road, someone I'd call a suspicious character, but I'm probably just imagining things. I didn't get much sleep last night."

Kurt raised his eyebrows flirtatiously, and she said, "Oh no. Nothing like that." The heat of her face meant she was surely blushing, and she thought maybe this was a bad idea.

"Well, we have our share of suspicious characters." Kurt's gaze was honest, steady. "And if he was on the main road, where he almost always is, that's probably the guy people call Crazy Eddie."

"You're teasing me."

"Maybe a little."

Alice studied her surroundings again now, more at peace. There were maybe ten tables—all of them occupied—and there was music, some kind of jazz, piped in. Two young girls around Abby's age had jewelry set up on a table near the path that led to the beach. They had flat foreheads and black-black hair and looked like they could have lived at Caracol in a long-ago century. "Do you own this place?"

"I do." Kurt seemed to nod approval at himself. "Going on ten years."

"Did you grow up here?"

He shook his head and smiled. "Well, I was born in California. And there's a lot of people between there and here who would tell you we're still waiting on the growing-up part." He looked down and tapped a finger on his beer bottle, seemingly embarrassed at having shared too much. He looked up again then. "So what brings you to Belize, Alice?" He eased back into his chair now, seeming more comfortable now that he'd gotten that confession out of the way. "If you forgive my saying it, you don't seem the type."

"Why *is* that?" Alice asked.

Kurt laughed, and Alice laughed, too.

"I'm serious." She took a sip of her beer. "What is it about me? Why am I not the type?"

Kurt stroked his chin, faux contemplatively. "You seem a bit refined, really, a little soft. I take it from your reaction to the walk into town that you're not an adventurous traveler in general."

Alice shook her head and thought, You got that right. She said, "My daughter's getting married here."

"Oh, one of those."

"I guess!" She wasn't sure what he meant.

"We generally get two kinds." He picked the book up, closed it, and put it down, front cover down, off to the side. Alice didn't recognize the cover art. "Real liberal earthy crunchy hipster types or blond sorority girls who've hardly traveled anywhere and have absolutely no idea what to expect when they get here and are usually horrified by what they find."

"She's the first."

"Re-he-eally." He assessed her again. "Who threw the apple then?"

"Her father, I suppose." It felt strange to refer to Jack that way. "She's over at his tree." She felt her ring on her finger, wondered if Kurt had even noticed it. "He passed away. Twelve years ago now."

He said, "Sorry to hear that," and sounded like he meant it, and Alice thought he was exactly the kind of character Jack would've gotten a kick out of meeting. But while she was usually all too happy to talk about her late husband, he was, for some reason, the last person she wanted to talk about now. Death was a hard act to follow, though.

They sat in silence for a moment, both watching the restaurant's guests or nothing at all. Alice imagined Kurt thinking, Great, a goddamn widow. What a great way to ruin an afternoon. Then he tilted his head down toward the board. "You play?"

Alice shook her head—"Afraid not"—and sensed their interaction coming to an end.

He flipped the board over to reveal a red-and-black side. "How about now?"

Alice smiled surprise. Checkers she could handle.

Dan sat on a ledge in the pool's shallow end and winced as another cramp sliced through his stomach. He'd made it this far—a solid two-minute walk from his cabana and toilet, after just one unpleasant b.m. this morning, post–pregnancy test—so it was definitely progress, but he wished the cramping would stop. It felt like an ornery crab had taken up residence in his gut. Every once in a while it did its sideways shimmy with its claws dug into the walls of Dan's organs.

He'd gone to the office earlier and arranged for the private island, with the final head count still to be decided, and pushed away that underlying feeling of being had. Trevor had effectively manipulated him into forking over the cash, but on the other hand, what good was a ton of money if you didn't occasionally indulge in, well, indulgence? And it would be a trip, for sure. Dan had actually applied to *Survivor* once—made the video, the whole kit and caboodle—and had had fantasies for weeks about getting accepted and using his cunning to win the million-dollar prize. But when he'd received his notice of rejection, he was sort of relieved. He actually tended to not like most people he met and thought one of the great joys of single, self-employed life in your thirties was the fact that you mostly didn't have to be around people you didn't like. You weren't stuck sitting next to obnoxious know-it-alls in college classes anymore. You weren't stuck swapping niceties with your kids' friends' parents. You didn't have to chat about TV by the watercooler. There were some annoying people on the co-op board of the McCarren, for sure, people who clearly had nothing better to do, but Dan hardly had to deal with them at all. So yeah, being stuck on an island with a bunch of people he'd probably hate would be torture.

"How are you holding up?" Becky had just done a lap and was breathing heavily but looking very much exhilarated. Dan checked his heart, but nope, still not in love with her.

"Just happy to be outside," he said, and she grabbed on to his knees, her body extended out behind her, her chin submerged in water. It was strange to be touched by her, and she must've realized this, too, that she'd latched on to him out of habit. And of course they were trying to be nice to each other, so she didn't immediately pull away. He had a thought about a night not so long ago, in his new kitchen with granite countertops in the McCarren, and of having sex with Becky's ass perched on the middle island—right after eating Thai takeout. It felt like that must have been somebody else.

He could barely stand to meet her eyes, he was feeling so sorry for himself, so conflicted about his life. He shifted his legs at a cramp, and Becky's hands slipped. She dropped underwater for a second and came back up, sputtering a bit and wiping water from her eyes.

"Thanks a lot," she said. "I got water up my nose."

"Sorry," Dan said. "Cramp."

Becky went to take another turn around the small pool, and Dan just watched as a woman wrangled three small children over to a nearby shower. She was Belizean, so were the kiddies, and she shoved them under the nozzle to get the sand from the beach off them. He wondered if they were guests at the hotel, or if she maybe worked there. If it was neither, he was about to start getting mad because the children were screaming and screeching, not to mention staring at him, and more so at Becky, whose skin was white enough to scare a ghost. He tried to picture himself and Becky with kids. Because a baby was one thing, kids were another, with their endless homework and annoying questions. He just couldn't see it.

"So I'm curious." Becky was upon him again, and Dan suddenly wished she'd gone snorkeling, hadn't been kind enough to martyr herself to him. Or maybe she just wanted to be close to a bathroom, so she could check for her period every five minutes. "What was your plan, anyway? With the autograph?" She stood up in the shallow end—about four feet deep—and walked over to sit on the submerged ledge beside Dan.

"I don't know, Becky," he said, as the crab opened a claw and closed it again, shimmied a little.

"Yes you do," Becky said. "Were you going to give it to her and proclaim your love?"

It felt like the crab was doing a very slow cartwheel. "Something like that."

"How do you even know it's real?"

"It feels real." Whenever he saw June, it felt more real than ever.

"No, Dan." She really did have the contempt thing down. "The autograph. How do you know it's even really hers? June Carter's?"

"Becky"—Dan started to make his way toward the pool exit—"I've spent the better part of the last forty-eight hours on the crapper with liquid shit coming out of my ass. You'll forgive me if I don't feel like talking about this right now."

"So much for being nice to each other." Becky rose, turned, took a deep breath, and then squatted into the water, pushing off with her feet and traveling the length of the pool without coming up for air. She climbed out of the pool's far end, grabbed her towel and her sudoku book with a pen clipped to it, and went over to sit on the beach. A crab's claw clutched Dan's lung.

After lunch on the little island, where there'd been some excitement over a shark sighting that Abby had chosen not to participate in—people were really crazy about animals—the boat went back out to another snorkeling spot, and everyone started to unload, jumping in, fins on. "What do you want to do, Abs?" Cash said.

There was no way in hell she was getting in the water again. Even though everyone said the shark was tiny, harmless, barely even a shark, snorkeling was clearly not Abby's thing. "I'll stay here."

"Are you sure?" Cash sounded sad. "I can stay right by you if you want to try again."

"No, I'm good." Abby pulled *Heart of Darkness* out. "I'll just hang out here."

Noting the title of the book, Cash said, "Wow. You must've *really* been freaked."

Abby said, "Yeah," and he patted her head then dove in with the others.

It was weird to be alone on the boat with the guide. He'd basically told them his life story while he carved up chicken and pineapples and bread and the other stuff they had for lunch, and she felt bad that she'd forgotten his name, if she'd even been told it, and she wasn't sure she had. He and his sister had run away from his parents' house to his grandmother's when he was little, and their grandmother had raised them from that day—had never let their father see them again. He'd only been like seven or eight, but he'd planned and planned

299

for his escape with his little sister from a father who beat them. Abby sort of wanted to pat him on the back but also was suspicious. Was his story even for real? 'Cause it sounded kind of crazy. Crazy things happen in life, for sure—like when those two girls in the news were in a car crash and one survived but was really mangled and then, when she woke from a coma, she told them she wasn't the girl they thought she was but the other one. They'd "buried" the wrong girl. That was about the craziest story that Abby had ever heard—she'd gotten chills because that was so seriously f'ed up. But what if this guy was just making it up? Hoping for better tips. Miller and Maggie had given her a twenty to tip the guy, if other people were tipping, and she felt weird about that, too. She sort of wanted to tell him that she'd had an asshole father, too, but all he'd done was cheat on her mom, which didn't really compare to beating your kids.

After lunch, everybody had just hung out and read on the beach, but Abby hadn't felt like reading—she couldn't get through even a page of *Heart of Darkness* without losing her sense of what was going on—so she'd plopped down next to Billy, who was reading a James Bond book, and tried to lie quietly, appreciating the sun's prickle. "I don't feel like reading," she'd finally said.

"So don't," Billy said, not taking his eyes off his book.

She had found a hair on his leg and tugged it. "Pay attention to me."

"Ow." He'd swatted her hand and smiled, and Abby had thought for sure she was making progress. Weakening his resolve—even in the Speedo. The kiss was inevitable. He just didn't know it yet.

Without warning, the guide dove into the water, leaving Abby alone on the boat. He disappeared under the surface, and Abby tried to count heads in the water. Cash. June. Billy. Trevor. Joe. All visibly accounted for. But what if something happened to one of them like right this second, and they needed to radio for help? Where the hell had the guide guy gone? He was underwater for longer than Abby had thought possible and, well, what if something happened to *him*? The Crocodile Hunter dude was proof that just because you were an expert in something didn't mean you were immune.

Looking around, Abby tried to count heads again, but they were farther away this time. Cash and June were almost out of sight, rounding the curve of this other little island. The guide surfaced then, threw a lobster onto the boat, and then dove again. Abby could hear it scurrying around, and she yelped. No one heard. Or if they did, they didn't do anything about it.

Again he was gone, and Abby looked around at blue seas and bursts of green and a massive sky and tried to think of a time in her life when she'd been this alone. She wished there were a mirror on the boat so she could sketch herself now: sitting on a wooden bench, red paint cracking under her legs, with nothing but ocean and sky behind her, the wind whipping her hair around, drawing pieces into her face. There would be white puffy clouds behind her and maybe an angry lobster reflected in her eyes, and the sun would make her skin seem to glow, even in charcoal strokes.

The guide surfaced and tossed another lobster onto the boat, and Abby flinched. He was on board in a few seconds and trying to contain the red beasts. "That's dinner for my family," he said, and Abby nodded. She said, "That really sucks about your dad."

Kurt had just opened a second beer and one for Alice, too. Her first one had gotten warm and she'd stopped drinking it, so Kurt had cleared it and replaced it with a cold one without asking. In the hour they'd been playing checkers, the sun had risen high, and even in the shade of the restaurant, it was hot.

"So are you having fun?" Kurt asked. "In Belize?"

"I'm not sure." Alice made a double jump, took two of Kurt's black pieces. She'd chosen red for herself, trying to get used to it as a color she associated with. "Sometimes, yeah. Maybe. I think."

He looked at the board, but his face showed confusion Alice knew wasn't over checkers.

She clarified. "I've always heard the mother-of-the-bride role is a tortured one, and I'm finding it to be true. I don't even really have anything to wear."

"Well, you should probably pick up *something*"—this man was a serious flirt—"lest you make a scene."

"Oh, I've got three dresses with me. Well, two now." He looked up, and Alice waved a hand. "Long story. But I don't want to wear any of them. I thought there'd be more, I don't know, shopping opportunities this week."

"What kind of dress we talking here?"

Alice tried to find words to describe it but couldn't. "I just know that I'd know it if I saw it."

A younger man with a clipboard came up to Kurt then, presented the clipboard and a pen, and said something Alice couldn't understand. Kurt signed, then the man walked off.

Alice asked, "Was that Kriol?"

"Indeed it was." Kurt made a jump then—Alice was sort of cornered—and got kinged.

Alice, not much caring about winning or losing, said, "So how'd you end up here?"

"Well, I retired early and came down here for a month to unwind, and then a month turned into two and then three. I liked it here, and I couldn't find a reason to move back to the

States. I'd traveled a lot when I was working, so I didn't feel like I had a home base anymore anyway."

"No family." He wasn't wearing a wedding ring. How could you help but notice? But that didn't mean anything these days.

He studied the board. "Parents have passed, and I have a sister in Florida with a gaggle of kids, so I go there twice a year or so. It's so close."

"You've done well for yourself here, by the looks of it."

"Well, I've taken a few hits." A man walked in and slid a few cases of bottled water onto the bar and looked at Kurt, who waved. "It's well known among expats that the second house you buy in Belize is twice as big and half as expensive. And I lost this place to Hurricane Iris and had to rebuild from the ground up."

Alice couldn't remember a Hurricane Iris and supposed it had never made that big of an impact on the States. Oprah would be disappointed in her America-centrism.

"Plus, most people don't understand why anyone from the U.S. in their right mind would ever move here, so there was a lot of suspicion about me at first, like maybe I'm on the lam."

"We're all on the lam from something," Alice said, and Kurt looked up, frozen, and smiled.

Alice said, "Oh, don't mind me. Belize has made me all sorts of, well, I don't know what, exactly."

"Go on."

"I'm sitting here with you, and you've got this restaurant that you own in Belize. And I look at my children and their friends who are here and they've all done so much"—Alice probably hadn't said this many words in a row since book club, when she'd gone on her rant about *The Memory Keeper's Daughter*—"and I'm feeling, suddenly, like I've wasted a lot of time. The band has traveled all over together—they talk about towns in Italy and Croatia like they're just a short drive away—and I can't help but feel like I missed out. I mean, I was of a different generation of women, of course. But I'm still kicking, you know. Only I'm not, not really."

"I lost you." Kurt squinted, and a starburst of lines appeared around his eyes. "The band?"

"I guess I didn't mention. My daughter's in a band. The groom, too. They're all here for the wedding."

"What are they called?" He jumped her again. Alice's pieces were down to three.

"The Starter House." She had no decent moves, began a retreat.

"Any good?" He jumped her again.

"I think so. Most of the time, anyway." She had a jump here, but it was a trap. She took it anyway. The game could not go on all day.

"They make a living at it?" He jumped her again.

"Not exactly. They all still have jobs. But not real jobs. It's a different world these days. Everyone's freelance this and free-lance that. Working in their pajamas. And June just got a great offer for a full-time job writing music for a new animated TV show. It's all very up in the air right now."

He said, "Sorry," and took Alice's last piece, then looked at his watch. "Are you in a hurry to get back?"

Alice looked at hers. "Not particularly. But I have to get this." She pulled out the piece of paper with the ointment's name written on it. "A spider gave my daughter a shiner."

"Come on, then." He got up. "The soccer match's starting, and the pharmacy won't be open until it's over."

Back out on the road that had brought Alice to town, everyone seemed to be heading farther into town, and she and Kurt joined the flow. Walking next to him, her steps seemed more certain. When she realized she was walking to the beat of a distant drum—there was a trumpet, too—the temptation was to break pace, but she didn't. She said, "Don't suppose there are any dress shops on the way?"

Becky and Dan had made up after their earlier fight at the pool, but some things hadn't changed. Like the fact that Becky was a napper, which was yet another thing on the long list of reasons why Dan and Becky weren't meant to be. Dan, who'd never napped in his life, had wandered over to the bar where, thankfully, there were no landscapers or football games, only Joe.

"Hey," Dan said. "Where is everybody?"

"I don't know." Joe shrugged. "Napping, I guess."

"Never was much of a napper myself," Dan said.

"Me neither."

Dan thought this might be the only thing he and Joe had in common besides friends. Still, there was only one tiki bar. "Mind if I join you?"

"Of course not."

Dan asked the bartender for a Belikin. "You went snorkeling, right?" Joe was drinking and nodding. "How was it?"

"Good." He was looking at the TV, which was playing *Law & Order*. "Abby almost died, but other than that, it was pretty good."

"She did?"

"Well, not exactly, I guess." They both looked up at the *Law & Order chung-chung* gavel. "But it was really choppy water, and there was like no instruction at all. Sort of crazy." He ran his hands through his hair then. He wasn't looking too happy.

"You all right?" Dan asked.

"Yeah," Joe said. "I mean, this probably sounds lame, but I miss the baby."

Yeah, pretty lame. The detectives were at a swanky apartment on Central Park West, and Dan thought he'd have to buy some artwork for his walls at the McCarren when he got home.

Dan said, "I can imagine," and tried it on for size. He supposed if you spent that much time with a baby—if it were your own and not somebody else's—it'd be significantly more interesting in general. He tried to picture himself, arms around Becky, studying their newborn for tiny clues, reflections of themselves. If there were a baby, hopefully it'd have Becky's nose, especially if it was a girl, since his was kind of flat and wide. He suddenly realized it was probably weird for him to assume, as he had from the first "I'm late," echoing out over *E. Coli* Falls, that Becky would keep the baby, and wondered now whether she would. It was probably the kind of thing you were supposed to talk about with people you were having sex with, but now that there was an actual chance she was pregnant, the topic seemed verboten. Did the fact that he assumed she'd want the baby mean that *he* wanted it—and that he was more ready for fatherhood than he'd thought? And did the fact that he pictured his arms around her mean there was hope for them yet?

Joe's Dad persona had been unleashed. "It's like I don't really know what to do with myself, you know? At home everything's so scheduled out."

"I hear you," Dan said, already growing bored by the topic. "So what do you think about all this stuff with June?"

Joe shrugged. He never was much of a talker, Joe. Not with Dan anyway. He said, "Having a kid sort of puts a lot of things in perspective."

"I bet," Dan said, and tried to think of another way to change the subject.

"Seriously, man, having a daughter." Joe was turning into a virtual chatterbox. "A son, I guess, too, but I wouldn't know yet. A daughter becomes the center of your world. And I've been watching kids' shows, and they could really use a few more people like June writing the music. God, most of it's torturous."

Yeah, so now officially bored. "That's cool," Dan said, but he *liked* being the center of his own world. "Do you know what time it is?" he asked.

"Probably time to clean up for dinner, right?" So maybe Joe was getting bored by him, too, because they had plenty of time before dinner.

That's when Becky arrived, shiny and sundressed, and said, "Hello, kind sir," to the bartender. "Could I please get a double vodka on the rocks?"

Another *chung-chung*, and now a sexy young female ADA was strutting her stuff in the courtroom, requesting remand without bail.

"Rough day?" Joe asked, and Dan's head pounded with a new beat of pressure as his blood pumped faster.

Becky smiled and said, "Not anymore."

Joe finished his beer and said he was going back to his cabana to shower. He'd see them at dinner. Dan turned to Becky when he was gone. "Does this mean what I think it means?"

"Yes, Dan." She was watching the bartender pour vodka over rocks at the far end of the bar. "You're off the hook."

"You don't have to be like that." He finished his beer. "You're just as relieved as I am."

"I think it's fair to say I'm a good bit more relieved than you are." She looked out at the ocean then and the wind blew her hair toward Dan; it smelled fruity, clean. "God," she said. "What a perfectly beautiful evening."

Dan said, "We don't need to split hairs."

"No, Dan. We really don't need to do anything at all."

"What's that supposed to mean?"

Her drink was placed in front of her, and Becky took a sip,

then breathed hard—shoulders rising and falling. She looked at Dan, and her eyes seemed glassy, like the vodka had gone straight to her eye sockets and pooled. "Let's just enjoy the evening, shall we?"

"Fine," Dan said. "Let's."

She leaned in and kissed him full on the lips. He wasn't sure he'd ever seen her happier. She ordered him another beer.

Alice wished she could just pick up the phone and call Mary-Anise. She'd tell her all about Kurt—the random meeting, the checkers, the unexpected trip to the soccer match. Mary-Anise would never be able to picture the scene—Alice, with a stunningly handsome man, in the bleachers of a small school field, shouting and cheering on the local Placencia boys' team. When they'd gone to that Cubs game one time, Mary-Anise had been disappointed with Alice's cheering skills, and Alice had explained, "Jack and I never really did sports."

"It shows." Mary-Anise had been clapping and yelling, *Way to watch it!* "You're like a robot trying to approximate a human at a baseball game."

"Sorry," Alice had said.

But she hadn't been a robot this time, not at the Belizean soccer game. This time Alice had given it her all. Something about being in Belize, in Placencia, with nothing but strangers, freed her to make an ass of herself. And the irony was that in being free to make an ass of herself, she no longer did. She seemed to fit right in.

But she would not call Mary-Anise. She sat, instead, through dinner, as if literally sitting on her secret, almost unable to keep herself in her chair. Already she was thinking about what she'd wear tomorrow, wishing it were already here. Already she was thinking she'd clearly lost her mind. But if this was what losing your mind felt like, then maybe Alice had clung to hers too long. Because if Oprah were single and an attractive American expat in Belize asked her to go out on his boat, Oprah would say yes, too. Alice was sure of it.

Tuning in to a conversation that June was having, Alice heard Maggie say, "I hope you understand. We're taking Minky on the Monkey River tour, then having dinner at Turtle Inn."

"Of course," June said, and Alice wondered whether she'd be let off the hook as easily. This seemed as good a time as any to find out, as dinner—Alice had barely paid attention to anyone or anything—was already winding down. She pulled June aside when she was done talking to Maggie. "I'm not going to go to the private island either."

"Oh, come on, Mom. Live a little." They were standing near Alice's chair at the table; it was hard to look at June, with that eye. Alice had already given her the ointment she'd bought after the soccer match.

"I plan on it," Alice said. "In fact, I already have plans for tomorrow afternoon and evening."

"Please don't tell me you're giving your money over to Coppola, too."

"No."

June grabbed her mother's arm. "Then please don't tell me you're going dress shopping."

Kurt hadn't thought the shops in Placencia would be much help, but Alice still wasn't convinced.

"Billy told me you've been torturing yourself. But Mom. Really. I don't *care* what you wear!"

"*I* care!" Alice was getting off topic, wanted to make sure her point was heard. Her secret was desperate to get out. "I met someone. He invited me out on his boat."

June's eyes lit with suspicion and surprise.

"A man." Alice played with the bottom edge of her top.

June looked left and right, as if about to cross the street, then back at her mother, voice lowered. "You haven't gone on a date in decades, and you decided to do it for the first time two days before my wedding?"

Alice hadn't really considered the event in context. "That's one way of looking at it, yes."

June's mouth half started to say something, then she stopped and tilted her head pensively, like a dog contemplating a faraway sound. She swooped in then and kissed Alice hard on the cheek. "Well, it's about time."

*T*hey are in the rehearsal space on a Saturday, playing the same song for the fifteenth time that day, and it still isn't working. Trevor thinks it's too slow. Joe thinks it's too fast. Cash, who wrote the song, thinks it's just right. June thinks the song just isn't very good. Though she hasn't really said so. They are recording their dreaded second record next week, though it's not quite as dreaded when only a few thousand people went out and bought your first. It's hard to have a sophomore slump if you've sort of been slumping all along.

Yes, they're filling better venues in the States now. No, they're no longer playing "It Ain't Me, Babe." But it's just not that easy to make it these days. Trevor has decided they should sign with a major label, and June has snorted a few times and said, "Oh, okay. Let's do that." She's taken out her cell phone and said, "Should we call 'em up right now?"

"Why don't we?" Trevor said at last Saturday's rehearsal, then took out his wallet and pulled out a business card for a woman who works in A and R at Sony.

Cash snatched it out of his hand. "Where the fuck did you get that?"

"She gave it to me."

"When?"

"The last show we played at Webster Hall."

"Why didn't you say anything?" Joe said, drumsticks in hand.

Trevor shrugged. "Because I didn't think she'd call."

"And . . . ," Cash said.

"And then she did."

And so Trevor had told her about their gig last week—at the Bowery Ballroom—and she said she'd be there. And she was. And June hated her at hello. After suffering the woman's industry jargon and bullshit promises over drinks after the show, June declared to the boys, "I won't sign with a major."

"There are four people in this band," Trevor said.

"And two songwriters," June said. She looked at Cash, expecting him to back her up, but he didn't. He was contemplating rocks and hard places and hoping that, for once, June and Trevor would just sort it out on their own.

"I think we should hear what they have to say, in terms of an actual offer," Trevor said, and Joe said, "Me too."

June looked at Cash and said, "Did you believe a word that woman said all night?"

Cash said, "That's really not the point."

"So you all want to just sell our souls to the highest bidder. Or the only bidder?"

"We just want to hear what she has to say," Cash said. "What's the harm in that?"

They are playing Cash's song for the sixteenth time because the Sony woman ended up flaking out on them, and now the band seems to be making June pay for being right about her all along. They all know she doesn't like this song at all, and it's as if they've latched on to it for that very reason. They are all insisting that it go on the record *even though it's still not in great shape and they could go in there next week and record nine of June's songs and the three Cash songs they're already planning on recording and come out with a real stunner of a CD.*

Cash is a good songwriter, mind you, way better now than he was when the Co-op Board became the Starter House, and lately he's on fire whereas June's all dried up—lyrically especially—but those last nine were her best yet.

Joe thinks this is going to be the one. The record that really puts them over the top. He doesn't think it really matters whether the song they're playing gets recorded because there are already a bunch of "singles"—not that they really release singles these days—on the record for sure. He has fantasies of taking Leah and Darla on tour with the band, of them all seeing the world together as he lives out his dream. He has nightmares about Leah telling him enough is enough, that it's time for him to grow up, if this record doesn't do something big. Something bigger than that opening slot at Radio City or a European club tour, which would mean pretty freakin' big. In Joe's nightmares, Leah doesn't mess around.

Trevor, being Trevor, has no expectation and no complaints, and he'll play the song sixteen times or six hundred or never again. He thinks the band's had a good run and he'll do his part to keep it going, but when he was in college and starting his first band he thought he'd do it until he was maybe thirty, at which point he'd be too old, then he'd retire his guitar picks and write the Great American Novel—about a blueblood college kid who goes up to Alaska to try to get a spot as a greenhorn on a boat during the last derby-style king crab season. He's one year past his imagined switch from music to words, but thirty-one doesn't feel quite as old as he thought it would, and so he's going to ride this thing out. He figures John and Yoko will bring the drama eventually and has started researching derby fishing, but he's also pretty revved up about a lot of the new stuff Cash is writing. It's good. Really good. No better than anything June's done, just different. And maybe more Trevor's vibe. He's being reminded of why he wanted to be in a band with Cash in the first place.

They are recording that song a week later because Cash went home that night and said, "We're putting it on the record," and June said, "Well, can we at least work on the bridge a little? Maybe try out a few different things," and Cash said, "Like what?" and then she took out her guitar and played and sang an entirely new bridge. He looked mad for a second but said, "Play it again," and she did, and then he said, "Fine," and she said, "Fine." She put her guitar down and he said, "Does this mean we just wrote a song together?" and she said, "I think it does." Putting on her best girlie girl, she said, "Gosh, Cash, maybe we should get married!" and he said, "If there's one thing you're good at, June, it's ruining everything."

Thursday

Dan woke from a dream about Harry Potter with a fierce pain behind his forehead. Becky's double vodkas had given him free rein, and he'd had more Belikins than he could remember. A moment passed before he remembered this: she'd gotten her period; they were off the hook. They'd partied together, the two of them, just like old times, except that they'd never really partied together before—except that one time, when Dan had gotten his check from the close of the sale of the dilapidated mansion. Remembering that simple fact—she wasn't pregnant—was wonderful beyond belief; it was the opposite feeling of when you woke up after something bad happened and had a moment in which you'd forgotten that no, this day was not one you wanted to face. This day Dan didn't mind facing. In fact, he was so happy—even with the hangover—that he wanted to pull Becky into a huge body hug, except she wasn't there.

"Becky?" His voice seemed to echo in such a hollow way that he knew, for sure, he was alone in the cabana. He listened to the breeze, blowing through trees and curtains, and then he remembered. She'd woken him up—he looked at the clock, 10:00 a.m., so it must've been a few hours ago—and she'd said, "Dan, I'm going on the Monkey River tour."

"What?" he'd said. "But the boat leaves for the island at—"

"I'm not going to the island. I need some breathing room." She'd moved away from the bed, and he'd seen her putting her backpack on. "I'll see you when you get back."

"Are you sure?" She was already out the door.

"I'm sure," she'd said from the porch.

Dan got up, and his brain seemed to sway inside his head, banging into the spot near his left ear, like cargo on a ship on rocky seas. Becky's ibuprofen was on the counter in the bathroom and he took two, with Peggy's tap water—he was feeling that good, that untouchable, in spite of Becky's abandonment. Because *she wasn't pregnant*. He took a leak then, and relished the simple standing-up of it all. The fact that he was peeing and nothing more. To boot, there hadn't been any crab walks in his ribs in hours. The worst was over! Nature had run its course, and he could go to the private island without fear.

He set about packing an overnight bag, practically dancing around the room singing a sort of cha-cha—*Beck-y-is-n't-PREG-NANT! Beck-y-is-n't-PREG-NANT!*—but realized there wasn't any rush at all; the boat for the island wasn't leaving until noon. So he ate a granola bar that was sitting on the kitchen table next to an empty wine bottle—he had no idea how either had gotten there—retrieved his book from the bathroom, grabbed his sunglasses, and climbed into a hammock on the porch. God, it felt great to be alone. It was just him and Colson Whitehead and the beach and the sea and the sky. He couldn't think of the last time he'd felt so relaxed, so carefree. And even though his head produced the occasional sharp pain—as if the ornery crab had simply migrated north—he would not be deterred.

He heard the smack of a door on the next bungalow over, then, and turned his head. Trevor was standing on his front porch in tighty-whiteys, stretching. "Dan the man," he said. "Top of the morning to ya."

"And to you," Dan said.

He went back to his book so as to discourage further conversation, but Trevor was having none of it. He was on Dan's porch, still in his underwear, and also wearing a wide-brimmed straw hat, in a matter of seconds. He settled in on the other hammock. "So I saw Becky taking off this morning like a bat out of hell."

"Yeah?" Dan kept his eyes on Colson Whitehead, who would never use such a cliché.

"Yeah, so what's the deal?"

"No deal." Still Colson. "She's doing her own thing today."

"So you guys are tight?"

Dan let the book fall to his lap. He was too hyped up to read anyway. "What's it to you, Trevor?"

"Jeez, man. Just making conversation."

"Yeah?" Dan could play that game. "How's things with the band?"

"It's just a band, man." Trevor shifted his hat so it covered his face, and his voice was slightly distorted when he said, "There'll be plenty more where that one came from."

"You don't mean that." Dan had spotted a spider on one of the porch columns and was wondering whether June's spider bite had calmed any overnight. God, it was awful to behold.

"What if I do?" Trevor reached down to the floor and pushed off to get his hammock swinging. "I mean, what am I supposed to do, beg her to stay? Fuck that. She's free to do whatever she wants. I've got some other offers. Other people doing some cool stuff asking me to play with them. I always land on my feet."

Dan looked at the open pages of his book. "Good for you."

He thought maybe Becky had the right idea about Monkey River being the better of the day's options.

"Yeah," Trevor peeked out from under his hat. "It is."

It had taken every ounce of Abby's self-control not to be snippy or to physically shove M and M and M out the door earlier that morning. They kept checking and double-checking that they had everything—packing and unpacking two daypacks—and Abby had thought she'd probably snap and kill one of them with a blast of bug spray to the face or a fatal blow to the head made with an especially firm bottle of sunscreen if they didn't get the hell out of there already! When they finally left, she had set about packing up for the private island, and was glad Maggie had been too frazzled to remember to take Abby's black bikini to Monkey River with her, just to guarantee it wouldn't be worn. Abby's having submitted to the boring Speedo these last few days had paid off.

When she couldn't bear to stay in the cabana anymore, Abby locked it behind her and went down to the front desk, where the private island people were meeting up. June's mom wasn't going either, so that meant it was only young people. Cool people. This was definitely going to be the best night of the trip. But then Dan arrived, and Abby said, "Where's Becky?" and he said she'd gone on the Monkey River tour, so that was pretty strange. From the way Becky had been hitting the vodka the night before, it was clear she'd gotten her period—and then she'd told Abby as much, in a happy slur by the ladies' room—and Abby half wondered if she was still conked out in bed, too embarrassed to show her face. Then June and Cash and Billy and Trevor and Joe arrived, and Dan explained again about Becky, and Trevor said, yes, that he'd seen her actually get up and leave, and they all headed down the wooded path again, to a boat. Some of the guys from Peggy's Place were already there, loading coolers and supplies on board, and then they were on their way, out of the canal, out into open waters.

Becky was probably dumping Dan's sorry ass now that she knew she wasn't having his baby. Abby had finally figured out what it was that she didn't like about him. It had taken days of observation, but this was it: he always seemed to have a little smirk on his lips, and he never really seemed to look people in the eye; always like a half an inch beneath the eye, almost. He didn't hold doors for Becky, and just generally didn't behave in a nice boyfriendly way at all. Becky could do way better than Dan for sure, and Abby sort of wondered why Cash was friends with him at all, but then if you judged her by her friends, you might not like her either. Hannah and Lisa seemed like dreams now—people she'd read about in a book—and Abby realized she hadn't had a conscious thought about them in hours, if not days. It was Thursday, so she'd be home in less than three days. But while she'd started the trip counting the days until she could go home, something had changed along the way, and now she was counting the days she could stay. There was today. Then two more full days in Belize, then that was it. She needed to get that kiss.

Maybe twenty minutes out, they slowed by a small island and the boat started making its way toward a dock. They'd been told that two dogs lived on the island, and they both came bounding down the dock, woofing, to greet the boat. They kept running right up to the edge, their feet dancing, and then when the boat was close enough, the brown one jumped aboard and ran around licking everyone and generally unleashing chaos. Abby's best guess was that they were retrievers. Billy bent down and tried to pet the one on board, but the dog was too busy running around to let him.

"Easy there, boy," he said, trying again, to no avail.

Abby liked that he was obviously a dog person. It wasn't the kind of thing you knew about people until you encountered an actual dog.

Abby was first off the boat once it was secured at the dock—a twenty-foot stretch of faded gray two-by-fours—and she bent down to greet the other dog, this one golden, after letting him sniff her hand. He licked it and then nuzzled his nose into the crook of her knee, and she was in love that quickly. "That's Jules," the guide said. "And the other one's Miles."

You could see the whole of the island from the dock, and Abby was both surprised it was so small and also relieved. There didn't seem to be anywhere for anyone to hide—which kind of sucked if you were looking for a private place where you could make out with somebody, but was good because there wasn't any place for a crazy person to hide. Not that Abby was scared of stuff like that in general, but she was expecting sleeping on a deserted island to be kind of creepy anyway, and at least now she could eliminate the fear of crazies, unless they crawled up out of the sea, all ghoulish and rotting and covered in seaweed. There were few trees, with a couple of hammocks strung between them, and then four huts on stilts in a big semicircle around three picnic tables and a fire pit. A volleyball net tilted in the wind on what looked like the island's flattest beach.

"Well." Cash put an arm around her shoulder. "What do you think?"

She smiled up at him. "It's awesome."

He was getting around a lot better on crutches now, but still wasn't putting weight on his ankle. "No volleyball for you, though," Abby said.

Cash patted her back and said, "Oh ye of little faith."

"Hold up, Manuel," Trevor shouted as a man from Peggy's walked past with a cooler. And how did everyone else know everyone's names? "Where you going with those beers?"

Abby was looking at the huts and doing some figuring. One for Cash and June; another for Trevor and Joe; another for Dan and Becky; and another for her and Billy? Was there any way anyone would let that happen, or was she supposed to be sharing with June? And now Becky wasn't even here, so maybe Dan and Billy would end up together?

"Hey, so . . ." Abby fell in step beside June, whose spider bite had taken on a sea green sheen; at the very least you could fully see her eye again. "Where am I sleeping?"

"Oh, just pick one," June said. "We were gonna have Billy on our floor, but now he can double up with Dan." She turned to the boys. "Billy. Dan. You guys are sharing a hut, okay?"

"Sure, okay." Billy said. "Whatever."

Abby decided on a middle hut—more people on each side to hear her scream if anything did happen—and threw her bag on the air mattress. It was sort of stuffy, so she opened the hut's two windows by pushing out wooden shutters that you secured at an angle with a sort of wooden handle, and released sun-bleached curtains that were held back from the windows by nails. Confident no one could see in, she returned to her pack.

Her bikini was way down at the bottom, and when she pulled it out and laid it out, she felt Christmas giddy. She took off her clothes and put it on, then pushed the curtains back again to let more light in. There was no mirror in the hut, but looking down at herself, she felt like a magical transformation had occurred; she was now Super Abby, and it was her job to seduce Billy in a single bound. She put on shorts but decided to let the bikini top do its job, then tossed a few things into her beach bag—book, sunglasses, sunscreen, sketch pad—and went back outside, where the boys were already playing volleyball. Cash, standing on one foot with one crutch for balance, wielded the other crutch like it was a bat, and Trevor, upon seeing her, started to whistle a song she recognized from a yogurt commercial—something about an "Itsy Bitsy Teenie Weenie Yellow Polka Dot Bikini." Billy turned and saw her.

"Hey," she said, as the volleyball sailed over the net and hit him on the head. She smiled and thought, It's on. But the bikini would probably not fare too well at volleyball. She went to a picnic table instead. June was down on the beach playing fetch with the dogs.

Abby had gotten some good advice from Billy about drawing things you were excited about, so she set out to compose her own still life, instead of just looking around for something that happened to be there. The urns and papayas by the river at Blancaneaux hadn't panned out in the end. Now she was going for a sort of typical Belizean still life, or typical Belizean *tourist* still life, and so put her copy of *Heart of Darkness*, sunscreen, bug spray, sunglasses, and snorkel on the table and arranged them just so.

"How's it going?" Billy said, after Trevor and Cash had beat him and Joe. Abby was thrilled he'd walked right into her trap.

"Good," she said. "I think."

He stood behind her and looked at the sketch so far. "Looks cool," he said. "And I guarantee you'll stand out from a helluva lot of fruit."

"Just one more to go after this."

"The self-portrait."

She'd had a million ideas for that one, but none that would stick. The "from observation" part was sort of a downer.

"Don't overthink it." Billy picked up the still-life sunscreen and Abby said, "Hey!"

"I'll put it back." He squirted some white cream into his palm. "Seriously, though."

"Yeah." Abby almost snorted but knew snorting wasn't sexy. "I mean, it's only my whole future that's at stake."

"Well, your future's not drawing. It's making clothes." Billy

322

was spreading sunscreen on his face, eyes closed. "I assume you have to turn in some of those, or some sketches of those, too?"

"Yeah, and I'm mostly set for that."

He opened his eyes. "My mother has this image in her mind of the perfect dress she wants to wear for the wedding, and apparently no stores in the whole state of Illinois sell one anything like it." He smiled and said, "You could've maybe made it for her," and Abby thought he couldn't be any sweeter or sexier if he tried.

Alice looked herself deep in the eyes in the bathroom mirror after lunch and said, "Don't do anything I wouldn't do." She ran a brush through her hair and said, "Scratch that. Don't do anything Oprah wouldn't do."

She was meeting Kurt in the parking lot in a few minutes and had already changed her top—and thus messed up her hair—three times. She'd settled on a pair of chinos and a blue V-neck T-shirt, but no matter what she did, she felt like she looked like she'd dressed up. Like for a date. She wiped the lipstick from her lips and put on a clear gloss instead, then grabbed her bag and started walking down the beach, sandals in hand. The sandals in hand contributed to a sense that she was sneaking off, tiptoeing around, but there was really no one left at Peggy's now that the boat had left for the private island and the Monkey River tour was well under way. She stopped at the bench near check-in to put on the sandals—navy blue flats—and Kurt was standing there, car keys in hand, when she looked up.

"Alice." He wore long khaki shorts and a white polo shirt, a step up from yesterday, and she didn't feel quite so awkward anymore. "Hello!"

She got up and said, "Hello," and he surprised her with a kiss on the cheek. "You got everything?" he said. His sharp cologne made her realize she'd forgotten to wear perfume.

"I think so," Alice said. She was prepared for pretty much everything and for nothing at all. She followed him out to his car—a Range Rover, it turned out—and then he started it up, shifted into gear, and pulled out of the parking lot. They were barely out on the road before Turtle Inn was upon them. It had seemed much farther away on foot.

Kurt said, "Have you popped in there yet?"

"No, not yet."

"Oh, you have to see it. Let's stop." He pulled off the road, effectively parking the car in a ditch.

"Oh." It was all happening so fast. Alice had only barely adjusted to the reality of her not being in her bungalow changing her clothes. "Okay."

"Unless you don't want to." His looked over at her, fingers poised on the key in the ignition.

"No, I want to." She put a hand on the door handle. "I mean, if you want to."

"We won't stay long." He took the keys out. "We'll just have a quick look around, maybe have a drink."

"Perfect." She opened the door, because really, the butterfly farm had been days ago. Who would even remember her?

A car zipped down the road as Alice rounded the back of the Range Rover, and Kurt put an arm out, a sort of protective barrier, then stepped forward into the road when the car passed. Alice followed, looking up at Turtle Inn, which seemed to get exponentially bigger with each step she took closer to it. It didn't seem real. Then again, neither did Kurt.

"A lot of people have mixed feelings about Coppola, but the man knows how to do resorts," Kurt said as they walked in. Alice eyes adjusted to the relative dark. "And he's also done a great job of raising the profile of Belize in the tourism indus-try. I think it's mostly been a good thing. He employs a lot of people."

Alice followed Kurt past a dark wood reception counter and a turnoff to a gift shop, and then into a huge restaurant—gear-ing up for lunch—with open walls and way-high ceiling fans hanging from an elaborate crisscrossed ceiling made of wood. Beyond the dining room, a pool and a bunch of cabanas like the ones from the Pine Ridge dotted the beach.

Kurt stepped up to the bar. "What can I get you?" He had a money clip in his hand.

"Oh, just a Coke or something," Alice said, and Kurt greeted the bartender and ordered a Coke and a beer. He gestured to a high bar stool, and Alice climbed up onto it.

"So I looked up the Starter House and found some free downloads."

"I'm sure I'm supposed to object to that." Their drinks ar-rived, and Kurt tapped his beer bottle to Alice's Coke bottle and then drank. She poured her soda into a glass of ice.

Kurt put his beer down, licked his lips. "Well, I'll buy a CD then, too."

"There are three of them."

He jerked his torso away in surprise. "Wow! You're like a hardcore band mom!" His body relaxed again. "I'll buy *all* of them, okay?"

"Better."

"I like the cover of 'It Ain't Me, Babe.'" He nodded ap-provingly.

"Everyone does. I think that's part of the problem." There was such a thing as the wrong kind of fame, Alice had been told; car commercials did not rock-'n'-roll legends make.

"I read some interviews with your June." His saying her name prompted Alice to imagine June in the room, and she wondered whether June would approve and thought she might;

325

though she'd never approve of the choice of adjective—*your* June; she was anything but. "She's a real firecracker."

Alice imagined sparks of color bursting from June's mouth and nodded. "She's the Fourth of July."

Kurt smiled. "How exactly did *you*"—he elbowed Alice gently, and she was pretty sure that even in this day and age that qualified as flirting—"end up with a *rock star* for a daughter?"

"Oh, my husband was a composer." The past tense always caught. "Industrial musicals."

Kurt's face pinched; Alice was used to explaining. "Companies used to hire people to write music shows for their big conventions."

Still pinched. "When was this, the sixties?"

She nodded. "Jack was one of the younger composers. Fell into it through a sort of mentorship when he was barely in his twenties."

"What kinds of things were they about?"

"Oh, cars, plumbing, paper, you name it." Alice and Jack had listened to his old recordings so many times that she could still hear most of the songs in her head; whenever she lay in bed at night unable to sleep, she'd pick a song and try to sing it all the way through. "He was writing a musical of his own, actually, when he died. I hoped maybe June would finish it someday, but Broadway's beneath her."

"What's it about?"

"You ever see the movie *What Ever Happened to Baby Jane?*" Alice, because of Jack's project, had seen the film more times than she could count, and it never lost one iota of its creepiness. Because feeding your sister a rat was never not creepy.

"It's a musical of *that*?"

"I know it sounds awful." Who in their right mind would write song-and-dance numbers about a demented former child star? "There was a poster for the movie, in the early sixties, with the line 'Sister, sister, oh so fair, why is there blood all over your hair?' and he wrote a song based on that, and then he just kept going."

"Well, *he*"—Kurt raised his beer—"sounds like an interesting man."

"He was." Alice's Coke was nearly gone, and she regretted not having had some rum put in it. "And his daughter thinks I'm about as interesting as a sloth."

Kurt shrugged. "Most people are boring, when you think about it." He played with the leather bracelet on his wrist. "I mean, unless you're off saving the world, or writing the Great American Novel, but then I've met a lot of novelists who are real windbags, too."

Alice felt a tug on her arm and turned. The woman from the butterfly farm smiled victoriously. "I *thought* that was you." Her eyes took on a flirty sheen, and she turned to Kurt. "And this must be your husband!"

Kurt—thank God—had a great poker face, and Alice said, "One would think!" The words "Yes, he is" just wouldn't come out.

Alice sought out Kurt's gaze, pleaded with her eyes. "We met at a butterfly farm up in the Pine Ridge," she said, then turned back to the butterfly woman. "But we didn't really meet. I'm Alice." She gestured toward Kurt. "And this is Kurt."

"And I'm Ginny." They all shook hands, and Ginny held Kurt's with both of hers. "Congratulations on your daughter's wedding!"

Kurt just smiled and nodded, and Ginny seemed to look back and forth between him and Alice, registering that something about this interaction wasn't quite right, whether she could pinpoint what it was or not. Rising to the occasion, Kurt put an arm around Alice. "Isn't she a beautiful mother of the bride?" He kissed her on the forehead then, and Alice had to fight hard to maintain composure.

Ginny clapped her hands together at the sweetness of the scene. "Well, I just wanted to say hello. So funny to run into you. Small world, I guess!"

"Like the top of a pin!" Alice said.

Ginny walked off then, and Alice and Kurt both watched her join a table of people while Alice pictured her and Kurt and June and Cash and Ginny all balanced on one tiny point. She couldn't even begin to imagine what Kurt must think of her. All she'd been talking about was Jack, and now he probably thought she did that everywhere she went, and lied about him, too, when it suited her. But she was so grateful for the role he'd played—and how he'd played it, never actually claiming to be June's father, the father of the bride. She didn't think she could've handled it if he had.

He asked for the check then, and Alice thought he might call off the rest of the afternoon.

"I don't know, Alice," he said close to her ear as he stood. "Maybe you're not so boring after all."

Dan took a nap—he could hardly believe it himself—on an inflated mattress in one of the stilted huts, then got up, feeling mightily refreshed. He decided to unpack a few things, settle in, while there was still light and before Billy invaded the space. He emptied his backpack of everything he'd brought with him, including the June Carter autograph. It was a good thing it was a napkin, already sort of crinkled, because it probably wouldn't have traveled as well had it been written on thicker stock.

Tonight would be his last chance to give the autograph to June. Their numbers were down, with all the elderlies back on the mainland, and they would only begin to grow when they returned to Peggy's the next day. The maid of honor was flying in for the weekend, as were some more friends and family members. So tonight was the night. He'd have to give it to June at the first opportunity—night or day—so he put the Ziploc in the largest pocket of his cargo shorts and went out. He wasn't really planning on swimming, and he was fully prepared for Trevor to mock him about it.

The boys were drinking beers at one of the picnic tables, so Dan slid right in. Trevor was leading one of his typical conversations.

"Yeah, but if they never came back to get us," he said, "who would wind up top dog on the island?"

"Not to worry, Trevor, I'm sure you would," Cash said, then turned to Dan. "So Dan," he said, "what's the deal with Becky?"

Dan shrugged. "Doing her own thing. So it's sort of like we already had our first tribal council."

Trevor snorted. "We'd vote you off before we'd vote Becky off."

Cash said, "Don't take this the wrong way, but—" He hesitated here. "Things haven't looked so hot between you two."

Dan shook his head. "They haven't been hot at all. We pretty much broke up."

Cash leaned forward a bit too excitedly. "You think she'll even still be here when we get back tomorrow? You think she'll come to the wedding?"

"I have no idea." Dan sipped his beer. "But it feels awesome to have her out of my hair."

Cash said, "She's not that bad."

"Yeah." Trevor laughed. "She is!"

The afternoon soon revealed itself to be playing out as a frustrating string of near hits. Because every time Dan thought that maybe he'd have a minute alone with June, it quickly became apparent that there wasn't really any privacy to speak of on this private island. Even though there were only seven of them—and wait'll Trevor realized that and tried to match them all up with the castaways on Gilligan's Island; Dan had no doubt he'd be cast as the bumbling millionaire, Mr. Howell, even though he didn't have a wife—someone would always pop up. He didn't want to have to force the issue—it'd be too conspicuous to say, "June, can I have a word?" in the middle of a volleyball game or a game of cards—but if it came to that, he would.

He actually missed Becky. Or, more accurately, missed being part of a couple. Because he didn't really have a safe place in the group here on the island. Cash was supposedly his best friend, but he wasn't feeling like much of a best friend, so he was never quite sure where to sit, whom to talk to, who might want him on their volleyball team. Mentally exhausted from it all, he decided he'd spend some time on the beach with Colson Whitehead and hope that June might wander over for a chat. He spread his towel out on a nice smooth strip, got himself situated while the dogs came over to check out the scene, then looked out across the water toward Peggy's. He couldn't help but wonder what Becky was up to right then. Maybe she was still cruising down some jungle-tangled river looking for monkeys and wondering how many monkeys you had to see to have it count as much as a jaguar. Or maybe she was on Peggy's beach with her pink book, learning that men were like buses, and that another one would come along soon.

A joyful golden dog greeted Alice and Kurt on the boat. Which Alice would have called a yacht, not knowing exactly what qualified a boat as a yacht or not. It's not that it was huge, exactly, but it was white and luxurious-looking with silver and black letters on the side: *The Lam.*

"All right, Brinks." Kurt petted the dog with two hands. "Calm down."

Alice thought for a second. "You're funny."

"I got Brinks here when I was the new kid on the block because he barks at the drop of any hat that isn't mine." Kurt revved up the dog's ears, then patted his back hard; Brinks went away happy. "Rob me once, shame on you. Rob me twice, shame on me."

"And the boat name?"

He held a hand out to Alice, and she stepped aboard. He said, "Now you're officially on the lam."

He started untying ties, and when he needed to get past Alice, he steered her to a seat at the back of the boat. "You sit here a minute, make yourself at home, while I get this show on the road." Alice let herself be deposited on a bench chair, then watched as he unhooked more ties, tossed ropes here and there, then climbed up a skinny staircase and took his place in his captain's chair. The boat vibrated at the turn of his key, and he waved and said, "Come on up!" So Alice climbed. He gestured to a chair beside his captain's chair, and then he thrust a lever forward. Brinks came up, too, and they were on their way.

Whenever Alice was on a boat, she wished it were the kind of thing she did more often. She and Mary-Anise had taken a sunset cruise on a catamaran in Hawaii—they'd seen dolphins, whales, the works—and Alice had been rendered giddy by it all. This time, she was content to just sit and watch blue-green waters sail by. When Kurt pointed and said, "That's Peggy's island there," Alice had no idea how many minutes or miles had passed. He smiled. "I can take you if you want."

She shook her head. "I don't have any stuff with me!" she said brightly—it was awful of her, really, to be so happy she wasn't there—and he said, "Oh, well, then! In that case!"

Now boating was a bona fide leisure activity. Boating Alice

could get used to. Because the second you were out on the water, everything else seemed to fade away. All you had to do was look around, and you were having fun. Would boating or sailing get boring after a while, though? Like most things did? Alice hadn't picked up *The Da Vinci Code* or *The Thirteenth Tale* in days and was starting to think that maybe book clubs were sort of ridiculous. Felicia never had anything interesting to say—quite the contrary at times—and the other girls were busier than Alice and didn't always finish the books. They seemed more interested in gossiping and drinking wine. And power-walking with Mary-Anise? What a ridiculous American pursuit this suddenly seemed like, and Alice resolved that if she and Mary-Anise ever went out walking together again, Alice would throw caution to the wind and just break out into a goddamn run. One minute she and Mary-Anise would be rounding a cul-de-sac, commenting on cars or landscaping or last night's episode of *CSI: Miami*, and then the next, Alice would stop and turn to Mary-Anise. Adopting Horatio Caine's naming-names tic from the show, she'd say, "Mary-Anise, I hope this isn't going to be a problem, Mary-Anise"—she'd pause dramatically for effect—"but, Mary-Anise, I'm going to have to see you later." Then she'd take off, and she wouldn't care if she was properly heel-toeing or pumping her arms. She'd be free from the shackles of *walking for fun* forever.

Kurt looked at her, and Alice felt that somehow her reverie was apparent on her face. She said, "You know what I've learned this week, *Kurt*?"

"What have you learned this week, *Alice*?"

"Well, *Kurt*."

He smiled, though Alice doubted he knew about Horatio and knew why it was funny at all. "I watch too much TV." She started ticking off shows on her fingers. "*CSI*—all three of them—*Survivor, The Amazing Race, Lost, Bones, 24, Grey's Anatomy, American Idol, Dancing with the Stars*—"

"Damn, woman." Kurt killed the engine, and the boat groaned and slowed. "But hey, if that's the worst thing about you, you're doin' all right"—he smiled—"*Alice*." He dropped the anchor, and Alice watched the rope on deck uncoil and disappear. "Hell, I drink too much."

"Really?"

"Sure! And on that note, how about a glass of wine?"

"Wine would be lovely." And when she got home, she wouldn't touch it for a month to make up for this week's excess.

"Come down on deck," he said, so she followed him to the front deck, and then he said, "Have a seat. I'll be right back."

Alice returned to the cushy bench seat and watched as a boat that had been small just a few minutes ago came into sharper focus. It was heading right for them.

"Looks like we've got company," Kurt said, when he returned with a bottle of wine and two stemless glasses. A man on board waved his arms overhead—an SOS—and weary bodies, shoulders hunched forward, slumped on the boat's benches. The sun glared down on them all, and Alice felt her skin turn cold. Brinks made a high-pitched mew.

There wasn't enough snorkeling equipment for everyone to go at once, and so Abby had taken a pass the first time out and hung out onshore with Trevor and Billy, who were playing a three-of-five single volleyball tournament with Abby as scorekeeper and line ref, when necessary.

Trevor had won his final point—he dropped to his knees on the sand, hands in the hair—just as the rest of the group came back from snorkeling, and Abby asked Billy and Trevor, "Will one of you go snorkeling with me?"

"We can all go," Billy said, and Trevor said, "I don't want to upstage you twice. I'm gonna just chill for a while. But you kids go. Have fun."

Abby watched as Billy thought twice about this, and then he said, "Let's do it."

So they geared up—Abby dropped her shorts—and then waded off one side of the island and started to swim. The breathing bit was, thank God, easier still this time, and Abby thought she might actually be enjoying herself. Billy swam over with an underwater camera, and she made a thumbs-up sign and then waved. He took a picture, nodded, and continued to swim. But this was the problem with snorkeling, and Abby was mad at herself for not having quite thought things through: You couldn't talk, and thus couldn't flirt, while you were doing it. Then she saw Billy again, waving and turning an index finger up and pointing. She surfaced.

"You have to see this," he said. He was standing in shallow water near another of the island's beachy shores. "Follow me."

He swam out away from the island, and this time Abby followed. He started doing a dead man's float and waved Abby over, so she came up by his side. He pointed at a spot, but Abby followed the line of his finger and didn't see anything but a big gray rock—was that even coral? She didn't know. She shook her head, and bubbles escaped her mouth. She clenched her mouth harder on the pipe as Billy moved closer and took one of her hands in his own and then pointed again with both their arms. He was clearly indicating the rock, and yes, now Abby saw the huge, big-eyed gray fish that was hanging out under it. She gave a thumbs-up, and then Billy moved on and she followed.

It felt like forever that they swam, then, and Abby was sure to never let Billy out of her sight. Snorkeling was disorienting, and she wasn't even sure sometimes which way the island was.

She trusted Billy to get them back safe, and if he didn't, at least they'd be stranded at sea together. They'd find a piece of driftwood to hang on to and they'd share all their secrets and dreams while hoping that the Coast Guard found them before the sun went down. Or if they were lucky they'd drift to an island—but not this one—and then they'd be alone with each other, without a care in the world. They'd catch fish, and cook them over an open fire and build shelter and make love, and there'd be nothing illegal about it.

Billy's body in front of her broke form, and he was treading water and she drifted almost right into him.

"Abby!" he was yelling, when she surfaced. "Swim to shore now!"

She took off swimming and then ran aground and stood, but fell, and then Billy's arm was under her arm, helping her up, and they were both rushing to the beach on the far side of the island from the docks, where they collapsed on the sand, heaving. "Ohmigod." Abby took her mask off, and it took a few hairs with it. "What?!?"

"I saw something. Like a stingray, I think. I swear it looked right at me."

"Holy crap," Abby said. "You scared the shit out of me." They were both lying on their backs on the beach and their arms brushed and Billy squeezed her hand and said, "Sorry." Abby turned her head to the side—away from him—and smiled. They lay there, and she could feel her breathing start to calm, his, too, and then she brushed his hand with her thumb. His hand twitched and moved away, but Abby moved her hand so it touched his again. She did the thing with her thumb again.

"What are you doing, Abby?" he said. He moved his hand to his stomach, and she perched up beside him on an elbow. He said, "Quit it."

She leaned in, then, and he put a hand up, firm on her shoulder. "Abby, don't," he said.

She looked up the beach; the angle of the island hid them from the others. "No one can see us."

"That's not the point."

"Just kiss me," she said. "I know you want to. I can tell."

"No," Billy said. "You can't." He went to get up, and she pulled him down by his arm and then they were face to face, just inches away, and she was looking at him and he looked at her and then at her lips, and he looked scared, and she knew even more than she'd known before—and she'd definitely known before—that he wanted her. She went in for a kiss.

"Abby." He held her strongly with a hand on each of her upper arms and said, "It's never going to happen." He got up, and he said, "I'm not attracted to you," and Abby watched him walk away, sand stuck in splotchy swirls to his back.

Tears came and Abby thought about the Crocodile Hunter and his cartoon accent and all the crocs and critters he'd toyed with in his day. She thought of the stingray that got him in the end, stabbing him straight through the heart.

Alice sat on deck with the passengers from the other boat and didn't ask anything at all about what had happened. She knew all she needed to know. They'd been snorkeling, they were down one, and a search was under way. The weather was all wrong, the heat and low evening sun entirely untragic.

"Do you have any water?" a woman in her forties asked, and Alice went downstairs in search of the fridge; it was stocked entirely with water and tonic. Upstairs again, she started handing out the water bottles, and thought of New Orleans and the Gulf Coast and rooftop rescues and tears. The woman in her forties was part of a couple, and there were two younger couples, too. All of them looked shell-shocked, and one of the younger girls kept wiping her eyes. She was crying and trying not to, and her husband—they wore wedding bands—had an arm around her shoulder. Alice went back down and into the bathroom and pulled tissues from a box. She took a few deep, calming breaths—*This is a tragedy, but not my tragedy*—and went back out and gave the tissues to the girl, who couldn't manage to say thanks, only nodded.

Alice remembered Cash's complaint about the lack of supervision on the snorkeling tour the day before—how the water had been too choppy, how the guide had left Abby alone on the boat so he could catch dinner. He'd been livid and, Alice had thought, rightfully so. But June, typically, had defended the man, saying he had a family to feed and hadn't they all heard how horrible a childhood he'd had? And compared to the tour company, he probably wasn't getting that big of a cut. They felt very far away now—June and Cash, all the others—and Alice was glad they'd passed Peggy's private island on the boat, so she could picture where they were. She said a prayer for their safety.

Alice thought of book club, of Yann Martel's novel about the boy adrift at sea with vicious animals on board the boat—and how the Bengal tiger feasts upon them all, and how the boy cunningly avoids being eaten. Felicia had taken some of the questions in the reading group guide very seriously and had decided to interpret the book one way—the boy's family had been with him, and the passengers on the boat had turned on each other, and so the animals were a sort of hallucination, a coping mechanism, none of it had really happened. The true story was one of cannibalism, brutality, survival of the fittest, Felicia claimed. But Alice and everyone else in book club took it literally. It was a story about animals, and one boy's courage, no more. Now she wasn't so sure.

They seemed to be heading for a resort on the canal just past Placencia, and the sign—Rum Runner's Cove—came into focus. The engine kicked off, and Kurt skillfully steered the boat in, stopping on the farthest end of the dock, where the water was no doubt deepest. He came down to throw ties and secure the boat and then stood on the dock, helping each passenger off. From the beach nearby came a few concerned tourists. A few men in uniforms approached, too, and Kurt spoke to them, though Alice couldn't hear what he said. He pointed out at a distant spot in the sea and then stood with hands on hips. They talked a minute more, shook hands. Alice was standing on the dock right by the boat when he returned to her.

"I'm going back out to help search," he said, and started to untie *The Lam*.

Alice nodded urgently and said, "I'm coming, too."

"Alice." He threw ropes aboard. "I just don't think—"

"Listen, I'm not entirely useless." Her hands formed fists at her side.

"I wasn't saying—" He stepped on the boat.

"I went down to the Gulf Coast to help after Katrina. I'm a nurse by profession and—"

And it didn't matter, nothing mattered except that she was going to go. She stepped back onto the boat, and Kurt sighed and climbed to the wheel. Alice went down below, where she'd seen a pair of binoculars, then came back up and took a seat near the bow. She wondered what animal she would imagine Kurt to be if she were desperately, delusionally lost at sea, if she were heroic and wise and living the life of Pi.

"So what are you waiting for, Junie? Divine intervention?" Trevor had taken up the roll of fire starter, and they were all sitting around the fire pit, watching the flames twitch in the wind. "Or maybe you need to ask the island to help you make your choice." Trevor took a new log from their stash of firewood and put it on the fire. The whole enterprise dulled.

"Oh, leave her alone," Joe said. Dan was pretty sure those were the first words he'd spoken all day. "She said she'd decide by tomorrow, so she'll decide by tomorrow."

"Maybe I'll just quit right now," Trevor said. "Put everybody out of their misery."

"You know what, Trevor? Go ahead, if that's what you want." June got up and walked away. Cash made a move to follow her, and Dan saw an opportunity. He simply said, "I'll go," then got up and followed June down the beach. She sat by lapping waves at the shore, and he sat next to her. He could feel the Ziploc in his pocket. It had been a very long wait, a very long day.

"You can't let him get to you," Dan said. One of the dogs trotted over, started sniffing around.

"Oh, but he's right." June had a twig in her hand and tossed it toward the water. "I mean, what's my problem? I've never been so indecisive in my life."

"It's just a job," Dan said. "There'll be others. If you're not ready. And by the same token, well, don't take this the wrong way, but it's just a band. It's not a matter of life and death."

"Speaking of which. Well, the life part anyway. What happened with Becky?"

"Well, as you may have figured out, she's not pregnant."

"Yeah. That vodka didn't stand a chance."

"And I have the distinct impression that we're breaking up."

"Over a pregnancy scare?" June shook her head. "Well, that's unfortunate."

"No," Dan said, "not so much about that as, well"—he reached into his pocket and pulled out the Ziploc—"this." He handed it to her, and she said, "A Ziploc bag?"

"Look closer." Already this was not the scene he'd imagined so many times.

She brought the bag closer, read the signature, and said, "I don't understand."

"It's real. I bought it for you."

"Seriously?" She looked excited, and then confused. "So she's pissed that you got us one of the coolest wedding gifts maybe ever?"

"It's not a wedding gift." Dan was in it now; there was no turning back. "I bought it a bunch of years ago. When we first met. Before you were with Cash. And then, well, it seemed too late."

"Oh." In the night her hair looked blond again, better.

"I was in love with you." Dan couldn't stop now; that fumble at the arcade, that Dance Dance Revolution, had always been leading to this. "I *am* in love with you." He let the words hang there and wondered, even then, if he really meant them. "And if you quit the band, and if things with Cash are tied up in that, well, I'm here for you." He felt oddly false, unconvinced, when he said, "I can give you everything you've ever wanted."

"Oh, Dan." June put the autograph atop Dan's knees and let go, and he had to grab on to it when it teetered there. She said, "Dan, Dan, Dan," and it sounded uncannily like the "No! No! No!" of "It Ain't Me, Babe," like she'd been singing it to him all this time and was disappointed he obviously hadn't listened, or heard.

She said, "You're not in love with me."

"Why does everyone keep saying that?" Dan snapped.

"Who's everyone?"

"Becky."

June squinted confusion and leaned in at the neck. "You told *Becky*?"

This was all going horribly wrong, and it was as if he'd always known that it would. Now that he was in it, he couldn't believe he'd actually done it. "She found the autograph. She said they asked her to go through my suitcase when they brought it back. To make sure nothing was missing. I have no idea if that's true or not, but there you have it."

June just nodded and looked down the beach, where Cash was limping from the beer cooler back to the picnic table. Dan was annoyed that she obviously wanted to be on her way already, that with that look, she was as good as asking if she could be excused,

"I want you to have it," Dan said, putting the autograph on her stretched-out legs, because at least there would be that. She'd look at the autograph over the years—maybe frame it and hang it in a future den—and wherever she was in life, and wherever he was, and whether they were still in each others' lives or not, she'd have to think about him. She'd think, *Dan Eshom gave me that autograph. Because he loved me.* Maybe at another point in her life that thought would bring her comfort. Or joy.

"I can't." She put it back on his knees, and he dropped them to sit cross-legged.

"Well, what am I supposed to do with it?" he said. There was an unintentional edge to his voice.

"Just get rid of it," June snapped. She looked down the beach again. "I mean, for God's sake, Dan"—she shook her head—"you're his *best man*."

She wasn't going to leave Cash for him, and he'd been an idiot to ever think she would.

"You've got some fucking nerve," she said angrily, slowly.

She had never looked more serious or disappointed, and Dan knew she was right. He had some fucking nerve.

"I'm sorry," he said, thinking that it was true on two levels; he was remorseful, yes, but also just a pathetic, sorry man. But then panic rushed in uninvited. "You're not going to tell him, are you?"

June sighed then, and the question seemed to float away.

341

She took the Ziploc and opened it and pulled out the cocktail napkin. She pulled it close to her face and studied the swirls and curves, and then she put it to her nose and smelled it, breathing in hard. She gingerly put it back in the bag, pressed the seal strip closed, and handed it back. "The fucked-up thing is," she said, "that was exactly what I needed."

She got up and Dan said, "I don't understand," but she was already moving down the beach.

She yelled, "Hey, Trevor," and he said, "What?" and Dan saw a poof of sparks escape from the fire into the black night air.

June did a cartwheel, and stood and wiped sand off her palms. "I quit!"

They are rehearsing above the bodega on a regular ole Wednesday night in September—except they're not. Apologies, folks, they're actually not, because the second record came out to some critical acclaim but seemed to do no better or worse than the first, and when the subject of practicing this Wednesday came up on Monday, June said, "Can't we just take a pass?"

Trevor was keen on working on some new stuff, a song of Cash's he was all revved up about but that June hadn't heard yet, which was weird, because he normally played things for her first. "It's my brother's twenty-fifth birthday," she explained. "And I'd like to go to dinner with him and his friends."

"But we've got a gig Friday," Joe said, sort of snippy, because he had already told Leah that he really had to rehearse Monday and Wednesday this week, and they'd already had a fight about it and about how Darla has two parents, if he hasn't forgotten, and how we can't all run off and be rock stars.

"I know," June said, and slouched in exasperation. "But we'll be fine. It's not like we're playing anything new."

"And whose fault is that!" Trevor said, because it wasn't just about Billy's birthday but about a Wednesday last month when one of June's friends offered her a last-minute ticket to the ballet, and a Wednesday the month before when her friend Lydia's middle child

broke her arm and June swooped in to babysit, and a Monday over the summer, after the barbecue at McCarren, when the newly engaged (which Trevor took to mean June, whether that was accurate or not) decided "they" wanted a quiet night in after such a big weekend.

Their gear is there, silent as the air conditioner—still sealed up with a variety of tape, now dark and dusty—because June thought that while they were on the subject of playing out, they might as well stay there, especially if staying there would help avoid the fact that she hadn't written an actual song in months.

"I didn't want to take the gig anyway," she said. "Our mailing list is tapped from the last two shows, and we really shouldn't even be playing low-profile places like Pianos anymore. We're above that."

"Oh, we are, are we?"

They'd had this argument maybe three times in the past three months. "I just think we should only play out when we can fill a room, and we should only fill rooms we really want to fill."

"That's not how it works, Junie," Trevor said, and June said, "Well, then, explain it to me, Trevor. How exactly does 'it' work?"

She is all sorts of guilty quiet with the key when she comes home, wine-drunk, because while she went out with Billy and a handful of his friends to a cool downtown enoteca, Cash was home, working on the song some more, so that it would be ready for the band next week.

She is stopping by the door, closing it real quietly, because the man she's going to marry in less than three months is still awake despite

344

the hour, and he's singing—"One day he'll see he's really scared of do-ing anything at all"—and playing guitar with a programmed drum track over more tracks he's obviously already laid down: some key-boards, a little bass.

She hears the lyric "He'll take a hammer to her head and try to tear down all the walls" and stands super still because the guy sitting next to her at dinner—a guy from Nickelodeon who was dating a girl from Nickelodeon who was one of Billy's best gal pals—said, "We were starting to wonder whether Billy was making up the fact that you were his sister."

"I'm sorry," June said, irked by the implication that she was somehow a bad sibling. "Have we met before?"

"No," he said. "That's sort of my point."

She is holding her breath as Cash sings on—and she doesn't have to see him to know he's standing at a mike stand with eyes closed—because she thought the Nickelodeon guy was being sort of rude. She said, "I'm in a band," then sipped her wine. "Things have been busy."

"The Starter House. I know." He drank from his wineglass. "I love your music. The lyrics not so much."

She is feeling the rush and weight of fate as Cash sings along with himself, having apparently decided to go ahead and record his own backing vocals on "He'll have his dollar and his day | He'll climb back up after the fall" because normally June would have been of-fended by what the Nickelodeon guy said, but she wasn't. She said, "You know what's funny. I've been struggling with lyrics lately." She slid her wineglass back and forth a few inches on the table, a tic. "*I've got tons of pieces of music, none of which seem to quite belong together, and I haven't been able to think up a* word *to lay over them.*"

She is walking toward Cash because the song is just amazing and beautiful and building now as two Cashes are singing, "*He'll set a fire under their feet | He'll try to show them all,*" *because the guy said,* "*You know what's funnier?*" *He drank from his wineglass again, and June wondered whether he was nervous.* "*I was about to tell you we're looking for somebody with a different perspective to music-direct this new show we've got in development. About a rock camp for girls.*"

"*Seriously?*" *June thought maybe he was putting her on.* "*I volunteered at one of those once.*"

"*Yeah. I heard. They recommended a few people to us. You were one of them.*"

She is moving closer to Cash and his guitar and getting ready to scare the shit out of him as he sings what it's all been building to—"*He's gonna burst*"—*because she said to the Nickelodeon guy,* "*Then maybe we should talk details,*" *and she knows now*—"*Yeah, he's gonna burst*"—*that they should.*

Friday

Alice awoke to strange angles and her brain went to work. *Kurt's place. Kurt's bed.* But they were on top of the covers, still fully clothed. His arm hooked over her at the waist and she lay extra still and let the emotions of the moment—guilt, sadness, invigoration, desire—wash over her like waves, one blending with the next and moving at her and then away. She slid out from under Kurt's arm and went to the doors to the terrace, looked out at the sea.

She was scanning the surface, still, for anything unusual, but she was also thinking of eels and octopus tentacles and jellyfish and sharks and everything she didn't like about the ocean. If she were lost at sea, she'd die of fear. She'd read new stories, of course, about people who survived for several days, who were picked up alive, having hallucinated their own rescues and the mundane details of their daily lives, but she didn't think she'd survive a night alone at sea any more than she'd cut her own arm off if it were stuck under a rock. It was depressing to know these things about yourself. Because was her will to live really so weak, just a faint pulse? Or was it the opposite? Had she constructed a life mostly devoid of adventure and risk because her will to live was so strong? Jumping off a bridge with a bungee cord strapped around your ankles didn't necessarily mean that you loved life. It meant, maybe, that you were cavalier about it, that you fancied yourself invincible.

By that thinking, she could make a good argument that Kurt's life here in Placencia wasn't any more adventurous than her own. Sure, he was a gringo living amid a variety of cultures foreign to his own, but even if he wasn't hiding from anything in particular, there seemed to be a way in which he was hiding. He served beers and endless plates of chicken stew and met new people every day, but he lived almost as on a constant vacation. Life wasn't a permanent holiday, Alice knew, and she wasn't sure she'd want it to be. He had his chessboard the same way she had her book club, and even if one sounded more interesting than the other, they were both just ways to pass the time. He seemed exotic, yes, but only to people like her. If a toucan came face to face with a regular garden-variety house cat, wouldn't the bird be intrigued? To a toucan, a jaguar was probably ho-hum.

"What's on your mind?" Kurt asked her now.

She smiled at her own idiocy. "You wouldn't believe me if I told you."

"Why don't you stay a few more days, Alice?" Kurt joined her by the terrace. "After the others have gone. I could give you the insider's tour."

"You're serious."

"Don't answer right away." He turned to go. "Come downstairs."

Alice was pretty sure Oprah would be as confounded as she was as she watched Kurt move around his kitchen—dicing potatoes and tossing them into sizzling oil and then taking eggs from the fridge, whisking them in a bowl from a top shelf.

"There's a funny thing people say down here that I think of every time I make eggs," Kurt said.

"Yeah, what's that?" Alice sipped her coffee.

"A chicken shits white and thinks she has laid an egg."

Alice laughed. "I don't know if I get it."

"It's a warning about being too full of yourself."

"Oprah says it should be a goal to be full of yourself," Alice said. "But I guess she means it a different way."

"Yeah." Kurt pushed the eggs around in the pan. "No more TV for you when you get home. For real."

He was a stranger, and yet she felt she could spend days with him here quite happily. But wasn't that how predators worked? Didn't they lure you into a false sense of security and then strike when you had no escape? Was there a place in the world—or in history—where thoughts like that wouldn't even occur to you? Alice hoped so, but she was living in an age of paranoia and *To Catch A Predator*, and it wasn't unfathomable that she herself could end up in a news story that would be filed under "Disasters."

She'd have to sleep with him if she stayed. She wasn't a schoolgirl, and he was no boy. That alone was reason enough to go—or to stay. She tried to picture it, tried to imagine herself naked. In bed. With Kurt. Moving her body that way. It was too bizarre a thought. And yet she pushed through the initial awkwardness of the scene in her head and tried to imagine instead of the first time, the second. How she'd feel if she ever got over that hump. She'd only ever been with Jack, and even the thoughts of Kurt seemed like a betrayal. Marriage was only supposed to last until death, but Alice had gone beyond the call of duty in the vows department. She looked at her wedding band then, wasn't sure she'd ever be comfortable not wearing it, but she decided, on a whim, to experiment. She put her hands under the counter and slid the ring off and switched it to her right hand.

"I wonder if there's news," she said, cupping her coffee mug. The ring felt heavy, funny.

"I'm sure there is." Kurt used his spatula to push eggs from the pan onto two plates. "One way or another."

So much of last night seemed like a dream, and Alice imagined that much of this trip would, too. Already, the toucan atop the Mayan temple seemed like a scene she'd made up. Already, dinner at Blancaneaux felt like another lifetime. Hawaii, too, being that much farther into the past, felt like a long-ago dream, and Alice wondered if that was part of the appeal of vacations—and of destination weddings, too. Whether they really were or not, in retrospect they felt like dreams come true.

How hard could it possibly be to find Becky in Placencia? Not very. So after getting off the boat that brought them back from the private island, Dan showered, then went down to the front desk and asked if anyone had seen or heard from Becky. The man working the desk said, "Tall girl. Brown hair. Freckles?"

"That's the one."

"Saw her walking toward town with her bags."

"Thanks," Dan said. Then he set out on foot, though he didn't have a plan.

He didn't have to go very far, though, before it all became crystal clear. Turtle Inn was right there, and Becky had developed expensive tastes since Dan's real estate boon. He went up to the front desk. "Hello," he said to the receptionist. "I'm trying to get in touch with one of your guests. Rebecca Wilson?"

Her full name sounded somehow exotic. It was as if he were talking about another woman entirely, and he wondered whether Becky would've held more mystique for him somehow if she'd gone by Rebecca instead. Becky was someone's kid sister. Rebecca could bring you to your knees.

The woman typed on the keyboard. "I'm sorry. No Rebecca Wilson."

"Oh, okay," Dan said. "Thanks anyway." He walked a few paces and saw a sign for a spa and felt increasingly certain that Becky was here. He approached the desk again. "I'm sorry, but could you check a different name?"

"Of course."

"Daniel Eshom. That's E-s-h-o-m."

"Yes, Mr. Eshom is here. Can I try the room for you?"

You had to hand it to that Becky. "Please."

The receptionist gestured to a nearby table with a courtesy phone, and Dan picked up. It was ringing on the other end, but Becky didn't answer so he returned the phone to its cradle and said, "Thanks." He thought he'd have a look around while trying to compose the right message to leave. And he pulled his wallet out of his pocket to confirm that, yes, Becky had taken his Amex card.

She was at the bar in a huge central restaurant. A small plastic turtle swam in her aquamarine cocktail.

"I suppose I'm paying for that drink?" Dan took the stool beside Becky, who looked up from her pink book, just a few pages shy of the end. Presumably the heroine would soon catch her man and ride off into the sunset with fancy shoes on her feet. Presumably Becky's faith in men—in love—would be restored.

"Yup." She raised her drink, smiled, and gestured with her left hand toward the bartender. "Can you get you a drink?"

"Very funny."

She poked her ice around with her straw and the turtle dove and then floated back up to the surface. She let her knee fall into his, then pulled it back. "I didn't think you'd have a leg to stand on, if you were mad."

"No, I don't suppose I do."

Dan ordered a Belikin, then half regretted not getting whatever it was that Becky was drinking. Something about that turtle floating around in there looked peaceful, and Dan thought peaceful was a good goal, after so much drama. He said, "I know it sounds trite, but I really would like to stay friends."

Becky shook her head softly. "We were never friends, Dan."

"We weren't?" Dan felt as if the ghost of that crab had created a phantom stab in his gut.

"Friends are nicer to each other than we mostly were." Becky folded the top corner of a page and slipped her book into the bag hanging from her bar stool.

"We had some okay times."

"Sure. We did." Her hand dug around in her bag then and came out with her wallet. "But I just don't really see us hanging out. I don't think you do either." She handed him his credit card, and the exchange prompted him to say, "I gave her the autograph. Or tried to."

"Yeah?"

Dan's eyes were straight ahead, reading unfamiliar labels on rum bottles. "She wouldn't take it."

"Good for her," Becky said, then elbowed him and said, "I mean, sorry."

"No. It's okay." Dan stroked his beer; it was half gone already. "I don't expect you to feel bad for me." He spun his stool to face her. "And I know it's a lot to ask, but I'd really like for you to come to the wedding with me."

"Oh, I'll be there, Dan." She looked at her watch, and Dan realized it was not for the first time, rather the fourth or fifth. "But not as your date." She looked around anxiously, and Dan realized that wasn't for the first time either.

"Speaking of dates—" Becky waved across the restaurant, and Dan turned. She said, "I've got one now. For lunch."

Dan studied the guy approaching: maybe thirty-five, wearing old-man plaid shorts and a yellow golf shirt. "You have got to be fraking kidding me."

"It's just lunch, Dan," she said quietly. "He thinks I'm a

yoga teacher scoping out the place for a possible retreat. Please don't make me have to tell him otherwise."

He was upon them now, and Becky got up and smiled and said, "Hey," and kissed the guy on the cheek. Dan got up, half smiled, and said, "Hey," to the guy, then said, "Well, it was nice to meet you." He shook Becky's hand. "And I'll definitely think about giving yoga a try."

Abby sat on the beach listening to the Starter House and feeling sort of bummed, thinking about the band and that boy she slept with and the sketches and the astronomical odds against her actually getting into fashion design school and then of actually making it after that. It was almost party time back at home—people were probably already getting ready, having their hair done, getting manicures—and instead she was here, feeling like a total loser. For a while there it had really seemed like the week was going to turn around, but it had proven to be a complete disaster. She was swearing off guys completely, for sure. Because first she'd been so way off about Colin, and then, *wow*, had she been wrong about Billy.

She'd pretty much disappeared into her hut after dinner with the gang last night, and she hadn't spoken another word to Billy all night. With absolutely nothing else to do, she'd picked up *Heart of Darkness* again, started it over from the beginning, and this time she felt Kurtz's loneliness, felt his fear, felt what must have been his sense of daring, adventure, and disappointment. And when Marlow got to that bit where he said, "Droll thing life is—that mysterious arrangement of merciless logic for a futile purpose. The most you can hope from it is some knowledge of yourself," she thought maybe, just maybe, she knew what he meant.

Abby hadn't spoken to Billy at all over their bonfire breakfast that morning or on the boat ride back to the mainland, and she was hoping she could just get through the wedding tomorrow and get home without having to look him in the eye. She was mortified. Humiliated. And dreading wearing the boring dress she'd bought for the wedding. It would be different if she could face him tomorrow feeling like she looked awesome. She kept replaying yesterday's scene in her head—the look of horror in his eyes, the way his voice sounded so cold when he'd said, "I'm not attracted to you." She hated the fact that he lived in New York now, because New York was pretty much ruined for her with him there.

The Starter House was no more, and there was nothing Abby could do about it. She flipped through her sketchbook and it was sort of like reliving the whole week. A lot of botched shoes and then, finally, the Converse All Stars. A handful of weird attempts at self-portraits, none of them quite drawn from observation, and then the Belizean tourist still life. That one had really turned out well, and it was probably because Billy had been watching. She'd busted out all of her tricks and skills.

"Abby, come on!" Maggie yelled from the porch.

M and M and M were waiting. Some of Abby's aunts and uncles had arrived that morning, and they were all going to have lunch together in town. Typically, Abby would've tried to think of a way to get out of it, but there was really nothing else for her to do except sit around and feel sorry for herself, and that would only get her in trouble with Maggie, who'd unleash one of her tirades about rudeness and how, really, Abby should put things in perspective. Her life was really nothing to complain about. Which was probably true—she wasn't among the earliest white men to make a harrowing journey into the heart of Africa, she didn't have to dive into the ocean to feed her family, she hadn't even had to run away from her father; he'd done the running first—but Abby just didn't feel like hearing it.

"Coming!" she called, and tried to shift Abby 2.0 into family mode. She'd have to be cheery and polite and talk about things like school, and her job at the Troc Center, and UC—and probably ziplining—and no one would have any idea at all what was really going on or who Abby really was.

"Hello, miss?" a voice called out from Alice's porch. She was in the kitchenette drinking water and replaying her good-bye with Kurt in the parking lot. He'd kissed her, really kissed her, and she wasn't sure whether that kiss represented a beginning or an end. She couldn't extend her trip; that would be crazy. And there really wasn't time to see him again while she was here. Soon more guests were arriving, so she'd have to be on hand just to, well, be on hand. And then they were having a sort of late-afternoon bachelorette party for June, then a rehearsal dinner, but no rehearsal. Tomorrow was the wedding, and then Sunday morning she went home.

"Yes, hello?" She went to the door.

"A package," the man said. "For you."

"Oh!" Alice couldn't imagine. . . . She opened the door and took the soft parcel out of the man's hands. "Thank you so much."

The screen door tapped shut, and Alice ripped the package open. It was something soft, a T-shirt, and Alice unfolded it and a white envelope fell to the floor. She spread the T-shirt out on the kitchen table. WWOD? stared back at her—hot pink letters on pale pink cotton—and she laughed, hand over mouth. She peeled off the plain yellow tee she was wearing and put the new one on, then she bent to pick up the envelope and opened it. "To the Rock Star's Mother: It cost me more money to ship this damn thing global express than it did to make it, so you better wear it well. Can't wait to hear all about it. Love, The Lawyer's Wife." Alice waved the card in front of her eyes to stop herself from crying. She read the P.S.: "You were right. What the heck is a Memory Keeper, and how can it have a daughter?"

"Mom?" June was at the door. "You ready?"

June had asked Alice to spend the early afternoon with her while she did some final wedding prep. Since Alice hadn't helped out at all before now, she was thrilled. Alice said, "Yes! Come in." She went to the bathroom, dabbed at her eyes, and came back out.

"What's that mean?" June frowned at the shirt.

"What Would Oprah Do?" Alice said. "It's a long story."

June's mouth curled into a wry smile. "What do you think Oprah would do if she were me?"

"Don't make fun." Alice started packing her purse, then stopped and considered. It was D-day, after all. "I think she'd take the job. She'd see it as putting in a kind of dues. And then she'd be so amazing at everything she did that down the line she'd be able to do anything she wanted, on her own clock, not necessarily a nine-to-five. And she'd just always—*always*—keep writing songs, since that's really what makes her happy."

"That's what I decided, too."

Alice gave June a hug. "I'm so excited for you."

"Me too." June pulled away. "I'm getting married!"

"I know!" They clasped hands.

"Come on." June's spider bite was a mere shadow now. "Leah's waiting."

Dan thought about walking into town, but from what he'd heard, there wasn't that much to see, and he thought he deserved some quality beach time after all he'd been through this week. It was sunny and hot—again—and this was probably the last window. So he went back to the bungalow, changed, and got ready to grab a lounge chair between the pool and the sea, but then saw June Carter's John Hancock sitting there on the kitchen table, right next to that empty bottle of wine. He picked them both up, cork and all.

It was time to make a clean start, and this was a nice, symbolic way to do it. Probably something he should've done a long time ago. The lack of waves here would make the whole thing a bit less dramatic than doing it back up near home, maybe somewhere in Jersey when a hurricane was churning up the Atlantic, exfoliating everything around with sand. But the time was now. He needed to be free of the autograph.

He'd have to go home and really get his life together now. Becky would come by the McCarren and get her things, and then he'd be alone in his life, with his money, and he'd have to fend for himself out there in the world again. Had he ever really been in love with June? The question had started haunting him and, well, maybe it hadn't been love, exactly. Maybe she represented the kind of girl Dan would want to be with if he were the kind of person he wanted to be. But he was not that person. Not yet, anyway. He was Dan. He had a lot of shit to sort out.

He thought back to those Dance Dance Revolution lunches and felt sad. And old. He'd be thirty-three next week. It seemed like so long ago, and Dan hadn't changed much at all since then. What a silly memory to have so lodged in your mind. To think he'd let one afternoon, one unconfirmed charge of chemistry, fuel his actions for so long when there was so much overwhelming evidence to the contrary that he and June would never be together and that that was how it should be. It was actually kind of sickening how perfectly paired she and Cash were, and Dan could only hope he'd find his own nauseating match someday.

Already, he missed Becky. Genuinely. She'd called him out on his bullshit, and if there was a person in the world who needed to sometimes be called on his bullshit, it was Dan. She'd looked calmer, happier, sitting there at the bar at Turtle Inn, waiting for her date, than she had looked, well, maybe as long as she'd been with him. She'd obviously been working hard to make it work, and now she didn't have to anymore. She was happier for it. It showed. It would be hard, he knew, to prevent himself from asking her if maybe they should give it one more try. Because she'd turn up tomorrow in a cute sundress or something, and her freckled face just belonged on a beach, and he'd want to at least take her to bed one more time. But he wouldn't. He'd dance a couple of dances with her, if there was even music for dancing, and he'd pay for her room at Turtle Inn and her cab home from the airport, and then that would be that. He'd wish her well.

He'd find someone, eventually, who only ever sneezed once at a time, and who didn't say "frak" or shop at Kohl's or read pink books or do sudoku. Preferably someone who'd never heard of the Starter House, which wouldn't be hard.

Sitting near the shoreline, he took the autograph out of the Ziploc and studied it. Becky was right. It could be a complete fake. Some chump with a big basement in Michigan or Ohio could have taught his wife how to copy the signature and made a fortune off less enterprising chumps like Dan. Holding it in his hands, the item and his frenzy over it seemed more foolish than ever before. It was silly to give an autograph that much power. He guessed it was neat to imagine that June Carter herself had touched this very cocktail napkin, but Dan himself wasn't much into hero worship. He held it close to his nose and smelled it like June had, but didn't feel any new clarity about his life. June was kind of flaky, really; he'd never realized that before. He did not feel the urge to do a cartwheel.

But he was snuffing out this ring of fire for sure. He needed two hands to pull the cork from the bottle—it was in there pretty tight—and so rested the napkin temporarily on his thigh. The wind lifted it then, and put it on the sand beside him, where it shivered for a split second before spinning into its own cartwheel down the beach.

"Shit."

Dan struggled to get up and then started chasing down the autograph, but a wave came then—one of maybe five actual waves Dan had seen over the last bunch of days—and floated the napkin up onto the beach and then back out. Dan waded over and lifted the napkin out of the water, and it clung to his hand, just an inch above the water, and then he decided to just let it go. It was already disintegrating into shreds.

It was all too perfect really. Fitting, somehow, in the end. The only thing more fitting would have been if he'd wiped his ass with it. Dan pushed the cork back into the bottle and took a running start so he could hurl it into the sea. He flung his arm forward and a muscle twinged and he said, "Ow," and watched the cloudy bottle fly through the air and hit the surface and bob. It was a message in a bottle, his own idiocy lost at sea.

Abby ditched M and M and Co. as soon as they all got back from town, and headed for the bungalow. She spotted Billy and Trevor sitting out by the pool and looked away just as she saw Billy raise a hand to wave. But Abby didn't turn or wave back. She had more important things on her mind.

In her room, she took the sarong and bracelet she'd bought in town out of a brown bag. She'd seen the sarong in the window of a shop they'd passed—with white flowers on a fuchsia background, it was maybe the prettiest pattern she'd ever seen in tropical colors—and she'd begged Maggie to let her go in because the second Abby saw the sarong she had an idea for how to turn it into a dress for tomorrow's wedding. The skinny wooden bracelet she bought in the same store was essential to the design.

She hadn't had any luck finding thread in town, but Maggie had mentioned Minky's travel sewing kit, so, having gotten permission, Abby went into Minky's adjoining room and took the kit back to her room.

Abby laid the sarong out on her bed and started playing around with it, folding it here, cinching in there, pulling one corner through the bracelet, to see whether the idea in her head could become a reality. It would be a sort of halter dress, with the circle of the bracelet as the centerpiece, resting on her breastbone where a pendant might be. There wouldn't actually be that much sewing involved, since the dress, once properly attached to the bracelet, where the cinching would be a little tricky, could basically function as a wrap dress. Then there would be straps, maybe pieces of fabric cut from one end and twisted up like thin ropes, to hook around both the bracelet and Abby's neck.

"Knock, knock!" someone called out, and Abby knew right away that it was Billy. She poked her head into the main room.

He was peering through the screen with his eyes cupped between his hands, and he saw her. "I wanted to apologize."

He looked monochrome on account of the screen door's gray mesh. Abby couldn't bring herself to actually say anything.

He said, "Can I come in?"

She said, "I guess." She was standing in the middle of the room now and didn't know whether to sit or not. She crossed her arms in front of her.

"I want to be very clear about something." Billy stood square in front of her. "Because I didn't mean to hurt your feelings the way I did."

Abby's knees felt wonky.

"I think you're great, Abby. Really great. I had a lot of fun with you this week." He ran a hand over his hair. "And yes, of course. I mean. You're incredibly attractive. Okay? I said it."

Abby's cheeks pulled toward a smile, but she managed to keep a straight face.

"But you're seventeen!" He shook his head. "And I mean, I know you and Cash are only stepsiblings, but still. We're practically going to be family. So it's just not going to happen."

Abby tapped a toe, and Billy turned to go. She said, "So you're attracted to me?"

"Yes." He turned back.

"So I wasn't completely wrong." She stepped forward.

"Well, you were wrong to push and push and push."

"But what I felt wasn't wrong."

"No, Abby." He sounded tired, amused. "And now I'm going to leave. And if you ever tell anyone about this conversation, I will deny it."

Abby followed him to the door and held it open as he stepped out onto the porch. He turned then and stepped back into the room faster than Abby knew what was happening and kissed her on the lips. Soft, sweet. Nothing more. He said, "I'll deny that, too," and Abby knew she wouldn't care if he did. She spun on her heels, went back to the sarong, and got to work. There wasn't a lot of time. She needed to make the most of it.

When Leah pulled the towel away from June's wet head, Alice smiled. Brown. Good old-fashioned brown. "Much better," Alice said, and then June said, "Eh-eh-eh. Not so fast."

"What now?" Alice asked. She was holding little Darla, who was smiling and blabbing baby babble.

"Just a couple of blond streaks."

"June, your hair's going to fall out if you keep treating it like this."

June shrugged. "I can't help myself."

"Fine." Alice smiled exaggeratedly at the baby, and the baby smiled back. "I'm over it."

"You're over it?" June looked up at Leah, who smiled and shrugged.

"Yeah." Alice shifted Darla's weight. "Over it."

"Oh," June said. "I have *got* to meet this guy."

Alice looked at her watch; her arms were getting tired. It had been a long time since she'd held a baby for this long; it was hard to believe June had ever been that small at all. "Maybe another time."

"Sure, Mom." Leah was using the back end of a pointy comb to isolate chunks of June's hair. "Next time we're in Belize together."

Alice shifted Darla to her other arm. "Stranger things have happened."

"They have?"

Alice shrugged. She was thinking of the toucan on the Mayan temple, of the butterfly that tried to hitch a ride out of the farm, of the iguana that she mistook for an evildoer, and the soccer game in town. She was thinking that this week had been nothing she'd hoped for and more.

June submitted as Leah pushed her head forward and down. "Name one."

*T*hey are up there, exchanging vows about sickness and health and richer and poorer, because this much was never in doubt: June and Cash were going to get married, and she was never planning on doing it with pink hair. Today it's brown and streaked with golden blond that matches the gold of her dress, and even Alice has to admit it looks more gorgeous with that gold than it would without.

This much was never in doubt, either. Cash's mother, Tamara, was never going to show up, and Cash knew it. Sometimes that's just how things are, so he already had his moment earlier this morning—a sort of woe-is-me moment—then he shook if off, boxed it up, and put it away.

Billy is up there, playing the role of maid of honor, because Lydia's middle child started running a fever of 103 and she missed her flight and there wasn't another that would get her there on time, even if she wanted to leave her family in that state, and she didn't. He is wearing Alice's gray dress—yes, you read that right—because he went to her cabana that morning, plopped down on the bed with a couple of shirts in his hand, and said, "I need help figuring out what to wear."

"Well, this *is a role reversal.*" *Alice still hadn't decided for herself.*

Billy explained about Lydia, and Alice said, 'Well, that's a shame," *and pointed up at the two dresses on hooks on the wall.* "I'll wear whatever one you don't."

Billy bent at the torso, propped up sideways on an elbow. "You're serious."

She hadn't been, but the smile on Billy's face triggered an image of Billy up there in a dress, standing up for June, and it made Alice want to laugh out loud. She said, "Try 'em on."

Billy stood and took his shirt off. "She's gonna flip."

"Well, they might not fit."

"Oh, they'll fit." *He rubbed his hands together excitedly, like warming them by a fire.*

Alice took the plastic off the red dress and helped Billy slip it over his head. He moved to the mirror in the bathroom as she zipped up the back, and they were both cracking up before it was even fully on him. "Oh. My. God," *Billy managed between laughs.*

"It's a little, I don't know," *Alice said,* "sexy?"

"Very funny." *He turned, and they went back out to the main room.* "Let's try the other one."

He let the red dress fall to his ankles, revealing his swim trunks again, and then Alice helped him step into the gray dress. He returned to the mirror as Alice trailed after him, zipping him up, and then they were both in fits, laughing hysterically, before she could even finish. Something about the look of the dress on Billy reminded Alice of Miss Piggy and Muppets and she had no idea why. This only made her laugh harder. "You look like Miss Piggy," *she said, then started cracking up again. Her stomach hurt.* "Ohmigod."

"Miss Piggy?" *Bill stomped his foot and laughed silently now, in heaves.* "What?"

Alice was able to compose herself. "I think you have to do it." *She wiped some tears from her cheeks.*

"I don't know if I can. I mean"—*Billy laughed more*—"look at me!"

"Oh, honey." Alice covered her mouth and took in the sight of him again. "I'm looking." She smiled mischievously and shrugged. "She said she didn't care what anyone wore."

Trevor is standing up and banging a knife on a Coke bottle half an hour later and saying, "Ladies and germs, if I could have your attention," because late yesterday afternoon he started rounding up the men of the group, who were scattered around the beach.

"What's up?" Dan said, allowing himself to be corralled to the tiki bar, and Trevor said, "Bachelor party."

"Oh crap," Dan said. "I should've organized that, I guess."

"Uh, well, yeah," Trevor said. "We have to do it now, before dinner, so it's sort of untraditional, but a man's gotta have a bachelor party." Dan joined a group already assembled at the bar, and Trevor said, "Dan. You want to lure Cash out here?"

"Sure."

Trevor is up there, speaking incredibly eloquently about his affection for Cash and June and his humble awe of their relationship—and Dan is telling Becky that shhhh, he'll explain later—because Dan approached Cash and June's cabana down the beach and knocked. He picked a small stone up off the porch and tried to hurl it into the sea, missing by a long shot: not a stone's throw from the water, after all.

"Cash?" he called out, because the screen door was, well, a screen door.

"Yeah!" Cash stepped into view. "What's up?"

Dan couldn't think up a story or excuse. "Would you mind accompanying me to the tiki bar for a minute?"

Cash picked his sunglasses off the table and stepped out onto the porch. "Everything okay?" He was no longer using crutches, and it struck Dan that Cash wasn't really bumbling through life anymore, and that maybe he never had been; maybe Dan was the one who had

been bumbling all along. Cash had somehow managed to get every-
thing he'd ever wanted in life, and what did Dan have?

"Everything's fine," Dan said as they walked down the steps and
across the beach. "But listen, man." Dan hadn't known he was going
to do this until this moment; he stopped walking, and Cash took an-
other couple of steps, then stopped, too, and turned. He heard June's
voice echo in his head—For God's sake, you're his best man—and
said, "I don't want you to ask me why, you just have to trust me. You
should ask Trevor to be your best man."

Voices carried easily on the wind, and Dan could hear Trevor say-
ing, "Here he comes, here he comes."

"But you're my oldest friend," Cash said.

"Yeah," Dan said. "I am. But he deserves it. You know he does."

Cash put his sunglasses on; between you and me, he'd sort of asked
Dan in order to avoid having to choose between Trevor and Joe, but
had later come to realize that Joe wouldn't have cared. "You realize
he'll never let me live it down," Cash said. "Asking him second."

Dan caught a glimpse of Trevor across the grounds, craning his
crazy goatee to see, and Dan said, "Actually, I have a feeling he
will."

Alice is over by the pool talking to Kurt, who is apologizing for crash-
ing the wedding—and with this kind of news—because Alice insisted
when she last saw him that he tell her news of the lost snorkeler the
second he had any. The body has been found. The cause of death—and
the tour company—will be investigated. But his family at least will be
able to bring him home.

Kurt is reiterating his invitation for Alice to stay a few extra days,
and Alice is declining again because first she's going to go home and let
Mary-Anise introduce her to the other Jack, and then maybe after that
she'll see if anyone else knows anyone they think she might get along

with. She is taking down Kurt's phone number and his address and then kissing him full on the lips good-bye because she thinks that's what Oprah might do and because the red dress ended up being the right one after all.

Abby is up there dancing with Billy—who has changed out of that awful dress—and the landscapers from Boston, too, and wishing she could live the whole week over again without the drama from home hanging over her, because after last night's rehearsal dinner, she worked into the wee hours on her new dress, then fell asleep and awoke to find that she still—whew!—loved it in the morning. So when she was getting ready for the wedding, she put the dress on and cued up one of her favorite Starter House songs and thought about how Chelsea Lambert's party was finally over and how she was glad she hadn't been there because if she'd been there she wouldn't be here, wearing this amazing dress. Now that the party was over, Abby was sure she'd go home to discover that it hadn't really lived up to the hype. Most things in life—sex, snorkeling, tiny fishing towns—didn't. She regretted that she'd be home soon and she'd forget the smell of a papaya after it's cut open, the taste of Belizean chicken stew, the tickle of a school of fish on her legs, the way it felt to have Billy's lips on hers, if only for a moment. Whatever else it was with him, it was real, and Abby already felt sad for how much of him—and Belize—would be lost to her when she was gone.

But that postkiss, new-dress moment—that particular morning's version of Abby—she'd capture. So when the next song kicked in, she sat on the bed with a mirror propped nearby and started drawing her reflection, and it looked good, the reflection and the sketch both. Guitars were jangling and rocking out in her headphones, and she drew and drew, and then she couldn't sit there anymore so she stood up and started tapping her left heel to the beat. It was a rare Starter House duet, with June's voice like an ethereal sort of ghost behind Cash's more screechy lead vocals. This was definitely the best of Cash's songs ever. Soon Abby's hips were moving—she loved the way the dress shimmied, knew she'd have to include it in her application portfolio—and then she was singing along and playing air guitar and then the song really got going. Abby let it all go and let her head fall this way and that and let her arms swing like a monkey's and God it felt good.

She is up there now, dancing in the tiki bar and chanting, "One more song! One more song!" with Billy and the landscapers because that morning, while she was dancing in her room, she was picturing the dance floor at Chelsea Lambert's Sweet Sixteen last night— all crowded and pulsing to some god-awful R & B—and thinking that, yes, definitely, where she was was better by a mile. She felt all at once like it was a rainy night or like something fantastic had just happened—or something awful—and it was all wrapped up in this one feeling of being so alive and so lucky to be able to feel music, to feel life, this way. The song sounded different to her than it ever had before. It seemed to capture everything that the Starter House had ever been—the soft and the raw, both—and the two sounds seemed to be doing battle and there was no way either one could win, and it seemed suddenly obvious then that the band would implode. It was a fire that raged and then burned out.

She is up there now, walking like an Egyptian with Billy—who is saying, "Cool dress, by the way"—because Maggie was right all along. There will be other boys. There will be other bands. And with any luck, many many more dresses.

They are up there, wasting away again in Margaritaville because it seems more appropriate, somehow, than "It Ain't Me, Babe" (it is, after all, a wedding), and June is up there, on the makeshift stage, playing her last gig with the Starter House, because poor delusional Dan bought her that autograph and it reminded June how Ms. Carter once said, "I could have made more records, but I wanted to have a marriage," and what June remembered her saying was that she could've made more records but wanted to have a life.

She is stepping over to Cash and throwing her arms around his neck and kissing him and smiling because earlier that morning, she turned to him and said, "It is *me, babe," and he said, "Yeah, yeah, yeah," like he was already over her, no big deal.*

She is kissing him now and soaking it all in—the sea, her mother like a stranger in a red dress, even the landscapers from Boston— because she doesn't know that when she yelled down the beach of the private island, "I quit!" Trevor muttered, "Good, cause we were about to kick you out anyway," and Cash and Joe both laughed even though it wasn't entirely a joke.

She is stepping off the stage to let her husband *finish searching for that lost shaker of salt by himself because somewhere out there a generation of girls awaits. They are in their messy living rooms or pink bedrooms, in high pigtails or low ponytails, watching TV or listening to the radio and feeling a sort of itch, an itch that June knows well. They are hearing music in their heads, dancing when no one's watching—maybe even wondering why* Scott Haslett *gets to play the piano, or guitar, or drums in the class play—and it's time to rock their worlds.*